Solemnly Swear

NANCY MOSER

Tyndale House Publishers, Inc.
CAROL STREAM, ILLINOIS

Library of Congress Cataloging-in-Publication Data

Moser, Nancy.
    Solemnly swear / Nancy Moser.
      p. cm.
    ISBN-13: 978-1-4143-0163-1 (sc)
    ISBN-10: 1-4143-0163-4 (sc)
    1. Laundresses—Fiction.   2. Hotel cleaning personnel—Fiction.   3. Trials (Murder)—Fiction.   4. Jury—Fiction.   I. Title.

PS3563.O88417S65 2007
813'54—dc22   2007025920

Printed in the United States of America

13   12   11   10   09   08   07
 7   6   5   4   3   2   1

Many thanks to the Kansas Eight,

my fellow writers who brainstorm

the bizarre plots that pop into my head:

Steph, Deb, Till, Colleen, Judy, Cheryl, Mel, Rene.

It's all your fault.

Prologue

Since your refuge is made of lies,
a hailstorm will knock it down.
Since it is made of deception,
a flood will sweep it away.

ISAIAH 28:17

*S*omeone is coming.

I'm in control but my heart still pounds. I can't let anyone see me this way. Calm. I have to look calm. That's the only way this will play out like I've planned.

I check my watch. Twenty minutes, thirty tops. I know where this person lives, how close it is. I know it won't take long to get here.

Things will work out. The way this whole thing set itself up . . . it wasn't a coincidence. I don't believe in such a thing. I believe in fate. Yet sometimes fate needs a little push. A well-planned push.

My watch again. Another minute gone. It's time to stage things and get in place. I already know my lines—and theirs. People are predictable. It's a fact I count on to get what I want.

I sluff off my suit pants and shirt from work, hanging up one, drilling the other into the laundry basket. I pull on my swim trunks and pause to look in the mirror. I flex my muscles. Six-pack abs, even at age thirty-five. But looking studly doesn't figure into tonight's scenario. The meeting that's coming down is mental, not physical. Luckily, my mental capabilities are also in A1 condition. My mark doesn't have a chance.

As intended.

I pour myself a glass of wine and take it—and the bottle— outside to the hot tub I put in last year. It's not one of those tacky lumber-store numbers but a hotel-quality, in-the-ground tub that can hold six people. It has twenty-eight jets and a hot-spot waterfall. Hey, why not? Don't I deserve the best? Besides, I didn't pay full price. I got connections. I *am* the connection. I make things happen.

My way or no way.

I slide into the tub, enjoying the sting of the hot water and the steam rising in the winter air. I keep it hotter than most. Some like it hot. Hmm. I got wit too. I got it all.

But I want more. Much more. As much as I can get.

After tonight's little transaction, I'll be richer by fifty thou. My mark didn't like the price and said it would be hard coming up with it. They always say that, but they always do it. What choice do they have? *My* offers can't be refused.

Not that I'd do a Corleone on them. I've never had to resort to that. Charm and brains. That's worth more than any thug technique.

I sip my wine and make a face—a reaction I reserve for moments when I'm alone. I still don't like wine, but I drink it because it fits the part I play.

I turn on the jets, letting the swirling water pulse against my lower back. My job requires me to stand a lot, and though my legs have gotten used to it, my back is weak. But I'm working on it. Four hundred crunches a day. Working with weights. I'm not arrogant enough to be blind to my weaknesses. Unlike most people, I do something about them. People don't have to be incomplete. All it takes is a little work.

And a little luck.

I hear a car. My neighborhood is in the boonies with
the houses sitting on acreages, giving plenty of privacy. The
flicker of headlights on the tree at the edge of the backyard
tells me a car has pulled into the driveway. I gave instructions
to meet me out back. I don't want anyone in my house. Plus
I want the advantage of creating a scene that's unexpected.
Blackmail works best if the victim is a bit put off, uncomfortable, uncertain. That's why I always pick my turf. Sure, it lets
them know where I live, but the privacy means I don't have
to worry about some stranger hearing or seeing what they
shouldn't. It's worked so far. I've never had problems with a
one of them coming back. I assure them what's done is done
and I won't be bothering them again. And I keep my word.
One blackmailing per customer.

There *is* such a thing as honor among thieves.

I turn off the jets to listen more closely. I hear footsteps on
the walkway that connects the front of the house to the back.

I wait just long enough.

"Welcome," I say.

The look of surprise is right on cue.

I turn on the jets, sending the water into motion. "Want to
join me? The water's great."

My victim wears a winter coat and gloves and carries a
gym bag.

The money.

My invitation is declined. "I want to get this over with."

"Excellent. Then let's get down to business."

———

My head is killing me. I lean my neck against the edge of
the hot tub and press a hand against the wound. Pieces of the
broken wine bottle litter the patio, reflecting the light.

I can't believe it went so wrong. Before today . . . everyone else paid their money and left. But this one wanted to discuss it. Then the discussion turned into an argument. It was totally unexpected. My marks always accept their guilt because they *are* guilty.

Hitting me over the head with the bottle was unplanned; I know that for a fact. It was followed by wide eyes, a gasp, and "Oh, no. I'm sorry. I'm so, so sorry" before a panicked getaway.

I mean, who says such a thing at such a time?

Someone who's innocent.

I can't think about that now. I need to think about me. I need to get out of this tub.

I try to sit upright, but the pain and the dizziness force me back in the water.

I can't do this alone. I need help. Suddenly the distance between neighbors is a bad thing. And my phone . . . it's inside.

A world away.

Hold on. I have to hold on.

I doze. . . .

I snap awake when my face hits the water. My grip on the sides is weakening. I'm weakening. If only the jets weren't going.

I need help.

Now.

The water bubbles around my chin.

It teases me, pretending *it's* innocent.

It's not.

I'm not.

It nibbles at my grip.

It grabs at me, pulling at me.

It wants me.

It . . .

It . . .

Wins.

One

Those who are wise will find a time
and a way to do what is right,
for there is a time and a way
for everything, even when
a person is in trouble.

ECCLESIASTES 8:5-6

*A*bigail Buchanan?"

"Here."

Abigail stood *without* pushing on the arms of the chair. She forced herself to walk faster than her normal gait. She willed her spine to be as straight as it was fifty years earlier when she'd gone on her first audition.

Being an out-of-work actress who was over seventy was the pits. Actually, the pits had started at age forty when leading roles had started to fade into character parts. The first time she'd played the lead's mother instead of playing the lead had been a wake-up call. Welcome to reality.

The young woman who'd called her name held the door. Not a wrinkle in *her* dewy soft skin. Abigail hated when people made statements such as, "I've earned my wrinkles. I'm proud of each and every one."

Pooh. Such declarations were the pitiful rationalization of a person consumed with panic, a person resorting to any kind of desperate validation they could muster. Abigail stood by her original statement: getting old was the pits.

Personally, although she hated wrinkles as much as the

next woman, she'd never succumbed to the knife, mostly because plastic surgery had been a touch and go procedure back when she'd first been tempted. Seeing one of her actress friends end up with a mouth as tight and wide as Donald Duck's had also been instrumental in her decision to wing it.

Yet she *had* tried every face cream, wrinkle reducer, scrub, and gimmick that promised to bar time at the door. It didn't take long to realize that those creams—when and if they worked—only offered time a coffee break. Time was relentless and insisted on getting back to work. Crummy job too, making days turn into months turn into years that made a person *old*.

Bummer.

"Stand over there," the sweet young thing said, indicating the space directly in front of two seated men who held Abigail's future in their hands.

She smiled, "Afternoon, gentlemen."

A nod. "You're Abigail Buchanan. . . ."

There was the slightest indication he'd heard of her. "That's me. Star of *Winsome Girl* on Broadway and *The Jackie Daniels Show* on TV."

The other man looked confused. She could go on to explain that she'd won the *Winsome Girl* role away from Mary Martin and had earned a full-time role on *Jackie* through the depth and breadth of her talent, but she had the feeling her explanation would gain her another blank stare.

"It says here you were on *Friends* once."

"Those kids were so sweet." *Kids. I shouldn't have called them kids.* Yet it was obvious by the men's appreciative nods that an appearance on *Friends* overrode dozens of more important performances in the too-distant past. "I also did twelve commercials as the Ivory Soap lady. . . ."

The first man—who had one of those annoying little

shocks of hair in the cleft of his chin—said, "You look older in person."

You charmer you. She didn't react.

Chin Hair sighed as if he'd already decided this was a supreme waste of time. He waved a hand at the girl. "Give her the script."

If Abigail had participated in a paying job in the past nine months, she might have tossed the pages back at him, saying something trite (but satisfying) like "I don't need this!" But since her rent was due and she really would like to eat something besides four-for-a-dollar mac and cheese for dinner, she took the pages and did her best.

When she was done, they didn't even confer. Chin Hair merely said, "We'll be in touch" and Cutie Pie popped out of her chair to show Abigail the door.

Don't call us; we'll call you.

At times like this, Abigail grieved divorcing her husband back in 1958. Not because she missed him (what was his name again?) nor because she thought they should have stayed together. But having him around would have at least given her the possibility of companionship. The whole marriage experience had soured her to commitment and she'd never found another mate—marriageable mate, that is. As a result she'd never had children—which would have also provided her with some company in her old age.

There it was again. Old age. Nasty devil.

As it was, she had to bear her disappointment regarding not getting the part alone. She was used to it, but that didn't mean she liked it. Once she'd entered the golden years (a dull yellow if you asked her) she'd found her bounce-back ability a huge bit wanting. And when she talked to her friends about wanting to work, they always made her feel moronic. "What are you thinking? Enjoy your retirement, Abigail."

Doing what? With what? And with whom?

"Stop it!" she snapped at the traitorous thoughts.

Alas, the empty elevator did not respond.

But it did offer a nice reverberation to her anger. . . .

Smiling wickedly, she said the words again, yelled them within the confines of the moving box, and added a few more for emphasis: "Stop feeling sorry for yourself, Abigail Buchanan!"

She imagined her words rising up the elevator shaft and ricocheting off the ears of some poor cuss waiting on the eighth floor with a cheek numb from Novocain.

Maybe she shouldn't have said her name.

As the elevator doors opened on one, she laughed. What did it matter if people heard her name?

As always, they'd forget it soon enough.

———

Abigail used her key to get the mail in the tiny foyer of her ancient apartment building—which had, at one time, been a stately Victorian home.

Looking through the mail, she realized how pitiful her life had become that she could get excited about offers for credit cards she didn't want, vinyl siding she didn't need, and cruises she couldn't afford.

C'est la vie.

She was disappointed there weren't any of the just-listed items but only a gas bill and a letter from some government agency. She shoved both into her shoulder bag and started up the stairs to her attic apartment. When she'd first gotten this place fifteen years earlier, she'd thought the stairs would keep her young.

Very funny.

The good thing about the stairs was that they were on the inside of the building and owned the essence of stately— somewhere beneath the countless coats of paint that covered what surely was oak or walnut paneling. A shame. A crying, dying shame. Though in theory maybe some thick coats of paint would keep *her* working too. . . .

She traversed the second floor landing and walked to the end of the hall, where a small door led to her own private, winding stairs, so narrow that, out of habit and for support, she put her hands on either side, letting the grime of the day transfer to an existing swath of dark against the white paint. She should clean it. One of these days. It's not like she didn't have time.

The stairs winded her, so after retrieving the letters from her purse, she fell into the mauve Queen Anne chair that really should be re-covered into some with-it color. If she cared.

Which she didn't.

She tossed the gas bill to the floor and zeroed in on the official-looking letter. Within moments, she sat up straight, fueled with a new energy.

Abigail kissed the letter. They wanted her to be a juror on a trial? Now there was a part she'd always wanted to play.

———

Ken Doolittle heard the water running in the master bath. It took him a moment to put a name to the person in the bathroom.

Loretta.

Lorena?

Since he couldn't remember for sure, he decided to keep his eyes closed and pretend he was still asleep. No need for poignant good-byes. At age fifty-five, *poignant* had never been

in his vocabulary. Or his game plan. As if he had one. One that
worked anyway.

The water stopped and he heard the light being flipped
off. The woman rustled through her purse and Ken nearly
opened his eyes to see what she was doing. . . .

But then he sensed her presence close. The scent of newly
applied floral perfume wafted over him. Then footsteps. Away.
On the stairs. He held his breath waiting for the front door to—

Click.

Ah. Safe.

The sounds of a car pulling away gave him permission to
sit up. He saw a note on the pillow next to him: *Thanks.*

He stared at the note. That was it? Thanks? Not *You were
wonderful. Call me.* Not even just *Call me.*

They always said *Call me.*

Well, usually.

Sometimes.

He glanced at the clock. One-thirty. In the afternoon? The
light streaming in the window was his answer. At least Lor-
whatever had stuck around. Of course they hadn't gotten to his
house until nearly five in the a.m. part of the day. He'd met her
at a bar where she waitressed. When she had gotten off work
at two they grabbed something to eat, then went back to his
house to . . . grab each other.

Ken sat up, swinging his legs to the side of the bed. He
moved his head carefully, testing to see if a hangover was in
the cards.

Free from that burden, he found his terry robe thrown over
the chair by the window, the robe he'd bought on a whim at a
golf resort in Arizona ten years ago. As he tied the belt around
his thickening waist he noticed there was a red stain across the
front of it.

Then he remembered. Wine. But not from last night. Wine

from a little tête-à-tête he'd had last week. Another pickup in a bar. Another woman.

He really should wash it.

One of these days.

He traipsed downstairs in search of coffee. And oatmeal would be good. Oatmeal was supposed to regulate his cholesterol. It was kind of late for breakfast, but Ken had long ago given up trying to adhere to regular hours. And who really cared? As long as he got to the Marlborough Country Club in time to give his private golf lessons his hours and diet were *his* business.

Ken turned the coffeepot on and put a bowl of instant oatmeal in the microwave. While he waited he perused the mail he'd tossed on the counter. Two days worth. At least.

Junk, junk, bill, coupon, bill, advertising . . .

What was this? A letter from the district court. His mind scanned any infraction they might be writing to him about. Parking tickets? That one DUI?

No. Those had been taken care of eons ago.

He opened the letter. Jury duty? What do you know? He never would have guessed. . . .

He read the letter with interest—and glee.

Women would be impressed by jury duty . . . especially if he got assigned to some scandalous trial. This might be fun.

———

Deidre Kelly sat in the principal's office with her twelve-year-old daughter beside her.

Crying beside her.

"This is not acceptable," Deidre told the principal. "Nelly should not have to endure the abuse of a bully." She turned to

Nelly's PE teacher, who stood near the door. "Where were you during all this?"

"I have thirty students to watch, not just Nelly," Ms. Hollings said.

"Are you telling me this has never happened before, to another child?"

"I'm afraid we can't say," the principal said. "A student's records are private and—"

"There was nothing private about Damon knocking Nelly to the ground and putting his foot on her arm."

She nearly caught Ms. Hollings in a shrug. "He's being disciplined."

The principal closed a file on her desk. "I assure you, Mrs. Kelly, we do not condone this sort of behavior at our school."

"But you also apparently do little to stop it. Damon has been harassing Nelly after school."

"Other girls too," Nelly said.

"I'm afraid we have no control over the children once school is over and they are away from school property," the principal said.

"It appears you don't have control over them ever." She stood and nodded to Nelly to stand also. "Boys who harass girls turn into men who assault women. I'm sure you can find a hundred statistics to bear that out."

"A correlation might be made, but Damon—"

Deidre led Nelly to the door. "Damon will not harass my daughter again, nor any other girl in this school, or the school board will hear about it."

"We don't appreciate threats," Ms. Hollings said.

"And I don't appreciate apathy. You have a problem in your school. You see a need, you see children who need help—then do something about it. Good day, ladies."

Once in the car, Nelly said, "Thanks, Mom."
"Anytime, sweetie. Anytime. Anyplace."

It was not something any citizen—patriotic or otherwise—looked forward to getting. A jury-duty letter.

After reading it once, Deidre read it again. No. Not now. She couldn't do this. She'd been so stressed the past few months that she'd turned into one of those nervous Nellies who jumped at sounds and focused on worst-case scenarios.

Speaking of Nellies . . . she had her own Nelly to worry about. Beyond the problems with bullies at school, Nelly had a schedule that rivaled that of the president of a country. Being a Carpool Mom and Mother Protector was as unglamorous as it sounded and often made Deidre feel as though she had no purpose other than negotiating the drop-off lane or meeting with an assortment of powers that be, suggesting they do their jobs.

Her husband, Sig, offered little help with the logistics of Nelly's schedule. He was a pediatric orthopedic surgeon and often traveled the world performing free surgeries with his Kelly Pediatric Foundation. The foundation's motto was "Bringing help to the helpless." An able goal, though helping Deidre with the occasional piano lesson or teacher conference would have been appreciated.

Now, with this jury notice . . . The world already sat heavily on Deidre's shoulders like the yoke of a milkmaid carrying sloshing pails. Her feet were in constant danger of getting wet, her shoulders were sore, and her breaking point was imminent.

Added to the intricate scheduling were the responsibilities she incurred as the *wife* of a pediatric surgeon. In order to help finance the foundation, she was required to attend countless banquets and fund-raising events. Deidre usually enjoyed playing the pretty socialite, smiling and saying all the right things to the right people to get the right results. She hadn't climbed her way out of near poverty to sit in the shadows. Yet sometimes being "on" all the time was a pain *and* a drain.

Though certainly not the same degree of pain and drain as what she'd endured in her life before Sig. Deidre's first husband, Don, had died five years earlier after a long battle with cancer. In the aftermath of his death—since there'd been no insurance—she'd been forced to sell their small home and move in with Don's mother, Karla. Karla had lived in the Polland family home, a crumbling fixer-upper that sported a refrigerator whose freezer only worked part-time, many lights that wouldn't work at all (but couldn't be fixed for fear that the electrician would say the entire house needed rewiring), and a furnace that clanked loudly as it spit out not enough heat.

The only perk to the house had been the presence of Karla. The typical mother-in-law jokes never applied to her. Karla was the nurturing mother Deidre never had. The three generations of Polland females had huddled together in the old house, sharing their grief, making do, striving to get from this day to the next.

Until Deidre met Dr. Sigmund T. Kelly.

After their whirlwind courtship and union, Deidre, little Nelly, and even Karla had moved into Sig's 7,500-square-foot mansion that sported an enormous stainless steel refrigerator-freezer, lights that wouldn't dare not work, and a furnace that softly purred as it made their life cozy warm.

Yes indeed, the life she was living held little pain and was very nearly perfect.

Back before Sig, Deidre—known as Dee-Dee back then— had been working as a med tech at Mountain Valley Hospital in Branson, Missouri. She'd come into contact with Dr. Kelly off and on and had been instantly attracted to him. More surprisingly, he'd been attracted to her. She was pretty enough, with long blonde hair and a body with just enough curves to be interesting. Physically, they were on an equal par. As for the rest of any Sig-Deidre comparison? She was a nobody, a peon pricking fingers and taking blood, while he was an internationally known doctor, famous for his philanthropy. Dee-Dee hadn't even known what *philanthropy* meant.

When Dr. Kelly had first asked her out, she'd kept her past private, as well as her current housing situation. Sig didn't need to know about her rough beginnings, her sorrows and insecurities, or her tough living conditions. Not until she'd charmed him into not caring.

Which she'd done with great skill. They had that in common—two charmers in search of an appreciative audience.

Not that there was anything wrong with that.

If only Sig didn't use his charm to attract other females. Last winter Deidre had overheard some women gossiping in the restroom at an awards banquet—gossiping about her husband and a woman named Audrey. She'd confronted Sig, but with great expertise he'd made her feel ridiculous.

Her memory of that night quickly sped past what had happened next. If only she could take back that night, that accusation, that . . . everything.

That everything that had changed everything.

And yet nothing had changed. Although Sig reassured her there was nothing to worry about regarding anyone named Audrey (or by any other name), Deidre didn't believe it. She knew what a catch her husband was—after all, she'd caught him—and so she remained on full alert, ready to pounce on any hint that something in their life was amiss. She was *not* going to lose all she had gained. No way. No how.

"Anything for me?"

Upon hearing her mother-in-law's voice, Deidre was yanked from the past and placed firmly in the present. She handed the rest of the mail to Karla. Actually . . . Karla might be her lifesaver in this current jury dilemma.

Deidre waved the court's letter between them. "I got called to jury duty."

Karla saluted. "Congratulations, O mighty citizen!"

"Don't tell me it's an honor, because I know it's random. There is no honor involved."

"There *is* honor in doing your duty." Karla leafed through a Chico's catalog. She stopped at the page with the coupon and ripped it out.

Deidre's first reaction was *Hey, that's mine!* but she silently reminded herself that since marrying Sig she could afford full price.

Karla couldn't.

Old habits—and frugalities—died hard. When Deidre and Don were married, she had never considered shopping at Chico's. Wal-Mart and clearance sales offering at least 70 percent off were the recipients of what little money she had to spend on clothes. Same with Karla. After all, she was Don's mother, cut from the same blue-collar cloth. Karla had never even heard of Chico's until she'd come to live with Deidre and Sig.

Many would (and did) say it was an odd arrangement, but Deidre didn't care. She loved Karla and Karla loved her—and Nelly. So when the maintenance of the Polland family home had become too much for Karla, Deidre had offered her a home.

She'd asked Sig, of course. Sig—being the kind of guy who helped the helpless—had agreed.

And honestly, what did he care? He wasn't around that

much anyway. And if having Karla in the house took him off the hot seat toward helping Deidre handle Nelly's schedule, he was all for it. In that regard (and others) Karla was a gem. She was only sixty-two, had more energy than Deidre could cook up on a good day, and possessed a wit and pizzazz that appealed to Nelly.

Deidre often remembered the time when Nelly had been down with strep throat, and Karla had donned a tiara and an old poufy petticoat and pirouetted into Nelly's room, making her laugh. Actually, it was the red sweatpants and tennies *under* the petticoat that had made the ensemble truly memorable.

Through all the turmoil of the past few months, Karla had been a lifeline to Deidre, an oasis of sanity and common sense and strength and humor. . . .

Karla interrupted her thoughts. "I'll take care of Nelly while you're on the jury."

Once again Karla had seen a need and filled it.

"That would be wonderful," Deidre said.

"Hey, maybe you'll get assigned a murder trial. Something lurid and juicy."

"Karla!"

She shrugged. "Who wants to listen to testimony about a robbery or tax evasion or some corporate mishmash? If you've got to sit there day after day, it might as well be interesting. Plus, you'd know you were doing something important, getting a murderer off the streets, making the world safe for mankind."

"It sounds like you've already convicted them. What happened to 'innocent until proven guilty'?"

Karla flipped Chico's shut and moved the Coldwater Creek catalog front and center. "That's good too. Saving an innocent person from a lifetime in jail. Heady stuff, my dear."

Deidre looked back to the letter. "I may not be chosen. Then all of this talk would be for—"

"Oh, you'll be chosen. Just be your sweet self—and wear your tan suit. You look authoritative in that."

"I don't think they want authoritative jurors."

"Hmm. Maybe the pink polka dot then. To look impressionable."

"Impressionable? Polka dots make me look impressionable?"

"Pink ones do." Suddenly, Karla pegged the page with her finger. "This. Ooh! I want this."

Deidre looked over her shoulder at the catalog page. "Which?"

After a moment's hesitation, Karla removed her finger and said, "The whole page. Yes, that's it. I want the whole page. Goodness, I love this catalog!"

"You help me get through this jury time and I'll buy you that whole page."

Karla's eyes sparkled. "You got a deal."

———

If Bobby Mann had to say, "Welcome to Burger Madness. May I help you?" one more time, he would combust into some nice ground-up something-or-other they could make into thin-as-a-dime patties. *Get me an extra-large fries and drink with that, and make it snappy.*

Yes, he was bitter. But also resigned. What twenty-eight-year-old man with a wife and two kids worked at a burger joint? If he were a manager, or even an assistant manager, that would have been one thing. But to just hand out burgers at a drive-through . . .

Pitiful.

As he turned onto Magnolia Lane, the street where he

lived, he checked his watch. He had two hours before his second job started—working concessions at the Higgins Family Variety Extravaganza show. Considering the way the smell of fries and popcorn made his stomach roil . . . he used to love fries and popcorn.

He used to love a lot of things. Like life.

He pulled into the driveway and parked behind his wife's '85 jade green Grand Prix that needed new shocks and a new paint job that would hide the trunk, which was pieced from a blue Grand Prix, and the front right bumper, which was tan. "My patchwork car" Becky called it—with no malice in her voice whatsoever.

Becky didn't do malice. Nor bitterness. Becky was a saint. *She has to be to put up with me.*

Bobby opened the screen door but noticed the real door was open. Probably to let the air flow through. It was a hot September day but air-conditioning was expensive. Again, Becky never complained.

He was just about to call out, "I'm home" when he saw her asleep on the sofa, a stuffed bear held to her pregnant belly. The pregnancy was sapping her strength and they still had two months to go. Actually, a bigger cause of her sapped strength was in the other room.

Bobby tiptoed up the stairs into the kids' bedroom. Four-year-old Tanner lay asleep on his back, limbs sprawled. Two-year-old Teresa was curled into a ball, sucking her thumb.

Nap time at the Mann residence.

He should join them. His shift at the theater didn't get over until midnight.

Yet he couldn't waste time sleeping.

Bobby detoured into the master bedroom and removed the green Burger Madness polo shirt, replacing it with a red

Mozart's 250th birthday T-shirt he'd bought at the symphony concert he'd taken Becky to a few years previous.

He moved through the house without making a sound and went out the kitchen door. Within a few steps he was in the one-stall garage that was his shop.

Once inside, once the lights were switched on, the stiffness in Bobby's body fell away. He breathed deeply and let the sweet aroma of wood shavings fuel his soul. He knew other people would think he was crazy for being so energized by a bunch of wood and tools, but that didn't change his reaction every time he came into his shop. His reaction was reliable, one of the few things he could count on in this unpredictable life. Besides Becky . . . he could always count on Becky. Sweet, dear Becky . . .

He carried the thoughts of her to the sanding table. On it was the top of an inlaid coffee table. While the bulk of the table was red oak, Bobby had painstakingly cut tiny triangles and squares of walnut and birch veneer, creating a decorative border two inches from the table's edge. It was a piece of art—if he did say so himself.

Which he didn't.

Because it was also busywork, a stupid dream, a fantasy.

These were not new thoughts and with a flick of his head, he shoved them aside. He retrieved the sanding block and started on the tabletop with long sweeping motions. He'd used the electric sander on the main part of the table, but with the veneer . . . he had to use finesse. He stopped sanding and felt the edges of the inlay. He closed his eyes to rely completely on touch. Just a little off the right-hand edge . . .

He leaned over his work, gingerly rubbing the offending edge. He stopped and felt again. Yes. Yes.

Bobby heard the door to his work space open.

Becky came in, offering her usual smile. "You should have woken me up."

"You looked too cute. Maybe I should get you your own teddy bear so you wouldn't have to borrow Teresa's."

She ran her fingernails up and back on his shoulder before kissing it. She held a stack of mail. "There's a letter for you."

"Let me guess. A bill?"

"Those too, but this one looks official." She held it out to him.

He checked the return address. District court? "I hope I'm not being arrested for anything," he joked.

"I'd visit you."

"Only if you bring your oatmeal raisin cookies."

"Open it," she said. She read over his shoulder. "Jury duty?"

Bobby shook his head. "I don't have time for this." He pointed to the table he was making. "I don't have time for *this*." He pointed at her. "I don't have time for you, for them. For—"

"Shh. It'll be all right. It's an honor, Bobby."

"Duty."

"Same thing."

Only in her eyes.

He tossed the sandpaper on the workbench. He wasn't in the mood. "It'll take forever. You've seen those trials that carry on weeks and weeks."

"Maybe it will be a little trial. In, out, done."

He thought of something else. "Maybe I won't be chosen." He shook the letter. "It says here I'm on duty for a week. I have to call in the night before and see if I'm supposed to come in. Then they either pick me or don't. Maybe I won't get picked. I can't. I have three jobs. Two and a half kids."

"I've got my Pretty Lady Cosmetics job. . . ."

They both knew her profit selling makeup from a catalog

was minimal. People ordered online these days. And in her condition, it wasn't as if Becky could sell door-to-door like those Avon ladies used to do.

Bobby headed out, flicking off the light. "I can't get chosen. That's it. I just can't—and I won't."

TWO

Do not twist justice in legal matters
by favoring the poor or being partial
to the rich and powerful.
Always judge people fairly.

LEVITICUS 19:15

I'd rather be flipping burgers.

It was an amazing thought considering Bobby Mann hated his burger job. He hadn't wanted to be selected for a jury, but when he was, he'd tried to think positively about it. Maybe it wouldn't be so bad. After all, he loved watching *Law & Order* and *CSI* on TV. He loved the forensic stuff and the give-and-take of the lawyers against the witnesses, especially when the lawyers made them break and tell stuff they didn't want to tell.

He hoped that would happen during this case—a murder case. The defendant, Patti McCoy, was a kitchen worker at a local resort. She was accused of killing her boyfriend, Brett Lerner, the restaurant's maître d', while he sat in a hot tub in his backyard. She hit him over the head with a wine bottle. Allegedly hit him. Or pushed him under. Or something.

The whole thing sounded pretty fishy, with good potential to hold Bobby's interest.

But so far, it had been boring. If he was bored this bad on the first day . . .

He found himself admiring the courtroom. The room was probably built in the 1930s when budgets allowed craftsmen

to paint the mural that swept the wall behind the judge: rolling hills and upright people, standing together with their chins
held high as they searched for justice. The budget had also
included intricate wrought iron chandeliers that hung from a
tin-roofed ceiling. The windows were high, letting in light but
no view. There would be no distraction from the job at hand.
At least not on their account.

But what impressed Bobby the most was the woodwork.
The massive mountain of oak that raised the judge on a
level above the rest of them was set off by layers of fluted
trim topped with carved corners. The half wall separating
the lawyers from the spectators, and the jury from the rest
of the courtroom, was created with large curved spindles
beneath a massive rail. *I can make spindles like that on my
lathe. . . .*

The chairs were also oak, yet were surprisingly comfortable because they had armrests and were designed to curve
around a person's back. They were classic. Timeless. Bobby
made a quick sketch on his notepad.

Maybe this wouldn't be a total waste of time.

The prosecutor could have been hired by central casting.
Abigail had seen his type in dozens of productions: a striking
man skirting the edge of handsome who made up for his lack
of hunky looks through his commanding manner, immaculate
grooming, and impeccable taste. He wore an expensive coal
gray suit, a white starched shirt, a cerulean tie, and polished
oxfords.

Actually, the color of the tie was unexpected. The standard
dress for a conservative man in power would have dictated
maroon. This flash of individuality piqued Abigail's interest,

making her pay more attention to the man—and his words— rather than less.

As intended?

She wouldn't doubt it. Lawyers were like that. Just as the ideal theater set did not contain a single prop that wasn't vital to the story, a savvy lawyer thought through every detail of his production—the trial. Visual or audible, everything was taken into account in an attempt to predict a response. An outcome. A verdict in their favor.

The prosecutor's name was also in his favor: Jonathan Cummings. Very authoritative and persuasive. The man wouldn't have had the same impact if his name had been Jon. Or especially John. What's in a name?

Plenty.

Abigail looked at the defendant. Patti. With an *i* not a *y*. By the looks of her, Abigail guessed Patti signed her name with a little heart to dot the *i*. It was hard to believe she was capable of murder.

And yet, by what Cummings was saying . . .

". . . will prove that Patti Jo McCoy had both the motive and the opportunity to take the life of her lover, Brett Lerner. Hers was a motive that is timeless and transcends all segments and sections of society." He paused in the middle of the court-room and turned toward Patti, managing a look that conveyed both pity and scorn. "Unmarried. Alone. She was carrying a child, and Brett was the unwilling father."

Abigail looked at Patti, watching for her reaction. The girl didn't try to hide her condition by looking ashamed or ignore it by staring straight ahead. Patti put a hand on her abdomen.

Ah. A love child. If that tidbit of information had been in the news, Abigail had missed it. A love child and the heel who wouldn't marry her.

Abigail knew she shouldn't jump to such conclusions

before the case was made. And yet . . . life was revealed in the details. One hand placed lovingly on one belly . . .

Cummings continued with a list of the evidence against little Patti. "The state will show through eyewitness accounts that Ms. McCoy was at the murder scene. Through fingerprint evidence we will show she touched the murder weapon. And we will reveal, through a neighbor's testimony, that upon killing her lover, she screamed in shock at her own actions. Overcome by guilt, she then ran away."

Guilty as charged. Case closed. Can I go home now?

Abigail was shocked by how quickly these thoughts appeared. She'd always prided herself on having an open mind.

But also a logical one. If there *was* hard evidence . . .

Poor little thing. As it stood now, Patti Jo McCoy was toast.

———

Ken Doolittle pinched a piece of lint from his khakis and let it fall to the ground between his chair and the chair of his fellow juror Jack, the car guy. Jack slowly turned his head and watched it fall, then looked at Ken as if he'd just witnessed something offensive.

Ken hoped their seating order wasn't set in stone because the thought of looking at Jack's grease-stained fingernails day after day . . . To tick Jack off, Ken plucked another— invisible—piece of lint from his pants and let it fly between them. *Bug off, buddy.*

Ken realized he hadn't been listening to the defense attorney's opening statement. Not that he was missing much. Stan Stadler was no more impressive than his defendant. Ken would bet his PING driver the man was a public defender. Stan was a good fifty pounds overweight and carried the majority of the fat in front. With no backside, he was constantly hitching up his pants, which balanced under his belly with gravity a constant enemy.

Stadler had made an attempt to slick his dark hair back, but it rebelled, leaving strays shooting from his head at odd angles as if the wisps didn't want to be associated with this obvious bad hair day. And when the man wasn't rescuing his pants, he was pushing his aviator-shaped glasses farther up his nose—which was the only skinny thing about him. Actually, when Ken thought about it, he realized the nose might be the only body part not affected by fat. Interesting.

With a deep intake of breath, Stadler wound things up. "The defense will show that the defendant, Patti McCoy, did not kill Brett Lerner." With a nod to the jury, Stadler returned to his chair.

That was it?

Patti looked hopeful.

Ken was not impressed.

Deidre Kelly was determined to soak in every word of the trial's opening statements. Sig would want a play-by-play that evening. When Deidre had been chosen for this particular trial, they'd both agreed it was an amazing twist of fate.

Deidre was glad the judge had said they could take notes because she had trouble remembering three items to get at the store without writing them down. She was no Abigail Buchanan—who seemed to be taking it all in but wasn't writing down a thing.

The defendant, Patti, was a bitty thing who could have benefited from some beauty parlor expertise. There was some natural beauty present, but with her minimal makeup, washed-out lips, and dull hair pulled back in a ponytail, Patti blended into the background, as unremarkable as the items that occupied the defendant's table, as inconsequential as her lawyer's briefcase, a manila folder, a yellow legal pad, or a pitcher of water.

Patti's job as a dishwasher at The Pines restaurant at the Country Comfort Resort and Spa was not a stretch. Patti was someone Deidre would have glimpsed through the kitchen door without really looking at her, an invisible service employee like those she'd come into contact with a hundred times. There, but not there. Although Patti had not spoken aloud as yet (would she be allowed to testify?) Deidre guessed her voice would be soft. *"You'll have to speak up, Ms. McCoy. . . ."*

Yes indeed. The girl would have to speak up if she was going to be acquitted of this murder charge. But if Patti didn't take the rap, who would?

Deidre knew justice was occasionally fooled or interrupted, but it was rarely completely blocked. Justice was relentless.

The truth would come out.

Deidre shivered.

———

Opening statements, then one lone witness—the coroner who said Brett was hit over the head with a wine bottle but died of drowning in the hot tub. There were no drugs in his system, just some wine and a corned beef sandwich. A deep blue wine bottle—broken at the neck—had been put into evidence. That was it for the first day. Although Abigail had found the two attorneys enjoyable to watch—each in their own way—she'd expected a little more action.

If this trial were a play, it would close opening night. To mediocre reviews.

Abigail wasn't dumb. She realized movies and plays about jury trials were a step beyond real life and were played for the dramatic moment. But since hers was a murder trial, she'd expected some excitement. Some surprises.

She chastised herself. It was only the first day.

Besides, getting off at four was a perk.

Inside her apartment building, Abigail's path was blocked by the little girl from the first floor apartment sitting on the stairs, head in her hands. Abigail could never remember her name. Harley?

"Hi there, uh . . . ?"

"Hayley."

Right. "Are you bored, in trouble, or just thinking? Hayley."

"I'm mad."

"A fourth alternative. Is it justified or are you pouting just to pout?"

Hayley stood, glaring down at her. "I'm mad at life."

Abigail stifled a laugh. "All eight years of it?"

"Nine," Hayley said, plopping back down on a step.

Abigail looked at the upper landing, wishing she were there, past this impediment to the rest of her afternoon. She put her foot on the first step, hoping Hayley would move.

She didn't.

Abigail sighed. "Have you talked to your mom about it?" *Whatever it is?*

"She doesn't know anything about theater stuff."

Abigail removed her foot from the stair. Her interest was definitely piqued, but she wasn't going to be pulled in so easily. "You shouldn't sit out here in the hall so anybody can nab you."

"This is Branson. No one lives in this house but us, you, and Mr. Larson. No one's going to nab me."

She had a point. The small number of tenants was one of the reasons Abigail liked the place so much. Especially since Mr. Larson—who lived on the entire second floor and was in the import business—was off in Asia most of the time. That left a full floor between herself and the noise of Hayley's family. (Abigail had seen a little brother.) Silence was golden.

"I'm nervous about the tryouts Thursday," Hayley said.

The girl definitely had a talent for making leading statements. Abigail had no choice but to bite. "What tryout?"

"For *Annie*."

"Who's doing *Annie*?"

"The community playhouse. You were in *Annie* once, weren't you?"

Abigail was impressed. "How do you know that?"

"I looked you up on the Internet."

Doubly impressed—and curious. "I'm on the Internet?"

Hayley shrugged. "Everybody is. I googled you."

"You what?"

Hayley stood on the third step, meeting Abigail eye to eye. "I've never tried out before. Would you tell me how it works?"

Although Abigail loved nothing better than talking about the theater, she'd had a long day, and it was going to be a long day tomorrow—if not through activity, certainly through boredom. Plus, not having any children of her own, she didn't relate well to the species. Kids and dogs. They always stole the scene.

"I liked you as Cynthia in that war movie."

"You saw that?"

"I rented it. You die good."

"Thank you. I guess."

Hayley changed her weight to the other foot. "So, Ms. Buchanan? Will you help me?"

The manipulative little thing. Abigail headed up the stairs. "Are you sure you're only nine?"

"I'll be ten next month."

None too soon. "You hungry?"

"Starved."

"A starving artist. Get used to it, girlie. And call me Abigail."

———

"Hi, honey. I'm home."

Becky appeared in the kitchen doorway, a paring knife in one hand, a potato in the other. "I didn't expect—"

Tanner and Teresa left their coloring books and ran to him, each grabbing a leg. "Daddy!"

It was such a lovely sound.

"Hey, chicapoo and chicapoo-poo. How do you do?"

They stood on his feet and he took them along as he hobbled to greet his wife with a kiss. "We got off early."

"I see that. But you've ruined the surprise."

"What surprise?"

She lifted the potato. "A special dinner. Minute steaks, scalloped potatoes, creamed corn, garlic bread . . ."

"And cake, Daddy! Chocolate cake for dessert."

Bobby flicked the tip of Tanner's nose. "Should I go outside and sit on the porch until you're ready for me?"

Becky turned back to the kitchen. "You could set the table and talk to me. Tell me how it went today."

The kids jumped from their father's feet and went back to coloring. Bobby washed his hands and got out plates that each had a daisy in the center.

"Not those," Becky said. "Get the china."

"Being on a jury isn't that big a deal, Becky."

"Having you home for dinner, not rushing off on your way to your other job . . . that's worth celebrating." He must have made a face because she added, "You *were* planning on being here all evening, weren't you?"

Actually . . .

She tossed the potato on the counter, where it rolled against the cookie jar. "You got permission from both week-day jobs to be gone while you're on the jury. You have permission; I know you do."

"But if I don't work, I don't get paid. I was thinking of working concessions tonight."

Becky's shoulders drooped. "I'd hoped we could have the whole evening together, get the kids to bed early, spend some time . . ."

He knew what she meant. Romance had been lacking of late.

She turned her back on him and retrieved the potato. "I have to get these in the oven. I'll hurry things along so you can get to work."

"Beck . . ." He was torn. Was being focused on providing for his family a bad thing? In a few months he'd have another mouth to feed. He wasn't getting squat for pay from the court while he was on the jury.

Becky looked over her shoulder at him. She took a deep breath, put her utensils down, and wiped her hands on a towel. She came to him, wrapping her arms around his waist, leaning her head against his chest. "I'm sorry. I don't mean to make you feel guilty. You're only doing what you think best."

Becky may have been a good woman in her moral being, but she was also good at doing what women did best.

He kissed the top of her head. "I'll stay home, Beck. Tonight I'll stay home."

Her smile was his paycheck.

————

Ken tossed his keys and extra change in the bowl by the front door of his town house. After being on the jury he thought he'd feel better than this, more important. Truth was, the whole day had been rather boring. A lot of stops, starts, and recesses. The judge had to have a bladder the size of a walnut the number of times he called for a break. Then there was the tedium of being led out then led back in. And he'd thought lunch was going to be served to the jury, gratis. That's what he'd always seen in movies.

But apparently that was only after deliberations started. Up until then they were on their own. Yet, since they couldn't talk to the other jurors about the trial, and since they didn't even know each other, it was awkward. Ken never relished eating alone. He got enough of that at home.

So when he'd spotted the pretty blonde juror he'd taken a chance and asked her to join him for lunch at the deli across the street. He'd guessed correctly that she too wasn't the type who wanted to eat alone. The classy way she dressed told him she was the sort who needed to be appreciated and noticed. He was happy to oblige.

The deli wasn't a regular restaurant, and they'd stood in one line to order their sandwiches and in another to pick them up. Ken had gotten pastrami on rye and the woman had ordered tomato bisque soup and a tuna sandwich—hold the mayo.

Watching her weight, no doubt. *I'll be happy to watch her weight. . . .*

As soon as they were settled at the only free table—by the

restrooms—Ken made introductions. "I'm Ken Doolittle. And you are?"

They shook hands over the table. "Deidre Kelly."

"So. What do you think so far?" Ken asked.

"We're not supposed to talk about the trial."

He shrugged. "It was worth a shot. But now that I know you're an honest woman, I won't try to lead you astray again."

"Are you married, Ken?" she asked.

"Divorced. You?"

"My husband is Dr. Sigmund T. Kelly."

Though the name sounded familiar, he knew it would make for more interesting conversation if he pretended it wasn't. "Sorry. I'm not familiar—"

Her face revealed an *Oh, really?* look. "He travels the world and operates on children, for free."

"Do you go with him?"

She dabbed her mouth with a napkin. "No. I have a twelve-year-old daughter. We have a daughter. She was mine before—" She dunked her spoon in her soup. "We got married and then Sig operated on *her*—he cured her hip joint problem."

"Marriage is one way to get a free operation." When she didn't smile, Ken realized he might have gone too far. "Sorry. I didn't mean anything by that. I'm sure you—"

"I don't know what we would have done if Sig hadn't come along."

Obviously, without meaning to, he'd hit the mark. Time to change the subject, though it was one he rarely visited. "I have a son."

"How old?"

"Twenty."

"Is he in college?"

A bitter laugh escaped along with a shake of his head. "I'd

love to say he was busy finding himself, but the truth is, Philip isn't that ambitious."

"Maybe it's just a phase."

"Maybe." Not.

For the rest of the meal they'd talked about safe subjects like travel and golf, and Ken was fine with the idea of avoiding further discussion about their families.

Odd thing, families.

Ken walked into his empty kitchen and saw that the light on the answering machine was pulsing. He hit the Play button.

"Hi. Dad. This is Philip. I . . . uh . . . how have you been? Anyway . . . I really need to talk to you. I want to talk to you. If you have a chance. I mean, if you want. I . . . here's my number. . . ."

Ken did not pick up a pen to write the number down, and it wasn't because he knew it by heart. He opened the fridge.

Odd thing, families.

———

"So?" Sig met Deidre at the door.

"Can I at least set my purse down?" she asked.

Sig stepped back, finding the edge of the counter for support.

She looked past him. "Where's Nelly?"

"She's at her piano lesson. Karla took her."

It took Deidre a moment to remember what day it was. And the time. It was four-thirty. "Why are you home so early?" she asked.

He sighed. "I can't work. I can't concentrate on anything. Tell me what happened at the trial."

Although his interest was a bit desperate, she enjoyed

owning control of the moment—enjoyed it enough to prolong it. "I need some iced tea."

She poured herself a glass and added a packet of Equal. She stirred, letting the *dink-clink-plink* of the spoon against the glass ring a moment. "Would you like a glass?"

"Deidre, please."

She'd pushed it far enough. She strolled into the family room. The television was on the evening news. She shut it off. Having Sig's full attention was a luxury she was going to milk without distraction. "They gave opening statements and we listened to one witness."

"Who's going to win?" he asked.

"We don't know yet. We haven't heard all the evid—"

He sat on the edge of his favorite leather chair. "Which lawyer is the best?"

"The prosecution. By far."

The kitchen door sprang open and Nelly and Karla came in.

"Hey, Mom." Nelly stopped at the edge of the room. "Dad? Why are you home so early?"

He huffed. "You'd think I was never home."

"You're never home this early," Karla said. "But lucky you, because now you'll be able to partake of my famous lasagna hot out of the oven instead of warmed up."

"And garlic bread?" Nelly said.

"A ridiculous, decadent amount."

Nelly headed for her room upstairs. "Tons and tons of cheese, please."

"You got it."

The three adults looked at each other an awkward moment; then Karla said, "You're not talking about the trial, are you? Because from what I've heard, jurors are instructed not to talk—"

Deidre looked to Sig. She wasn't sure what to do. She *had* been instructed not to talk about it.

"I'm her husband. She tells me everything."

Not everything.

Karla put her fingers in her ears and chanted, "I'm not listening. I'm not listening."

Sig waved a hand at her. "That's your choice. But I want to hear, so if you'll excuse us?"

It was not like Sig to be rude to Karla. They got along amazingly well considering they weren't even related.

Her mother-in-law seemed unsure how to react. She made a face, then retreated toward the front hall. Probably going downstairs to her apartment . . .

Sig sighed. He looked wiped out. "Finally. Now go on. Tell me everything."

So much for milking the moment. Deidre gave a quick recap of the day's events, including a description of the lawyers. "Looks do matter in these things."

Sig nodded. "You mentioned a witness?"

"The coroner." This was her drama card for the day. "Brett died of drowning."

He sat forward. "Not from being hit over the head?"

"It was implied the bonk on the head dazed him and made him sink into the water. Where he drowned."

Sig sat back against the soft leather of the chair. "Oh."

Deidre's attention was drawn toward the front hall. There, against the marble floor, she spotted a shadow—the shadow of Karla? Listening?

Sig needed to stop talking. *Loose lips sink ships. . . .*

She stood and said, "I'm going to work on dinner." She pointed toward the foyer and mouthed "Kar-la . . ."

Sig offered another defeated sigh but grabbed the remote and turned on the news.

Deidre could certainly teach her mother-in-law a thing or two about being sneaky.

Three

I replied, "But my work seems so useless!
I have spent my strength for nothing
and to no purpose. Yet I leave it all
in the LORD's hand; I will trust
God for my reward."

ISAIAH 49:4

She reminds me of Mama.

Bobby Mann was surprised by the thought. But as he sat in the courtroom on the second day of the trial and looked at petite, fragile Patti McCoy, the present raced back to collide with the distant past.

He hadn't seen his mama since he was fourteen. Actually the last time he'd seen her . . .

He squeezed his eyes shut against that particular memory: looking up from raking the leaves in the side yard, only to see his mama walk down the front walk of the house, her arms cradling herself as if she was cold.

Get a sweater on, Mama.

He remembered thinking that. He'd been brought up to be a practical boy, and a caring one, aware of the needs of others. Mama was always after him and his two brothers and three sisters to get a sweater on—most likely because *she* was cold. She was always cold. There wasn't enough meat on her to keep her warm in any weather below sixty.

But on that day in the fall of his fourteenth year Mama hadn't worn a sweater. She hadn't really needed one, because she wasn't outside that long. Just long enough to walk down the front path, walk between two cars parked on the busy street, and walk out into the ever-present traffic.

He'd never forget the sound of it, the awful thump as car met flesh.

Bobby shook his head. Mama couldn't help herself. She'd been distraught over the death of her husband—who'd accidentally died while walking in front of other traffic, on another busy street. But Daddy had been drunk. Mama was sober.

Drunk with grief?

Bobby knew the feeling. Losing his dad, then his mom, then having all the kids get split up . . . He'd only seen his siblings a couple times since. But now, double the age he was then, even if they did miraculously find each other they'd be strangers, like playmates who were conjured up only in snapshots and snippets of memories.

Bobby had gone to live with his grandpa in Branson. Teddy Mann had been a crotchety old cuss. The best man Bobby had ever known.

Suddenly, Bobby was yanked back to the courtroom as Patti McCoy looked directly at him. She smiled just a little, her expression changing from fear to . . .

Bobby looked away. *She reminds me of Mama.*

———

Finally. The good stuff.

Ken crossed his legs, getting comfortable for the first witness of the day. Officer Carter. The first officer at the scene.

The prosecutor began. "What did you find when you answered the 911 call to 1248 Bonham?"

"I answered the call with my partner, Officer Randy Moore. Actually, we weren't far away when the call came, so we got there within a couple minutes. My partner was driving, and when we pulled up, I saw a woman open the door to a car which was sitting in front of the house. When she saw us, she bolted. She ran down the street, between some houses—they are acreages out there—and I ran after her."

"What did your partner do?"

"He yelled that he was going to check the house."

"Did you apprehend the woman?"

"I did." He nodded toward Patti. "It was the defendant, Patti Jo McCoy." He smiled. "She may be small but she was feisty." He seemed to catch his smile and got serious. "Feisty for a moment. I got her calmed down soon enough."

"Did she say anything to you?"

"She kept saying, 'He's dead! I can't believe he's dead!'"

"Meaning Mr. Lerner."

Carter nodded. "Of course I didn't know that at the time, but yes. That's the only DB we came upon that night."

"DB. Dead body?"

"Yeah. Yes. Sorry."

"What happened next?"

"I took her back toward the house and secured her in the back of the squad car. By then my partner, Randy, was coming to the front to get me. He led me round back."

"What did you find there?"

"I saw the victim, Brett Lerner, floating in a hot tub. There was blood on his head and in the water."

"Was the water still or bubbling?"

"Still."

"What else?"

"There was a broken wine bottle beside the hot tub, a toppled wineglass, and a rumpled towel."

"Dry or wet?"

Officer Carter looked to the ceiling. "Dry."

"Anything else? Anyone else at the scene?"

"A man in jogging shorts and a T-shirt came around the house, into the backyard."

"Who was that?"

"The neighbor who'd called 911, who'd heard the defendant scream. And he said—"

Cummings held up a hand. "We will call the neighbor, Bill Daltry, to the stand to make his own testimony, Your Honor."

The judge nodded.

"What happened next?"

"An ambulance came, and Lerner was pronounced dead. Then the crime unit showed up to process the scene."

"What happened to the defendant?"

"We were going to question her more right there at the scene, but she was in a bad state, hugging herself, rocking, shaking her head. It was getting crazy at the house too—TV cameras had showed up; we don't have that many murders in Branson, you know—so we took her to the station for questioning. For her own good."

"Was she a suspect?"

"Not officially. Not yet. But a person would have to be dumb not to see the connection and—"

"Objection!"

"Sustained."

It was obvious Officer Carter didn't like being cut off. Ken agreed with what he was going to say. Patti had been trying to escape the scene in her car, and when the cops came she ran. . . . Yes indeed, a person would have to be dumb not to see the connection. She was guilty. Of something.

"What happened at the station?"

"First off, we fixed her hand up. It was bleeding. Not bad, but she'd cut herself on the wine bottle when—"

"Objection!"

Officer Carter didn't wait for the judge to rule. "She told us that herself. About how she'd been cut."

"Overruled," the judge said.

"Continue," Cummings said.

"After she told us about the cut, we had no choice but to consider her a suspect, so we read her her rights."

"Did she waive those rights?"

"Yes, sir, she did."

Cummings moved to the evidence table and held up a bound stack of paper. "Your Honor, I would like to offer the transcript of that interview into evidence."

"So noted."

Cummings held the transcript but returned to the place in front of the prosecutor's table. "In short, what did the defendant say happened?"

Officer Carter took a deep breath. "She said Lerner was her boyfriend and she'd gone over to his house after work, wanting to talk to him about something important."

"Which was?"

"She was pregnant."

"He was the father?"

"Well . . . that's what she said." Carter's voice was skeptical.

"Objection, Your Honor."

"Sustained. No embellishments, Officer. However subtle."

"Yes, Your Honor." He cleared his throat. "She knocked on the front door. When he didn't answer she went around back because she knew he liked to get in the hot tub most evenings, it didn't matter how cold. She didn't see him, but the hot tub was bubbling. She saw the broken wine bottle and picked it up. Then the timer on the hot tub stopped and when the bubbles cleared, she saw him."

"Did she call 911?"

"No, sir. The jogger did that."

"If she was innocent, why didn't she call for—?"

"Objection, Your Honor! Calls for conclusion."

Cummings waved a hand. "Withdrawn." He stroked his chin a moment. "How many years have you been on the force, Officer?"

"Nine."

"In those nine years have you ever apprehended a suspect who was running away from a crime scene?"

Carter snickered. "They don't just stand there and wait to be arrested."

"Is that a yes?"

"Yes. Many."

"Have you personally apprehended an innocent person who was running away from the scene of a crime?"

Stadler rose. "Your Honor . . ."

The judge nodded. "I'll allow it." He turned to Officer Carter. "In your personal experience only, Officer."

Carter nodded. "In my experience, no. If they were running, they were guilty."

"Nothing further."

Stadler rose for his turn. "When you encountered Ms. McCoy, did you cuff her?"

"No, sir."

"But if every person who runs from a crime scene is guilty, shouldn't you have assumed she was guilty?"

"We didn't know there was a crime yet. The 911 call said there was a woman screaming."

"In your vast experience as an officer of the law, do people scream for no reason?"

"No."

"So why didn't you cuff her? Obviously something frightening or bad had happened at that house."

Officer Carter squirmed in the wooden chair.

"Officer?"

"It was just that . . . she was just so little."

"So drawing on your vast experience, she didn't look like your usual criminal?"

"Well, no."

"And when she said . . ." Stadler turned to the court stenographer. "Can you read me back Officer Carter's quote of what the defendant said, please?"

The stenographer read, "'He's dead. I can't believe he's dead.'"

Stadler nodded. "Not 'He's dead! I can't believe I killed him!' but 'He's dead. I can't believe he's dead.'" Stadler looked at the officer. Waiting.

The officer looked at Stadler. Waiting.

Cummings stood. "Your Honor, is there a question?"

"Get to the point, Counselor."

"Excuse me, Your Honor." Stadler turned to Carter. "Could it be that the main reason you didn't cuff her—even after you discovered there was a dead body involved—is that you knew she didn't do it? She was a witness, not a criminal?"

"I didn't know any such thing. As an officer of the law, I have to take into account everything—"

"I'm through, Your Honor."

As the officer stepped down, Ken was very confused. If she was innocent, why had she run? And yet . . . Patti McCoy did *not* look like a killer.

———

Once again, the prosecutor, Jonathan Cummings, looked classy, this time in a dark suit, a starched shirt, and a red tie sporting gold fleurs-de-lis. He was definitely easy on the eyes and Deidre realized he looked slightly familiar. She wasn't sure whether it was from the media attention from some previous trial or whether they'd met at a social event. Either way she found comfort in his presence. They were on an equal social plane. The other people on the jury . . . although the jury hadn't gone into deliberations yet, so they hadn't had a real chance to introduce themselves and talk, Deidre remembered enough of the voir dire questions to know that the majority were middle-class working people. Not that there was anything wrong with that, not that Deidre hadn't lived in that social stratum—or lower—during all but the past three years. It was just an observation.

Or was it?

With a start she realized how snobbish it was to arrange these people according to worth. Jonathan Cummings was worth more than Bobby, who'd said he worked at a burger place, or Joe the ponytailed truck driver. And Susan the schoolteacher and the other woman, Ann, whom Deidre had seen showing off pictures of her kids . . . they were someplace in between. Or so weighed the levy of her first impression.

Her eyes were drawn to the defendant. Patti was on the low end of the placement. A dishwasher with no sense of style, little education, and few chances to move away from the mediocrity of her—

Just like you. She's just like you. Were. Once. Not that long ago.

Deidre shook her head, then realized anyone watching

might think she was reacting to something the prosecutor was saying.

She had no idea what the prosecutor was saying. And wasn't it inexcusably vain to even think that anyone would be watching her during a trial? This trial wasn't about her.

Not exactly.

Her thoughts were interrupted by the movement of the juror in the seat beside her. The woman's nails were at least an inch and a half long and were painted magenta with little rhinestones imbedded in the polish. Now there was something Deidre would never see at one of their black-tie events. . . .

Deidre curled her own fingers under. She'd had the acrylic nails taken off because she kept breaking them. And in the past few months she'd gotten back in the habit of biting her own nails . . . a nasty habit. Nasty, nasty habit.

Fingernails. Fingerprints. They were swearing in the fingerprint expert. Next to DNA, it was often the most damning.

Deidre had seen the forensic TV shows where they could get prints from nearly anything now; just one print was all it took.

A sobering thought.

Cummings stepped forward, his face all business. "Mr. Maddox, what is your title?"

"I'm a criminologist with Taney County."

"How long have you worked there?"

"Ten years."

The defense lawyer stood. "We accept Mr. Maddox as an expert in his field, Your Honor."

"Noted," said Judge Abrams. "Proceed, Mr. Cummings."

Cummings went to the evidence table and brought over the broken wine bottle. "Did you find fingerprints on this bottle, the bottle used to hit Mr. Lerner over the head?"

"Yes." Maddox nodded at Patti. "The victim's and the defendant's."

"Any others?"

"No."

Cummings strolled toward the jury box. The jurors couldn't help but look at the murder weapon. The sharp edge of the bottle made the teacher in the front row draw back.

"Were other items checked for fingerprints?"

"The house was, as was the patio area."

"Your findings?"

"The house was full of fingerprints belonging to three dozen individuals, as well as the victim's. Of course."

"Of course. And of those three dozen individuals, did you find the prints of the defendant?"

"Yes."

"Where?"

"In the entry, living room, kitchen, bathroom, bedroom, master bath . . ."

Cummings held up his hand. The picture was clear. Patti had the full run of the house. "Let's focus on the patio area, near the hot tub."

Maddox shifted in his chair. "Unfortunately, there weren't a lot of surfaces that were conducive to prints. The tub was Plexiglas, it was wet, and it was the kind that is built into the concrete. Though we did find some of the defendant's prints on a chair on the far side of the patio."

This didn't seem to help the prosecution. . . .

The face of the witness brightened, as if he remembered something. "But her prints *were* on the wineglass we found toppled near the tub."

"Thank you, Mr. Maddox." Cummings nodded and walked toward the prosecutor's table. "Nothing further, Your Honor."

"Mr. Stadler?" Judge Abrams said.

If Cummings made Deidre feel she was in the company of a peer, Stan Stadler made her cringe. He was the before to Cummings' after makeover.

The defense attorney rose, hitched up his pants, and pushed his glasses onto his nose. "Mr. Maddox, how many wineglasses were found at the scene by the hot tub?"

"One. It was on its side."

"Were there any other fingerprints on the glass?"

"The victim's."

Stadler angled toward the jury and raised his left eyebrow. "So it seems highly probable that the victim was drinking alone, and upon discovering his body, the defendant merely moved his glass out of the way, hence getting her fingerprints on the glass."

Cummings stood. "Again, Your Honor, is there a question?"

Stadler nodded. "Does it seem highly probable that the victim was drinking alone, and upon discovering his body, the defendant got her fingerprints on the glass by moving it out of the way in order to give him aid?"

"I wouldn't say probable."

"Possible?"

"Sure. It's possible," Maddox said.

Stadler shrugged. "Nothing further."

Deidre found she'd been holding her breath. She let it out and grabbed a new one.

————

At lunch break, Abigail saw Bobby sitting on a bench in the courtyard. He wore headphones and was taking food out of a brown paper bag. She went to join him. "May I?" she asked, nodding at the free space on the bench.

He moved his earset to the side, and she was surprised

to hear classical music weave its way through the air. She'd
expected country or bluegrass.

"May I join you?" she asked again.

"Sure." Bobby scooted over, giving her more than enough
room. He took off the headphones and shut off the music.

Abigail spread her voluminous purse wide and pulled out
a tuna sandwich. She looked at the sandwich sitting on his
flattened sack. "Whatcha got?"

He lifted the top piece of bread. "Bologna and mustard."

"Want half a tuna for half a bologna?"

"Sure."

He certainly had that word down.

They traded sandwiches. Abigail wasn't too keen on
bologna and wasn't even sure why she'd offered to trade.
She loved tuna. She usually ate it twice a week. She couldn't
remember the last time she'd succumbed to bologna—if ever.
Yet there was something about Bobby Mann that was appealing. The self-deprecating way he tried so hard to listen well,
taking careful notes while hunched over his pad like a student
worried about a pop quiz.

Abigail hadn't taken any notes yet. A finely honed
memory was perhaps the biggest perk of being an actress
for fifty years. Directors were always shoving a new page
of dialogue in your face. "Here. We changed it." She'd
have a few minutes to forget the old and insert the new. So
far the evidence had not taxed her brain. Even the last bit
of evidence from the jogger neighbor, before lunch. He'd
heard the scream and called 911. Check. He'd seen Patti
at Lerner's house many times. Check. The only tidbit that
had sparked any interest was when he'd added with a smile,
"But she was one of many."

So the victim was a cad. The plot thickened. And sick-
ened. Poor pregnant Patti.

Bobby ate his sandwich, looking forward. Looking nervous. Maybe it wasn't such a good idea to invade his space. Not everyone liked company the way Abigail did. Not everyone liked Abigail's company.

"You're an actress, right?" Bobby asked.

She quickly swallowed. "Yes. Abigail Buchanan, star of stage, screen, and soap commercials."

He turned enough to eye her. "You do look kinda familiar."

"You flatter me, Mr. Mann."

He shook his head adamantly. "No, I don't. I *have* seen you act. Somewhere."

She made a by-your-leave motion with her hand. "That's good to hear. An actor's worst nightmare is not being seen. Or remembered."

"Do you do shows around here, in Branson?"

"I've been in a few." But none lately.

He nodded, then took a bite of a green apple.

"What do you do, Mr. Mann?"

"Bobby."

"And I'm Abigail. I remember you mentioning a restaurant?"

He laughed. "Burger Madness. I work concessions at one of the theaters too. And drive a taxi on weekends."

"I'd say your work ethic is superb."

"Or desperate. I have a wife and two kids, and another one on the way."

"I admire you for being such a good provider."

He shrugged. "Someday . . ."

Ah. An opening. "Someday what?"

He glanced in her direction, then away, as if catching himself. "Nothing."

Abigail angled in her seat to block his disclaimer.

"Nothing, my left shin. It's something. Tell me what you want to do someday."

He bit the corner off the tuna sandwich, chewed, and took a few deep breaths. "I like woodworking. I like to make furniture."

Abigail let her eyebrows rise. It was not what she expected. "You're an artisan?"

"Not yet."

"But someday?"

He smiled. "Someday." He held a Baggie full of Cheetos toward her. She took a couple and enjoyed the cheesy crunch. "You have kids?" he asked.

"Alas, no."

"Married?"

"Was once, back in the fifties."

It was his turn to raise an eyebrow.

She raised a hand. "I know, I know. The dark ages."

"Sorry," he said. "It's just that you don't look that old."

Abigail laughed. "Your wife is a very lucky woman, Bobby Mann. Very lucky."

He didn't take the compliment well. "That's not true."

She didn't pursue it. "Tell me about her. About your kids."

"I met Becky because she spilled her popcorn. At a movie. She was with someone else." He twisted the stem of the apple until it broke off. He put the stem in his sack. "She accidentally spilled her popcorn and her date got mad that she'd wasted his money, and I came to the rescue and told the guy to beat it and helped her clean it up."

"Her knight in shining armor."

"Most likely a T-shirt and jeans."

Abigail shrugged. "How long have you been married?"

"Six years. We have a son, Tanner, who's four, and Teresa, who's two."

"When's the baby due?"

"Six weeks."

"Is it a boy or a girl?"

"We don't know. We don't want to know. We'll know soon enough."

"Do you have a *T* name picked out?"

"Mmm?"

"Tanner. Teresa. A *T* name."

He nodded. "Theodore or Tally. My granddad and Becky's grandmother."

"Seems you have it all worked out."

"Hope so."

He put the half-eaten apple in his sack. "Becky's a wonderful mom. Patient, loving, smart, pretty . . ."

"You don't have to be pretty to be a wonderful mother."

Bobby blushed. "The pretty's for me. She's beautiful to me."

Abigail felt a pang of a long-forgotten ache. She'd never had anyone adore her like Bobby adored his Becky. "You're both very lucky," she said. She was appalled her voice cracked. Was she becoming a sentimental old woman?

"Blessed," Bobby said. "Becky doesn't believe in luck. But she does say we're blessed."

Although Abigail was more familiar with the luck involved with "break a leg" rather than "God bless," she didn't argue with him.

———

Deidre was glad Nelly and Karla were out doing errands. She wasn't up to watching her words with Sig. . . .

She leaned her head against the cushion of the love seat in the master bedroom and rubbed the place between her eyes.

"The first witness after lunch was a forensic expert saying there were other long hairs—presumably female—in the hot tub. As well as Patti's."

Sig paced before the fireplace. "Looks like he had other girlfriends."

As do you?

She must have made a face because he stopped pacing. "Don't go there, Deidre. I told you there's nothing to worry about. When are you going to believe me?"

How many times had she heard that in the past six months? Sometimes she wished she were brave enough to have it out, give Sig an ultimatum: *"It's me or them."*

But every time she even imagined such a scenario, she backed down. She couldn't risk her life, Nelly's life, even Karla's life, in a fit of jealous pique. She'd gone to great pains to create this reality for the three of them, and it would be totally selfish of her to take it away because of something as inconsequential as her ego. As long as Sig was discreet . . .

Discretion . . . What was that old saying? "Discretion is the better part of valor"? She wasn't sure about that, but it sure was the better part of survival.

In the past months, Deidre had felt the insecurities—and determination—of the old Dee-Dee return. She'd always been the sort to do whatever needed to be done. When Don had been sick she'd handled it. When he'd died and she'd found herself a single mom with serious financial issues, she'd handled it. When Nelly's hip problem had gotten worse . . . when it became clear that her daughter was not going to walk normally or have a normal life unless something drastic was done . . .

Dee-Dee had come through. She'd done what needed to be done. She'd found herself a rich, capable, pediatric ortho-pedic surgeon—and married him. He'd taken away her financial problems *and* fixed her daughter's hip. Two birds with one stone.

Only then had Deidre finally been able to relax, to rest and let someone else do the thinking and handling for a while. No one had been more surprised than she at how fast she'd relinquished the reins of her life.

Yet in these past few months, since hearing the gossip about Sig's affairs, since . . . since all the rest, she'd been forced to take up the reins of her life again. If she didn't do it . . . It was kind of sad that the three years she'd had coasting along on the strength of Sig's care were gone. Deidre had hoped to never be forced into survival mode again.

Never say never.

"Deidre? Hello, Deidre?"

With her eyes closed she'd nearly fallen asleep. She sat up, forcing energy through her veins. "Sorry. What did you say?"

"I asked if there was any other evidence."

"Just someone from the police who said they'd found lots of e-mails from Patti to Brett on his computer. Love notes."

"That doesn't sound like it will help us. Were they threatening? incriminating?"

"No. But they did sound obsessive. Like she was trying too hard. It was obvious he wasn't responding like she wanted him to."

"She sounds loose, a younger woman who wanted something from an older man."

"Or vice versa." She hoped he caught her innuendo.

He did.

"Don't, Deidre. I've told you . . . don't."

Yes, he'd told her. He never wanted to talk about Audrey—or the others. And she was too chicken to do anything more than sneak in a snide comment when the occasion arose. A marriage counselor would surely urge her to confront her husband in order to conquer the issue—which is why she avoided such experts.

"So . . . is she loose? A groupie type?"

Deidre arched her back. "If anything she's naive, smitten by a suave man who knew how to get what he wanted from her."

Sig plucked a marble egg from a brass stand on the mantel. He tossed it from hand to hand. "Do you think the verdict will go against her? There's motive; there's opportunity. She acted suspicious running like that."

"I don't know, Sig. It's pretty circumstantial. The defense gets to bring its witnesses tomorrow."

"What do the other jurors think?"

She was confused. "You know we can't discuss the trial until we go into deliberations."

He put the egg down. "I know you shouldn't, but I was hoping . . . I need to know where this is heading. Don't you have lunch together? Breaks?"

She didn't mention that today she'd had lunch with another juror, Ann. But with Ann being the mother of four they'd talked about kids. "We're on our own for lunch." She stood and headed for the master bath. After sitting on a hard wooden chair all day she needed the relaxation of a session in the whirlpool tub.

Sig stopped her in the doorway with a hand to her arm. "Can't you do something? Anything to make sure . . . ?"

"I have to be careful, Sig. I can't break the rules and risk getting kicked off the jury. You wouldn't want that, would you? Want me kicked off before we even get to the deliberation part where I might do some good?"

"You have to swing the vote our way, Deidre. I need to feel some hope here. Yet every time I get a glimpse of it, you squash it."

Compassion and stress collided. "I'm just telling you the truth. You want me to lie?"

The befuddled look on his face was strangely satisfying.

———

There were two messages on her answering machine. A busy day in the life of Abigail Buchanan.

She punched the Play button. *"Ms. Buchanan, this is Carl from the Newland Theatre. I'm sorry, but we chose someone else for the part. Please try us again. We're going to have auditions for the next show in three months and . . ."*

"Pooh to you," Abigail said, talking over the blah-de-blah details. She needed work now. Yesterday.

"Hey, Ms. Buchanan, this is Doris, the casting assistant for the Century Cell Phone commercial? I'm sorry but—"

Abigail's finger hurt from jamming the Off button. So be it. Nobody wanted her. She was a has-been. She was a tarnished trophy on the shelf, a trophy so old nobody could even remember its significance, a trophy someone would find in some junk store on sale for a buck.

I need a long, deep, hot bubble bath.

If only she had a tub. She used to have a tub. A whirlpool. At stressful times she used to make herself a cup of minty tea, light some candles, blow up her bath pillow, and soak until she pruned or the water got cold—whichever came first.

But that was two residences ago, when she was working regular and had money. When she lived in NYC, in Soho, she used to hang out at 21 with her theater cronies after the show. She'd worn the latest Bohemian styles, eschewing Jackie Kennedy's or Audrey Hepburn's matching dresses and coats for gypsy skirts, hippie beads, and Birkenstocks. Actually, it had not been unusual for Abigail to wear an eighteenth century corset top—borrowed from the costume department of her newest play—with a miniskirt and go-go boots. Eccentricity was a religion, attention its mode of worship.

Abigail fell onto her couch that was covered with an Indian throw (to conceal the cigarette holes in the upholstery from its previous owner). Her other furniture—what little there was—was a mishmash of styles. After her opportunities in New York folded in the late seventies, she'd followed the work to LA, where she'd submerged herself in movie, TV, and ad work. But her true love was live theater, which had been why she'd ended up smack-dab in the middle of the country, in Branson, Missouri. She'd been lured by her dear friend Andy Williams and had moved out for a gig in his new Moon River Theatre. But even that gig had ended and since then, other than a sprinkling of parts, she was an out-of-work hoofer, actress, and crooner.

Abigail lit a candle. Her collection of candles and incense burners were a holdover from her hippie days, although she now preferred the more subtle scent of vanilla over patchouli.

She leaned back, letting a dramatic sigh have its moment. Her eyes skimmed over the framed programs and posters from her past that dotted the walls, a collection that had highest priority whenever the need to move intruded. It was quite impressive. Forty-two shows on Broadway (and off, and off-off Broadway), eight movies, twelve TV shows, and nineteen ads.

Her smiling Ivory Soap face glared down as if saying, *"See what you once were? Too bad you're nothing now."*

She grabbed a crocheted afghan and lay down on her side, her back to the mocking wall of her past.

———

"But, Bobby . . . last night was so wonderful."

Bobby buttoned the shirt of his concessions uniform. "I know, Beck, but when I have the chance to work, I need to take it. One of the girls called in sick."

Becky scooped a helping of spaghetti into Teresa's bowl and cut it into small pieces. "The trial shouldn't last more than a couple weeks," she said. "That's what the lawyers told you. You can be away from work a couple weeks. Your bosses said so."

"But if I go into work, I get paid. They told me that too."

"Use your vacation time."

"I want to save that for when you have the baby."

In a motion that had become a habit whenever the baby was mentioned, Becky stroked her belly. "It *would* be nice to have you here then."

"Ghet!" Teresa said. Becky had paused in serving her spaghetti.

With a few more cuts to the pasta, Becky gave her daughter the bowl. The little girl took a handful to her mouth.

"The fork, little one," Bobby said, putting the pint-sized utensil into her hand. The parents' discussion was put on hold until Teresa managed to scoop a forkful of spaghetti into her mouth.

"Yay!" Becky said, clapping.

Bobby joined in. "Yay!"

Teresa grinned and tried for bite number two.

"I can eat with a fork too," Tanner said, showing his expertise.

"I know you can," Becky said. "You're quite the big boy. You can show your sister how it's done."

With that challenge given—and taken, as Tanner started

talking to his sister about forks and spoons—Bobby motioned his wife toward the back door, where his jacket hung on a hook. "You know I'd be here if I thought it best."

Becky changed her weight to the other foot and nodded. She looked adorable pregnant. She was one of those women who carried the change in physique as if it truly was her calling. Although it was a trite saying, she glowed from the inside out.

Actually, Becky always glowed. There was a calm assurance about her that rarely wavered. It was one of the first things he'd noticed when they'd started dating. One time he'd asked her how she could always be so calm, so confident. So glowy.

She'd shrugged and said, "I just try to remember that whatever's happening, God's got it. Knowing that, how can I worry . . . much? I do worry, but I try not to."

The answer had put him off, sounding way too Holy Roller. And yet, Becky hadn't pressed the issue, hadn't gone into a sermon about how he too could glow with the love of Jesus if only he believed.

Bobby appreciated that. It wasn't that he was against Jesus, or ignorant. His grandpa had been a Jesus man—albeit a bit crusty. Bobby had gone to church with Grandpa most Sundays, and he'd liked what he saw. He'd come really close to going up front one Sunday when the preacher had invited anyone who wanted to commit their life to the Lord—

But he hadn't. Though his heart was willing, his mind had been jumbled that morning because one of his brothers had shown up at Grandpa's the night before, running from the police because he'd stolen a car. The police had come with lights flashing and arrested Chuck. But the worst of it was that Bobby's carefully molded life, the one he'd created since moving into Grandpa's, had come tumbling down. Suddenly people knew he had a brother, and soon after that some kid at school found out his dad died a drunk and his mother committed suicide. . . .

After church that day Grandpa came up to his room and sat on his bed. He'd said, "Own up to your roots, Bobby. It's who you are. A maple tree can't pretend it has an oak tree's roots. But that doesn't mean it's any less of a tree. It can be the best maple tree there is. Rise above, boy. Rise above."

Suddenly, Becky stood on tiptoe and kissed his cheek. "Be home as soon as you can. I love you, you know."

He knew. And it sustained him.

I will not eat alone again.

Ken stood by the phone in his kitchen and leafed through his little black book. He got a kick out of having such a thing, and yes, it did contain the names of many, many women. One of whom would have the privilege of eating with him this very night.

Lunch break during the trial today had been humiliating. He'd asked the pretty little blonde juror with the button nose—he thought she was a teacher—if she cared to join him. She'd had the gall to say no, she had other plans. And then she'd waved at a sandy-haired man standing by the stairwell wearing jeans and a slumpy red T-shirt emblazoned with the message "No, I Will Not Fix Your Computer."

She preferred a geek to moi?

Apparently. And so Ken had sauntered out of the courthouse and down the street two blocks to a Wendy's. Luckily, he didn't recognize anyone from the trial inside.

That was then. This was now. He was hungry and in need of a little companionship.

Easily remedied . . .

His first thought was the waitress who had shared his bed most recently: Loretta (or was it Lorena?). She was so recent that he didn't even have her name recorded in the book yet. He opened the junk drawer and found the matchbook from the bar where she'd written her name and number. Loretta Dawson. He dialed.

"Hey, Loretta, this is Ken Doolittle."

"Ah. The man I dallied with nearly two weeks ago but haven't heard from since?"

Oops. "I was called to jury duty."

"I'm happy for you."

He moved the phone to his other ear. "How 'bout some dinner?"

Silence.

"Loretta?"

"I'll pass."

"Why?"

"Because you expect me to go."

"That's not a—"

"Bye, Ken. I think it would be best if you lose my number."

She hung up and Ken looked at the phone, incredulous. "The nerve." He tossed the matchbook in the trash and moved on to the next name.

No.

The next? Some other time.

Six noes. When he got the reaction "Ken who?" from a woman named Martha he scratched out her name, closed his little black book, and grabbed his keys. If his existing women friends didn't want his company, he'd get himself a new one.

Within twenty minutes he was in the parking lot of one of his favorite bars: Jet. He turned on the dome light of his Mercedes and checked his reflection in the rearview mirror.

With the careful stroke of a finger, he moved a stray hair into place.

He heard laughter to his left and watched as a curvy twentysomething flirted with a hunky companion. Across the parking lot he saw another young couple make their way to the bar. No one was going in alone.

Not that he would leave alone, but . . .

But suddenly the thought of playing the part of debonair golf pro offered little excitement and filled him with an overwhelming weariness.

He couldn't do this. Not tonight.

On the ride home, his body embraced the weariness like a long-lost relative, so by the time he unlocked his front door he barely had the energy to undress before falling into bed.

The silence was heavy and condemning.

Ken turned on the television. He ran through the channels twice, landing on a shopping channel. After watching the spokesman rave about a set of top-of-the line steak knives, Ken dug one of his Visa cards out of the drawer of the bedside table.

A man could never have too many steak knives.

Four

We are in this struggle together.
You have seen my struggle in the past,
and you know that I am
still in the midst of it.

PHILIPPIANS 1:30

*T*he state calls Lucy Delgado."

Patti smiled and offered Lucy a little wave as the woman moved past the defendant's table to the witness stand. Lucy returned neither gesture but held her arms stiffly against her short, stout frame as she walked. She looked like she was going to the gallows.

Abigail's first reaction was *uh-oh*. Although Patti had innocently greeted the woman as a friend, Abigail was astute enough to realize whatever Lucy had to say wasn't going to be in Patti's favor. After all, Lucy was a prosecution witness. Didn't Patti realize that?

Abigail studied the defendant. As Lucy was being sworn in, Patti was still smiling. She even looked expectant, as if she was eager to hear Lucy's words. It was painful to watch someone so clueless.

Jonathan Cummings stood and also smiled at Lucy. And *his* smile she returned. Double *uh-oh*.

Cummings settled into the space halfway between the witness box and his table as if a piece of tape on the floor marked the perfect spot. Abigail had often placed such marks on a stage. . . .

"Ms. Delgado," he said. Abigail was once again impressed by the fullness in his voice. He would have made a good actor. Perhaps he *was* a good actor?

"Yes, sir?"

"Would you tell the court your relationship with the defendant?"

"She's my friend." Lucy glanced at Patti, then focused on the lawyer in front of her.

"How did you meet?"

"We work together at the resort. We both work in the kitchen. I make the salads. She washes dishes."

"Do you spend time together outside of work?"

"Sometimes."

"Doing what?"

Lucy fidgeted in the chair. Although Abigail couldn't see the woman's feet, she doubted they reached the floor. "We go out to dinner sometimes. Or to a bar. We went shopping once. At the outlets."

Cummings smiled. "Are you married?"

"Was. My husband died six years ago." She smiled. "But I'm engaged to a wonderful man now." She held out her left hand, revealing a ring with a small diamond.

"Congratulations. In your time together with the defendant did the two of you ever talk about romance? your love lives?"

Even from the jury box Abigail could see Lucy blush. "Quite a bit."

"So you were aware of Ms. McCoy's relationship with the deceased?"

Stadler rose. "Objection, Your Honor. Anything she has to say will be hearsay."

Cummings turned to his opponent. "It goes toward evidence of intent, Your Honor."

"Overruled."

Cummings began again. "So you were aware of Ms. McCoy's relationship with the deceased?"

"Oh yes. She talked about him constantly. She was really smitten." She hesitated a moment then added, "She said she loved him."

"To your knowledge was the relationship a smooth one?"

Lucy shook her head. "They were always fighting."

"About what?"

"Hearsay, Your Honor," Stadler said.

"Sustained. Get to the point, Counselor."

"Did you ever hear the defendant threaten the deceased?"

Lucy looked down. "Well . . . yes, sir. I did."

"What did she say?"

Lucy hesitated. The words were obviously hard to say. "She said, 'I could kill him. I'm going to kill him.'"

Abigail looked at Patti, whose smile had been replaced by a gawk. Clearly she had not expected this.

"'I'm going to kill him'?"

"Yes, sir."

"When did she say this?"

"A week before he died."

There was a collective *oh* from the gallery.

"Nothing further, Your Honor."

The judge looked at the defense table. "Mr. Stadler? Do you have any questions for this witness?"

Stadler pushed his chair back with a rattle and stood. "I certainly do."

Unlike Cummings, Stadler was a roamer, a habit Abigail found disconcerting. As an actress she'd learned not to move unless there was good reason because unnecessary movement diluted the moment and was a distraction from the importance of the words.

As it was in Stadler's case.

"Ms. Delgado, how many years were you married?"

"Twenty-two."

"During those years did you and your husband ever argue?"

Cummings stood. "Objection, Your Honor. Relevance?"

"I'll show relevance, Your Honor."

"Overruled. But make it quick."

Stadler strolled past the jury box then turned back toward his desk. "Have you ever said the words *I could kill him. I'm going to kill him*?"

Lucy lifted her chin. "Never."

Stadler stopped roaming and turned toward her. "Never after a big argument, perhaps while talking with a confidante?"

She shook her head. "Never."

"Then you had a better relationship than the rest of us."

Cummings stood. "Is the counselor admitting to dire intentions of his own, or perhaps even a more serious deed?"

The judge pounded his gavel. "Enough, gentlemen. Mr. Stadler, do you have another question for this witness?"

Stadler scratched his left eyebrow then faced Lucy. "Did you ever see the two of them together? Did you ever actually see Ms. McCoy with Brett Lerner?"

Once again, Cummings rose. "Your Honor, I don't see the point of this question. By her own admission the defendant is pregnant by the deceased. Obviously, they were together, witnessed or otherwise."

Abigail had to bite back a chuckle. Others in the courtroom were less successful.

The judge pounded his gavel. "Order!"

Wisely, Stadler made a beeline for his chair. "Withdrawn. Nothing further, Your Honor."

Prosecution: 1, Defense: 0.

Ken Doolittle couldn't help but enjoy the humiliation of
Stan Stadler. Actually, the way he felt that morning—after
suffering his own bout of humiliation the night before, after
spending over five hundred dollars on various shopping channels—Ken didn't much care which lawyer was humiliated.
As long as someone was. The fact that it was someone who
had no taste whatsoever and needed to lose fifty pounds was
a bonus.

Ken pinched a piece of lint from his navy trousers and was
almost disappointed that the greasy-nailed juror wasn't beside
him to see it. Since that first day Ken had managed to sit
elsewhere. Yesterday he'd sat beside the pretty teacher who'd
shunned him for Techno-nerd, and today he'd positioned
himself next to Mary, a thirtyish Hispanic woman with good
taste in shoes. He was disappointed—but not deterred—to see
that she wore a wedding ring.

The next witness was Howard Smithsen, a burly guy who
obviously used a gym more than twice a week. Ken looked at
Patti. She wasn't smiling. In fact, since the last witness, she'd
slumped in her chair, making her already small frame appear
even smaller.

"Mr. Smithsen, what relationship do you have with the
defendant?"

The witness looked shocked. "None. We've never dated."

Cummings smiled. "Are you her neighbor?"

"Oh. Yeah. I live right next to her—4D. We share a
common wall."

"Which wall?"

Howard smiled. "The bedroom one."

Ken sat up straighter. This could get interesting.

With a nod to Stadler, Cummings asked, "Did you ever *see* the defendant with the deceased?"

"Lots of times."

"Did you ever hear them argue?"

Howard smiled again. "Lots of times. Out front and through the wall. More than once I heard her break something against that wall. A vase or something glass."

"How do you know it wasn't the deceased acting so violently?"

"Because she—Patti—she told me she always broke things. Once I met her on the stairs bringing out a wastebasket full of a blue broken glass."

Cummings looked like he was surprised, but Ken knew he wasn't. "Blue glass? Was it a wine bottle?"

Stadler shot out of his chair. "Objection!"

Cummings sighed and said, "He saw it, Your Honor. Mr. Smithsen is a direct witness."

"Overruled."

"Was the blue glass you saw in the trash a wine bottle?"

"Yeah. The pouring part was still there."

Not good, Patti-girl, not good . . .

"Perhaps she'd dropped the bottle by accident?" Cummings offered.

Howard shook his head. "Nope. She told me she'd thrown it across the room. Then she laughed and said, 'I need to stop doing that. It gets expensive. And messy.'"

"Nothing further, Your Honor."

The judge turned to Stadler. "Any questions, Mr. Stadler?"

"Nothing at this time, Your Honor."

It took a wise man to know when to fold 'em. Yet the score had changed. It was now Prosecution: 2, Defense: 0. Mr. Frumpy Dumpy better get his act together. And soon.

———

The prosecution rested. It was the defense's turn and Bobby was ready for them. He wanted to hear something positive about Patti McCoy. Although there seemed to be flaws in some of the evidence, the last two witnesses who'd testified about Patti's anger, and her threat . . . it would be hard to counter that.

Actually, the worst thing about hearing the coworker and neighbor testify was how it brought back memories of his father's tirades. What had the neighbors heard coming from the Mann residence? What did people say about them after Bobby's father got run over while he was drunk? after his mother's suicide?

He shuddered and was glad he'd been so absorbed in his own grief and the uncertainty of what would happen next that he hadn't been aware of any gossip. Ignorance had indeed been bliss.

If called, would his childhood neighbors say anything good about the Mann household? Had they ever witnessed his mother tucking them into bed every night, stroking their hair behind their ears, saying special prayers for enough money, enough protection, and enough happiness? Had they ever heard his little sister, Cass, sing "Jesus Loves Me" in a voice so pure the air hung on to the notes a moment longer than usual as if sad to let them go?

Or had they only heard his father threaten his mother? Had they cringed when they'd heard his older brothers nearly come to blows with their dad on the front lawn? Had they heard the front door being kicked in when his mother locked his father out?

Would any of that have been held against Bobby like it was being held against Patti?

Bobby was hopeful the defense witnesses would do

Patti some good, but another coworker, a high school friend, and some distant aunt, all saying Patti was a sweet girl and wouldn't hurt a fly, had as much impact as a fly hitting a screen.

Patti the fly. Too easily swatted and flung away.

———

Deidre didn't trust psychologists. She'd been to one when she found herself still mired in grief a year after Don had passed away. Her insurance had supplied three free sessions, so why not? She'd quit going after two.

"So . . . how does your husband's death make you feel?"

"Like I was pushed into a huge pile of dog doo."

When the therapist had nodded politely at her analogy as if Dee-Dee had said something profound, she'd realized the man was of the I'm-okay-you're-okay-everything's-okay bent. If she kept seeing him she'd probably hear all the right words, but they'd be like froth on a cappuccino—tasty, but gone too soon. If only he'd yelled at her, "Come on! Snap out of it!" she might have respected him.

It wasn't as though she hadn't been handling things. Dee-Dee Polland prided herself on handling whatever was thrown her way. Nurse a husband? Check. Bury a husband? Check. Raise a crippled daughter? Check, check. Zoning in on her feelings would only upset the cart of her emotions. As it was, her day-to-day survival had been a precarious balance. The Polland family home, where she and Nelly lived with Karla, was a money pit. Every week something broke down and needed fixing. Between Karla's income as a receptionist at a CPA's office and Deidre's hospital job, they'd barely gotten by. Dee-Dee didn't need some almost-a-real-doctor telling her she'd be okay if only she let it all out.

If she'd done that . . .

The psychologist brought to testify today was Dr. Bridget
Rand. The defense attorney was about to begin his question-
ing. Deidre needed to forget her past and be in the present.
She needed to listen. Too much was at stake.

"Dr. Rand, have you had a chance to speak with the defendant, Patti McCoy?"

"I have. At length."

"What are your findings?"

Jonathan Cummings stood. "Objection, Your Honor. None
of us want to be here for days. Can we have a more specific
question?"

"That would be preferable," said the judge. "Mr. Stadler,
please rephrase."

Stadler hitched up his pants. "In your professional opinion, what is the defendant's temperament?"

"She's generally a needy personality. But she's also very
giving and has a servant's heart. She'd do anything for anybody.
She's meek, nonaggressive, and nonconfrontational to the point
of being a doormat. She's not a leader but a follower." She
appeared finished, then added, "And she's terribly naive."

"Do you believe she genuinely loved Brett Lerner?"

"I believe she did."

"And through her naiveté, did she believe he would marry
her—in her delicate condition?"

"I believe she did."

Cummings stood up again. "Is this leading anywhere,
Your Honor? This is a rehashing of known facts."

"Get to the point, Mr. Stadler," said the judge.

Stadler cleared his throat and pushed his glasses into
place. "In your expert opinion, do you believe Ms. McCoy had
the temperament, the wherewithal, and the inner constitution
to kill someone?"

Dr. Rand leaned toward the microphone. "No, I do not."

"Nothing further, Your Honor."

Cummings popped out of his chair. "I have a few questions for this witness." He walked around the prosecutor's table and took his place. "I'm a little confused, Doctor. You state that Ms. McCoy is nonconfrontational to the point of being a doormat, yet previous witnesses have testified to her violent outbursts during arguments, throwing bottles against walls, and making threats to kill the deceased. That doesn't sound very meek and nonaggressive to me. Nor does it sound like a follower. It sounds very much like Ms. McCoy was ready to *do* something with her anger."

It was Stadler's turn to rise. "Your Honor? Is there a question?"

The judge nodded at Cummings. "Ask a question, Mr. Cummings."

The lawyer nodded once. "How do you explain the discrepancy between your assessment of the defendant's temperament and her verbal and physical actions?"

"Everyone gets angry once in a while."

Cummings looked shocked. "Not according to you. According to you Ms. McCoy is needy, nonaggressive, nonconfrontational, meek. . . ."

"Everyone can get pushed past their breaking point."

Cummings beamed. "As was Ms. McCoy the night she killed her lover. Nothing further, Your Honor."

Dr. Rand stepped down. Deidre's opinion of psychologists had not altered.

———

Abigail had just put Nat King Cole on the CD player, had just sat down with a bowl of bean with bacon soup

and a glass of milk, when there was a knock on her door.
"It's open."

Hayley came in, beaming. She held something behind her
back. "Guess what I have."

Hello to you too. "A million dollars in small bills."

"Nope." Hayley revealed a newspaper. "I've been reading
about your trial. I know everything about it."

Abigail put a hand in front of her face. "Number one, it's
not my trial; it's Patti McCoy's trial. And number two, get that
thing away from me."

Hayley's smile disappeared. "Why? I saved it for you."

Abigail let her voice soften. "As a juror I can't read anything
about the trial. I can't watch or listen to the news either."

"Why not?"

"I have to remain impartial." She pointed to the stove.
"There's some soup if you want."

Hayley looked as if she'd just been told there would be no
Christmas this year. "But I read it for you, so I could talk to
you about it."

"I can't, girlie. Sorry. I have to base my final decision on
what I hear in court and only what I hear in court."

"That's no fun."

She had a point. Abigail blew on her bowl of soup, waiting for the girl to leave.

She didn't. Instead she fell into a rattan bowl chair. "Every
time I think about the audition I want to throw up."

"Bathroom's over there." Abigail ate a spoonful of soup.
Warm and creamy.

Hayley rolled the newspaper into a tube, peered through
it, and did a quick scan of the room, looking like a pirate with
bad posture. Then she tossed it on the floor with a sigh. "I'm
never going to get the part of Annie because Kathy Button is
trying out."

Abigail laughed in spite of herself. "Kathy Button? With a name like that, she can't be much of a threat."

"She can sing. Really sing."

"So can you." She paused. "I assume. Yes?"

"She was the lead in our school program three times. Whatever part she tries out for, she gets."

Abigail had dealt with a few of those types herself. Victoria Mason, Zoe Marshall. Marguerite Albertini. She used to cringe whenever she'd see one of them at an audition. These three women possessed a certain aura, a confidence, a presence, that seemed to make any director buckle to their charms. And talent. They did have talent. The cretins.

When the intro to Nat's song "When I Fall in Love" started up, Abigail set her soup aside and stood. She extended a hand to Hayley. "Come on."

"What?"

"Join me. It's sacrilegious to sit still while the King is singing."

"Elvis?"

"Never! Nat King Cole."

"Who?" But Hayley let herself be pulled into the dance. Abigail took the male role and led expertly, singing along. "'When I fall in love, it will be forever.'" She swung Hayley under her arm and back again, making good use of the small space. She ended with a deep backward dip, then bowed. "Thank you, mademoiselle. I'd like to see Kathy Button do that."

Hayley headed back to the chair. "She probably could. She can do anything."

Abigail intercepted her, took her hand, and swung her around so they were face-to-face. "*You* can do anything, girlie. Don't worry about other people. You can't control them. Just go out there and do your best. Then, whether you get the part or not, you can walk away free and clear."

"Feeling crummy."

Abigail gave her one final spin and let go, sending her sprawling into the chair. "That's part of it too, little girl. We don't always get what we want—or even deserve. Get used to it."

Hayley made her feet dangle. "I was wondering . . . would you go with me tomorrow night? If you were there, if I could look at you when I tried out, I'd do my best. I know I would."

Abigail knew it was always helpful to play to a specific person in the audience. But this girl's presumption . . . until the other day, their friendship had consisted of a few words while passing in the hall.

"Come on. Help me. People will think it's cool, you being famous and all."

Considering Abigail's lack of exposure of late . . . a little adulation would be appreciated. "Sure. Why not? You can even introduce me to Kathy Zipper as your acting coach."

"She'll just die."

"That's the plan."

―――

Becky was waiting for Bobby right inside the door. She stood there, arms crossed, a piece of paper in her hand.

Bobby unzipped his jacket and hung it on the hall tree. "Hey, hon." He leaned to kiss her cheek but she jerked just out of reach. He glanced at the paper she held. It was yellowed.

"Where are the kids?" he asked, needing a diversion from whatever Becky had on her mind.

"Mrs. Ross has 'em next door." She took a deep breath, making the baby in her belly rise. "I went to the bank today."

"Why?"

"To see about getting a second mortgage."

Bobby's stomach slid into his boots. He had no idea what to say but managed, "Oh."

Becky's eyebrows rose. "*Oh?* That's all you can say?"

"Beck, let me explain."

She moved to the Queen Anne chair with the frayed arms. She perched on the edge of its cushion, placed the yellowed paper in her lap, and set her hands on top of it. "I'm waiting."

He sat on the couch, as far away from her as possible. He was very glad the kids weren't there because this was not going to be pleasant. "We don't have a mortgage."

"So I was told." She held up the paper. "The mortgage was paid off in 1993, by Theodore Mann, your grandfather."

"Where did you find that?"

"In a box of old papers in the attic."

He was going to get after her for snooping but wisely did no such thing. What was his was hers. He'd been the one who'd crossed the line. He'd been the one to lie and keep secrets.

"I lived here with Grandpa from the time I was fourteen until he died when I was nineteen. He gave me the house in his will."

"A house you own, free and clear."

An entire paragraph full of explanations turned into one word. "Yes."

"So all your talk about needing three jobs to get by, to pay the mortgage . . . all that was a lie."

The one-word answers kept coming. "Yes."

"So all the times you could have been here with me and the kids, you chose—you *chose*—to be gone from us, earning money we didn't need."

"That's not entirely true," he said. "We do need the money."

"For what?"

He ran a finger over a tear in the couch upholstery that
Becky had sewn together. It reminded him of a surgery scar.
He'd had his appendix out when he was eight. . . . "You
deserve better." He swept an arm around the room. "This place
has the same carpet it had when Grandpa was alive. The walls
need painting, the bathtub has chips in the enamel, the maple
tree out front has dead limbs that are going to fall on the house
one of these days and cause some real damage, you and I
never did get a proper honeymoon, and—"

While he'd been reciting his want-to-do list, she'd risen
from the chair and strolled toward him. After the mention of
the honeymoon, she stopped his words with a finger to his
lips.

"You are mistaken, Bobby Mann."

"No, I'm—"

"Shh."

He could not speak. He could not go against her will, not
with her finger touching his lips, not with her eyes looking
down at him. He didn't know if he believed in auras and stuff
like that, but he couldn't think of any other term that fit the
effect his wife had on him. Having her close was like standing
on the edge of a riverbank, fishing with his grandpa, content to
watch the river flow as if it had all the time in the world to go
nowhere or everywhere. In his memories, his grandpa sang an
old hymn.

> When peace like a river attendeth my way,
> When sorrows like sea-billows roll;
> Whatever my lot, Thou has taught me to say,
> "It is well, it is well with my soul."

Becky reminded Bobby a lot of his grandpa, the quiet
manner, the deep faith, the comfort radiated by their presence.

Even though it had been nearly ten years, he missed Grandpa so much. . . .

"Bobby?"

He blinked and the song and memories stopped. "Mmm?"

"Tell me about your family. The rest of your family."

Family? *Wasn't she talking about the mortgage?* He welcomed the change of subject. "My parents died when I was young. I've told you that."

"But your brothers and sisters . . ."

His heart jumped. He'd never told her about any of them. Had he? Nor *how* his parents had died.

Becky moved to the mantel and brought him an old photo— of his family. His entire family when he was about six.

"Where did you get this?"

"In the attic."

He looked up from the picture. "What were you doing up there anyway? Just leave it alone, Beck. There's no reason for you to go through all that old junk."

"Family photographs are not junk." She pointed at the youngest boy—at Bobby's image. "This is you, isn't it?"

"How can you tell?"

She looked at him, then the photo. "Your eyes. Your kind eyes. You had them even then."

She'd done it again. Defused any possibility of anger. "You should have been a diplomat. Nations wouldn't dare go to war with you around. You'd charm them into peace. You missed your calling."

"I'm living out my calling." She moved to his side to see the picture better. "Tell me who's who."

Bobby went through the picture. "That's my mom and dad, then Martin—the oldest, Chuck, me, Cass, Katie, and Vicki."

"I wish I'd had brothers or sisters. Aunts and uncles for

our children. With the possibility of cousins for our children to play with."

He shook his head vehemently. "I don't know where they are. After our parents died, we were spread around. I lost track."

She stared at him, mouth agape. "Lost track of family? of siblings? How could you do that?"

He let her hold the picture and stepped away from her, to the recliner, where he took off his shoes. "We were kids. We didn't have any say. My brothers ran off; my sisters went to live with my dad's sister in Chicago or something. I got the best deal of it, here with Grandpa."

"Didn't *he* want to see the rest of them? stay in touch?"

Bobby remembered a few visits. . . . "I was plenty for him. He was an old man. His health wasn't that good."

Becky gazed down at the photo and ran her fingers over the faces. "How did your parents die?"

He did *not* want to go into this. Ever. He'd be willing to talk about the mortgage rather than this. "You still haven't explained *your* comment. I was telling you what you don't have, what you deserve, and you said—"

"I said you were mistaken."

He set his shoes to the side of the recliner. "And why is that?"

"Because I have plenty. I don't need more *things* bought with wages you earn by working three jobs. I need *you*. Here. And the kids need you, here."

He held out his hand. Becky set the photo down, came to him, and he pulled her into his lap. "I know."

Her eyebrows rose. She'd obviously expected a fight. If she only knew her power over him, as well as his intense desire to keep the past past.

She wrapped her arms around his neck. "Care to tell me the real reason you're working three jobs?"

"I want you to have—"

She shook her head. "I know why you're working so much, and it has nothing to do with money."

"It doesn't?"

"It has to do with fear."

He tried to laugh. "What am I afraid of?" *Want to see a list?*

She moved her index finger close to her face, looked toward the garage, and pointed.

"My shop?"

"Your art."

"My hobby."

"Your grandpa's legacy."

He had no response to that. "Grandpa never sold anything. He dinked around, making furniture for fun."

"He taught you what you know."

Bobby hooked her hair behind her ear, to better see her profile. "That he did."

"He'd be proud of you."

"I haven't done anything yet."

"You've sold a few pieces."

"Stuff I had around, just sitting. To friends."

"You could do more. Make custom pieces. You *will* do that. If you give yourself permission. If you give yourself time."

"Even if I do make furniture, how would I ever sell it to strangers? How would I get people to know I exist? How—"

She stopped his words with a soft kiss. "I don't know those answers, but somebody does. God does. He's already made you a carpenter like his Son, and I think he wants you to share that gift with others. I know it."

"How do you know it?"

She put a hand to her heart. "I just do."

He couldn't argue with her. Becky knew such things. She and God were close.

"I also found out about our savings account today," she said. "I didn't realize we had one."

He felt horrible for withholding these things from her. "I'm sorry. I don't know what I was thinking. I was saving for repairs and trips I hoped we'd take and . . . I don't know."

She grinned. "I was really mad at first. But then I thought about all the men who keep *debts* secret from their wives, and I realized it was kind of unique that you have secret *savings*." She looked at him, willing him to meet her gaze. "The repairs can wait, but your talent can't. Quit a job, Bobby, one job. I don't care which one. Then use that time to be with us and pursue your art."

"What if nothing happens?"

She kissed his forehead and with his help, managed to stand. "To have faith, have faith." Once on her feet she looked down at him. "It's not that hard, Bobby. I promise."

Bobby wasn't so sure but took solace that Becky never broke her promises.

———

Ken set his shopping bags down in front of the display of Ralph Lauren polo shirts. He picked up a yellow one. It felt like butter in his—

"Excuse me, sir. But don't you already have at least one yellow polo shirt?"

Ken turned around to see Ronnie, his ex-wife. "You got your hair cut," he said.

She put a hand to the nape of her boyish hairdo. With her red hair and pale skin she looked ten years younger than forty-five. "Do you like it?"

"It's drastic."

"I wanted easy care."

"Why?"

She cocked her head and looked incredulous, as if he should know something he didn't. He thought about asking for details but didn't want to get into it. Since their divorce six years previous, they'd agreed to let their personal lives remain personal. Actually, that had been Ken's intent throughout the entire marriage. If only a few of his personal indiscretions hadn't ceased being discreet . . .

"You look pale compared to your usual George Hamilton tan," she said. "You're still the pro at the club, aren't you?"

He didn't tell her that his gaggle of private students had tapered off. "I'm on jury duty right now. A murder trial."

She moved her purse to the other shoulder. "How did you manage that?"

"I didn't manage it. I was chosen. As a citizen."

Ronnie stifled a laugh. "When was the last time you voted in an election?"

He couldn't remember. He held the polo shirt toward her. "Feel this fabric."

She complied, though halfheartedly. "Uncle Davey died."

The shirt was forgotten. He'd always liked her uncle Davey. "When?"

"Last Friday."

"His heart?" There'd been a few scares over the years.

She shook her head. "A small plane crash in Wyoming."

Ken's mind grabbed on to flashes of newscasts from the weekend. "I think I saw it on the news. Could I have seen that on the news?"

Ronnie shrugged. "He was going deer hunting."

Ken nodded. "His annual trip. I went along that one time."

"I know. He still talks—or talked—about how you nearly caught your shoes on fire."

"I'm not a campfire kind of guy." He put a hand on her shoulder. "I'm so sorry, Ron. I always liked Davey."

He watched her face as she struggled for control. With a deep sigh, she kept the tears at bay. "Since I ran into you . . . would you go with me to the memorial service Friday evening?"

It was not how he liked to spend his Friday evenings.

"Please?" she said.

"Sure."

All the way home from jury duty, the psychologist's words about the accused hung around Deidre like birds waiting to land. *Needy. Meek. Nonaggressive. Nonconfrontational.* She knew from experience that these traits—most often construed as negative—could also be positive under the right circumstances. It was very confusing and she didn't want to feel confused right now. Not more than she already was.

She slammed the car door shut, hoping to trap the words inside.

No such luck.

She hurried into the house and flipped on the kitchen light, hoping its cheery brightness would make the words fly away.

Nope.

Even a handful of M&M'S didn't do the trick.

And though Deidre usually didn't mind coming home to an empty house, today she would have relished Sig's questions, Karla's effervescence, and even Nelly's adolescent rambling.

But it was Wednesday and Nelly and Karla were at

choir practice and Sig had a board meeting and would be home late. She checked the clock. She had time to enjoy the silence.

To let the words land.

It made little sense that the description of an uneducated, needy dishwasher would bother Deidre, a socialite whose idea of having zeros in her bank account brought to mind something far different from the zeros that most likely plagued Patti's. Deidre was a woman who was far from meek, plenty aggressive, and not averse to confrontation. Most confrontation.

Deidre got a Perrier out of the fridge and took it, along with the entire bowl of M&M'S, to the deck off the family room. The deck swing beckoned. . . .

She and Don had installed a swing on the front porch of their fixer-upper Victorian. They used to sit there for hours, talking, or even not talking, just being.

"You and Nelly are everything to me, Dee-Dee."

She smiled at the sudden memory of Don's words. Somehow with him as the father, with herself as the mother, and with little Nelly as the daughter, they'd been a family who needed each other—in a meek, nonaggressive, and nonconfrontational way.

She stopped swinging a moment, letting the notion sink in. Maybe that's why she'd been so bothered by the testimony. Years ago, these character traits—presented as negative when possessed by Patti—had made Dee-Dee feel strong. She'd come into her marriage to Don *needing* plenty. Yet in his household she'd let go of her intense desire to *take* and had been able to shove aside the bad things in her past. Under Don's love and care she'd grabbed on to a life where aggression and confrontation were unknown. Unacceptable. Unnecessary.

They'd been a family in the finest sense of the word. There had been no need for one to be above the other or control the other or wield power over the other. Each of them had possessed a unique function and they had come together as three parts of a whole.

"A triple-braided cord is not easily broken."

She blinked. Where had that come from?

It didn't take long to remember. It was a Bible verse Don used to quote. Like his mother, Karla, he often quoted the Bible. Deidre had even learned a few verses, though she didn't have their knack for remembering.

It was Wednesday night. If Don were still alive it wouldn't be just Nelly and Karla at church. All four of them would have spent the evening there, at the weekly congregational dinner, at choir rehearsal. . . .

"'O God, our help in ages past. . . .'"

Hearing herself sing was a surprise. Deidre had a good alto voice and always preferred harmony to the boring melody. Why had she stopped singing in the choir?

Deidre knew very well why. With Don's death the song had gone out of her. As had God and all things *church.* As had all things that involved finding strength in the middle of a peaceful life. There was no peace in the panic and desperation she'd felt after his death, after losing a level of happiness she'd never imagined possible. She may have gone into her marriage to Don harboring ulterior motives, but Don had broken through her tough facade and had allowed a new, gentler Dee-Dee to emerge.

Then he'd left her alone and the toughness returned out of necessity. Her neediness increased, and her ability to sit back and enjoy the serenity of all Don had shown her was buried with him.

But now she was married again. Financially, her life with

Sig was even more stable than it had been while married to Don. In that respect, she certainly wasn't needy anymore.

So . . . where was the peace? Where was the freedom to be meek, nonaggressive, and nonconfrontational? Where was the freedom to just *be*?

She felt the vibration of the garage door opening.

Sig was home.

And Don . . .

Was not.

"Can I talk to you a minute, Deidre?" Karla asked later that evening.

Deidre already had one foot on the stair, heading to bed. "I'm really tired."

"It will only take a minute." She looked upstairs. "Sig and Nelly . . . how about we go downstairs to my apartment?"

"This sounds ominous."

Karla didn't answer.

They went downstairs to the basement where Deidre— with Sig's money—had created a space for Karla to call her own: a bedroom, sitting area, kitchenette, and full bath. There was a rec room and pool table area that Nelly and her friends often used, but Karla didn't seem to mind sharing. In truth, the space was far better than what she'd been used to. Deidre had loved taking Karla furniture shopping and telling her she could get whatever she wanted. Get *new,* not *used.*

They headed to the sitting area. Deidre sat on the couch.

Karla did not. She stood with the coffee table between them. "I want to know what's going on."

"With what?"

"With this trial."

"I can't talk about the trial, Karla. You're the one who said—"

"I'm not asking you to talk about the trial. Not directly. I'm asking you to explain why Sig is so interested—overly interested—in it."

"He's not; he's just—"

"He is. The other night I overheard you talking in your bedroom and—"

"You were eavesdropping?"

"No, of course—" Karla sighed. "Well, yes. Guilty as charged. When Nelly and I got home from errands and you two weren't downstairs . . . I went upstairs to find you. I heard you. The door wasn't closed."

"Because we thought we were home alone."

Karla shrugged. "I should have made my presence known. I admit it. But the point is, I overheard a few odd comments from Sig. Him saying some testimony didn't help *you,* and reminding you that you needed to swing the jury vote *your* way. *Your* way, Dee-Dee. What does that mean?"

Deidre's throat was dry. "It's complicated."

"I suspect so."

Deidre pulled a pillow into her lap. "You don't need to concern yourself thinking about the trial, Karla. For one thing, Brett Lerner doesn't deserve your concern. He was a heel, a creep, and an evil man. No one should care two hoots if he died or not. If I had my way I'd let Patti go free and make sure no one took any blame for his death. The world is a better place without—"

Deidre stopped talking. Her breathing had turned heavy and there were wads of pillow clutched in her fists.

Karla's eyebrows had risen into alert mode. "What's got you so riled? Neither the paper nor the TV has portrayed Brett like that. He was the victim. He—" Suddenly she put a finger to her mouth. "Did you know him? Did you and Sig know him?"

Sig didn't know him.

"I've never heard you mention his name . . . so how . . . ?" Karla was not going to let up.

Maybe Deidre could tell her part of it. But she'd have to be careful. Very careful.

"Yes, I knew him. Ages ago. Before Sig. Before Don."

"Did you date him?"

An odd laugh escaped. Did it reveal too much? "Sort of," Deidre said. But then her hatred swelled. "The Brett Lerner I knew was an arrogant, despicable, horrible man. If anyone deserved to die, he did."

Karla looked aghast. "Do you hear what you're saying?"

Deidre forced herself to calm down. She couldn't let her emotions take over like that. She set the pillow flat on her lap and stroked it once before letting her hands settle on top of it. "Please don't tell Sig I knew him. He doesn't know anything about my past before Don."

"Actually, neither do I. Well, just the one thing, but nothing else."

"That's all you need to know."

The way Karla stood there, looking at her . . .

Deidre stood. "If we're done I'm going—"

Suddenly Karla took a seat beside her and pulled Deidre into a hug. "You don't need to feel badly for things that happened years ago, Dee-Dee. God returns to us the years the locusts have eaten."

Deidre pulled back. "What's that supposed to mean?"

"He forgives the past, the years that seem stripped of anything good. He lets us move forward, unencumbered."

I don't think so.

"You can count on it."

Although Deidre didn't believe what Karla said about being unencumbered, she did what she always did when memories begged for attention. With practiced skill she shoved the past into a storage room and flipped the dead bolt. Then she stood, ready to go upstairs. *That wasn't so bad. So she knows I knew Brett. No harm done.*

"You don't believe me," Karla said. "You don't believe you can be free of all that."

Deidre was done. "It sounds nice."

Karla looked at her skeptically. "You're patronizing me." *Completely and utterly.*

Deidre moved away from the couch, her need to leave increasing. "I'm tired, Karla. I really appreciate your concern, but there's nothing to be worried about that a good night's sleep won't—"

"When did you last see him? see Brett?" Karla asked. "Your anger is so fresh. I mean . . . did you see him recently? Right before he died?"

In the twist of a moment Karla had reopened the door to the past that Deidre had just locked away. *So much for receiving forgiveness for any locust-ravaged anything.*

Deidre's mind scrambled as she tried to determine if telling more of the truth would be advantageous. Long ago she'd learned it was often best to tell the truth—as far as it would go. . . .

And in this case it *might* go a little further. "Remember the bad argument Sig and I had last winter?"

"You never did tell me what that was about—not that it's any of my business, but if I could help—"

Sig's infidelity was *not* Karla's business. "When I left the house the morning after the argument, I drove to a resort, to get away for a few days. Brett worked there. I didn't know that, of course, and would never have gone there if I had, but when I went into the restaurant, I saw him and he recognized me and wanted to talk and—" She took a fresh breath. "And that's that."

"Did he contact you after that?"

"I wanted nothing to do with him." Deidre walked toward the stairs. "You want more details, ask him."

Luckily Karla couldn't ask Brett.

Because Brett was dead.

A good thing, all around.

Five

Let the one who has never sinned
throw the first stone.

JOHN 8:7

$\mathcal{T}$he defense calls Patti McCoy."

Abigail glanced at the other jurors. Although they hadn't
been allowed to talk to each other about the trial, she guessed
she hadn't been the only one wondering whether Patti would
testify. She was glad to see it. The prosecution's case wasn't
ironclad, but with the witnesses testifying about Brett and
Patti's rocky relationship and Patti's outbursts . . . the girl
needed to tell her story.

For Patti's sake, Abigail hoped the defense had coached
her well. So far, Stadler hadn't done a bang-up job with his
costuming choices for the girl. Up until now Patti had sat at
the defense table in nondescript skirts and tops, not wearing
enough makeup to reach even her attorney's notice. When the
psychologist had called Patti meek, Abigail had nodded, based
solely on her appearance.

But today, during her one chance to set the record straight,
Patti had turned glamour girl. She wore a shorter skirt than
was appropriate, one that was unflattering to her slightly
chubby legs. Her first act in the witness box was to tug on it.
And her top, though not maternity, should have been. It pulled

across her midsection, implying that Patti was in the awkward stage of pregnancy where she appeared more overweight than pregnant, that stage where people might wonder if she was expecting but would be wary about asking.

The mousy brown hair that had always been pulled into a low ponytail was loose and fluffed like a Texas beauty queen's, hair spray mandatory. The makeup was also worthy of beauty queen status. Even from a distance Abigail could see rouge on her cheeks and blue eye shadow. And bright red lips, à la Marilyn Monroe.

What was Stadler thinking? If it *was* his doing, he'd turned the innocent girl who'd been duped by a slick man into a femme fatale who was quite capable of doing her own seducing.

Although Abigail had an open mind about the outcome of the trial, she couldn't help but wonder if this one costuming detail might be a fatal error.

———

I should ask her out.

As soon as the words reached Ken's consciousness he shook his head, appalled. Patti was the defendant. She was on trial for murder. What was wrong with him that the sight of a pretty young thing hurled him into wolf mode?

She does look good today.

He forced the small of his back into the hardness of the chair.

———

Bobby was confused. Patti's voice did not match her looks. It matched her old looks, the way she'd looked every day of the trial so far. Today her looks called for a seductive voice, smooth yet confident, the voice of a woman used to getting whatever she wanted. Instead, her tentative voice elicited a request that the microphone be moved closer so she could be heard.

Which woman was the real Patti? The sexy lady or the sweet young thing?

"State your name for the record, please."

"Patti McCoy." She looked to the judge. "Actually it's Patricia Jo McCoy."

"What is your occupation?"

"I'm a dishwasher at The Pines restaurant."

"How long have you worked there?"

"Two years."

"Do you enjoy your work there?"

She shrugged. "Would you like washing hundreds of dishes every day with steaming hot water?"

Although the judge smiled, he said, "Answer the question, Ms. McCoy."

"I can think of better things I'd like to do. But it pays the bills."

"Where and when did you first meet Brett Lerner?"

"At work." She smiled at the jury. "He was the maître d' and one Saturday before the busy season last year, management put on a barbecue for all the employees. Brett and me had talked before then, but just during work, about work. The barbecue was the first time him and me actually got to talk about other things." She beamed broadly. "*He* came up to *me.*"

Stadler's eyebrows rose and he nodded slowly as if this was particularly significant. "Did he make advances toward you?"

She shook her head. "Not at all. He was a complete gentleman. We just sat at a picnic table under a big elm tree and talked."

"About what?"

"Not much really. Just flirting talk."

"Flirting talk?"

"You know, teasing each other about the weather, our jobs, old bosses. Stuff we had in common."

"When did you first go out on a real date?"

She hesitated. "Brett wasn't a real-date kind of guy."

"So what did you do when you were together?"

Patti blushed and looked at her lap. "We did go on drives sometimes. But mostly we stayed in."

"In?"

"We were either at my apartment or his house. I cooked for him a lot. I'm a good cook. He really liked my meat loaf and corn bread. It's my mom's recipe."

"Did you move in together?"

She shook her head emphatically. "I said I wouldn't." She straightened her shoulders and looked at the jury. "Not without being married."

Bobby mentally filled in what the defense handily left out. *But you had no trouble sleeping with him. . . .*

"Did you love him?"

Her face turned serious. "Very, very much."

"Did he love you?"

She hesitated just a moment, then nodded. "Very, very much. He told me so. He did."

Bobby didn't believe it. Though Brett wasn't there to defend himself, Bobby found it odd that he and Patti never went anywhere. It sounded like Brett wanted the perks of Patti without the public scrutiny. A maître d' and a dishwasher. In the hierarchy of a resort, they were as far apart as a prince and a pauper.

"We've heard testimony from witnesses who overheard you arguing. Did you argue?"

"Of course." She looked at the jury. "Everybody argues."

Bobby agreed, but he and Becky never threw things. Broke things.

Stadler flipped a page on his yellow pad. "On the night of January thirteenth, why did you go to Brett's house?"

"I often went there after work. Lots of times. Like I said, he liked my cooking."

"Were you going to cook for him that night?"

"Maybe. Or else we'd order takeout. Brett loved Chinese. Kung pao chicken was his favorite. He liked things spicy." After a moment, realizing the innuendo, she blushed. "Well, he did."

"Take us through the events that occurred on the night Brett died."

Patti moved her hands from her lap and gripped the arms of the chair as if gaining strength from their presence. "As I said, I went over to his house when I got off work. I pulled up front and parked across from his house, then went to the front door. I rang the bell tons of times then knocked. He didn't answer."

"Why didn't you leave?"

"Because he was supposed to be home. We'd talked about me coming over."

"So what did you do?"

"I went around back. Brett liked sitting in the hot tub, especially when it was cold out."

Her hands returned to her lap. "I didn't see him at first. But the tub was on, and it was bubbling and steam was rising from it and . . . that was the first thing I heard when I came around the corner to the back. The jets going full blast."

"Did you hear or see anything else?"

"As I got closer I saw there was a toppled wineglass next to the tub and a broken wine bottle. I didn't understand what was going on. I looked around the yard and—"

"Did you search the yard?"

"No. I just looked around. From the patio."

"So the person who murdered Mr. Lerner could have been hiding in the trees or in the—"

"Objection, Your Honor. Speculation."

"Sustained."

Although Stadler had been shot down, Bobby took note of the possibility someone had been hiding. . . .

Stadler pushed his glasses to the bridge of his nose. "What did you do next?"

"I was worried about the broken wine bottle. If Brett had dropped it, why hadn't he cleaned it up? I mean, you don't want broken glass next to a hot tub where you're going to be barefoot. That's when I started thinking he'd gone inside to get a broom and a dustpan. Thinking that, I bent down and starting picking up the mess. To help."

"So you touched the bottle?"

"Sure. All over the place. I moved the neck part of the bottle—the biggest part—to the side and started putting the littler pieces in my hand." She mimicked this motion, placing invisible shards in the palm of her hand, looking at the space just beyond her knees as if making sure she didn't miss any. "There was wine spilled all over the concrete too. It was white wine so it didn't stand out, but I could smell it, and I recognized the bottle as a kind we'd drank together before. But then I noticed a little bit of red on the concrete, right where the neck part of the bottle had been sitting. . . ."

Suddenly Patti closed both hands and sucked in a breath. "And just when I was thinking how odd that was and wondering what that red could be, the hot tub stopped bubbling." She turned her head to the left, one hand moving to her mouth. "That's when I saw him. Saw his . . ." Both hands were at her mouth now, as if trying to stop her from saying the words.

"I saw his hand first, floating at the top. Then his head, then his shoulders . . ." She covered her face, bursting into tears. "He was facedown, just floating there, and there was a gash, and blood in the water and . . ." She sucked in a breath.

Stadler pulled a tissue out of his inner suit coat pocket. "Here, Ms. McCoy."

She used the tissue but kept crying.

"Would you like a short recess?" the judge asked.

"No!" Stadler said, almost too quickly.

With a glance to her attorney, Patti collected herself slightly and said, "No. I'll be okay."

It was then Bobby realized Stadler *wanted* his client to cry on the stand. He needed her to cry and didn't want a recess to break the moment. Bobby looked at Patti with new eyes— though her tears *seemed* real enough . . .

Stadler walked back to the defense table, where he got another tissue, making Bobby wonder if this prolonged scenario also had a purpose.

Stadler gave Patti the tissue.

"One more thing . . . When I saw Brett, that's when I cut my hand on the pieces of glass. I must've flinched and got cut, and . . . I dropped all the little pieces of glass back on the patio." She held up the tissue he'd just given her. "Thank you."

"You're welcome." He waited while she dabbed her eyes carefully, beneath the lashes, like women did when they didn't want to ruin their makeup.

"After discovering Brett's body, what did you do?"

"I think I screamed. I don't really know, but I seem to remember hearing a scream, and since I was the only one there, it must've been me."

Stadler cleared his throat and she continued.

"I was upset and shocked. I ran to my car. I just needed to be home. Somewhere far away from there."

"But your car wouldn't start?"

"It does that. I've been saving to get it fixed. And when the police drove up—"

Stadler lifted a hand, obviously not wanting her to take the lead. "A police car drove up. What did you do?"

"I panicked. Again, I just wanted to be home. So I ran. I know I shouldn't have, but I was upset."

"When the police officer caught up with you, accosted you, what did you do?"

"I stopped running. I went with him. Everything changed then. Just seeing another person, being able to talk to them, to tell them what I'd seen . . . suddenly that became more important than getting home."

"So you answered their questions willingly?"

"Of course. By that time I was thinking more clearly and I knew someone had killed Brett and I wanted the cops to get 'em. Arrest the murderer."

Stadler nodded once. "So, Ms. McCoy. Did you kill Brett Lerner?"

Patti took a deep breath and sat up straight. This answer she knew. "No, sir, I did not." She looked at the jury. "I loved him. Loved him more than I've ever loved any man."

"Nothing further, Your Honor."

Jonathan Cummings took his time moving from the prosecutor's table to his *spot*. Abigail admired how he didn't hurry and gave the jurors time to adjust to his presence. It wasn't hard. Where Stadler was annoying like a sty in the eye, Cummings was a balm.

"Ms. McCoy, did you try to get Brett out of the tub?"

"I couldn't."

"Did you try?"

"No. He's a lot bigger than me, and . . . he was facedown in the water. He was dead."

"So you're an expert?"

"Objection."

Cummings lifted a hand, conceding. "Why didn't you call for help?"

"I would've. But I didn't have my phone with me. It was in the car. If I would've got the car started, I would've called."

"Why didn't you go into Brett's house and call?"

"It was locked."

"The back door was locked? Most people don't lock their back doors if they're out on the patio."

"Actually, I didn't try that door. The front was locked. . . ." She hesitated, then looked at Cummings. "But if he was dead, 911 wouldn't have helped anyway, right?"

Cummings shrugged. "Most people would have called. It's instinctive."

Stadler rose. "Objection, Your Honor. Supposition on what 'most people' might do."

"Sustained. Move on."

Cummings brought his index finger to his lips and held it there a moment. Then he nodded, as if completing a thought. "So . . . you didn't call for help. I guess the big question that needs to be answered is, why did you run? I know you said that you wanted to get home, but somehow that doesn't ring true."

"I . . . I heard sirens."

"Do you usually run when you hear sirens?" Cummings made a sweeping gesture around the courtroom. "People hear sirens every day and don't run."

Stadler rose. "Supposition again, Your Honor, as to what people do or don't do."

Cummings looked at Stadler. "Do you run when you hear sirens, Mr. Stadler?"

The judge banged his gavel. "Enough. Stick to what the defendant did, Mr. Cummings."

"Yes, Your Honor." Cummings put his hands behind his back. "What you did, Ms. McCoy, is run away. Or try to. Your car wouldn't start, correct?"

"Yes."

"And when the police came, you didn't wait to talk to them, to tell them your lover was in trouble or even dead. You ran."

"I wasn't thinking straight. It was . . . instinctive."

Abigail had to smile. For little Patti to use the prosecutor's own terminology . . . Chalk one up for the underdog.

"Can I say something?" Patti asked. She looked to the judge.

"If it's relevant."

Patti turned toward the court. "I'm not a complicated person. I reacted without thinking about it or planning my next move. I am who I am. I don't pretend to be anything more."

Cummings allowed a moment of silence. "Is that all?"

Patti looked up, then at him. "Yes, I think so. Thanks."

Such a simple girl. In so much trouble.

———

Patti was a goner. Any thought of dating or even being attracted to her had long evaporated from Ken's mind.

The prosecutor, Cummings, leaned against the edge of the prosecution table, his whole demeanor shouting cool and confident. "Let's backtrack a bit, Ms. McCoy. When you first came to Brett's house you knocked on the door. So you didn't have a key?"

"Brett said he didn't give out keys. To anyone."

Ken wasn't into giving out keys either. A man needed his privacy.

Cummings nodded but continued. "And you parked in front of Brett's house, yet across the street. . . . Why not in the driveway?"

"Brett told me he didn't want grease on the driveway."

"Does your car leak oil?"

She blinked. "Not that I know of."

"So . . . maybe there was another reason he told you to always park across the street, not directly in front of his house?"

"Objection," Stadler said. "There is no way Mr. Cummings or even Ms. McCoy could know the intent of the deceased."

"Sustained."

Although Cummings was not making any deep points, he was raising questions in Ken's mind.

"Did Mr. Lerner know you were pregnant on the night he was killed?" Cummings asked.

"Objection, Your Honor," Stadler said. "I object to the use of the term *killed*."

Cummings turned to the judge. "Your Honor, my colleague objects to me saying *killed*. . . . What term, pray tell, does he wish me to use? Mr. Lerner did not hit himself over the head with a wine bottle. I will gladly use the term *murdered* if he would like."

"Can the sarcasm, Mr. Cummings," said the judge. He looked at Stadler. "Objection overruled. Mr. Cummings does have a point, Counselor. The deceased did not pass away of natural causes. If he had we wouldn't be here."

Ken wondered if Stadler had caused more harm than good by bringing it up. The words *murdered* and *killed* had gotten more attention during the objection than they had by being a part of a question.

"Let me ask the question again," Cummings said. "Did Mr. Lerner know you were pregnant on the night he was killed?"

"Well . . . no."

"Wasn't the real reason you were going to see him that night so you could tell him?"

"Yes . . . I mean, I hoped the chance would come up so I could tell him. But I didn't tell him. When I got there he was dead."

"Because you killed him."

"No! I loved him. I'm going to have his baby. I wanted the baby to have a father."

Cummings appeared unimpressed by the outburst. He calmly walked around to the prosecution table, where he retrieved a piece of paper from a folder.

"Let's backtrack one more time. I'm a bit curious about your many violent, volatile arguments with the deceased."

Stadler rose. "Your Honor, do we really need such dramatic descriptions?"

"Overruled. But watch it, Mr. Cummings."

"What did you argue about?"

Ken decided that every time Patti shrugged it made her look younger, more immature. More pitiful. *The shrug that was worth a thousand words.*

"Give us a few examples, Ms. McCoy."

"Well . . . he didn't want to meet my family. That was a big one."

"Did he say why?"

"He . . . he said he wasn't into families much."

"So your supposition that he would be happy about the pregnancy was based on . . . ?"

"I . . . I . . ."

Cummings raised a hand. "Withdrawn. One more thing, Ms. McCoy. In your heartfelt declaration of innocence you stated—" he looked at the paper in his hand—"'I loved him. Loved him more than I've ever loved any man.' Is that correct?"

"Oh yes."

"I'm a little curious about the 'any man' you mentioned. Have you ever had another relationship on the same level as the one you had with Mr. Lerner?"

"Objection, Your Honor. The defendant's past is not on trial here."

"No, it isn't, Your Honor," Cummings said. "But she herself opened the door when she compared her love of the deceased with other loves in her life."

"Overruled," the judge said. "Answer the question, please."

"Yes, I've had other boyfriends."

"Boyfriends you slept with?"

"Well, yes."

"Have you ever been pregnant before?"

"I . . . just the once."

Ken heard his own gasp added to others. So she wasn't such an innocent after all.

"Where is that baby?"

Stadler was out of his seat. "Objection, Your Honor. The location of this baby is not—"

"There is no baby," Patti said, interrupting. "He made me get an abortion!"

The courtroom was silent. Although sympathy skirted the top of Ken's thoughts, the emotion that took hold was incredulousness. Patti's relationship with Brett was a pattern. She slept with men, got pregnant, and most likely gave them

an ultimatum. The first man had refused to play along. They'd
never know how Brett would have reacted.

Or did they know? Had she told him that night and they'd
argued?

Cummings had one more ace. "Wasn't that man married?"

Patti looked ready to cry. Her voice was small. "Yes; yes,
he was. I didn't know he was, not at first. But that's why he
couldn't marry me. That's why he didn't let me have the baby.
But I loved him! I really did."

Ken sat forward in his chair. The dumb, dumb girl. Patti
McCoy had just dug her own grave.

———

Deidre was in no mood to hear about Patti's affair with a
married man. What made women do such a thing?

What made Audrey have an affair with my husband?

Patti's exuberant "But I loved him!" rang in the courtroom.

It was countered by another question. "Like you loved
Brett?"

Patti's forehead pulled. "Nobody loves two men the same.
But I did love them. I loved both of them."

"And you wanted both of their babies."

"The babies weren't planned. They just happened."

Cummings nodded. Was the statement the essence of
naiveté? Or manipulation?

"What did this married man do for a living?"

Stadler stood. "Your Honor, this has nothing to do—"

"I disagree, Your Honor," Cummings said. "You will come
to see it has much to do with the reason we are here."

"Objection overruled. But make it quick, Mr. Cummings."

Cummings folded the paper in half and creased it. "What

did the other man you loved, the father of your first baby, do for a living, Ms. McCoy?"

"He owned a restaurant. A chain of restaurants."

Cummings nodded, as if he was impressed. "And what job did you hold at the time?"

Deidre watched as Patti's face clouded. Even Patti realized how incriminating her answer would sound. "I bused tables."

"In one of his restaurants?"

"Yes."

"So, it appears you make a habit of falling in love—or at least in lust—with men of authority in your workplace. Men who have the power to perhaps help you rise in the company, or at the very least, men who have money to take care of you."

"I don't care about their money."

"Then why do you care if they marry you?"

"Because I was having a baby. I wanted the baby to have a father."

"You wanted to be the wife of a successful man."

Deidre's stomach flipped. This was way too close to home.

"Doesn't everybody?" Patti asked.

"Touché, Ms. McCoy." Cummings set the paper on the table and moved closer. "Did you know Brett Lerner was married—was still married—at the time of his death?"

Stadler was on his feet. "I object, Your Honor."

"On what grounds?"

"On the grounds that . . . I don't see the relevance."

Cummings held his ground, turning slightly toward his adversary as if instructing an underling. "The relevance is that if the defendant knew he was married, or rather, found out he was married after she found out she was pregnant—for the second time, by a married man—that could intensify and solidify the motive."

"Objection overruled. Can the lecture, Mr. Cummings. And answer the question, Ms. McCoy."

Patti bit her lip. "I . . . uh . . ."

Cummings held up a hand. "Let me refresh your memory. My question is, did you know Brett Lerner was married when you killed him?"

Stadler was on his feet. "Your Honor! That is an unanswerable question."

The judge concurred. "Mr. Cummings."

"Pardon me. Rephrase. Did you know Brett Lerner was still married at the time of his untimely demise?"

Deidre watched Patti's shoulders slump, and by that simple action, she knew what the girl was going to say.

"Yes, I did."

There was no need for deliberation. With the combination of the circumstantial evidence, the forensics, the witnesses who'd testified against her, and the double motive of her pregnancy and finding out her lover was married . . .

Deidre would have good news to tell Sig tonight.

Then why did she feel so bad?

———

Deidre had never been a crier, but after coming home from jury duty, she collapsed in a blubbery mess, finding solace in bed.

It had a lot to do with Patti's testimony; that much was sure. The testimony was over. Tomorrow they'd hear closing arguments. Soon. It would all be over soon.

But would it ever really be over?

That Patti's testimony had affected Deidre so deeply was a surprise. She should be happy with today's events. Unless Stan Stadler could pull a rabbit out of his hat . . .

Deidre had come home to an empty house—which was odd because it was Thursday and Nelly always came home right after school on Thursdays. Karla was gone too. But Deidre wasn't worried. They were probably off on some errand together. Their absence was a blessing. She didn't want either of them to see her in such a state—which she wouldn't be able to explain.

To them. Much less to herself.

She didn't worry about them until Sig got home before they did. This was not like either Karla or Nelly. Both were good about calling if they were going to be late.

Sig came into the bedroom, pulling his tie from the confines of his collar. "Where is everybody? And what's wrong with you? You sick?"

If it would keep her from having to discuss the trial she'd be as sick as necessary. "A little. I just don't feel right. As for Karla and Nelly? They weren't here when I got home either."

He talked to her from the closet. "I suppose I could make you some soup."

"That sounds good." Comfort food.

Sig appeared in jeans and a polo shirt. He headed to the door of the bedroom, and Deidre thought she was home free until he hesitated, then detoured to the bedside.

"Are you feeling sick because it went badly today?"

So much for escaping free and clear. "It *was* very emotional."

"Patti was due to testify. Did she?"

Deidre nodded.

"Any new revelations?"

"She's been pregnant before, by a married man."

Sig sat on the edge of the bed. "A pattern forms."

"And Brett was married."

Sig's eyebrows rose. "Really."

"Patti wanted him to marry her but—"

"But he couldn't because he was already married."

Deidre shrugged. She heard talking downstairs. "They're home."

Sig stood. He lowered his voice. "Brett being married adds to her motive."

Deidre shrugged again.

"Don't you agree? Didn't she come off as guilty?"

"Actually she did."

"Good. That's what we—"

There was a tap on the jamb of the opened door. Karla came in—tentatively. "Hi."

"Where's Nelly?" Deidre asked.

Karla looked to the hallway and a reluctant Nelly moved into the doorway.

"Come on," Karla instructed. "All the way in."

Deidre could tell by the forlorn look on Nelly's face that something was wrong. "What happened?"

Karla looked to Nelly, but the girl remained silent. "Go on. Tell them."

"They'll just get mad."

"I guarantee we'll get even madder if we have to pull this out of you," Sig said. "Tell us what's going on."

Nelly looked at her father, then at Deidre, and suddenly rushed to the bed, where her mother sat against the pillows. She threw herself into Deidre's arms. "I'm sorry. I really am. But he pushed me too far."

Torn between comforting her daughter and getting the truth from her, Deidre reluctantly pushed Nelly upright. "Who are we talking about?"

"Damon," Nelly said.

"Who?" Sig asked.

"The school bully," Deidre said. "What did he do to you?"

"He cornered me again. He's been better since you talked

to the principal, but today he came after me at afternoon recess. He wanted money."

"You don't have money."

"I had ten dollars."

"You aren't supposed to take money to school."

"Nana and I were going to go shopping after school for Dad's birthday present. Damon must have heard me talking about shopping and the money with Jennifer. He wanted it. Said if I didn't give it to him he would tell our teacher I cheated on the math test." She looked directly at each of them in turn. "I didn't cheat. I got a ninety-two on my own. I promise."

"I believe you," Deidre said.

"You should have called for a teacher," Sig said. "Or run away."

"There weren't any teachers close, and he had me cornered in some trees near the swings, so I . . . so I . . ."

"She whammed him with a soccer ball," Karla said. "In the face."

Way to go, little girl.

Karla continued the story. "She broke his nose. It bled all over. Their teacher heard him scream and came running. She took both of them to the office, where the nurse took care of Damon's nose, and then they both sat before the principal. That's when they called here. You were at the trial, so I went to school to take care of it. They called Damon's mother too. We've been there ever since."

Nelly's tears started up again. "I'm sorry for throwing the ball at him. I didn't aim at his nose. I just wanted him to go away, leave me alone. And I couldn't have him telling lies about me. I didn't cheat. Honest, I didn't. My teacher has been talking about me going to a math fair. If she thought I cheated . . ."

Karla wagged a finger at her. "I told her violence is unacceptable. Even if Damon told lies about her, that was no reason to resort to violence."

Sig looked at Deidre and she read the look on his face. This was way too close to home.

Karla put her hands on her hips. "Come on, you two. I could use a little support here."

Sig cleared his throat. "You shouldn't have hurt Damon."

"But we understand why you did," Deidre added. "Sometimes people push us too far and—" She looked to Sig for help.

"And a person is forced to do something they normally wouldn't do."

Karla shook her head, incredulous. "I don't believe this. I've just spent the past three hours telling her that violence is never appropriate and now the two of you say it has its place?"

Deidre lay back against the pillows, ready to play the sick card again. "We'll talk about it later. Karla, thanks ever so much for handling this. Nelly, don't you have some homework to do before dinner?"

"I told her she wasn't getting any dinner," Karla said.

"She needs to eat," Deidre said.

"She also needs to be punished for her actions."

"No . . . dessert then," Sig said.

Nelly's look of surprise revealed she'd expected much worse. Her surprise turned to relief as she hugged Deidre, then went to her father. "Thank you. Both of you. I'm really sorry. Really I am. I won't do it again."

Sig lifted her chin to look down into her face. "No, you won't. One mistake like that per person, per lifetime." He glanced at Deidre. "Right, Mom?"

His implication hit the mark. "Right."

"I'm going to do my homework now."

"You do that," Deidre said.

Nelly left the room, leaving a dumbfounded Karla behind. "What just happened? This was serious business. The boy's nose was broken. Harassed or not, Nelly overreacted. Damage was done. She needs to be punished more than taking away a dessert."

A sick feeling attacked Deidre. She didn't need to pretend to be unwell. "I'm not feeling up to dealing with this right now, Karla. We appreciate you taking care of it in our absence, but it's over."

"Just like that. No real consequences."

Sig moved toward the door, ushering her out. "Nelly was pushed into a no-win situation. Sometimes circumstances dictate extreme action," he said. "Come on. I was going to make Deidre some soup."

They left her alone.

Deidre—and her conscience.

———

Coming home and seeing the light blinking on his answering machine always made Ken's day. It was pitiful. His inane need to be needed. To be *somebody*.

Actually, he hoped someone from the club had called. Since getting off for jury duty he'd expected irate calls from his clients, upset because he wasn't there to tell them to keep their head down, their knees flexed, their shoulder turned . . . but so far, nothing. Not one call. The other two pros had said they would pick up the slack for him, but was it that easy for the golf world to go on without the expertise of Ken Doolittle?

Don't answer that.

He punched the Play button while he sorted the mail on the kitchen counter.

At the sound of his son's voice he stopped with a gas bill in midair. *"Hi, Dad. This is . . . well you know who it is. I would really like to talk to you. I know, I know, I haven't wanted to talk before recently, but now . . . I need . . . Just call me, okay?"*

Ken tossed the bill in the important pile. If Philip thought it was that easy to erase two years of neglect and rude behavior . . . let him deal with rejection awhile. Let him see what it felt like to leave messages and not get them returned.

The notion that he was behaving childishly came. And went. He flipped through a catalog of golf clothes and waited for the next message to play.

Thankfully, there *was* a next message.

"Heya, handsome. Cindy here. It's been too long, babe. I'm feeling the need for a Ken fix. And I'm hungry for sushi. You game? Call me."

He tossed the mail aside. Cindy with the long brown hair and legs up to here. He picked up the phone and dialed.

It was nice being needed.

———

Abigail's skin tingled and her stomach did the tango—with deep dramatic dips.

Auditions always had that effect on her. That this was just an audition for a community theater production of *Annie* apparently didn't matter. Show biz—of any form—ran through her veins.

Abigail spotted Hayley's nemesis right off. Kathy Button in all her arrogant, strutting glory. You'd think it was Oscar night and the oddsmakers had predicted Little Miss Nose-in-the-air the winner. The way she swished as she walked, as if wearing a gown with a train . . . it was laughable.

Hayley was not laughing. Whatever confidence Abigail had instilled in her housemate evaporated as soon as Kathy accosted her and said, "Oh. I didn't think you would still try out."

The unsaid but implied *Why waste your time?* prompted Abigail to put her hand on Hayley's shoulder and say, "Excuse us, but it's imperative my client warms up before she's called to perform."

Abigail led Hayley into the next room, where the two of them burst into laughter. "That was so cool!" Hayley whispered.

"Much of success has to do with perception, my girl. In fact, I want you to play a part right now."

"What part?"

"The part of a girl auditioning for *Annie* who gets the lead. Of course she doesn't know it at this point in the story, but that *is* where she's headed." Abigail leaned close, painting a picture in the air with a sweeping hand. "See the audition? See her stride to the front, not cocky like she deserves to be, yet with her head held high, with a feistiness that makes the director turn to his assistant and whisper, 'Oh my. There she is!'"

Hayley played along. "There I am."

Abigail slapped her on the back, putting a period to the scene. "There you are."

A woman with a clipboard came out of the auditorium. "Come, everyone. It's time to begin."

Abigail was glad to see Hayley stride inside as if she was that confident girl who would get the part. Abigail entered too, though her stomach betrayed her with a wringing of nerves. Her highest hope was that Hayley would do her best.

And Kathy Button would crash and burn.

———

Abigail had no trouble applauding with gusto for Hayley's performance and even found a twinge of compassion as little Ms. Button forgot her words and asked to start her tryout song over. Twice. Hayley was a shoo-in—if not for the lead, at least as one of the orphan girls.

The auditions for the kid parts were over and the session to cast the adult parts was about to begin. There was no reason to stay for the rest, and Abigail and Hayley were just gathering their things when the director approached. Hayley grabbed Abigail's hand and squeezed.

But the director's eyes weren't on Hayley. . . .

"Abigail Buchanan? Are you Abigail Buchanan?"

"Yes."

He held out his hand. "I thought that was you. I'm Tony Novotny. I am such a big fan. I've been following your career for years. Your talent is amazing."

Abigail took a quick scan of the other people nearby. Good. She had an audience; the compliment had not been wasted. "Why, thank you. You're very kind."

For the first time, he seemed to notice Hayley. "Is this your daughter?"

Granddaughter is more like it. Brownie points suitably earned and logged.

Abigail drew Hayley front and center. "No, this is my neighbor, Hayley . . ." She faltered. She wasn't sure of Hayley's last name. "I'm sure you remember her audition just a little while—"

"Of course, I remember," the director said. He smiled at Hayley and gave her a wink. "I'll be seeing you again. We'll be contacting people about callbacks tomorrow."

Hayley beamed. "Wow. Thank you."

He turned his attention back to Abigail. "Are you auditioning for Miss Hannigan?"

The crusty, churlish, conniving keeper of the orphanage? The part she'd played decades before? "I hadn't thought—"

He took her hand in his own. "Oh, please do. You don't know the boon it would give this production to have you involved. In fact, you wouldn't even have to audition. If you want it, the part is yours."

Oh my collided with *Really?* and finally slid next to *Why not?*

"I'm honored you'd consider me, but I would insist on auditioning with the others. Over the years I've learned that everyone deserves a fair chance."

"As you wish." He put a hand on her shoulder and led her back toward the auditorium's seats. "We're just about to start with the adults."

"I need to fill out a form, yes?"

He smiled. "Yes, I suppose you do." He snapped his fingers and the girl with the clipboard brought a form for Abigail.

She took a seat and began filling it out. The question about previous experience was especially satisfying.

———

"Bobby . . . Bobby, wake up!"

Bobby's eyes shot open. Moonlight cut a swath across the bottom of the bed. He looked to Becky's side, but she wasn't there.

"Bobby?"

He turned in the other direction. She was standing beside the bed, dressed. It only took a moment for his thoughts to fall into place. "What's wrong?"

"I'm getting contractions."

"But it's still six weeks."

"I know. I tried to ignore them, hoping . . . but they're not going away. I called Dr. White. We need to go to the hospital."

His feet hit the floor and he grabbed the jeans and shirt he'd worn the evening before. "What about the kids?"

"I called Mrs. Ross. She's coming over. She should be here any—"

There was a soft tapping on the front door. Bobby swept up his shoes and socks and ran downstairs to get it. Their neighbor Mrs. Ross stood before him, wrapped in a yellow fuzzy robe, jogging shoes, and pink foam curlers. Under normal conditions he would have indulged in some mighty teasing.

But not tonight.

"How is she?" Mrs. Ross asked.

"I'm fine," Becky said from the stairs.

Bobby scrambled up the steps to help her.

"Let the kids sleep," Becky told the neighbor. "There are packets of oatmeal and English muffins for breakfast."

Mrs. Ross waved her concerns away. "We'll be fine. Just take care of yourself. And let me know what's happening."

Hopefully nothing was happening. . . .

False labor. The baby was fine, but it was important it not be born just yet. At thirty-four weeks the lungs weren't fully developed. Each day the baby grew in the womb was a plus.

Becky was resting comfortably and the contractions had lessened in intensity. The doctor said she should be able to go home in an hour or so. Bobby sat beside her bed, leaning his head against the edge of the mattress. It was one o'clock in the morning. Was it possible to call in sick to jury duty? He didn't want to cause a mistrial or anything. Yet he couldn't leave Beck—

She put a hand on his head. "I'm fine, hon. The baby's fine. Why don't you sit in the recliner over there and get some sleep."

He kissed her hand and shook his head. "I want to stay awake until I get you home."

"Go get some coffee then."

A good idea. He stood, leaned down and kissed her, then left with an assurance he'd be right back.

Out in the hall, he sought a directional sign. Hospitals were so confusing with all their wings and hallways.

Cafeteria. To the left.

He headed that way, and when he saw a patient being pushed toward him, he moved to the right side of the corridor. Another middle-of-the-night crisis. Since Becky wasn't there to do it, he said a quick prayer for the woman. Becky was always saying prayers when an ambulance went by or when she saw an accident or—

As the gurney was wheeled past, Bobby did a double take. It was Patti McCoy!

He stopped and watched her being wheeled around the corner. An officer in uniform walked past him, and he stopped her. "Hey. What's wrong with her?"

"She lost her baby. Not that it's any of your business." The officer gave him the once-over. "Is it?"

"No. Sorry. I hope she's okay."

The officer shrugged and moved on. "She'll survive."

Bobby stood immobilized. Patti had lost her baby? Becky had lost a baby before Teresa was born. He knew firsthand the emotional pain of losing a child. As if Patti needed any more stress on her plate.

He remembered the task at hand. Coffee. And getting back to Becky.

Thank God *she* was all right.

Six

Get the truth and never sell it;

also get wisdom, discipline,

and good judgment.

PROVERBS 23:23

*A*ren't you going to be late?" Becky asked.

Bobby knelt beside the bed—their bed, in their bedroom. Becky had been released from the hospital at three in the morning with instructions to take it easy. Upon their arrival home, Mrs. Ross had returned to her house with a promise she'd be back by eight this morning to help out as long as Becky needed her. Right now she was in the kitchen making the kids oatmeal with raisins.

Bobby stroked her hand. "I don't want to go."

"I'm fine. The doctor says so. He wouldn't have let me come home unless it was true."

Bobby nodded. There was another reason he was hanging around. . . .

"There's something else, isn't there?" she asked.

Nothing slipped by this woman. Nothing. He stood and removed his cell phone from his belt clip. Maybe he'd missed a message?

Nope.

"Out with it," she said.

"Last night at the hospital I saw Patti McCoy, in the hall, on a gurney."

"The defendant?"

"That's her. The officer accompanying her said she'd lost her baby."

Becky's hand moved to her mouth. "Oh, Bobby. How awful."

"I know. And because I know . . . I was thinking they might not have court today. To give her a day to recuperate."

"They should."

"That's what I thought." He checked his phone again. "But they haven't called. So I guess it's business as usual."

"That seems cruel."

He shrugged. "Maybe it's just as cruel to put it off. I'm sure she wants this whole thing to be over."

Becky shook her head. "She needs a chance to mourn. She's not going to be in any shape to even listen to the proceedings."

"I feel sorry for her; that's for sure," he said.

Becky slipped lower on the pillow, and Bobby adjusted it for her. "Everyone will."

Bobby stopped his fluffing. "They will, won't they? No one's going to want to convict her when they find out she's lost a baby, the baby that was supposedly the motive for her—" He realized he wasn't supposed to discuss it.

"I bet the prosecution doesn't want anyone to know."

It was a good point. "But the defense *will* want people to know. Will want *us* to know. They've probably already been to the judge and discussed it."

"As if the death of her child is a mere trifle, a legalistic point to be wrangled." She turned on her side, facing him. "That's cold."

"That's the law."

"The law doesn't have to be cold."

"It's based on facts, Beck."

"The fact is, a woman just lost her baby. That should be the only fact presiding over the day." She adjusted a pillow between her knees and pulled the blanket over her shoulder. "You'd better get going. The law is waiting."

———

As soon as the jury filed in, Bobby looked at the defendant's table. Was Patti there?

She was.

But she was a far different Patti McCoy from the one presented the day before. Gone were the short skirt, the fluffy hair, and too much makeup. In their place were a dowdy pair of black pants and a generic white shirt. Her hair was almost straight, the way Becky's looked the day after she'd done it up curly, with any style once removed. It was droopy. Actually that was a good way to describe Patti. For today her stance was droopy, her shoulders slumped forward, her chin down as if her neck didn't have the strength to support her head. Even her eyes were downcast.

When Bobby glanced at the other jurors, he saw that they too were looking at Patti; they too had seen the difference—and were wondering what was wrong.

I know. I know!

The older lady on the jury, Abigail, caught his eye, gave a quick nod toward Patti, and offered a questioning look. He shrugged even as he ached to tell the secret. He'd grown up with secrets and had often been told "Don't tell," but this time, for the first time in his life, he had a secret that fairly begged to be shared. A secret that would even gain him a momentary spotlight and position of knowing something *nobody* else knew.

He ached to tell it. Share it.

But then the bailiff said, "All rise" and Judge Abrams came in. Would he make an announcement? *"We are sorry to inform you, but the defendant lost her baby last night. Our condolences, Ms. McCoy."*

The judge began. "Let us proceed with final arguments." He looked to the prosecution. "Mr. Cummings? Are you ready?"

"Of course, Your Honor."

Bobby wanted to jump from his chair, wave his arms, and say, *"But Patti's in mourning! We need to give her some time! I know, because my wife and I lost a baby and—"*

Mr. Cummings interrupted Bobby's mental monologue in Patti's defense and began his final attempt to further ruin her life.

It was obvious to Deidre that whoever had provided Patti with glam lessons the day before was no longer on duty. She looked horrible, like a half-drowned, shivering puppy, cowering in a chair. Deidre explained it away by recognizing that today was the day of final arguments, and by the end of the day the jury might even have time to deliberate. It could all be over today.

I'd cower too. In fact . . .

Jonathan Cummings had no such life-and-death pressure on him. Sure, his reputation was at stake, but by the smooth way he'd handled everything in this trial, Deidre doubted he got too worked up about anything. You win some, you lose some. Actually, you win most and lose a few. At least that was Deidre's guesstimate.

Cummings approached the jury box. "Good morning, ladies and gentlemen." There were a few mumbled responses,

while the rest nodded. "A man is dead. That's why we're
here." He pointed at Patti. "That woman, seated at that table,
is responsible. There are three things that lead to guilt: means,
motive, and opportunity. Ms. McCoy had all three. Let's go
through them now."

He held up one finger. "Means. The victim, Brett Lerner,
was hit over the head with a wine bottle, left dazed and hurting in a hot tub, where he sank into the bubbling water to
drown. It was not a cause of death that required brawn or even
cunning. Even someone as petite as the defendant had no
trouble taking advantage of her lover's vulnerable position.
She had the means."

A second finger was raised. "Motive. We've all heard the
saying 'Hell hath no fury like a woman scorned.' Patricia Jo
McCoy was just such a woman. She tells us she loved Brett
Lerner. She became pregnant with his child. She wanted a life
together, as a family. But he was a ladies' man, a man who
oozed charm and power. A man who had no intention of being
tied down with a mere dishwasher and her child."

Cummings raised a hand. "I know that some of what I say
is speculation. We don't know with certainty how Mr. Lerner
felt about Patti, yet we *have* heard witnesses testify that their
relationship was often confrontational. The simple fact that he
went to great lengths to keep their contact private . . . common
sense says that Mr. Lerner would not accept the reality of a
child of Patti's with open arms—or a proposal. Besides, he
could not. He was still married."

Cummings let the words ring in the room. They fell on
Deidre's shoulders and added to her own guilt. It was not
hard for Deidre to understand how Patti, meek and naive, had
embraced the attention and taken it to the next level. She had
also succumbed to Brett's charms.

A lifetime ago.

Two lifetimes ago.

That Brett had not readily agreed to take his relationship with Patti toward true commitment was not surprising. Deidre glanced at the other jurors. Everyone on this panel could have predicted the outcome of such a match. Murder was above and beyond most people's predictions, but conflict had been inevitable. And breakup. If any of them had known Patti personally as she went through the relationship, they would have advised her, "It will never work, Patti. Get out while you can."

If only someone had said those words to Deidre.

But now it was too late. Now Patti was in. Way in. Up to her eyeballs.

As was I.

Cummings was rambling on and on about Patti's motive. He painted a picture of her circumstances that made murder a viable solution, her only way out of a no-win situation.

Deidre understood this completely. As Sig had mentioned last evening when dealing with the Nelly-bully scenario, there *were* situations that offered no way out. There were times when panic took over. There were times when even a good person could make a mistake.

And be forgiven for it? *Not* be held accountable?

Suddenly she felt herself wanting Patti to be found innocent. But then she shook her head at the betrayal of the plan.

Patti *had* to be found guilty. Had to.

Cummings raised three fingers and touched the third one with the index finger of his other hand. "The third point of guilt is opportunity. Patti had knowledge of Brett's habits. She knew he often liked to relax in the hot tub. She knew the layout of his house and patio. She knew that once in the hot tub, he would be vulnerable."

He put his hands behind his back and shrugged. "Did she go to his house intending to kill him? No. I don't believe she did. What the state believes, what the evidence shows, is that she went to the home of her lover intending to tell him she was pregnant. To confront him with this fact." He pointed a finger at the jury. "Yes, confront. Because even someone as naive as Patricia Jo McCoy could not have assumed that a man like Brett Lerner would be happy about the news. She went to his house expecting confrontation, her blood pumping, her nerves on edge, on the offensive, ready to defend her dream of having a family with him, of escaping the drudgery of being a dishwasher, leaving behind the stress of living paycheck to paycheck. In the eyes of Patricia Jo McCoy, Brett Lerner was a successful man who was an icon of the good life. She'd been spurned before. Hurt badly by men. She wasn't going to take it anymore. Not this time. She'd worked too hard to let her dream die."

He paused to great effect before continuing.

"It came down to her dream or Brett. One of them was going to die that night. That both died is something Ms. McCoy—and Brett Lerner—would like to change. Alas, it can't happen. Mr. Lerner is dead because the defendant killed him. Is she sorry?" He shrugged. "So strong is her desire to hold on to the dream of family that she lives in denial, unwilling to accept responsibility for her actions."

He strolled to the middle of the room and faced Patti and her lawyer at their table. "I am sorry, Ms. McCoy. I am sorry your dream is dead. But you must be held accountable. You must pay the consequences."

As Cummings stepped away, his monologue over, Patti burst into tears, covering her face with her hands. The sound of her sobs filled the room. The judge pounded his gavel. "Let's take a ten minute recess."

As the jury stood, Deidre's heart went out to the girl. And yet, by her outburst . . . had she just admitted her guilt?

Deidre had to hold back her own tears. Her fellow juror Ann offered her a tissue while dabbing at her own eyes.

Deidre shook her head at the offer. She would *not* let the tears come.

She could not.

For once that dam was broken . . .

Deidre bit her lip, relishing the distraction of the pain. *This* pain she could handle.

As for the rest?

———

Bobby shook his head. *No. No. No.* He knew why Patti had gotten so upset. Cummings had mentioned the death of her dream. Her dream was to have a family. She was no longer pregnant. That's what she was crying about.

And yet, Bobby also realized that to the other jurors who were ignorant of her miscarriage, her outburst seemed an admission of guilt. An *I'm sorry! I'm so, so sorry!* A release of emotion. If only an announcement was made as to what had happened last night . . .

The jurors fanned out during the break, a few heading outside for a smoke, a few heading to the vending machines on the next floor, and a few sitting on the benches in the hall, their eyes closed, their bodies slumped in off-duty mode.

Bobby used the break to check on Becky. He was glad when she, rather than Mrs. Ross, answered. He needed to hear her voice. "How you doing, hon?"

"I'm okay. Mrs. Ross took the kids to the park so I have the house to myself."

Although Bobby knew such quiet time could be a balm to a harried mother, he didn't like the idea of her being alone in her precarious state. "You're resting, yes?"

"Yes."

"You have the phone close?"

"I got it on the first ring, didn't I?"

"Any more contractions?"

"One. But very mild."

Bobby looked toward the exit. If only he could get home. "You stay in bed. Don't do anything that will—"

She cut him off. "I'm not on complete bed rest, Bobby. I can get up and move around. I'm just supposed to be careful."

He pictured her cleaning out a closet or deciding she just had to wash the windows. "This is your first day home. Rest this one day. For me? Please?"

She sighed. "I suppose."

"Thank you. I'll be home as soon as I can."

Bobby hung up and noticed Abigail and Latisha sitting on benches across the hall. They were watching him.

"Everything okay at home?" Abigail asked.

They were women. They would understand. "My wife's expecting. She had some false labor last night. We were at the ER until three. She's okay now, but I—"

Latisha slapped a hand on her thigh. "What *are* you doing here, mister? Get home to your wife."

Bobby blinked, unsure. Could he go home? Was that possible?

Abigail touched Latisha's knee. "He can't go home. He's a devoted citizen." She nodded at him. "You get the prize for dedication to duty; that's for sure."

Bobby looked up and down the hall. How easy it would be to add, *"At the hospital last night I saw Patti. She lost her baby. She's the one who ought to get a prize for dedication to duty."*

The bailiff interrupted, calling from the courtroom door to return to session.

The chance was gone. Just as well. The main point was, if Patti could be here today, he could be here too.

It was the defense's turn to lay their case on the line—not that they had much case to lay. Not that Stadler would have any talent in presenting it. Ken knew he shouldn't have such preconceived opinions, but he couldn't help it. Presentation, if not everything, held a lot of weight in the world. He should know. He'd gotten his first job as a golf pro solely by presenting himself as a golf pro. He'd dressed the part, talked the talk, schmoozed the schmooze. Before that he'd tried to get golf jobs but had been repeatedly rejected. His ex, Ronnie, had been the one to point out that he might have lost the opportunities because he hadn't fully played the part. She'd been the one who'd dressed him for his first successful interview. And he'd been dressing the part ever since.

Stadler could have used a session with Ronnie, to utilize her makeover expertise.

The lawyer sauntered toward the jury box, hitching his pants, then pushing his glasses up. . . . His shoes needed polishing. And a tie tack would have kept his tie in place.

Where Cummings always spoke without notes, Stadler held a cheap spiral notebook that still held the remains of torn-out pages caught in the coil. Ken could see a bevy of blue chicken scratches on the page, with many cross-outs and arrows. The man hadn't even taken the time to recopy it.

Stadler offered a smile but even missed in that regard, making it look like an afterthought. An *I should smile now* action.

He cleared his throat and began. "A man is dead. That, ladies and gentlemen, is a fact no one can contest. How did he die? He was struck over the head and drowned in his own hot tub. Neither party disputes that fact either. But who wielded the bottle? Who accosted him when he was most vulnerable and struck him down?"

Stadler paused. "The sad fact is, we don't know. But after hearing what kind of man the victim was . . . it's inevitable he had enemies. Suave users-of-others leave behind a wake of bad feelings. Obviously someone was hurt enough to enact the ultimate revenge. Until we find the guilty party we will never know whether Brett Lerner was killed through a premeditated act or in a fit of anger. But what we do know is that this woman—" he walked over to the defendant and looked at her with some version of compassion—"did not kill him. She would not. It's against her nature and against her own best interests. She's preg—" He cleared his throat. "She found out she was having his baby. She was thrilled with the prospect because she loved him. She wanted to be a family. She wanted to settle down and be happy. Isn't that something we all desire?"

Yes, it was. If only Ken had realized it sooner.

His mind wandered to thoughts of Ronnie when they were first married. Wanting to be happy was a given, but had he really wanted to settle down at age twenty-five? He'd liked the idea of it. After all, who wouldn't want to play house with a leggy redhead with brains and wit and the ability to make pasta from scratch including an Alfredo sauce that made him swoon?

So much about Ronnie had made him swoon. He'd been a lucky man.

Then why had he blown it?

Stadler's voice cut into his thoughts. "Brett Lerner liked women. Lots of women. And as my colleague Mr. Cummings stated, hell hath no fury . . . but the defendant was not scorned by him. She was looking forward to telling him she was pregnant with their child. She went to his place anticipating a special evening. . . ."

Ken remembered the night Ronnie had told him *they* were expecting. She'd made a birthday cake and met him at the door. "Happy birthday!"

"It's not my birthday," he'd said.

She'd just stood there, grinning at him.

"Come on, Ronnie," he said, pushing past her to get inside and hang up his coat. He'd had a hard day selling copy machines. He hated his job. "It's not your birthday either."

"You're right," she said, moving by the closet, unrelenting with that stupid cake. "We're celebrating a future birthday, the birth date of our child."

He'd stopped hanging up his coat to see her grinning at him, the cake up near her chin in presentation style. He knew what he was supposed to say, what she wanted to hear, but instead . . . "This isn't what we planned."

The cake moved from chin level to waist, her expression following the downward movement. "We haven't planned anything about kids. You'll never discuss it."

"So you decided to take matters into your own—?"

She left the entry hall, heading to the kitchen. "I did no such thing. I wouldn't do that. But it happened. And I'm glad."

He shut the closet with extra emphasis. "I'm happy for you."

Ronnie came back into view, the cake gone. "I'm happy for *us*. We'll be a real family now. And baby makes three."

Stadler's words intruded on the memory. "Mr. Cummings's three points of guilt can each be disputed. Means. Ms. McCoy did not have the means to kill Brett Lerner. She did not have the constitution for it. She's a happy person, a good person. She tries hard to please. She is a nurturer. I will read to you from the psychologist's testimony: 'She's generally a needy personality. But she's also very giving and has a servant's heart. She'd do anything for anybody. She's meek, nonaggressive, and nonconfrontational to the point of being a doormat. She's not a leader but a follower. And she's terribly naive.'" Stadler looked up and shoved the loose sheet of paper into his notebook, bending an edge. "Those are not the traits of a person who has the *means* to kill. Anyone."

He walked away from the jury box enough for Ken to see that the back of his right pant leg was caught in the back of his shoe.

"Point two: motive," Stadler said. "She was in love with him; he was in love with her. They'd been together three months. She was *not* a one-night stand. She had no reason to believe he would not be pleased about the baby—but she never had a chance to tell him because when she got to his house, she found him, already dead." He repeated the words. "She found him, already dead."

If only I'd acted pleased about the baby . . . I was pleased. Eventually. Once Philip had grown past the baby stage, Ken had enjoyed being a father. There was something irresistible about having another being on earth with a slightly large nose and dark, curly hair just like himself. Especially when that kid liked what he liked. Ken had first taken Philip golfing when he was six. It had been their *thing*. And no one had been prouder of Ken when he'd played the circuit than his son. Afterward, they discussed the games in great detail.

But then. But then . . .

Ken's career had faltered and he'd lost his place in the tournaments. His ego had suffered greatly, and it had *not* been assuaged by Ronnie. At least not enough. And so he'd found women who would drool over him, who didn't know what a mediocre putz he was, who bought into the package, who didn't want to unwrap the pretty trappings and see who the real Ken Doolittle was.

As if Ken knew . . .

The affairs were just that. Affairs. Brief flings meaning nothing beyond immediate gratification. If only Ronnie had understood and been able to forgive. If only Ken had been able to stop. He realized his insatiable need for adoration was off-kilter. He never felt as if he had enough of whatever he needed at any given moment to stop looking for *it*.

Philip had been thirteen when they'd divorced. And though Ken had tried to keep their golf pairing alive, Philip had been old enough to understand infidelity and had been angry at his father for hurting his mother.

Ken didn't blame him.

And so Philip had grown up pretty much without his father. They'd moved away from each other in so many ways. During the first semester at college Philip had discovered his own escape—drugs. School had been forgotten and his days had been spent in pursuit of the next fix. Ken hadn't seen him in two years.

But now he was calling. Whatever he had to say . . . it couldn't be good. Ken didn't want to hear—

"I don't want to hear any more about how Ms. McCoy had the opportunity to kill Brett Lerner," Stadler said. "In that regard, who *didn't* have the opportunity? He was home alone, soaking in a hot tub, available to anyone who had a grudge. Ms. McCoy did not have a grudge. She loved him. She did not kill him, and no amount of wishful thinking by the prosecution can change that." With a nod, Stadler walked back to his place.

Wishful thinking . . .

Ken wished he could turn back the years and stop Philip from taking drugs, and not be unfaithful to Ronnie, and not get cocky and think he was a better golfer than he was, and be home more, and, and, and . . .

As the judge asked the prosecutor if he had anything else, Ken straightened in his chair. . . .

"I only have one thing to say." Cummings stood at his seat and looked at the jury. "No matter how much the defense tries to whitewash the events of January thirteenth, the evidence does not lie. People lie. People do things they never thought they'd do. But forensic evidence does not lie. Patti McCoy killed Brett Lerner. Period."

With a nod, he sat down.

Great. Can we go home now?

Ken wanted this trial to be over. He was tired of hearing the same facts skewed in different ways. He was tired of not knowing what to believe and not trusting and not understanding what to do next and—

The judge was speaking again. "We'll take a lunch break. Afterward, I will give the jury their instructions. They can begin their deliberations at that time."

Goodie.

———

Twelve of her peers? *My big foot. I'm the oldest one here. By decades.*

Although the realization was not a new one for Abigail, it still had the power to put a dent in her ego. She did not think of herself as seventy-six. Although her body often confirmed her age, her mind was sitting somewhere around fifty. Maybe even forty-five.

The other jurors—six men and five women—were certainly a cross section of society, and if Abigail made a list, she guessed she would have been able to say she'd played many of their types on the stage or screen. Couldn't this fact be an advantage during deliberations? Insight into character (or pinpointing whether a person even had any) was never wasted.

As they settled around the large rectangular table in the windowless jury room, waiting to begin, a man with salt-and-pepper hair, wearing a pink polo shirt under a gray blazer, remained standing. "Excuse me," he said, looking over the lot of them as if they were his subjects. "If no one else wants the job, I'll be foreman."

The man's words caught Jack, the burley auto mechanic halfway to sitting. He aborted the movement and stood, making Mr. Pinky-pink look like a rosebud ready for squashing. "Well, that's rich of you." He looked around the table, possessing his own kingly air, albeit *general* might have been a more apt title. "We haven't even gotten a cup of coffee and you want to take over?"

"I'm just volunteering."

Jack looked around the room. "I want a real vote. A fair vote."

Abigail raised her hand. "I do too."

A pretty woman named Mary nodded. She had lovely chocolate brown eyes and had told Abigail she was a data processor. "For now I think we should go around and tell a little about ourselves. That way, when we vote, we can decide better."

Deidre, the doctor's wife, raised her hand. "I think that's a good idea."

Mr. Pinky spread his hands in surrender and sat down. "Fine. Who'd like to start?"

Jack also took his seat but with a wicked grin said, "On this, I defer to you. Go ahead."

The man sat back in his chair. No . . . *sat back* wasn't an apt description. The man leaned into the maroon vinyl until it tipped and rocked, as if he'd already broken it in, as if he was a pro at acting casual and relaxed.

"My name is Ken Doolittle, and I'm a professional golfer."

Bingo.

"I won the John Deere Classic and the Valero Texas Open."

Blank faces. By the look on *his* face he'd obviously expected oohs and aahs, or at least an impressed *"Oh, really?"* Abigail actually felt sorry for him.

"I'm a golf pro now, at the Marlborough Country Club."

Jack snickered. "Those that can't do, teach."

"Hey!" said Bobby. "Be nice. We're going to be together a long time."

"I certainly hope not," Abigail said. She hadn't meant for that to come out so she defused it by saying, "I'm hoping for short and sweet so we can get back to our lives."

Nods all around.

Jack nodded at Bobby. "You go next."

Bobby reddened. "My name's Bobby Mann. And I can't name a job that I haven't had, nor one I can be proud of."

"You a criminal or something?" asked a blonde across the table.

"No." His grin was infectious. "But you might say I'm a jack-of-all-trades—as long as they pay that jack minimum wage."

"He's also an artist. He makes furniture," Abigail said. Bobby shouldn't dismiss his true calling.

Bobby shrugged. "I dabble."

"Where do you work now?" the blonde asked.

"Guess." He cleared his throat. "Would you like that giant-sized today?"

"Burger Madness?"

Bobby touched the end of his rather sharp nose. "That defendant out there? That Patti? A dishwasher? I probably have more in common with her than with any of you."

"I think we've all had our share of nowhere jobs," said a black man who'd previously told Abigail he was a fireman. "I'm just glad we can finally talk about the trial."

"Amen to that," Abigail said. "Your name's Gus, right?"

"Gus Walters. Been a fireman twenty-one years."

"Ever get hurt?" Deidre asked.

"Once or twice."

Abigail hated waiting her turn. She raised her hand. "I'm Abigail Buchanan. I'm an actress." She didn't wait for them to respond, not wanting to suffer the same fate as the golf pro. "I was in the original *Poseidon Adventure*, and I was in one episode of *Friends*. I was the old, crotchety neighbor who—"

"Typecasting?" Ken asked.

"Absolutely, so watch out." She took a fresh breath. "I've done dozens of commercials and also played with Gwen Verdon on Broadway."

"Gwen who?" the blonde asked.

Gus spoke up. "One of the old people in the movie *Cocoon*."

Abigail took offense on Gwen's behalf. "She was an amazing dancer, singer, and all-around performer. She was nominated for six Tony awards and won four. She was very famous in her time."

Blank stares. *Her* time was obviously not *their* time.

Deidre raised her hand. "I'm Deidre Kelly. My husband is Dr. Sigmund T. Kelly. He's a pediatric orthopedic surgeon and runs the Kelly Pediatric Founda—"

"Hey, I've heard of him," Gus said. He eyed Deidre. "Have I seen your picture in the papers with him? All dressed up?"

"Probably. The foundation is involved in a lot of social events."

"That's all fine and dandy, but what do *you* do, honey?" asked Letisha, a hefty black woman with jewels on her long fingernails.

"I'm a mother. And I help Sig whenever I can."

"You hold his scalpels for him?" asked a burly man with an unkempt ponytail. He had *Joe* on his name tag.

Deidre reddened. "Nothing like that."

"Don't be mean," said a petite redhead. "I'm *just* a mother, and that's not nothing. Deidre and I shouldn't have to defend ourselves." She seemed to catch herself and added, "I'm Ann. Four kids. One husband. Two cats. And an accounting degree I haven't used in ten years."

The others filled in the blanks with their introductions. When they were done, Abigail decided a summary was in order: "So—" she began going around the table, starting with herself—"we have myself, Abigail, an amazingly talented actress; Deidre, the wife of a pediatric surgeon who does not help with the actual surgery." She took a fresh breath. "We have Ken, a golf pro who likes pastels."

"Uh!" Ken said.

Abigail ignored him. "There's Bobby, a Burger Madness aficionado, hold the mustard. And Mary, a data processor with amazing brown eyes . . ."

"Thank you," Mary said.

"Then we have our blondie, Susan, who's a second grade teacher and will probably make us sit in the corner if we don't behave; and Joe, a truck driver, who looks like he would eschew Susan's tamer punishment and elicit his own in a more, shall we say, vigorous manner."

"I don't know about schew-anything, but you got the last part right," Joe said.

Abigail extended a hand of introduction to the far end of the table. "We have Gus, a fireman, who I'd let save me anytime. Jason, a waiter, who will be in charge of taking our lunch orders."

"I'm off duty," said the twentysomething with mousse-spiked hair.

"A person with skills is never off duty, young man. And the final two . . . there's Ann, a busy mother who probably is very familiar with the go-to-the-corner technique—"

"You got that right."

"And finally, on my right, Letisha, a beautiful beauty operator with scary nails." Abigail took an exaggerated breath. "Quite the ensemble cast."

"I suppose *you* want to be the star?" Ken asked.

Abigail shrugged. "I—"

"How did you remember all that?" Bobby asked. "You didn't take a single note."

"I can remember the order for a table of eight without writing anything down," Jason said.

"So what's my name?" Letisha asked.

Jason's face went blank. "I can remember food, not people."

"Hence the lunch duty," Gus said.

"I vote for Abigail to be our foreman," Letisha said.

Susan said, "I second it."

Bobby raised his hand. "Third."

Ken shook his head. "We don't need a third. And besides, who says it's time to choose a foreman? Jack said—"

Jack flipped a hand in the air. "I'm all for voting. We'll have it done."

"This is ridiculous," Ken said.

Gus stood. "Those in favor of Miss Abigail being our foreman, raise their hands."

Abigail pretended not to take note of those who were hesitant, but it was not surprising that Ken, Joe, and Jason were the last to concede. It didn't bother her. She'd handled tougher hombres than them.

"It's passed," Gus said. "You're the man, Miss Abigail."

"Now *that's* a part I haven't played."

This might be fun.

Or not.

———

Deidre was glad they took a vote right off. Maybe the whole thing could be done today and she could go home and find her life again. Maybe. Hopefully.

In a basket in front of Abigail were twelve slips of paper. She began to read them off. "Innocent."

"Yay!" said Ann, the mother of four.

"Shh!" Gus said. "I don't think we should say anything. Not yet."

"I think we can say what we want," Joe said. "I plan on booing if things don't go my way."

"Which means you think she's innocent too," Gus said.

"Why do you say that?"

"Because we've only heard one vote and it was innocent, and you didn't boo."

Joe sniffed. "Maybe."

Deidre suffered a silent sigh. A quick vote, in and out, was obviously not going to happen—especially when there was already an innocent vote. Guilty. Guilty had to be the unanimous verdict.

Abigail picked up another slip of paper. "Guilty."

"Boo," Joe said, glaring at Gus.

Yay.

"Guilty. Innocent. Innocent . . ."

The final vote was six guilty and six innocent.

Joe waved a hand toward Gus. "Now can we go around and tell our vote? We're going to know soon enough."

"I agree," Susan, the schoolteacher, said. "I'd like to know where people stand, so we can start discussing it."

"Start winning people over to our side," Jason said. He pounded a fist on the table, "I say she's guilty."

"Let's go round the table," Abigail said. She pointed to Letisha. "You next."

"I voted innocent."

Letisha, Susan, Ann, Mary, Bobby, and Joe had voted innocent. Deidre, Abigail, Ken, Jack, Gus, and Jason had voted guilty.

This was going to be harder than Deidre expected.

In so many ways.

Abigail tapped a spoon against the table, a makeshift gavel, calling for attention. "It does no good to argue and all talk at once. If you have something to say, everyone needs to hear it. That's the only way we'll get a unanimous decision."

Jack, the auto mechanic, tossed his hands in the air. "We're six to six. There's no way we'll ever sway half of us to the right side—which is my side. Guilty."

Letisha pointed a red-painted nail at him. "You bet your greasy fingernails we're not swaying. Not guilty is the verdict we need—and you, my man, need a manicure."

Jack glanced at his fingers, folded them over, then put his hands under the table. "No thanks. I don't want fancy-man nails like Ken or that there waiter guy over there."

"The name's Jason, and I'd be fired if I had dirty hands like you."

"You'd be taking the bus if people like me didn't have dirty hands."

"What's wrong with the bus?" Ann said. "My kids take the bus every day." She looked at Deidre, who was shaking her head. "Doesn't your daughter ride the bus to school?"

"Actually, my mother-in-law lives with us and usually drives her," Deidre said.

"In a limo no doubt," Joe, the truck driver, said.

"At least you have kids." Susan, the teacher, seemed surprised when her words stopped all conversation. She looked from face to face. "Sorry to put a damper on this lively discussion about kids in school, but some of us haven't been blessed, and—" She squared up the napkin under her coffee cup. "And that's all I want to say about that."

Bobby raised a hand. "Speaking of kids . . . Patti lost her baby. Last night."

These two definitely know how to still a room. "How do you know?" Abigail asked.

"I was at the hospital because my wife went into false labor and—"

"And you're here?" Ann asked. "Is your wife okay?"

"She's fine. She's at home, taking it easy."

"When's the baby due?" fireman Gus asked.

"Six weeks. Every week that goes by makes the baby's lungs stronger and—"

Joe made a time-out T with his hands. "Sorry for your troubles, Bob, but let's back up to the bombshell. Patti lost her baby?"

Bobby nodded. "I was in the hall at the hospital when she was wheeled in. A policewoman was with her. She told me Patti lost the baby."

"No offense," said Ken, "but why would she tell *you* that?"

Bobby shrugged. "Probably because I asked."

"And you do have an honest face," Letisha said.

"Oh, please," Jack said.

"Well, he does. A baby face—no offense, Bobby."

"None taken."

Not fifteen minutes into deliberations and Abigail questioned the wisdom of becoming foreman. These people could zip a conversation onto a side road faster than any race car driver; chance of collision imminent.

She stood at her place, wishing—not for the first time—that she were statuesque instead of petite. A Sigourney Weaver type instead of a Sally Field. "People, please!"

She might not have had the stature, but she had the voice. She hadn't performed six shows a week on Broadway (sometimes seven if there was a Sunday matinee) without learning how to use her voice to best advantage.

The room quieted. "We must stay on task. I, for one, have no desire to be in deliberations for days on end. We must be strong and do the work."

"And not get sidetracked," Ken said.

He'd done his share of off-roading, yet Abigail welcomed his support. "Let's keep the discussion tuned to the trial. During lunch and breaks if you want to compare lives, go for it. But while we're in session . . . focus. Please."

There were a few nods, and she assumed the rest were agreeing. What wasn't to agree with?

"Super-duper." Abigail turned her attention to Bobby. "Are you sure Patti lost her baby?"

He made a crossing motion over his heart. "I'm sure."

"Then why didn't the judge tell us?" Gus asked.

"Probably because he thought it could influence our decision," Mary said. "We'll feel sorry for her."

"So we'll say she's innocent?" Jack asked.

"I already think she's innocent, so it only reinforces my feelings," Mary said.

Finally, they were focused on the trial. Abigail sat down but said, "I think we should go around and state why we feel the way we do—guilty or innocent. Ken? Why don't you start?"

One by one, they gave their opinions. The distinctions between guilty and innocent were based on the forensics against Patti (for those who thought she was guilty) versus the innocent voter's gut feelings that she couldn't have done such a thing. Or wouldn't.

"She wanted a family," Susan said, summing up what most of Patti's supporters had said. "She wouldn't kill the man who would make that happen. I know. I want a family too, and if I ever had a chance to get one, I certainly wouldn't do anything to mess it up."

"But what if Brett didn't want a family?" Gus said. "Maybe she lied about not having the chance to tell him about the baby. With that one lie, a bevy of other scenarios opens up. She tells him; he feels trapped; she's hurt; they argue. He gets rude; she panics because her dream is on the edge of oblivion and she conks him over the head."

"Wow," Susan said. "It *could* have happened like that."

"Exactly." Gus sat back, obviously pleased.

"What Gus just said brings up a good point," Abigail said.

"Exactly," Gus repeated.

She admonished him with a look. "I don't mean the specifics of his what-if scenario as much as the power of one lie. We have to keep in mind that a witness can tell a hundred truths, but with one lie, everything can change."

"Great," Joe said. "How are we supposed to pick out the lies?"

No one had an answer to that one.

One lie can change everything.

Now *that* was the understatement of the century.

Deidre had planned to be more interactive once the jury deliberation started but found that sitting back, letting the rest of them talk, had its advantages. It allowed her the gift of observation. Let them show their hands. If she spoke too soon, pushed too soon for a guilty verdict, she might lose her ace.

Which was?

She had no idea.

Deidre took a sip of tea, trying to calm her stomach.

"Now that we've heard from everyone, let's do another vote," Ken suggested. He checked his watch. "I'd like to get out of here. I have something to do tonight."

"Starlight golf?" Jack asked.

"Actually, an uncle died. I have to attend his memorial service."

"Oh," Jack said. "Sorry." He looked to the rest of them. "I'm all for another vote. Abby?"

"Let's do it. How about a show of hands this time?"

Susan raised a hand, but not to vote. "Won't that be intimidating if someone's changed their mind?"

"Like you?" Joe said.

"No, not like me. But I'd much prefer we do a ballot."

"Everyone's going to know our vote when we keep talking about it," Gus said.

"Besides," Letisha added, "if we're unanimous, we're done."

"Fat chance," Jack said.

Abigail took over. "A ballot then." She set the basket in motion around the table. When it came back around she tallied the votes. "Guilty: seven." There was a gasp. "Innocent: five."

"Okay," Joe said, "who's the traitor?"

"You're just mad because someone came over to our side," Ken said.

"You bet I'm mad."

Abigail spread her arms, trying to make peace. "No one's going to get mad about anything. We're here to deliberate, to talk, to compromise—and to change our minds. People *will* have to change their minds or all this will have been for nothing."

"We're also here to get at the truth," Mary said.

"Fat chance," Jack said again.

Deidre looked at the wall clock above the coffeemaker. "It's four-thirty. Can we call it a day? start again Monday?"

Bobby raised his hand. "I second the motion. I'd like to get home to my wife sooner rather than later."

"I'll get permission." Abigail got up and went toward the door.

A few minutes later she came back. "We can go home. Be back here at nine on Monday. No discussing the trial, etcetera, etcetera."

Ken rose. "Yeah, yeah. See you Monday."

The part about not discussing the trial . . . Deidre knew *that* wasn't going to happen.

———

Sig met her at the door and, with a flourish, pulled flowers from behind his back. Peach roses wrapped in green tissue. Her favorite.

"What are these for?" she asked.

"For going through all this. For me." He kissed her cheek. "I heard on the news you didn't reach a verdict and were calling it quits for the day."

She waited for him to ask about the initial vote. She knew
he wanted to know. Which is why she didn't tell him. After
breathing in the luscious scent of the flowers she said, "I need
to get these in water."

He followed her to the dining room hutch, where she
retrieved a vase. Then to the kitchen sink for water. He was
like a puppy. If she walked across the room in a zigzag would
he follow the pattern?

She tore open the packet of flower preservative and
poured it into the water, where it gracefully danced its way
toward the bottom. "Where's Nelly?"

"She's at a friend's until eleven."

"Where's Karla?"

"Having dinner and playing bunco with her friends."

Deidre was surprised when he snuggled up behind her, his
lips in her hair, his hands on her waist. "With all that's been
going on with the trial, with Nelly, with . . . I thought it would
help if we had an evening alone. I made reservations at Da
Vinci's."

She didn't feel like a romantic evening—because it
wouldn't be about romance. She didn't feel like sitting across
the table from her husband, knowing that talk would focus on
the trial. He'd surely be disappointed at the initial jury vote
and would offer advice about how to sway people their way.

She just couldn't deal with it right now.

She turned to face him, finding the space tight for her
as she was between Sig and the counter. She offered him
a pained smile. "That sounds nice, but I just can't. I'm
exhausted and I don't feel very well." As soon as she said it
she realized she was playing the sick card way too often but
she couldn't think of another excuse. "I have a headache, and I
couldn't eat—"

He stepped back.

She'd hurt him. Again. She busied herself arranging the flowers. "Being in court all day, listening to testimony, then starting deliberations . . . it's hard work."

"So is sitting on the sidelines, having absolutely no control. I'm feeling desperate, Deidre. On the verge of doing something—"

"Something what?"

He shook his head.

She felt for him, she really did, and put a hand on his arm. "I know it's hard. I'm doing the best I can. Really, I am."

He moved his arm, propelling her hand away. "Whatever." He stormed into the family room, grabbed the remote, and fell into his chair.

Deidre stuffed the rest of the roses into the vase and went upstairs. Actually she would have loved a good dinner. She was starved. But since she'd said she couldn't eat . . .

Hunger was a minor consequence she'd have to live with.

———

When Bobby got home he did not expect to see Becky standing at the stove, making dinner.

"Where's Mrs. Ross?"

"Oh, hi, hon. I sent her home."

"But why? You need to be in bed."

"Who says?"

"The doctor."

She salted whatever was in the pot and stirred. "He did not say that. He said I should take it easy, but like I told you before, I'm not on total bed rest." She took a taste from the spoon, then added more salt. She looked at him. "You want me healthy, don't you?"

"Of course."

"Then you can't make me a prisoner in my own home. I have to be able to move about. To be useful. To live."

He moved toward her. "But the baby—"

Becky raised the spoon to stop him. "Hold it right there. Are you implying I don't care about the baby?"

Oops. "Of course not."

"Good. Because if that was what you were implying, I'd have to splatter sauce on you."

He lifted an arm. "I come in peace. May I approach?"

She started stirring again. "I was hoping you would."

He stood behind her and encircled her with his arms. "I just want everything to be okay. I want you to be okay, the baby, the kids . . ."

She pressed her free hand against the side of his head. "It *will* be okay. We'll be fine."

Suddenly, Bobby felt tears threaten. He didn't think he made a sound, but Becky let the spoon go and faced him, her eyes searching his. "There's something else wrong, isn't there?"

And there was, though he hadn't realized it until that very moment. "Patti lost her baby. She has nothing. Yet . . ."

"Yet what?"

"Yet I'm beginning to think she's guilty."

Becky's pale eyebrows rose. "But you told me she was innocent."

He stepped away and sank onto a kitchen chair. "I want her to be innocent. I don't want to believe she could kill her boyfriend, but the evidence is strong against her, and though I want to save her I . . . I'm doing my best to think this through but—"

"Daddy!" Tanner ran in the room, waving a picture torn from a coloring book. "Look what I made."

Teresa toddled in after him "Looky, Daddy, looky!" She

held out her own picture, which was a green scribble on top
of a line drawing of Cookie Monster.

"Mine's better," Tanner said, putting his picture on top of
Teresa's on the table. "I stayed in the lines. Mostly."

"Mine!" Teresa pulled her picture free.

Bobby lifted each child onto a knee, then held up the
pictures. "Well, let's see. . . . Tanner, you did a fine job of
coloring. But isn't Elmo supposed to be red?"

"He got tired of red fur. He's wearing purple today."

"Ah," Bobby said. He looked at Teresa's scribble. "And
you, little one. I see you agree with your brother about a new
color. I like the green instead of Cookie's usual blue."

"Boo!"

He snuggled both of them close, once again reveling in the
scent of their hair and their huggable frames. He was so blessed.

"I'm proud of both of you for doing your best. No one can
ever ask more than that."

Becky tapped the spoon against the edge of the pan, then
pointed it at him.

Oh. Yeah.

Point taken.

———

"No one loved life more than Davey. And if he could have
chosen a way to die, going down in a plane while on a hunting
trip would have been in his top ten. Though other scenarios
like getting his neck broken while bull riding or having his
parachute not open or even choking to death on a bone from a
fish he'd just cooked in a cast iron pan over an open fire would
also have been right up there."

Ken nodded and felt Ronnie squeeze his hand. Uncle
Davey was a character. A man who lived life to its fullest—
to the very end.

The eulogist was Davey's brother Oscar, another good guy. Actually there were a lot of good people on Ronnie's side of the family. Ken missed them almost as much as he missed Ronnie. His own family was rather staid and stodgy. The uncles on his side thought fun was talking about tax shelters over a rousing game of pinochle. Whoop-de-do. His family didn't *do* outside, and Ken's love of a sport (albeit "just golf") was never looked upon as a serious occupation. It was a game. "When you going to get a real job, Ken?" was a mantra heard at most Doolittle family gatherings. Since he obviously could never provide them an answer they would accept, he'd stopped gathering. And since losing the companionship of Ronnie's side of the family in the divorce . . .

Is it any wonder I seek companionship elsewhere? A man's got to have people.

Such as they were.

To wrap things up, Davey's brother led them in a rousing rendition of "Roll Out the Barrel." He even got the preacher to join in. Davey would have loved it.

There was no graveside service as Davey's remains had been cremated and tossed onto a mountain lake he particularly loved. Ken was sorry for that, only because he hated to lose Ronnie's company so soon.

As they made their way down the pew toward the center aisle, Ken spotted a couple of Ronnie's cousins. There were back slaps and a couple "How you been?" questions.

How had he been?

Fair to partly cloudy. Chance of rain 90 percent.

He didn't have much sun in his life anymore.

Out on the front steps, the skies had clouded up. How appropriate.

"Well then," Ronnie said, buttoning her coat. "I really appreciate you coming with me, Ken. It meant a lot to the whole family. They were glad to see you."

"I was glad to see them too." He took her arm, steadying her as she went down the steps in her heels. "And being in your company wasn't half bad either."

She stopped at the bottom. "Care for an encore?"

"Who else died?"

Her laugh made the sun shine. "No one, thank God. But I do need an escort for a fund-raiser tomorrow."

"Where they'll ask me for money?"

"That's the plan."

A funeral and a fund-raiser. Two of his least favorite events. "I don't know, Ron. I'm not in a generous mood right now. This trial . . ."

She slipped her hand around his elbow. "What if I tell you to leave your checkbook at home? What if your sole purpose is to be my companion?"

"Well . . ."

"It's a dinner. Food?"

"Bland chicken and a side salad?"

"Probably."

He sighed. "I've always been a sucker for bland chicken and a side salad."

She kissed his cheek.

———

Abigail was flying high.

Power was the culprit. She was the jury foreman. Yee-ha and take a bow. She'd been chosen above a fireman, a golf pro, a computer wiz, a teacher, and a socialite—among others. The old lady had done it.

Not that she'd ever expected to be foreman. It hadn't been a part she'd tried out for. But wasn't that the way? One of her best parts had come about in just such a manner. At age thirty she'd gone into a production of *Fiddler on the Roof* hoping to be cast as the eldest daughter but had ended up playing the mother, Golde. Sure, they'd had to make her look older, but having scene after scene opposite the lead, Tevye? The mother had much better songs too. She'd wowed them with "Sunrise, Sunset" and "Sabbath Prayer."

The success she'd had with the jury that day might be carried over to the callbacks of *Annie*. Last night the director had recognized her and asked her to try out for one of the leads. Why not? Such moments of serendipity could not be ignored—or thrown away.

Hayley sat in the car, biting her nails. Abigail reached across and moved her hands away from her mouth. "Stop that. You'll be fine."

"I'm nervous. I can't help it."

Abigail leaned a bit toward the middle of the car and lowered her voice. "So am I."

"Really?"

It wasn't true, but if it helped the girl . . . "Nerves aren't necessarily a bad thing. Here's a trick." She held out her right hand. "Dig your fingernail into your thumb until it hurts. Come on. Do it."

Hayley complied. "Ouch!"

"See? It's hard to be nervous when your thumb hurts."

Hayley rolled her eyes. "That's dumb."

"Hey, if it works . . ."

Whatever works. That motto had gotten Abigail through more than her share of tough spots.

———

I could lose this part.

During the last three minutes, witnessing Margaret Timmons run through *her* callback for the part of Miss Hannigan, Abigail lost all cockiness. The woman was good. Real good. And her look . . . physically she was a better match for the part than Abigail.

Bummer.

Not that Abigail hadn't done her best. She'd wowed them and had garnered effusive gushing from the director. "Wonderful, Ms. Buchanan. As expected. Thank you for gracing us with your presence."

But now, all praise aside, it looked like she could lose the part.

Wouldn't that be a downer.

Margaret Timmons finished, and the director said, "Very nice, Margaret."

According to the old praise-o-meter, Abigail won, hands down.

But there was still that nagging doubt. And humiliation. To lose a part to an amateur? A part in a volunteer production?

Luckily Hayley had done well, and though Abigail wouldn't want to bet on her own chances, in her eyes, the child had clearly beaten Kathy Button. Schmooshed her under her heel.

The director stood and stretched. "Well, that's it, people. We'll make decisions by tomorrow and will call with the news. Thanks for all your hard work."

Hayley bopped up beside Abigail. "I did good, didn't I?"

"You did great. How 'bout some ice cream?"

A double dip of rocky road had always been Abigail's celebratory choice.

After a long bath—and downing the remains of a bag of Oreos she found in Sig's bedside stand—Deidre went to bed, playing out the part of not feeling well for the second evening in a row. But given the chance to sleep, it eluded her. Her thoughts kept returning to the trial. Although she'd voted guilty, she had more than a reasonable doubt that Patti . . .

The girl was innocent. And though it was imperative she was found guilty, Deidre found her thoughts drifting to another what-if. What if Patti was found innocent? Then what?

Then you could lose everything.

Her eyes opened and fell upon Sig's empty place beside her. The vacancy only fueled the thought.

She needed Sig. Sig had saved her from poverty and widowhood. Sig had saved Nelly from a handicapped life. Sig had saved Karla from living in a dive after the Polland home became too much for her.

Sig had saved the three of them, as he continued to save children around the world. Sig was a good man. Even if he made mistakes, he was *good*.

She couldn't lose him. She couldn't lose this life he'd given her. Given Nelly. Given Karla.

She'd worked hard to win him over. If she wasn't completely happy? If she had to deal with a few infidelities on his part? It was a small price to pay for security.

Sig was a man of passion. Deidre had seen that.

And used it.

It hadn't been a seduction of *just* the physical that Deidre had employed when she and Sig had first started dating. She'd spotted a need in him to help the helpless. And who was more helpless than a struggling widow with a handicapped child? Sig's ego ached with the need to help. Was it wrong that she'd fed that need? Sure, she'd lured him into marriage with the ulterior motive of gaining health for her child, obtaining financial stability for all the Polland women, and becoming one of the beautiful people. They'd fed one another. What was wrong with that?

She pressed her pillow into her face, hiding from her own evil. What kind of woman was she anyway?

A practical one. One who would do whatever it took to survive and take care of her child. Sig was the second man who had saved her.

Would he be the last?

Toward that end she sat up, retrieved a pad of paper and pen from the bedside table, and listed the names of the jurors and their votes. It was mean to keep Sig in the dark. Maybe this would appease him.

She put it on his pillow and lay back down just as she heard him in the hall. It was after ten. He was coming to bed.

Sit up. Open your arms to him. Make up for all your horrible thoughts.

But instead of doing what she should have done, Deidre closed her eyes and pretended to be asleep.

It was easier than pretending to be a good person.

———

Deidre still couldn't sleep. She slipped downstairs and put a mug of water in the microwave. Maybe some chamomile would calm her.

As the microwave dinged, she spotted Karla on the edge of the kitchen. "You scared me!" Deidre whispered.

"I thought I heard someone up. You still feeling badly?"

"I'm fine. Or I will be fine. I'm making tea." Normally she would ask Karla if she wanted some, but she didn't want to encourage her to stay. "You can go back to bed now. I'm fine."

"Care if I join you?"

Deidre could *not* suffer another private moment with Karla. She didn't want to be told once again that they'd mishandled Nelly's situation with the bully. "Actually, I think I'll go back to bed. I don't feel much like tea after all." She handed Karla her mug of hot water. "Here, use—"

Karla put her hand on Deidre's. "Please tell me what's wrong. Yesterday, that whole thing with the bully? You're a loving mother, but up until now I thought you were also a mother who disciplined when it was appropriate—to teach the proper life lesson for Nelly's own good."

"I don't want to talk about that anymore, Karla. It's over. Do you understand?"

Karla neither shook her head nor nodded. "It's Patti, isn't it?"

Deidre didn't know what to say.

Karla continued. "I've been thinking. . . . Patti was pregnant by Brett. She wanted him to marry her."

"I don't want to discuss Nelly's upbringing *or* the trial, Karla. I really—"

"This isn't about the trial. It's about having a child out of wedlock. About having the father of the baby refuse to take responsibility for the child."

Deidre glanced toward the stairs. Sig and Nelly were in bed but she lowered her voice just the same. "Don made a much better father than Nelly's biological father ever would have made. Don was her father in every sense but one. I was lucky Nelly's father didn't . . . Patti is lucky Brett didn't want to marry her. He wasn't an honorable man. He didn't care about women. He only cared about using them, abusing them, hurting—"

Deidre realized she'd said too much.

"You *did* date him, didn't you?"

Uh-oh. "Karla, please."

"You know so much about him, it sounds like you were personally hurt by—"

The truth burst out, unexpected. "He raped me, all right?
Will that little fact finally get you to stop asking questions?"

Karla sucked in a breath. "Oh, Dee-Dee . . ." She came
close, her arms ready to comfort.

Deidre sidled away. "I don't need pity. I just want you to
leave this alone. Leave everything alone. Yes, I dated Brett.
Yes, he raped me. *Date rape* is the correct term these days,
though Brett certainly didn't see anything wrong with it.
I never had anything to do with him after that. Ever. Even
when—Good riddance."

Suddenly, Karla's face changed from disgust to revelation.
"Oh, my goodness . . . oh, dear . . . is . . . is Nelly *his*?"

Deidre turned on her, her finger pointing. "She is Don's.
She is *your* son's daughter."

"But she was ten months old when you married—"

Although Deidre whispered the words, she applied as
much strength to them as she could. "Nelly is Don's child.
End of story."

Hardly.

Deidre escaped upstairs.

If only there *were* a way to escape . . .

Seven

Trust in the LORD with all your heart;

do not depend on your own

understanding.

Seek his will in all you do,

and he will show you which path to take.

PROVERBS 3:5-6

To sleep: perchance to dream . . .

Ay, there's the rub.

Shakespeare could have been writing about Deidre's situation. For to sleep meant to dream, and to dream meant being assailed by doubts and fears and lapsed morals and the shame of being a victim and the horror of living in uncertainty and doubt. . . .

Although Deidre returned to bed after her late-night discussion with Karla she did not sleep. Seeing Sig asleep beside her added to her confusion, twisting sane and logical thoughts into feelings that were stretched, frayed, and distorted.

After a long hour of private tumult, she returned downstairs, taking solace in the most private room in the house—Sig's study.

She loved this room, especially after the sun went down and the deep patina of the oak paneling and the solidity of the floor-to-ceiling bookshelves made a cozy shelter. She was quite content to curl into the tufted leather love seat, tuck a fleece afghan around her toes, and pull it up to her chin. She

did so now. And by the glow of a single lamp, the shadows of
the room were nearly as comforting as the light, providing a
muted layer to her cocoon. She was not in the mood for hard
edges and bright lights. Her conscience would not tolerate
the glare.

Deidre had no idea if Sig knew she occasionally used his
study as a late-night retreat, as a place to fold within herself,
to find comfort and strength. Somehow this one room, experienced alone in the midst of the darkness outside and the
silence within, was a way to recharge and regroup so that she
could go on, the capable Deidre Kelly, mother, wife—

Liar.

Deceiver.

Manipulator.

Like a child, Deidre pulled the afghan over her face, closing her eyes against the truths that haunted her. She didn't
want to hold any of these titles. But what choice did she have?

When Brett had raped her, she'd been so shocked, so hurt,
so humiliated, so . . . without worth. She'd felt completely and
utterly stupid. How could she have been so blind and not seen
what kind of man he was?

Yet she'd never had an easy go of it with men. The problem had deep roots. She and her father had never bonded.
He'd had more important things to do than care about a
scrawny girl. And when Deidre's mother hadn't been able to
have any more children and her father had realized Deidre was
it, he'd withdrawn the scrap of love he'd originally offered.
Her mother had suffered too, and when he'd moved out, it was
more relief than tragedy. To live in a house with someone who
didn't want to be there, who didn't want *you* to be there . . .

"That was his problem."

Deidre hadn't meant to speak aloud, but the presence of
the words beneath the confines of the afghan made her lower

it to her shoulders. She took a few breaths, relishing the fresh air. Then she shook her head, dispelling any residual memories of her father. Long ago she'd vowed not to be the sort who made excuses, blaming her behavior on a crummy childhood. *My childhood made me do it.*

No sirree, Deidre was responsible for her own life. Yet she did hold Brett accountable for what *he'd* done to her. No woman deserved to be forced.

When she'd discovered she was pregnant she'd never considered telling Brett he was going to be a father. Besides, he was long gone. She'd kicked him out of her life and had even threatened to have him arrested. Maybe if she'd pressed charges back then . . .

Deidre wished she'd considered the pregnancy a blessing, but such a lofty declaration would have been a lie. Her first reaction upon seeing the pregnancy test show its indisputable plus sign was to scream, "No!" Her next reaction was to throw the test across the bathroom where it bounced off the wall and ended up in a philodendron like a white signpost among the green.

A signpost reading: "Life will never be the same."

An understatement.

After the initial shock, Deidre considered abortion—but only briefly. It just seemed . . . wrong. Life was a miracle, even when it was forced, inconvenient, and didn't make any sense whatsoever.

The sense came when Deidre first held Nelly in her arms. *This came from me?* And in that initial moment of bonding Deidre had felt true love for the first time. True love given and true love received. For even though baby Nelly didn't know she was showing love, she was by the very way she fit into Deidre's arms, calmed when held against her chest, and eventually smiled at Deidre's voice.

Deidre ached with the magnitude of such love.

She still did.

Nelly was the reason for everything she'd done ever since. Marrying Don, marrying Sig . . .

It wasn't that she didn't—hadn't—loved these two men who had become fathers to Nelly. She had. In a way. But she'd often wondered, if she'd been a woman unencumbered with a child . . . would she have married them? Would she have been so drawn to them, so adamant about catching them?

Catching two men who were completely different from each other.

Don had been a rock—a rough-hewn boulder, occasionally handsome in the eye of the beholder. He'd been unpretentious and genuine, solid in build, strong in heart, and unmoving in character and faith. Since Don's death from skin cancer (all those sunburns while roofing had finally taken their toll) Karla often said, "God made a good one with my son, didn't he?"

To which Deidre always replied, "The best."

Neither woman exaggerated. Don was the best man Deidre had ever known. That God had chosen to let him die . . .

Deidre had asked God why. Screamed, "Why?" Whispered it. Sobbed it.

She had not received an answer.

Probably never would.

It was this silence that had made her shove God aside. He obviously didn't care about Deidre and Nelly, thus leaving Deidre to do the caring for both of them. She was the one who made ends meet to pay the bills. She was the one who dealt with the bone-numbing weariness at the end of the day when the walls of their home loomed far too close.

Had God blessed her diligent efforts? Nope. God had added to her list of problems by making Nelly's hip problem worse. Pain, limping . . .

Karla had prayed about it and had urged Deidre to pray too. Deidre had found it far more advantageous to take action. Enter Dr. Sigmund T. Kelly.

At first Deidre had only targeted Sig with the intent of getting Nelly accepted as one of Sig's freebie surgeries. Poor widow and her poor crippled child . . .

But when Sig had shown interest beyond that of a surgeon, had shown interest in Deidre as a woman, Deidre had adjusted her strategy. She would have been stupid not to. Why settle for Cinderella's ball when the handsome prince was offering life at the castle?

Deidre tucked the afghan around a foot that had gotten free of its warmth. Once again settled in, she let her eyes scan the study. It was more than an office; it was a library, a den, a sanctum, a cozy chamber—with the top-of-the-line accoutrements of solid wood, leather, and brass. Don would have felt uneasy in such a room and would have lingered on its fringe like a visitor in a museum.

But Sig . . . he owned this space with every movement, breath, and breadth of being. If Don had been a rough-hewn boulder, Sig was highly polished granite, pretentious not in its attitude but in its very presence. Where Don was solid in stature, Sig was lean with a model's build and grooming. Even while lounging around the house Sig gave the impression that the presence of a camera would not faze him. He was always on, ready for public consumption.

Not that there was anything wrong with that. It was part of his job. The foundation needed funding, and Sig's persona and place in society were essential to making things work.

Actually, both men shared a strong sense of compassion.

Although Don's sphere of influence had been small and Sig's large, both men possessed a giving steadiness of character.

And faith?

Faith had been huge to Don. Giving back was as necessary as breathing. Being in the choir, serving as a deacon and then an elder . . . And Karla. At first Deidre had gotten involved for both their sakes, and Nelly thrived under the loving dome of the church. But eventually she'd felt her own faith grow and had participated of her own accord. By allowing the family of the faithful to become a part of her life Deidre experienced genuine love and true fellowship. She'd let it envelop her in a gentle, constant embrace.

The Kelly family went to church too. But the faith behind the act was far less intense and far more . . . social.

Not that Deidre minded. After her foray with God, she was ready to step back and—

"Deidre?"

She looked to the door of the study, where Sig stood in his flannel pajama bottoms and T-shirt. "Hi," she said.

"What are you doing in here?"

This was the first time he'd caught her here. She quickly sat upright and gathered the afghan. "I'm sorry. I'll get—"

"No, no." His hands made a sit-back-down motion. She expected him to take a seat behind his desk, but instead he moved to the ottoman. "Neither one of us able to sleep . . . are you okay?"

Deidre was going to say, "Sure" but found she didn't have strength for the farce. "Not really."

He adjusted the afghan around her legs. "Of course you're not. I woke up and found you gone and . . . I realized what I'm putting you through. Putting Nelly and Karla through too. I've been so caught up with what needs to happen that . . ." He sighed and rubbed his eyes. "It's awful business, isn't it?"

"Very."

"Do you think it will turn out all right?"

His uncertainty shocked her. Sig was never uncertain.

"Will it?"

"I . . . I hope so."

"If I could turn back time, I would, you know." His voice was incredibly weary. "One night. One impulsive act. One . . ." He shook his head. "The if-onlys are killing me."

"Me too."

He put a hand on her knee. "If there was any other way you know I'd choose it."

"I know."

He left the ottoman and sat beside her on the love seat, at the end where her head had been lying. "Here," he said, "lean on me."

Deidre couldn't remember the last time they'd snuggled or had even thought about snuggling, but once her head found the crook of his arm, once her ear lay against his chest and heard his heart, she felt herself relax.

A moment of calm before a storm?

She hoped not. But for the moment, she'd take what she could get.

———

You'd think I was waiting to get a nod from Broadway.

Abigail forced herself to stop pacing. She usually slept until nine or ten on Saturdays, but this morning she'd been up with the dawn. As if they'd call this early?

To distract herself she'd decided to clean her kitchen cupboards. Did she really need three bottles of soy sauce or twenty and one-half Tupperware containers? (Where had that one lid gone, anyway?)

When she heard a knock on her door, her heart jumped and it took her a moment to realize the director, Tony Novotny, would not be sending a messenger with the news; it was not fame calling.

It was Hayley. She burst into the room. "I got a part. Not Annie, but I'm one of the orphans!"

She heard already? Does this mean I haven't got a part? Abigail tucked her disappointment away and hugged the girl. "Congratulations! I knew you'd get it."

Hayley took possession of the room with expansive arms. "I didn't know it. I mean, I hoped, but with Kathy Button trying out I was never sure and—"

"Did Ms. Button get a part?"

"I don't know. The assistant director just said I got a part as one of the orphan girls." She stopped all movement. "Didn't you get a call?"

Abigail fluffed a tasseled pillow. "No."

"But you have to! You played Miss Hannigan before. You need to play her again. And you're famous! You'd bring tons and tons of people to the show."

That's what I thought. She stopped fluffing the pillow, punched it, then threw it back on the couch. *Act, Abigail. You're a big girl. Act happy.* When she turned around to face Hayley she succeeded at getting into character. She smiled. "We should celebrate. How about we go out for an early lunch?"

Hayley shook her head. "Mom and Dad are having a celebration for me. That's one reason I came up here, to invite you down at one o'clock for lunch and cake. Mom's making it right now."

Abigail did not feel like celebrating. She wanted to wallow in despair, pout with passion, get thoroughly mad, have a proper tantrum, and—

The phone rang. They exchanged a look.

"It's them!" Hayley whispered.

"No, it's not. Other people call me, you know." But very few at ten on a Saturday morning . . . She picked up the phone.

"Ms. Buchanan, this is Tony Novotny, the director at the Hillside Community Theatre."

"Yes, Mr. Novotny." *I've been waiting for your call.*

"I wanted to call you personally to ask if you would be willing to play the part of Miss Hannigan."

Ha! Abigail nodded to Hayley and the girl yelped and clapped. To Novotny she said, "I would be happy to play the part."

The director gave her details about the first read through—which was the next afternoon at one. She hung up and immediately raised a hand for a high five with Hayley.

"This is going to be so fun!" Hayley said. She hurried toward the door. "I have to tell Mom to put your name on the cake too! Now you have to come to the party."

Abigail never missed a got-a-part celebration.

———

Abigail was stuffed beyond comfortable. She knew what she was doing once she got home: a little Pepto-Bismol and a nap.

"Would you like another piece of cake?" Hayley's mother asked.

"No, no," Abigail said. "I'd burst."

"More ice cream!" Hayley's little brother, Joey, held up his plate.

Clive, his father, flashed him a look. "What do you say?"

"Please?"

The mother, Della, spooned another scoop onto his plate. "I don't know where he puts it."

"Kids have hollow legs," Abigail said. She put her hands on her midsection. "As we get older, our legs get filled up and we can't eat as much without it spreading outwards."

Joey stopped the spoon's journey to his mouth. "Really?"

Hayley whacked his shoulder. "No, silly. She's kidding." She looked at Abigail. "Aren't you?"

Abigail looked at Hayley, incredulous. Apparently she'd have to watch what she said. She hadn't thought kids were that gulli—

Hayley grinned. "Gotcha."

"My, my. You are a good actress."

Hayley bobbed her head and licked frosting from her finger with a loud *thwop*. "Thank you." She hopped to her feet. "Let's sing something for Mom and Dad."

"Like what?"

"Like 'Tomorrow' from the show."

The family clapped. "Yes, do! Sing for your supper!"

How could they refuse?

———

Taking Nelly shopping was done on a whim, but was much needed—and appreciated. With jury duty Deidre had been gone all week, and even when she'd been home she'd been preoccupied. And with Sig acting stressed and—using his own word—desperate, Deidre knew that grabbing on to a bit of normalcy was a worthy goal.

But normal wasn't in the offing. . . .

On the way to the mall Nelly asked, "What's going on with you and Dad? Why are you two acting so weird?"

"Weird?" Deidre said. "No one's acting—"

"Yes, you are. Both of you."

Deidre felt like turning around, driving home. Maybe this one-on-one time wasn't a good idea. "We're just a little stressed, that's all. Dad's busy and the trial has me gone when I'd rather be home."

Nelly shook her head, not finished. "Even when you're both home you've got your heads together, whispering."

It was true. Entirely true.

"It's nothing you should concern yourself with, sweetie," Deidre said. "It's just the trial. It's put a lot of strain on me and—"

Nelly hit the dash with her hand. "It's not the trial! You've been acting different for a long time. Months and months. Like you're worried about stuff. You're constantly giving each other looks, like you have this big secret that nobody else knows."

An understatement.

"What aren't you telling me?" Nelly asked. "I want to know."

But you can't know. Not ever.

Deidre summoned a smile. And a lie. "I assure you nothing is wrong. Nothing that an outing with my best daughter won't fix."

"Only daughter."

"Which means I'm prepared to lavish all my attention— and credit cards—upon you."

"Are you trying to bribe me?"

Although Deidre's stomach tightened she held on to the smile. "Is it working?"

"We'll see," Nelly said.

———

"Will this be all?" the clerk asked.

Deidre opened her wallet and laughed. "I think it's enough. Don't you, Nelly?"

Nelly was beaming. "I really like the jean skirt."

The clerk folded it. "It's very cute. Especially with the pink top."

Suddenly, Deidre noticed the clerk's name badge: *Audrey*. Audrey?

Sig's mistress? How many Audreys were there in Branson? Twentysomething Audreys?

"Mom, you just dropped a fifty-dollar bill." Nelly retrieved it from under the checkout counter.

Audrey smiled. "Throwing money around?"

Ha-ha. While Audrey finished checking them out, Deidre studied her. She had blonde longish hair, a pretty smile . . . Deidre was surprised her build was athletic. She would have though Sig would have chosen a more buxom type. Maybe she wasn't the right Audrey. . . .

But then, when the clerk excused herself to go get some sacks from the back room, Deidre noticed she had a pronounced limp.

It figured. Sig wouldn't be turned off by her infirmity. Just the opposite. And as such she was probably so grateful for his attention that she went gaga over him, making him feel like an Adonis.

"That will be $185.34," Audrey said.

Deidre handed over her credit card. Audrey glanced at it and did a double take. "Deidre Kelly? You're Sig's wife?"

Bingo. Just the way she said "Sig" oozed with familiarity. And for Audrey to be so peppy about it and acknowledge their relationship, right there in front of—

"And . . . you must be Nelly. Hi, I'm—"

Deidre snatched the credit card from Audrey's hand, grabbed Nelly's arm, and pulled her toward the exit. "We have to go."

"Mom? What are you doing?"

"Don't you want the clothes, Mrs. Kelly?"

Deidre kept walking, finding it difficult to fight against Nelly's contradictory pull.

Once out of the store, once she got Nelly one store away, Deidre let go of her arm. People were looking. People would think she was abusing her daughter.

"Why did you do that?" Nelly yelled.

"Shh!" Deidre said, nudging her to keep walking. "I'll explain later."

"But I loved those clothes. We just spent an hour picking them out."

"We'll get you other clothes."

"I don't want other clothes. I want those—"

Deidre pulled her to a stop. "I can't buy those clothes in that store, from that woman."

"Why not? She was nice. She knows Dad."

Deidre noticed they were standing in front of another clothing chain Nelly would like. "Let's go in here. I'm sure you'll find something."

"It's more expensive in here."

Deidre walked inside. At this particular moment, money had no meaning.

———

Appeasing her daughter had cost Deidre an additional $210.34; a price she willingly paid.

Not that she didn't have regrets. If she'd been a more mature human being she would have simply done the chitchat thing, paid the bill, and walked out with one happy daughter in tow. Not made a scene. Not raised all sorts of questions in Nelly's mind. And saved herself $210.34.

And yet . . . maturity was highly overrated. Didn't she

deserve a hissy fit once in a while? Did she always have to play the part of the perfect socialite wife? What she should have done is slapped Audrey in the face and yelled (for everyone to hear), "Stay away from my husband, you floozy!"

Not that she'd ever used the term *floozy* in a sentence, even if it was appropriate.

Luckily, as soon as Deidre and Nelly got home, Nelly invited a friend over to see her stash. Which left Deidre pacing the floor, wondering where Sig had gone off to. The good thing about seeing Audrey in the flesh (such as it was) was that it pushed Deidre into facing reality. She and Sig had not discussed her since the night of their big argument, after the awards banquet when Deidre had first heard Audrey's name as a point of gossip in the restroom. All he'd said then was, "I can't go into it, Deidre."

Won't go into it was more like it.

And then . . . other things had taken precedence and Audrey had been a bad dream compared to a full-blown nightmare. Yet Deidre had kept her eyes open to any evidence of sexual dalliances on Sig's part. If he was continuing the affair—or having others—he was very discreet.

But no more. Discreet or not, this had to stop. They had enough pressure in their lives. Deidre wanted everything cleared up, fixed, put to bed.

No pun intended.

Deidre wandered through the first floor of the house, her body as unsettled as her mind. She played through what she would say to Sig as soon as he got home. She needed to be done with this or die from anger.

And fear.

And guilt.

And exhaustion.

Deidre was startled when she and Karla nearly collided

at the top of the stairs leading to Karla's apartment. "Whoa, woman!" Karla said. "You nearly gave me a heart attack!"

Deidre backed away. "Sorry. I wasn't looking where I was going."

"And where are you going? It sounded like you were walking a marathon up here."

"I'm waiting for Sig."

"It looks more like you're stalking Sig." Karla pointed at Deidre's face. "There is a hunter-waiting-for-the-hunted look in your eye."

Deidre forced her hands to unclench. "I have to talk to him about something."

"Talk? Or pounce on him with claws bared?"

The phone rang, sounding like the bell in a fighter's ring, calling an end to a round—or the beginning of one? Deidre answered it. It was Sig.

"I need you to meet me."

"I need to talk to you, Sig. I—"

"We will talk. But . . . do you have a pen? Write down this address."

"Why should I?"

"Deidre. Please. Just come to 384 Mockingbird. You know the area?"

"Maybe. Probably. But why—?"

"Just come. Now. It's important."

He hung up, preventing her from arguing the point that she was the one who wanted to talk with *him*, and she wasn't in the mood to give in to one of his whims and go where he wanted her to go.

"What does Sig want?" Karla asked.

"He wants me to drop what I'm doing and meet him."

"If it will stop your pacing . . ."

"I hate that he snaps his fingers and I jump."

"You wanted to talk to him, yes?"

"Yes, but—"

"Then go talk to the man. The tension around this house is so thick I could tie a string around it and send it through the mail, which sounds tempting if only I had some string."

Deidre wasn't in the mood for one of her witty analogies. "We have a lot on our minds; that's all."

Karla got Deidre's coat out of the closet and held it open for her. "Then let those minds meet so things can get back to normal."

Deidre put her arms in the sleeves. "I'm not sure that's possible."

Karla adjusted the coat into place and hugged her from behind. "Of course it is, Dee-Dee. You know better than that." She whispered in her ear. "Remember what Jesus said. 'I am leaving you with a gift—peace of mind and heart. And the peace I give is a gift the world cannot give. So don't be troubled or afraid.'"

"I gave up peace for Lent."

Karla gave her an extra hug. "You had peace once. You can have it back. All you have to do is—"

Deidre pulled away, not looking back. "I gotta go."

She left her mother-in-law and her false promises of peace behind.

Deidre drove with the slip of paper in her hand: 384 Mockingbird. It was a residential neighborhood of small, nondescript homes built in the sixties. Pastels were the exterior paint color of choice. It was like driving through a basket of Easter eggs: blush pink, sky blue, moss green, and baby yellow.

She stopped looking at addresses when she spotted Sig's

SUV in the driveway of a yellow house with white trim. She tried to remember if anyone they knew lived in this neighborhood. Someone she and Don might have known would be more likely.

Deidre parked and went up the front walk, her nerves at attention. Did Sig want her to meet some child he hoped to operate on? Was this the home of some rich old lady who wanted to contribute to the foundation but wanted to meet "the wife" first? Or—

Sig was at the door before she could even ring the bell. "Come in," he said.

The inside was simply but tastefully done. The pastel colors outside were carried within. The place had an airy feel.

"Sig, why have you brought me—?"

Deidre's words were cut off when she saw Audrey come out of the kitchen.

"Hello, Mrs. Kelly." She extended a hand. "Nice to meet you. Again."

Deidre let her mouth hang open and shook her head. "I don't need this." Then she turned toward the door.

Sig blocked her way.

"Hear us out, Deidre."

A bitter laugh escaped. "Hear you out? Do you think I'm actually going to stand here while you tell me how much you love each other and—?"

"It's not like that," Audrey said.

Sig led Deidre to a couch. "Sit. Please."

She sat only because her legs were about to give out on her. "I don't want to hear this, Sig. Any of it. I can't believe you've had me come here to meet your lover, your little chippie, your . . . whatever you want to call her. I thought after overhearing the gossip back at the awards banquet that you'd have the sense to break it off, the decency to be faithful to your wife. Especially after all I'm doing to help you get out of the fix you got yourself—"

"Stop!"

The room fell into silence.

"I've brought you here to explain. To tell you the truth."

"Hmph."

"I've had a really hard day, Deidre. I did something earlier today, nearly did something that . . . anyway, I'm weary of more things than you can imagine. But in *this* one thing . . . I can set this right. I should have done it sooner. I don't know why I didn't." He glanced at Audrey, who stood in the doorway between kitchen and living room. "When Audrey called me this afternoon, saying she'd met you and Nelly . . ."

Here it comes. Audrey's given him an ultimatum. "It's me or them, Sig. It's time you decide."

"I didn't mean to upset you," Audrey said. "I kept the clothes aside, in case you want to come—"

"I don't want the clothes!" Deidre yelled. "I don't want anything you've touched. And I will never shop in that store again. In fact, what I should do is call the manager and tell her that she has an adulteress in her employ. See if she wants to keep you on after that bit of information!"

Audrey put a hand to her mouth. She began to cry. "Excuse me." She ran down the hallway that led to the bedrooms.

"Why did you do that?" Sig asked.

"I—"

Deidre watched incredulously as Sig went after Audrey. She heard him knocking softly on a door. "Come out. It's okay. She just doesn't know. She doesn't understand. It's my fault. But I'll make it right. I promise."

Deidre heard a door open and in a few moments Sig and Audrey appeared. She had a tissue to her eyes, and he had his

arm around her shoulders. "Deidre, I would like you to meet
Audrey Cannell, one of my patients."

Involuntarily, Deidre looked down at Audrey's leg. The
limp. She remembered thinking Sig was attracted to her
because she needed his medical expertise. She crossed her
arms and sat back in the chair. "Do you give this kind of attention to all your prospective patients?"

"She's not a prospective patient," Sig said, looking at
Audrey. "I already operated on her. And botched the job."

"My limp is better than it was."

"You're being kind. It's worse, and because of my error, it
will never be better."

"So you're having an affair because you feel sorry for
her?"

"We're not having an affair."

Audrey shook her head. "No. Not at all. Sig is like . . ."
She looked at him. "He's like a father to me."

Like a father? This did not compute.

Audrey continued. "I never knew you thought he and I . . ."

Sig led Audrey to a chair and stood between the two
women. "I've kept both of you in the dark. It was for the sake
of my reputation that I've kept Audrey a secret—and not for
the reason you think." He breathed deeply, then spoke again.
"First off, you have to know that I have never been unfaithful.
I wouldn't do that. Ever."

He seemed sincere, and yet . . .

"Secondly, as I said, Audrey was one of my patients.
One of my first patients. I operated on her leg. On her hip.
She had a similar problem to the one our Nelly had. But
with Audrey . . . I blew the operation. She will always limp
because of me."

"People make mistakes," Audrey said. "You were only
trying to help."

"I was only trying to be your savior. Save the poor crippled girl and be the hero."

Audrey smiled up at him. "You are a hero. You've gone above and beyond."

Sig shook his head. "I was young and cocky and thought I knew more than I did." He wrapped his arms tightly around his torso. "Audrey's father was dead, and her mother wasn't healthy. Her mother could have sued me for malpractice, but she didn't. She was a very good, forgiving woman. She brought her daughter to me, trusting me. . . ."

Audrey nodded. "She died four years ago, when I was eighteen."

Sig took up the story. "Suddenly, Audrey had no one. Both parents dead, a bum leg, no money for college or a good future. So I stepped up and started to take care of her. I paid for her education. She graduated last May in fashion merchandising." He looked at Audrey proudly. "She is already the buyer at Sassy's."

"Assistant buyer," Audrey said. "Among other duties. And on the side I design costumes for a few of the music shows around here."

"The point is, Audrey was a patient of mine. That's how I know her. That's why she's in my life."

The doubt and anger and angst of the past six months juggled before Deidre's eyes. "Why didn't you tell me? Especially when you heard the gossip about the two of you. If you're doing a good thing for her . . . you should be proud of it."

He shook his head. "I'm doing a good thing—now. But I ruined her life, Deidre. There are no number of bills I can pay that will change that. And I didn't tell you—or anyone— because frankly, I didn't want people to know that I've ever messed up. Pride kept my secret. I didn't want to risk my reputation by having anyone know that the great Dr. Sigmund

T. Kelly screwed up. Having them think I was unfaithful was preferable to having them thinking I was inept."

Deidre was stunned. Every thought, every accusation . . . off base, and oh, so wrong. Her husband had his faults but . . . he was an honorable man.

He sat on the couch beside her and took her hand. "I'm so sorry, Deidre. I'm sorry for Audrey, I'm sorry for not telling you, I'm sorry for putting you through . . ."

The great Dr. Sigmund T. Kelly began to cry.

As he should have.

Of his three jobs, Bobby enjoyed driving a cab the most. He liked to drive because it gave him a feeling of control and freedom and often gave him time to daydream. Plus, he met some interesting people. Some rude people. Some nice people. And some weird people.

Although he was still thinking about Becky's suggestion that he quit one of his jobs, he was pretty sure the cab job would remain on his résumé. For one thing, it paid the best. But the downside was that it took him away on weekends. Time away from his family—and his art. One, he regretted; the other, he embraced.

Chicken.

Today he was assigned the airport. It was one of his favorite runs because sometimes he got to meet famous people. With all the celebrity shows around Branson: Andy Williams, Bobby Vinton, the Oak Ridge Boys . . . He'd picked up Debbie Reynolds once. She was as adorable now as she was in those old Tammy movies.

But no stars today. Not so far at least.

He picked up a petite woman with a rolling carry-on.

"Welcome to Branson. Where to?"

"The Excelsior."

He pulled into traffic. "In town for business or pleasure?"

"Pleasure, though it could turn into business. I wasn't planning on it being for business but . . ." She sighed. "In the plane I was thinking about Branson and all the big shows going on here. . . . Are they hiring?"

"Depends on what you do. You a performer?"

She laughed. "If I sang or danced, they'd clear the auditorium. But I have done quite a bit of work with lighting in various shows. A lot of theaters are using computers to run the lighting and the sound. I know how to use all that. It's amazing what computers can help create nowadays."

"You a computer whiz?"

"I have my moments. Actually, I recently got my degree in theater—with a minor in production design."

"Congratulations. I never went to college."

"It's not for everybody."

Or available to everybody. It was a huge regret in his life. But Grandpa hadn't had the money, Bobby hadn't the inclination, and when Grandpa had died . . . And then Becky had come into his life.

"Do you like living here?" she asked.

"I do. It gets a bit crazy with all the tourists, but if you go out of town a ways, into the hills . . . there's nothing prettier. I've been here since I was a teenager."

"My grandpa used to live here. I visited him once, but we lost touch."

"Too bad—losing touch."

Her voice softened. "Yeah. It is."

They rode in silence until he pulled into the hotel. "Here you go."

He heard her take a deep breath. "Suddenly, I'm nervous.

I mean, I was coming here for family but am suddenly thinking of a career change? It's crazy."

"You'll do fine. One thing leads to another. That's the way
life works. And you'll never know if you don't try."

"I do want to create something. Be a part of something
that makes people happy."

"I agree with that one. That'll be $9.50."

She handed him fifteen. "I'm feeling generous; keep the
change." She got out of the cab, lugging her small suitcase
to the pavement. She leaned down to make a parting remark.
"My mama always said, 'The only true happiness comes from
squandering ourselves for a purpose.'"

Bobby's stomach flipped and he looked at her for the first
time. "William Cowper, right?"

"Right. Wow. Small world." The girl was a pretty thing.
Not stunning. Cute, with short ruffled hair.

The doorman took a step toward the cab and with a
sweeping hand gesture, motioned Bobby on. "Have a good
one," Bobby told the girl.

"Thanks."

Bobby pulled forward so another taxi could move in
behind him. But he paused at the edge of the street and looked
back to the hotel entrance. The girl had not moved inside. She
stood there, looking after him.

His stomach grabbed. *No. It can't be.*

Another taxi drove up behind him, wanting to exit.

He sped into traffic.

Bobby pulled to the side of the road and got out his cell
phone. He had a phone book in the cab and looked up the
Excelsior Hotel's number. He dialed.

As soon as the hotel operator answered, he suddenly realized he didn't know if Cass had married. She hadn't mentioned it. And she was just out of college.

"Hello?" the operator said for the second time.

"Sorry. Do you have a Cassie—maybe Cassandra—Mann registered?"

"Let me check. Yes. She just registered. Would you like me to ring her room?"

All courage left him. "No. No thanks."

He disconnected the phone.

But not the thoughts about his sister.

———

All day long there were at least two people in Bobby's taxi. Himself, his sister, and occasionally a passenger or two.

He hadn't seen Cass more than once or twice since he was fourteen and she was eight. After his parents had died, his two older brothers had gone off on their own and the three younger sisters had left to live with an aunt in Chicago.

His oldest brother, Martin, had run away and never come back. His second brother, Chuck, just sixteen, had run away too but had shown up at Grandpa's a few years later, first with a stolen car and later wanting money for drugs. Besides not having any extra cash, Grandpa was of the mind not to give a loser money to dig himself any deeper, and so . . .

Chuck had gotten mad and trashed Grandpa's shop. Bobby would never forget the pained look on Grandpa's face when he'd seen the destruction. But in true Theodore Mann fashion, he'd taken a deep breath, let it out, and said, "Well. 'Pears we have some work to do."

Together, Bobby and Grandpa had put the shop to order. Chuck's name wasn't mentioned again. And he hadn't returned. A few years later, when Grandpa died, Bobby thought about trying to find him but didn't make the effort. The way Chuck was going he was headed for an overdose— which became a reality a few years later. Bobby received word because Chuck had Grandpa's phone number in his wallet.

Some family he had.

But as Bobby pulled into his driveway on Magnolia Lane, the driveway to Grandpa's old house, as Tanner waved at him from his tricycle on the sidewalk, as Teresa and Becky sat on the porch . . .

Becky waved.

Tanner zoomed toward the car. "Hi, Daddy!"

Yes indeed. Some family he had.

————

Ronnie wanted to meet at the fund-raiser because she needed to go in early to help. Ken was grateful for that. He didn't want to be at this thing any longer than necessary.

But when he walked down the long corridors of the hotel toward the ballroom, when he saw the sign outside the room saying, "AIDS BENEFIT: Help Us Find a Cure!" he balked. AIDS? He didn't want anything to do with that charity. Why hadn't he asked Ronnie what kind of fund-raiser it was?

He knew the answer. He'd been so pleased with the idea of spending more time with her he hadn't cared.

But he did care. He hated fund-raisers but hated them even more when they played the sympathy card for people for whom he felt no sympathy. He'd imagined an evening spent listening to people laud the merits of the opera or new play-ground equipment, not giving depressing statistics about death and disease.

I'll just go home. When Ronnie calls I'll tell her I don't

feel well. It won't be a lie. The very thought of sitting through
this kind of evening makes me feel sick to my—

"Ken!"

Caught.

He turned toward her voice, resigned. Maybe if he wrote
a big check up front he could bow out of the rest of it. He
wasn't in need of a chicken dinner that much. At the moment
Burger Madness held more appeal.

Ronnie rushed toward him, looking lovely in a royal blue
dress that flowed in her wake when she walked. She kissed
him on his cheek and slipped her hand around his elbow. "I'm
so glad you came."

"You should have told me," he said.

"What?"

He nodded toward the sign. "AIDS? Frankly, that's not my
kind of charity."

She let go. "It's not anyone's kind of charity, Ken. Nothing would make us happier than to not have to be here."

"You don't have to be here."

"There you're wrong." She led him toward the opened
double doors. "Let's go sit down. Just do what you do best."

"And what's that?"

"Pretend."

He didn't have time to react. She drew him into the ballroom that was set with round tables for eight. There must have
been fifty of them. He did the math: four hundred people?
Gathered for AIDS? The upper crust too. He recognized a
few celebrities from the stage shows in town and the female
anchor for the evening news out of Springfield. People dressed
in their Sunday best. For AIDS?

As they walked, Ronnie greeted people, smiling, chatting.
As the principal at one of the high schools in town, she knew
a lot of people by name. A few tables in, Ken's mood light-

ened as he realized someone might recognize him. Maybe the evening wouldn't be a total waste. He could use a recognition hit. . . .

With that goal in mind, they reached their table too soon. Three people were already seated. Ken recognized the man as the manager of one of the country music theaters. Bob something?

The man stood as they approached. "Ken! Ronnie said you were coming. Long time no bogey—because of you."

Bogey Bill. Ken extended his hand. "Bill. Nice to see you."

"You remember my wife, Helen?"

"Indeed I do. I still haven't gotten over that peach-colored golf skirt you wore in the women's tourney."

"Oh, you." Helen blushed and accepted his peck on her cheek.

For the first time, Ken noticed the third person at the table, the man who'd had his back to their approach.

"Hello, Dad."

Ken shot a look toward Ronnie, but she wisely avoided eye contact by hanging her purse on a chair—one seat away from Philip. Leaving an empty chair between them.

Ken felt like a lobster in a trap.

Philip stood and Ken feared he might try to hug him. He chose the trap and sat down. "Hi, Philip."

By the look of discomfort on Bill's and Helen's faces, it was obvious the moment appeared as awkward as it felt. But luckily, another couple approached the table and the chitchat of introductions took over. Ken wouldn't have been able to repeat their names if a gun had been placed to his head. His mind railed with accusations and anger. He'd been tricked, trapped, and deceived. By Ronnie. His honest, honorable ex. It was something Ken would have done, but not Ronnie.

Ken felt his son's eyes. He did not look in his direction. He took too many sips of water and became preoccupied with placing his linen napkin in his lap, just so. Ronnie also vied for eye contact but he vowed to give neither of these conspirators the satisfaction.

Luckily, Bill supplied a distraction. "So, Ken, what's the gossip on the circuit?"

Although Ken hadn't been on the circuit for ten years, he chatted on about the pros, using the knowledge he'd gained from watching the tournaments on TV. Drawing on his past contact with many of the golfers, he managed to embellish enough that it sounded like he was still a player.

When the new guy at the table joined the discussion, Ken knew he'd successfully dodged the bullet.

———

Ken made it through half his salad doing the small talk thing. But when Bill asked Philip what he was up to lately, Ken pushed his chair back and stood. He tossed his napkin on his seat and walked out of the ballroom without even an "Excuse me" or "Nice talking to you" to his tablemates. A man could only take so much. . . .

The corridor was full of people as though another event had just let out. Ken slid into the crowd. Yet after going only a few yards he was shocked to hear his name called— by Ronnie.

"Ken!"

He kept walking.

"Ken!"

The female half of a couple walking in the opposite direction pointed toward Ronnie. "I think you're being paged."

Ken did a halfhearted job of pretending he'd only just

noticed: he did a quick glance toward Ronnie, slowed, and told the woman, "Thanks." He stopped while the couple moved on.

Ronnie caught up with him, in spite of her heels. Her face was red—and not from the physical exertion. She took his arm and, pasting on a smile, pulled him to the side of the corridor near a potted palm. She turned her back toward the exiting masses. "How dare you!"

"How dare *you*," Ken said, even as he tried to keep a happy face for the public's view. He lowered his voice. "You tricked me. You trapped me."

"Only because you haven't returned Philip's phone calls."

She knows about those? "So you're the one who told him to call?"

"No, no. It's his doing. He's the one who wants to make contact again."

"Why now? After two years?" Over his ex-wife's shoulder Ken saw Philip approaching. He quickly looked to his right, but the plant blocked his escape. And to the left was the wall. . . .

Philip joined them, adding to the blockade. "Don't run from me, Dad. I won't bite."

"I don't need this," Ken said.

"But I do."

The calm tone of his voice made Ken look at him.

"I'm the one who's been wrong, Dad. These past two years. Even before that. It's my fault."

Ken blinked. This was not the arrogant kid he'd last known, the one who'd glared at him with hatred and said, "Get away from me! I want nothing to do with you! Ever! I wish you were dead!"

For the first time that evening Ken looked at his son. He was taller. At least an inch taller than Ken. His dark curly hair was shorter than before and neatly trimmed. He wore a gray suit. And a tie. Who was this person standing before him?

"I'm sorry you feel tricked into coming tonight. When Mom told me she'd run into you at the mall and you'd agreed to go to Uncle Davey's funeral, I—"

"Why weren't you there?"

"I have a cold. It's better today."

"It was my idea to invite you here tonight," Ronnie said. "Philip wasn't gung ho about the idea, guessing you'd feel . . . like you feel. I shouldn't have—"

"No, you shouldn't have."

She lifted her chin and gave him a look he'd seen dozens of times before. "And *you* should have returned your son's calls."

She had a point.

"Just talk to me, Dad. Just once. See how it goes."

"Why don't the two of you go to lunch tomorrow?" Ronnie suggested.

"That'd be great," Philip said.

The trapped feeling returned—but with less vengeance. It was obvious this new Philip was not like the old Philip. It might be possible to be in the same room and not argue. It might be possible to actually talk.

"Do it for me," Ronnie said. "I want to see my two favorite guys get along."

Philip shook his head. "Do it for *me*, Dad. Please."

Ken looked at Ronnie. He looked at his son. Although he wasn't eager to open a slammed door, he wasn't sure he wanted to lock it either.

"Fine. Okay. Fine."

———

When Deidre returned home from her visit to Audrey's house, Karla was there waiting for the details. "So?"

There was no way Deidre would tell her. Could tell her.

Not that Sig or Audrey had asked Deidre to maintain silence. But what good would it do to have Karla think badly of Sig's professional skills? She looked up to him. She respected him.

Deidre hung up her coat and shut the closet door with a gentle click. "Things are better now."

"So you did receive peace of mind and heart?"

Oh. The verse. "Yes, I guess I did."

"Good for you."

Good for me. Good for us.

———

Deidre did not see Sig the rest of the day. Soon after she returned home, he phoned to say he'd been called into surgery for a two-vehicle accident, and one surgery had turned to two when another victim from the crushed van needed his services.

That night, for the first time in months Deidre longed to have him in bed beside her. She needed him.

But he wasn't there.

She drifted off to sleep while watching a *M*A*S*H* rerun. If she couldn't have her own surgeon beside her, she'd watch other surgeons . . . *helping the helpless.*

Deidre opened her eyes when she felt Sig get into bed. The room was dark. He'd turned off the TV. She started to sit up.

He put a hand on her shoulder. "Shh. No, no. It's not time to get up. It's nearly one in the morning. Complications with the surgeries. I'm so sorry. Go back to sleep."

Just the way he said it . . . so considerate. So kind.

Deidre lay back down, but once he was settled with his back to her, she moved close, hugging him, nestling together like two spoons seeking a common place within the space of the other.

Sig found her hand and pulled it to his chest.
He held it there.
Near his heart.

———

Knocking?

Abigail opened her eyes and listened, trying to see if the knocking in her dreams was part of the dream or—

Someone knocked at her door.

She looked at the clock. Green numbers glowed back at her: 2:15. Who would be knocking at this time of night?

"Abigail?" It was her neighbor Della's voice, a harsh whisper. Worried. Plaintive.

Abigail got out of bed and went to the door. Standing before her was Della holding a pajama-clad Joey. Hayley stood beside her, also in her pj's. "There's been an emergency. Can they come in with you?"

Still not grasping what was happening, Abigail *did* have the sense to step aside. Della carried Joey into the living room and deposited him in the circular rattan chair. He immediately curled into a ball, his eyes never opening.

"Dad was shot," Hayley said as she sat on the couch.

"Shot?"

Della tucked the afghan around her son. "He's a night watchman. A burglar . . . I have to get to the hospital."

"Is it serious?"

Della gave her the look she deserved. "He's been admitted." She kissed the top of Joey's head, then her daughter's upraised face. "Be good. I'll call when I know something." She hurried to the door.

"Is there anything I can do?" Abigail asked.

"You're doing it. Just take care of the kids. And pray."

Unfortunately, Abigail wasn't adept at either.

After locking the door behind Della, Abigail returned to the living room to find Hayley curled up on one end of the couch, her feet tucked between two cushions for warmth.

"I'll get you a blanket." She retrieved one from the closet and tucked it around the girl, then did an extra tucking of the afghan around Joey. She sat on the coffee table in front of Hayley. "You okay?"

Dumb question.

Hayley gave a wiser answer. She shrugged.

"Can I get you anything?"

"Will you pray with me?"

Ask me anything else.

"Please?"

To admit she wasn't a practiced prayer was not something Abigail wished to do, so she nodded and bowed her head. Hayley's hand appeared in the space between them and Abigail took it and held it against her knee. She waited for Hayley to pray.

Silence.

Surely the girl doesn't expect me to pray aloud?

Hayley opened her eyes. "Go ahead."

As if she had a choice? Abigail closed her eyes. She was good at improvisation. She could do this. "God? Help us—all of us. Show us what to do. And make Clive good as new." She hesitated a moment, then realized she had covered the main points. To herself she quickly added, *And help me help the kids.* "Amen," she said.

"Amen." Hayley snuggled deeper into the cushions. "Is Dad going to die?"

The impulse to say *Of course not* came. And went. "I don't know. I hope not."

Oddly, Hayley seemed satisfied with that answer. "I'm glad we're here with you."

"Me too," Abigail said. "Try to get some sleep."

If only that were an option.

Eight

Don't keep looking at my sins.
Remove the stain of my guilt.

PSALM 51:9

*D*eidre awoke to the sounds of the shower running—and Sig singing "Love Me Tender." He had such a nice voice. . . .

She glanced at the clock. It wasn't even seven yet. And he was up. On a Sunday? After getting home from surgery so early in the morning?

The shower turned off. Deidre swung her legs over the side of the bed and rubbed her face, trying to get her brain in gear.

Yesterday the truth about Audrey had come out. Her husband had *not* been unfaithful.

It was a new day.

Sig popped his head out of the bathroom wearing a white terry robe, rubbing his hair with a towel. "Hey. You're up."

"So are you."

"Good morning."

Was it? A good morning? If so, it was the first in many a month.

He tossed his towel on the counter and came into the bedroom. "I know we've gotten out of the habit, but what if we go to church this morning?"

Deidre felt her eyebrows rise. For months they'd rarely

gone. It was hard enough keeping secrets, much less going into God's house with them tucked away in a pocket.

Obviously noticing her skepticism, he came to the bed and sat beside her. "Come on, Deidre. With all that's been going on . . . maybe it would help. Besides, after yesterday, I feel cleansed. At least about Audrey. I'm so glad I told you. Finally told you."

"But church?"

He shrugged and fingered the belt of the robe. "I'm tired of worrying about the trial and . . . like I said the other night, I hate that the brunt of this is falling on you. I'm sure you want it done with as much as I do."

You have no idea.

He continued. "Yesterday with the surgeries, I had a chance to remember who I am and what I do. I helped three kids yesterday and—"

"I thought you had two surgeries."

"While you and Nelly were shopping I went out to . . . to do one thing, but ended up . . . I pinpointed the problem in another child, the cutest little boy named Orlando. I'm going to do some surgery on him. He might never have had a chance to be cured if it weren't for me."

Ah. *This* was the Sig she knew. A do-gooder. Confident and driven.

He raised a hand. "I know. You've heard it before. I've never been one to *not* toot my own horn. But in this case, I know it's true. The mother said so."

"I'm happy for you."

"Be happy for the kids."

Deidre was slightly taken aback. Although her husband had a soft spot for needy kids it was usually equaled by an assertive passion for his own talent. There was something different about him today. Softer. Submissive.

He took her hand and held it captive in his. "I don't know what's going to happen with the trial. But the mother of the boy I met yesterday said that there's no such thing as coincidence, that God can turn even bad things into good, so I'm hoping that this horrible thing that's been dogging us—" He took a fresh breath. "I hope somehow, someway, it will turn out okay. I mean, if God is behind my talent and my talent can help people, then surely he's got a plan to make this entire mess work out."

Was she in a movie? Or in the middle of a novel? This total change in her husband could only be explained away by a glitch in plotting.

"So is church okay this morning?"

"I suppose."

It couldn't hurt.

———

Deidre hadn't paid close attention during church in years. When she did attend, she did so with a chip on her shoulder. *Okay, God, I'm here, but don't expect to reach me 'cause it ain't happening.*

Yet today . . .

Pastor Miller caught her attention by telling a story about his three-year-old daughter–how she played a game where she covered her eyes and said, "Daddy, you can't see me!"

Deidre liked stories about kids in sermons. It made the message tolerable. And today . . . the story made her remember Nelly doing the same thing the pastor's daughter had done. It was such a cute—

The pastor interrupted her memory. "We laugh at our children's games, but are we playing the same game with our heavenly Father? Covering our eyes, pretending he can't see us?"

Deidre's happy thoughts of Nelly evaporated.

Pastor Miller continued. "Do we have the attitude: if I don't think about God, then he won't think about me?"

Pretty much.

"Let me assure you, he thinks about you—all the time. He sees you—all the time. 'The Lord looks down from heaven and sees the whole human race. From his throne he observes all who live on earth.'" The pastor smiled and whispered into the microphone. "He knows what you're doing and what you've done." He stood upright, his voice carrying across the sanctuary like a heavenly proclamation. 'For the Lord sees clearly what a man does, examining every path he takes.' 'The Lord is watching everywhere, keeping his eye on both the evil and the good.'"

Deidre felt a creepy-crawly feeling in her gut. She put her purse in her lap and pretended to need a tissue. Anything to defuse the moment.

"'People may be pure in their own eyes, but the Lord examines their motives.' But 'commit your actions to the Lord, and your plans will succeed. The Lord had made everything for his own purposes, even the wicked for a day of disaster. The Lord detests the proud; they will surely be punished.'"

That's what I'm afraid of. . . .

Punishment. Its threat loomed.

Suddenly Deidre couldn't listen a moment longer. Not when the words were so full of condemnation.

"The good thing is," Pastor Miller said, "God knows all you've done and loves you anyway. If we were smart we would stop hiding, introduce ourselves to him, be honest with him—since he knows it all anyway—and stop trying to live life under his radar. We need to work *with* him and let him work within us. Let him release us from the battle of handling things alone. If we do this, he guarantees—"

A shudder coursed through Deidre, one strong enough for Sig to give her a questioning look. She didn't look back at him. She couldn't.

Each breath came with pained deliberation. Her heart pounded.

"Are you all right?" Sig whispered.

She shook her head, stood, and sidled her way out of the pew.

Deidre hurried outside the church where she gasped for breath—breaths free of *him*. They did not come easily and she lifted her chin, straining to make the airway clear.

"Deidre?" Sig joined her on the front steps. "What's wrong?"

"I . . . can't . . . breathe."

He led her to the ledge of a stone planter. "Sit. Relax. In. Out."

An usher stuck his head out the door, but Sig reassured him everything was all right. Deidre was glad for that. She didn't need an audience.

In fact, she would have preferred if Sig weren't here. How was she ever going to explain what had brought about this panic attack; how her own sins overshadowed his? There was no way Sig could fathom what a bad person she really was. Her motives were selfish—*evil*, if she wanted to use the word Pastor Miller had used. And she was proud—in the worst way possible. Oh, so proud and sure of herself. She could handle things. She didn't need—

She *did* need . . . a lot. Too much. The secrets she'd ignited years ago had never left her. No matter how hard she tried to run away from them they perched on the edge of every moment, waiting. . . .

They aren't secrets to me. I know all about them. Let me in, Deidre. Let me help—

She shook her head, pushing the inner voice away. She couldn't let anyone—especially God—be privy to the inner workings of her mind and heart. Or her past. No one would want to have anything to do with her if they knew how she'd manipulated . . . And no matter what Pastor Miller said, God wouldn't want anything to do with her. Especially after she'd repeatedly told him she wanted nothing to do with him.

Sig sat beside her, stroking the place between her shoulder blades. "All the talk in there about secrets . . . are you still upset because of me keeping the Audrey secret from you? Or did Pastor's words about God seeing everything . . . ? They hit *me* hard. Even though you didn't know about Audrey, God knew and he didn't like it, and then there's the other thing he saw. . . ." Sig shook his head. "He knows, Deidre. He knows it all. I've tried to ignore that, but I don't think I can any longer." He sighed deeply. "I've got a lot to think about."

Tell me about it.

Deidre wanted to run far, far away—from Sig, from everyone. Yet what good would that do? Sig would only follow her and this moment would be repeated. Apparently he needed forgiveness for Audrey. Maybe if she assured him everything was all right he would move on.

She, on the other hand . . . it wouldn't be so easy for her. For there was no one who could pronounce a holy "I forgive you" over Deidre and make her feel new. She'd hurt too many people and told too many lies.

Sig was waiting—waiting for her to say what he needed to hear? She put a hand on his knee. "It's okay, Sig. I understand why you kept the secret about Audrey. On my part, I shouldn't have believed gossip like that. I'm guilty too." *Of so much more than that . . .*

He leaned his head close until it touched hers. "I've made so many mistakes."

Yes indeed. They were a pair.

"Let's go home," he said.

They might as well. Home was as good a place as any to seal a wound.

While others gaped open.

———

Abigail felt something touch her arm.

Her eyes shot open and she pulled back an inch, unbelieving. There, directly in front of her, was four-year-old Joey, his hand resting on her forearm. His light brown hair was tousled every which way, and his face looked soft and smooth as luscious cream.

He's flawless.

And in her bed.

She carefully turned in the other direction with the intention of getting up, but there on the other side was Hayley, on her back, arm sprawled over her head.

She was surrounded. There was no way she could move without waking them.

So she forced herself to relax, letting the soft sounds of their breathing lull her back to sleep.

———

When Abigail next awoke, she was alone in the bed. Did she smell toast?

She got up, wrapped her yellow chenille robe around her body, and walked through the hanging beads that separated the sleeping area from the rest of the apartment.

"Hi," Hayley said from the kitchen. She buttered a piece of toast. "Want one?"

"Mine has peanut butter," Joey said from his place on the couch.

Although Abigail regularly ate from his position, the thought of toast crumbs in the cushions spurred her to say, "Will you sit at the table, please?"

"Told ya," Hayley said over her shoulder.

Reluctantly, Joey moved to the table, only tipping his plate once. Abigail took solace that he had not dropped it, for surely the toast would have landed sticky side down.

"Strawberry jam or peanut butter?" Hayley asked.

"Both."

Her answer made Hayley frown. "That's the way my dad likes it."

Ah. The father who'd been shot. How had it slipped her mind? "Your mother hasn't called?" It was not a good sign.

Hayley shook her head. "I was wondering if we could call her cell."

"Sometimes those aren't allowed in hospitals."

"Can't we call *someone*?"

Yes, they could. Abigail got out the phone book and dialed. "I'm calling to check on the status of a patient who was brought in last night. Clive Wilson."

Hayley stood by her side, and even Joey left his toast behind. Abigail wiped some peanut butter off the corner of his mouth with the end of her tie belt. "I'm on hold," she told them.

"Is Daddy dead?" Joey asked.

"No, no, of course not," Abigail said. But considering Della hadn't called . . .

Hayley pulled her brother in front of her, laying her arms over his shoulders, meeting at his chest. He took hold of her hands, completing the circuit. Their position moved Abigail. It was clear they loved each other, were protective of each other.

Too bad you have no one to love and protect.

What an obtrusive thought. Where had that come from?

A woman came on the line. "Mr. Wilson has been admitted. I'll connect you to his room."

"ICU?"

"No, just a regular room. Room 425. I'll connect you now."

She flashed the children a smile. "He's still there. He's in a room. A regular room."

Joey cocked his head to look up at his sister. "Is that good?"

Hayley nodded. "I think so. I—"

"Shh!" Abigail said as soon as she heard Della's voice on the line. "Hi, Della. This is Abigail. How's he doing?"

Hayley pulled on the phone, forcing Abigail to tilt it so three ears could hear. "He's going to be all right," Della said. "The bullet nicked his liver and they had to operate, but he's going to be fine."

"That's gr—"

Hayley grabbed the phone away. "Mom! Can we talk to him?" As her mother responded, Hayley nodded.

"I want to talk too," Joey said tugging at her arm.

Hayley acquiesced. "Here's Joey."

While Joey talked to his mother, Hayley said, "Mom says he's sleeping. Can we go see him?"

To her own disgust Abigail said, "We have the first meeting today, for the play."

"We can do both, can't we? You can take us to see Dad, and then we can go to practice."

Possibly . . .

Joey handed Abigail the phone. "Mommy wants to talk to you."

"Abigail," Della said, "I know all of this has been an

imposition, and I want to thank you for taking the kids in like that."

"No problem."

"But I'm going to have to ask you if they can stay a little longer. I really need to be here."

"I was going to bring the kids by."

"That would be fine. Maybe on the way to your practice?"

Great minds . . . yet . . . she could handle Hayley, but—"What about Joey?"

"That's right," Della said. "Joey. It's all right with me if he goes with you to the meeting."

That's not what Abigail had meant. "But—"

"It's just the intro meeting, maybe a read-through, right?"

"Right, but—"

"Surely the director will understand once you explain."

Talk about drama. Abigail sighed. "Don't worry about a thing. We'll be fine."

She hung up and looked at the two children standing before her. "It appears we're stuck with each other all day."

"You're taking Joey to the meeting with us?"

"That's the plan."

"When we go, can we stop and get Chick-O-Rama?"

That sounded good. At the moment Abigail felt the need to wallow in a few thousand grams of fat, calories, and chemicals.

———

This was *not* Ken's type of restaurant. Especially at Sunday noon. The whole place was full of families coming from church, assuaging their guilt with the reward of something steeped in fat, calories—and flavor.

He couldn't eat like that anymore. It wasn't just his high

cholesterol but the way his stomach simply couldn't take it. Middle age was a triple bogey.

He was early but scanned the restaurant for Philip. Not that his son had ever even been on time for anything in his—

"Hi, Dad."

Ken turned around and saw Philip coming in the door. Philip moved a step closer than usual, as if to hug him, but luckily an elderly couple needed the right-of-way, and the hug was aborted.

Philip nodded toward the hostess. "Have you put our name in yet?"

He shook his head. "I just got here."

Philip stepped to the podium. "Two, nonsmoking, please."

"Right this way."

Philip took a step back and let Ken go first. Ken was blown away. That the simple act of getting a table should have made him feel this way added to the shock. But for Philip to be so poised, so grown-up, so polite . . .

Where was the brash, slumping loser who smelled like cigarettes—or worse? Where was the kid who looked like he wanted to punch the world in the stomach or spit on anyone who dared wield authority?

The hostess handed them menus. "Thank you," Philip said.

My, my, my. The world had definitely blown a cork.

"The biscuits and gravy are good here." Philip reached across the table and pointed to the entry on Ken's menu. "You can get an egg, too, and sausage links. I remember how much you like biscuits and gravy."

What else did Philip remember? What would Ken prefer he forget?

Ken found himself dreading the answer. He hadn't been a good dad. After the divorce, Ken had not taken advantage of all the visitation the courts allowed. He hadn't handled teen-age rebellion well. And when Philip had dropped out of college because of drugs . . . he went into rehab and tried hard to beat it, but Ken didn't have the patience for such things. Why would the kid take drugs in the first place? Didn't he have any self-control?

The waitress brought water. "What would you like to drink?" *Get me a double.* "Coffee for me."

"Me too, please," Philip said. He pulled the container of sugar and sweeteners close.

Ken pointed at it. "You always did have a sweet tooth."

Philip nodded.

Ken tried to think of something else to say. He zeroed in on Philip's red polo shirt and black pants. A polo shirt similar to the one he had on. He would have bet a million dollars his grown son would never wear a polo shirt. "You look nice. You didn't have to dress up for me."

"I didn't. I came from church."

Ken nearly choked on a piece of ice. "Since when?"

"Since recent."

Ken snickered. "Why?"

Philip shrugged. "I like the comfort of it."

"You like all that namby-pamby stuff?"

For the first time, Philip's face took on a hard edge. "So real men don't need God?"

"Real men don't need to sit in a pew to know God."

"So you know God?"

Ken smiled wickedly. "I've heard of him."

The waitress brought their coffees. "You ready to order?"

Ken hadn't looked at the menu but closed it. "Biscuits and gravy, an egg over easy, and sausage links."

"Ditto," Philip said. When the waitress left he tore open a packet of Equal and stirred it into his coffee. "It was nice to see you last night. At the fund-raiser."

"Sorry for running out so fast."

"Sorry if you felt tricked. Mom just wants us to get back in touch." Philip cradled his coffee mug in his hands and looked down at it. "Why haven't you returned my calls?"

Ken leaned against the aqua vinyl of the booth. "I . . . I've been pretty busy with this trial, being on the jury."

Philip nodded once. "Mom told me. How long is it going to last?"

"We had our first afternoon of deliberations Friday. It will take as long as it takes." Ken was glad Philip didn't ask for details. Not that he would. Philip had never cared much about what was going on in Ken's—

"I have HIV."

When the words flew across the table and hit him, Ken happened to be looking at a baby in a high chair across the aisle. The baby had dark, curly hair. . . .

"Did you hear me, Dad? I have—"

"I heard you!" Even the baby turned toward Ken's voice. He lowered it. "I heard you." He couldn't think of anything else to say. *I heard you I heard you I heard you.*

"It's under control. It's not AIDS—yet. And it's not a death sentence anymore, but—"

"Are you gay?"

Great. Three more awkward words to add to the day's inventory.

Philip leaned toward him. "I got it from a drug needle."

Ken realized his head was shaking no. How could this clean-cut, polite, totally transformed boy—*man* of twenty— have HIV? He'd obviously beaten the drugs. He'd turned his life around. Only to have it cut short?

Ken saw that Philip's hand had traversed the space between them and was on top of his own. "It will be all right, Dad. It will."

Ken pulled his hand away and hissed, "How will it be all right? How?" He looked toward the window as a blue van pulled into a parking place and two parents and three kids piled out. A family. Would Philip get the chance to marry and have a family?

Philip seemed to guess his father's thoughts because he said, "I'm in an early stage. I may live ten years or more." He looked Ken straight in the eyes. "Ten years. How many of us can state with certainty we will live for another ten years?"

He had a point.

"There are consequences to choices, Dad. Mom always told—" He faltered, then continued. "Both you and Mom tried to tell me that, but I thought I knew better. I wouldn't listen. And now I'm paying for those decisions." He shrugged.

Ken didn't know what to say.

"I take full responsibility, Dad."

Ken felt this throat tighten. Who was this man before him? For he was a man now—no thanks to Ken.

The waitress approached with a tray. "Here we go. I don't need to ask who gets what because you got the same. Like father, like son." She did a double take at the two men and added, "Hey, you *are* two peas in a pod." She nodded at their polo shirts then turned a finger in a curlicue motion near her hair.

Philip looked to Ken.

Ken nodded. "Can we get more coffee? When you have the time."

Time.

Would never be the same.

As if I don't have enough to worry about.

Bobby knew it was a horrible attitude to have while sitting

in church, but he couldn't shake it. The stress of being on
the jury and having Patti's fate in his hands; Becky's precarious pregnancy; her desire for him to quit one of his jobs; the
ever-present lure of his furniture making; and now, his sister's
appearance in Branson, which conjured up memories that
ached with the bite of bittersweet.

Should he follow through with his initial impulse to
contact her?

If I wait long enough, she'll be gone and I won't have to.

He shook his head, causing Becky to glance in his direction. He looked forward, pretending to be paying attention to
Pastor Collins.

"The New Testament verse for the day comes from
Second Corinthians, chapter 4, verse 8: 'We are pressed
on every side by troubles, but we are not crushed. We are
perplexed, but not driven to despair.'"

Wanna bet?

Despair was precisely what Bobby felt. Overwhelming
despair.

And worry.

Yet when he looked to his right to see Becky, he received
a smile for his trouble and a squeeze of her hand in his. Becky
never seemed to worry. She approached every bump in the
road with a calm determination to keep going. If the bumps
were bad enough to require a detour? Keep going. If the road
was washed out? Find another way but keep going. She was
the little engine that could. *I think I can. I think I can. I know
I can.*

Pastor Collins's voice interrupted his thoughts. "The
Old Testament lesson is from Second Chronicles, chapter
20, verse 17: 'But you will not even need to fight. Take your
positions; then stand still and watch the Lord's victory. He is
with you, O people of Judah and Jerusalem. Do not be afraid

or discouraged. Go out against them tomorrow, for the Lord is with you!'"

Becky was always telling him not to worry, that God would take care of it and would do the fighting for them. "You worry too much, Bobby. Let it go."

Let go and let God.

And there it was. Even though the saying was on everyone's trite list, on this particular morning, at this particular time, it came to him with fresh meaning. Could he really stop fighting for everything, stop mentally fighting about everything? Just take a position, stand still, and watch the victory play out?

The service entered a time of silent prayer. Bobby almost laughed at the timing. But he didn't waste the moment either. He bowed his head and gave it a shot. *Take all of it, Lord, all the things that are eating at me. Make them work out. Your way. Do it, God. Do your stuff.*

He smiled at his choice of phrasing. Was it proper to ask God to do his stuff?

The congregation sang a response. The service continued.

It was too late to be eloquent now.

———

"Bobby, who's that on the porch?"

Bobby finished his turn into the driveway. A young woman stood up from the wicker rocker and moved to the top of the steps.

Oh, my goodness . . .

It was Cass.

Bobby turned to Becky. "That's my . . . I had her in my cab yesterday and I thought . . . but . . ."

"Who is it, Bobby?" There was an odd lilt to her voice.

"It's Cass, my sister."

Becky beamed. "I know. Isn't it wonderful?"

Bobby stared at his wife. "You know?"

"Surprise!" Becky laughed and waved at his sister. "When Cass called me yesterday she said she nearly had a conniption when she realized it was you driving the cab, but by then you'd driven away and . . . besides, we had a plan and she didn't want—"

"You and my sister had a plan?"

She reached across the middle console and touched his arm. "I called her."

"But I didn't know where she was."

"It wasn't that hard. Father's sister, Chicago . . . Your aunt sounds very nice."

"You talked to my aunt?"

"Of course. She's the one who gave me Cass's phone number. Your other sisters' too."

"Out, Daddy!" Teresa said from the backseat.

"Me too!" Tanner said.

Bobby put the car in park, turned off the engine, and let the kids out of the van. They raced toward the front door, oblivious that a family moment was about to unfold.

"Whoa there, cuties!" Cass said, making herself small as they zipped around her to go inside.

Becky was the first to reach the steps. She held out her arms.

Cass came down to greet her. "Hi, I'm Cass, Bobby's little sister."

They hugged like he'd often seen women do—even women who barely new each other, even women who were just meeting. . . .

"It's so nice to meet you!" Becky said.

Then it was his turn. "Hi, Brother," Cass said. "Again."

Bobby took a step closer but still hung back. "Why didn't you say something in the cab?"

She shrugged. "I didn't know it was you—at first. My brain was geared to meeting up with you later, not in a cab. It was the Cowper quote that was the clincher, wasn't it?"

"Not many people—"

"Just Mama."

Cass stood with her hands in her jeans pockets. "Do I get a hug from you too?"

It was beyond awkward, but he opened his arms and she filled them. Her smell was sweet, with a bit of spice to it. It wasn't a perfume. It was just . . . just Cass. Was it possible that a scent memory from fourteen years ago could remain intact? Yet there was good reason he would remember her scent. She'd been the sister who'd often sat beside him on the couch, wanting him to help her with her reading. The fall their mother had killed herself, Cass had been on a *Ramona the Pest* kick.

Cass pulled away but kept her arm around his waist as she turned toward the house. "This is Grandpa's old place, isn't it?"

"It is."

"After Mama died I think I was here once. Doesn't it have a shop out back?"

Becky piped in. "It does. Like I told you on the phone, Bobby's a wonderful furniture maker."

"Very cool." Cass looked up at him. There was a good six inches difference in their height.

Bobby wished Becky hadn't brought up the shop. "I fiddle with stuff. That's all."

"Oh, he does more than that," Becky said. "Bobby, go show Cass the shop." She headed up the porch steps. "I have to check on the kids."

Brother and sister were left alone.

———

Cass stood just inside the doorway and inhaled deeply. "I remember this smell."

Bobby sidled past her, suddenly noticing the sawdust on the floor. Since he hadn't been working that much, he hadn't really cared if things were tidy. "Sorry it's such a mess."

She moved to the table he was sanding and ran her hand across the top. "This is beautiful. I love the inlay." She looked up, wiping her palm on her jeans. "Who's it for?"

"Nobody."

Becky came into the shop with Teresa and Tanner in tow—now dressed in comfortable play clothes. The kids moved to a box of wood scraps and began building towers. "The table's for sale," she said. "He'll give you a generous sister discount."

Cass's eyebrow lifted. "So you do sell to the public?"

"Occasionally. When he wants to," Becky said.

"Beck . . . I sold a few pieces to friends."

"But you *could* sell to anybody. Everybody." She accepted his scathing look with, "Sorry. I just get excited about your work. It's so beautiful."

"Yes, it is," Cass said. She looked pointedly at Bobby. "Do you want to open a store?"

"Oh no," Bobby said.

"I think he should," Becky said. "I could run it so he could work on his art full-time."

"It's not art, Beck. It's just furniture."

"It is not just furniture," Cass said, stroking the table again. Suddenly she looked up. "Do you at least have a Web site?"

Bobby laughed. "To do what? Show off furniture I haven't made?"

"To show off furniture you have made so people will order more. You can't have a business if no one knows what you do."

"I don't have a business," Bobby said. "I can't have a business. I need jobs that pay the bills."

Becky slipped her hand through his arm, touched her head to his shoulder, but kept her eyes on Cass. "Your brother has three jobs that keep him from doing what's in his heart."

"What do you do besides driving a cab?"

"I work at the concessions stand at a theater and at a burger joint."

"Jobs way below his expertise," Becky said.

Bobby shook his head. "I'm not proud. I'll do whatever it takes to care for my family." He nodded toward Becky's burgeoning belly. "My expanding family."

Cass stood silent, chewing the end of her thumb. "But this is what you need to do."

Bobby turned toward the door. "Maybe when I have time. When I retire. Come on, kids. Let's go inside for lunch."

Cass seemed reluctant to leave the shop, but Bobby waited for her to go first, letting himself be the one to turn off the light and shut the door.

———

You'd think Cass and Becky had known each other their entire lives. The two women made lunch and set the table with an ease that was enviable. It was a moot point that fifteen minutes earlier they'd never met. The fact that Bobby had been to blame for them not even knowing of each other's existence was handily set aside in the quest for a family meal.

Set aside until later. He *would* have to explain himself. The truth *would* come out.

It always did.

But thanks to the deep-seated gift of grace in his sister and wife, it was postponed until after dessert.

"So," Becky finally said, sitting back in her chair in the dining room. "Why didn't you tell me you had a sister? many sisters? two brothers?"

"And why didn't you keep in touch with me, Katie, and Vicki?"

Bobby wanted to be anyplace but here. He took a drink of iced tea. "Why didn't you keep in touch with *me*?"

"You're passing the buck?"

"I wasn't the only—"

"Us girls were little, Bobby."

"I was only fourteen. Still a kid."

Cass hesitated a moment then said, "We are both to blame—and neither to blame. We'd been through a lot. All six of us." She pushed her plate that held the last few bites of pumpkin cheesecake out of the way. "Do you know where Martin and Chuck are?"

Bobby shrugged, but as soon as he did, he wished he could take the action back. "They ran away when I moved in with Grandpa. I haven't seen Martin since."

"But Chuck?"

Bobby traced the rim of his coffee cup. "He got into drugs, came back wanting Grandpa to give him money. When Grandpa refused, he trashed the shop, then left town. He died of an overdose a few years later."

Cass's mouth dropped. "One dead and one missing?"

What could he say? He changed the subject. "Are Katie and Vicki okay?"

"They are. They both live in Chicago with our parents—Aunt Judy and Uncle Ben. Technically aunt and uncle, but we call them Mom and Dad. They legally adopted us the year after Mama killed herself. They're wonderful."

Suddenly Becky raised both hands in front of her, palms out. "Killed herself?"

When it rains . . .

Bobby knew it was his secret to tell. "Our father was a drunk and got killed by walking in front of a car. Our mother was so distraught that a few months later she did the same thing. On purpose."

"She left her children without a parent?"

"She was upset."

Becky's head shook back and forth, back and forth. "I don't care. She had no right leaving six kids to fend for themselves or to be pawned off on relatives."

"Mama tried," Bobby said. "But with there being six of us . . . and she'd never held a job outside the home and—"

Becky pushed back from the table and stood. She took a couple dessert plates toward the kitchen.

Bobby was left looking at his sister, who said, "You should have told her. About all of this."

"I couldn't. I didn't want her to think badly of me."

"None of it is our fault, Bobby. It's just our life. It is what it is."

She went to help Becky with the dishes.

———

Playing the part of a mother . . . it was not a part Abigail had often played. But today—like it or not—it was hers.

When Abigail entered the auditorium, the director, Tony Novotny, stood, clapped his hands together once, and hurried toward her. "Ms. Buchanan!" He took her hands in his, kissing both cheeks. "I'm so glad you're joining us."

"My pleasure."

A young woman with a clipboard followed close behind

the director. She held out her hand. "I'm Sandy, Tony's assistant. So nice to officially meet you, Ms. Buchanan."

"Nice to meet—"

"Wow," Joey said. "There are tons and tons of chairs in here."

"Shh!" Hayley said, taking his hand.

Sandy looked at the children. "Are these . . . yours?"

There was the slightest hint of disapproval in her voice. Abigail was tempted to take possession of them, creating some fascinating story about having had an affair with a twentysomething Frenchman during her last play, but Hayley took the opportunity away from her.

"He's my brother. I'm Hayley Wilson. I'm one of the orphans. Abigail's taking care of us today because my father was shot last night. He's in the hospital."

Tony and Sandy both looked to Abigail for confirmation. Stories of young French lovers were usurped by the truth. "It's true. Their father is a night watchman. There was a burglary. Their mother brought the kids to my house in the mid—"

Some women sitting nearby came close. "Oh, you poor things. Come sit with us. We'll take care of both of you."

The kids were herded into a row of chairs where some other actors closed ranks.

So much for them needing me . . .

Abigail realized she should feel relieved. So why was she disappointed?

"Come sit up front with us, Ms. Buchanan," Tony said.

There were no other actors in the director's row. Abigail reveled in being singled out. She took the seat offered, but then Tony and Sandy excused themselves for last-minute preparations. The meeting was due to start in five minutes, they said.

Abigail felt a tad uncomfortable sitting there alone, and

busied herself by removing her sweater and draping it just so in the next seat, then getting a tissue out of her purse. She waited for her fellow thespians to come greet her, pay their respects. But they did not.

Intimidated. That's what they are. Remember, Abigail, this is volunteer theater. None of them are professionals like you are.

This rationalization made her feel a little better, but still unfulfilled. One did not embrace the theater as a profession without acknowledging a desire for attention. A need.

As she rummaged through her purse—for nothing specific at all—she heard two women a few rows behind her, talking softly. One said, "Do you know who that is?"

"No."

"It's Abigail Buchanan."

"So?"

"She was famous once," said voice number one.

Ouch.

"She's playing Miss Hannigan," the woman added.

"Don't you think she's a little old?"

"You know Tony. Always looking for a way to sell tickets."

"Miscasting a part doesn't do anyone any good."

Abigail couldn't move. Realizing she'd frozen in place, she forced her hand to continue its excavation of her purse. *Nonchalant. Act nonchalant.*

The moment was broken when Margaret Timmons started down the row toward her seat. Margaret Timmons who'd tried out for Miss Hannigan. Who'd been very good at reading for Miss Hannigan. But who hadn't gotten the part of Miss Hannigan.

Margaret smiled and took the seat next to Abigail. "Well, here we go," she said.

"Here we go."

They shared an awkward pause. Then Margaret said, "I want to congratulate you on getting Miss Hannigan. I know you'll steal the show."

It was hard for Abigail to get out the words that had to come next. "Thank you. You're very kind." Beyond kind.

At that moment Tony strode across the front of the stage, clapping his hands to get everyone's attention. But Abigail had a hard time concentrating on his introduction. Margaret's words haunted her:

"You'll steal the show."

She'd stolen something all right. . . .

———

After coming home from his lunch with Philip, Ken turned on the TV. He sat in the chair where he always sat. He flipped with even more zeal than usual because every channel reminded him of his troubles.

The advertisements for dating services reminded him he was alone.

The golf shows reminded him of past glory, now gone.

The how-to shows reminded him of the home he gave up in the divorce.

The Travel Channel reminded him of places he'd never seen and had no desire to see alone.

The car advertisements reminded him of cars he couldn't afford.

And the pharmaceutical ads reminded him his son was dying.

Round and round we go. . . .

He turned the television off. The sudden silence spooked him, surrounding him with a nothingness that was worse than the mindless chatter and mocking condemnation of the tube.

And yet . . . it was an apt representation of his life.

Nothing.

Nada.

Void. Over and out.

The sudden ring of the phone jolted him upright and made his heart race. His feet left the ottoman and hit the floor, poised to answer it.

But he didn't move. He just sat there, frozen in place while the rings sliced through the air.

He stared at the phone in the entryway, willing it to stop its torment. He didn't feel like talking to anyone right now.

Maybe never.

Mercifully, after four rings the answering machine clicked on. He heard his own voice: "This is Ken. Leave a message."

How appropriate that the message he left the world was short. Without embellishment. Without personality.

Ronnie's voice yanked him out of his thoughts. *"Hey, Ken. I'm just calling to find out how your lunch with Philip went. I'm so glad you got together. It's a good thing, Ken. Really it is."*

Her voice stopped and the machine clicked off. He looked at the phone, incredulous. Good thing? Their son having HIV was a good thing?

He threw the remote toward the machine, where it ricocheted into a cup of pens, sending them flying.

Whatever.

———

Bobby was watching the late news in the family room when he realized Becky wasn't around. He'd noticed her go upstairs a half hour before but had expected her to return.

He shut off the TV and went to look for her. He found her in bed, the lights off.

It was a relief. Cass had stayed the day and somehow Bobby had managed to keep the additional conversation away from the Mann family history. Then after dinner Tanner had spilled some finger paints all over the kitchen floor, and once that was cleaned up the evening had slipped by with giving the kids baths, reading to them, and tucking them in. He'd been relieved, because he didn't want to deal with why he'd kept his past secret from his wife. He didn't want to talk about any of it.

As quietly as possible, Bobby got undressed and eased himself onto the bed, gingerly lifting the covers just enough to slip in and—

"Why the farce, Bobby? Why didn't you tell me?" Becky turned toward him, adjusting an extra pillow around her belly.

So much for not talking about it.

"I was ashamed, Beck. Once I moved in with Grandpa I created a new life for myself. Even my friends in school didn't know about having a drunken father and a suicidal mother—at least not at first. You should have been here when Chuck came back. . . . I wasn't thinking how great it was to see him again. The whole time, I was just hoping he'd leave town ASAP, so no one would even know I had a brother—much less a druggie brother. It wasn't just you. I never told anyone. I was ashamed of the truth."

She studied him a moment. In the moonlight her pink cheek was a beautiful contrast against the baby blue of the pillowcase. "Never be ashamed of the truth, Bobby. Let the past go, move on, rise above it. But don't be ashamed of what was. Sometimes we have nowhere to go but on. What happened in your past is all a part of where you are today, and what makes you *you*."

218 / Nancy Moser

"What makes me *me* is you," Bobby said, touching her
arm.

Instead of taking his hand and kissing it—as he hoped
she would do—she pulled away. "I can't be your everything,
Bobby. I don't want to be. That's too much responsibility.
I'm here for you. I hope to complement you. But beyond
that . . ."

"You're the only good thing that's ever happened to me,
Beck, and—"

She pushed herself to sitting. "That is a lie. Your family
was good—before the tragedies. Your siblings were good.
Even your brothers were good before bad choices dragged
them down. And your grandpa was certainly good, taking you
in like that. . . ." She looked straight at him. "He's a big reason
why you are the good man you are today."

Bobby felt the threat of tears. "But I don't feel good. I feel
like I'm spinning without direction. I'm in the middle of a big
intersection and I don't know which way to turn."

She gave him one nod, then said, "'I have swept away
your sins like a cloud. I have scattered your offenses like the
morning mist. Oh, return to me, for I have paid the price to set
you free.'"

"How do you do that?" he asked. "You're always doing
that. Bringing up just the right verse at just the right time."

She did it again. "'For everyone who asks, receives.
Everyone who seeks, finds. And to everyone who knocks,
the door will be opened.'" She shrugged. "I look for God's
answers. And I find them."

She did not say, "You should do the same." She didn't
need to.

Bobby held his hand, palm up, in the space between them.
"I love you."

This time he got the reaction he hoped for.

———

"The director sure is happy you took the part."

Hayley's words, said with sincerity, followed Abigail through the rehearsal, nudged her past the children's reunion with their mother (their father was expected to come home from the hospital tomorrow), and dogged her to the edge of sleep. The words were true. Tony Novotny gushed and oozed over Abigail's presence in a way that normally would have filled her attention cup to overflowing. But after surreptitiously overhearing the two women's opinions of her, after enduring her competition's gracious congratulations, the gushing had not elicited gratitude or pride but embarrassment and shame.

She rolled onto her back, took another pillow, and pressed it over her face. What had she been thinking, trying out for a part in a community play? She didn't belong there. She'd only tried out because Tony had pressed her pride button. Deep down she'd known she was too old for the Miss Hannigan part. The character should have been no older than forty-five, preferably thirty-five. She would be seventy-seven on her next birthday. The makeup job they would have to do on her would surely test the skills of the most experienced Hollywood makeup artist. And even if they got her looking far younger, anyone who knew who she was would do the math and realize she was pushing the part. They'd even guess the truth—that she'd gotten the part to help with ticket sales.

Because of her past. Not because of her present.

Not because of her talent.

Needing to breathe, she moved the pillow aside and took a cleansing breath—that did nothing to rid her mind of the thoughts. Even though she hadn't had a lot of paying jobs lately, she certainly had played a lot of parts. Mother, jury foreman, and now Miss Hannigan . . .

Who was she kidding? She should be booed off the stage. She was a farce, a pretender.

And worse, a has-been.

———

Karla knocked on the doorjamb to Deidre's walk-in closet. "I'm heading for bed and . . . what are you doing?"

Deidre realized she was standing in the middle of their closet, staring at nothing. How long had she been there? She made an excuse. "I'm figuring out what to wear tomorrow for court."

Karla nodded. "It's supposed to be cooler tomorrow. You might want to wear a blazer."

Deidre nodded.

"I've been wanting to ask you about this morning, but you seem to be avoiding me. From the choir loft I saw you run out of the church. What—?"

"I didn't feel well. It was nothing."

"That's what you said, what Sig said."

"You don't believe us?"

Karla shrugged. "*It was nothing* always means it was something."

"Not in this case."

"I'm a good listener."

Yes, she was. If only Deidre could talk about it, confess to someone.

"It's like the world is on your shoulders, Dee-Dee. I can see it bearing down on you."

And suddenly, with that one offer of compassion, Deidre covered her face with her hands.

Karla was immediately at her side. "Oh, honey. Please tell me what's wrong."

The tears were unexpected, yet in an odd way, welcome. If they had not found release Deidre would have self-destructed. Her entire inner being would have evaporated, leaving nothing but an empty shell.

Karla hugged her, rocked her, murmured comfort in her ear. "It will be all right. You've been so strong, taking your responsibility as a juror so seriously. Of course it's difficult dealing with your regular life and holding the fate of another person's life in your hands. Of course you should feel a bit overwhelmed."

"It's too hard," Deidre said. She focused on the trial. "I don't like having this responsibility, judging Patti when . . . when . . ."

"You're a lot like her?"

Deidre pulled back, incredulous. "I'm not like her."

Karla pushed a stray piece of hair behind Deidre's ear. "Aren't you?"

Deidre moved away. "Just because we both knew Brett doesn't—"

"You both knew Brett, were attracted to Brett, both got pregnant—"

Deidre pointed at Karla. "What Brett did to me was against my will. What he did to Patti, she wanted. Encouraged."

"So it's a crime to go after a better life by setting your sights on a man who's above you socially?"

Deidre opened her mouth to say yes but closed it in time to prevent another lie. The root of her sins lay in her own desire to grab on to a better life.

Karla adjusted a pink blouse that was hanging precariously off a hanger. "I'm not condemning Patti or anyone who takes drastic measures to survive. In fact, I'd say she was lucky to have you on the jury. You, who might understand and—"

Deidre ran past her, out the door, out of the bedroom, down the stairs.

Karla called from the landing, "Where are you going?"

Deidre grabbed her purse and keys but didn't answer.

Because she wasn't sure herself.

———

Deidre ended up at the hospital, Sig's hospital. During the fifteen-minute drive she pinpointed the reason she'd left the house so quickly. She needed to find Sig immediately. She needed to tell him she could not guarantee a guilty vote—from herself, much less anyone else on the jury.

Patti was innocent.

Ignorant and gullible, but innocent overall.

Brett had played on those traits, teasing her with false promises, tempting her with a better life, pretending to love . . .

Brett was not capable of loving anyone but himself.

It was the signature of an evil man. But just because Patti had fallen for his lies and charm—as had Deidre—that did not mean Patti should pay for his death. Deidre would let the jury decide, fairly, impartially, and responsibly. She would not try to sway them because Sig wanted her to. She couldn't do that.

It wasn't fair to Patti. And even more than that, it wasn't right.

I've been skirting right far too long. . . . I'm tired of swaying people to get what I want. Surely it would be easier just to let things play out the way they play out. I'm tired of pushing, of making things hap—

"Hello, Mrs. Kelly," said a nurse at the main station of the pediatric ward. "What's got you out so late?"

"Hi, Brenda. Is my husband around?"

She pointed down the brightly painted hall. "Room 243. Just checking on a little boy who was having some . . . issues. He'll be done soon."

"Thanks."

Deidre strolled down the corridor and parked herself outside room 243. As soon as Sig came out, she'd pull him aside and tell him the deal was off. She had no idea what he would do. Argue, certainly. Or maybe, just maybe, he'd come up with a plan B. At this point she'd take plan B, C, or Z.

She heard his voice inside the room. "Yes indeedy, Jason, you are going to be better than new."

"Will I be able to run?"

"Run, jump, and do cartwheels if you'd like."

An adult voice added, "Thank you for stopping by so late, Doctor. We were worried, but now . . . even beyond the surgery, just seeing you . . . the change in our Jason here is so astounding, so amazing. You're a miracle worker, Dr. Kelly. What would the world do without you?"

A scale popped into Deidre's mind. On one side was her husband's life, heavy with worth. And on the other was the life of Patti McCoy, an uneducated dishwasher. Whose life held true importance? purpose? promise? Who would be missed if they went to jail?

Not Patti.

But Sig . . . if he went to jail for the death of Brett Lerner . . .

He couldn't. Guilty or not, the world should not have to lose the services of this great man.

So much for letting things play out. If she didn't intervene . . .

Deidre retreated down the hall from whence she had come.

She had no choice. Plan A was still in place.

Patti McCoy must be found guilty.

So Sig could remain free.

NINE

They sweep past like the wind
and are gone.
But they are deeply guilty,
for their own strength is their god.

HABAKKUK 1:11

*T*he morning after the first meeting of the *Annie* cast, Abigail was not in the mood to be jury foreman. She was not in the mood to be in deliberations on any jury. She was not in the mood to do anything but stay home and watch game shows and soap operas all day, perhaps indulging in a large bag of Fritos and a half liter of Dr Pepper.

Her fellow jurors gathered in the jury room, getting coffee and donuts, settling in for a new week of deliberations. Heaven forbid it would take a week.

Gus took a sip of the coffee in his Styrofoam cup and made a face. "You'd think with all the taxes I pay they could provide a decent cup of coffee."

Jason the waiter stood over the donut tray. "You'd think with all the pay we don't get paid for doing this, they'd give us fancier donuts than plain old sugar and glazed."

"I could bring in a coffee cake," Susan said. "I make a great cinnamon crumble."

"I'm not sure they'd allow it," Jack said. "They have rules for rules around here."

"What's she going to do, bake a weapon into it?" Joe said.

He took a bite of donut, making it rain sugar onto the table. "That's one good thing about driving a truck. I get to eat great food at truck stops."

"Fried food, you mean," Letisha said. "But answer this, Mr. Trucker. I want to know why you don't weigh three hundred pounds." She caressed her own ample hips. "Sometimes I hate men. Most of them can eat and eat and not gain a thing. I just look at that donut, and . . ." She shook her head and gazed longingly at the pastries.

"I wish they had more than one kind of tea bag," Deidre said, dipping one in her cup. "Cinnamon or Earl Grey or Lemon Zinger."

Although Abigail accepted all the gripes as apropos, in Deidre's case, there was something disconcerting about seeing a Styrofoam cup in her hand. Not that the surgeon's wife had demanded china teacups, but Abigail was fairly sure she was not used to disposable dinnerware. And no donut for Deidre. Probably on a diet. Women like her were always on a diet. Where was the fun in that?

Abigail set her own place with a sugar donut and coffee, which was white with two cream packets and some Splenda. Might as well get this over with. "Come on, people. Let's get down to business."

Abigail watched as Mary took a seat directly across the table. She overheard her say to Deidre, "I met your husband Saturday."

"My husband? Really?" Deidre said.

"He's going to help my son. He's going to do surgery on him."

"Really?" She sounded genuinely surprised.

Joe—on Mary's other side—shoved a bite of donut to the inside of his cheek. "And why would he do that?"

Mary looked up, obviously surprised anyone had overheard. "He's a doctor. That's the kind of man he is."

Joe looked at Mary, then back at Deidre. "You're just trying to win her over to the guilty camp."

Deidre put a hand to her chest. "I'm doing no such thing. I have no idea what she's talking about."

Mary smacked Joe on the arm. "Dr. Kelly didn't seek me out. It just happened. I was having a garage sale. He stopped by, happened to see my son, noticed his hand problem, talked to me, and—"

"Sig went to a garage sale?" Deidre asked.

Mary nodded.

"See?" Joe said. "It's rigged. He rigged it."

"And why would he do that?" Abigail asked.

Joe hesitated a moment, then shrugged. "I don't know, but you gotta admit it's fishy."

Deidre shook her head. "Sig often goes up to people with children and talks to them about any medical problem he thinks he can help with. He really does. He performs free surgeries all the time. That's what his foundation is all about."

"That's really nice," Bobby said.

"He must be a really nice man," Letisha said. "A good man."

"He is," Mary said. "He's a godsend to our family, one who—"

Joe crossed his arms. "But with Deidre wanting a guilty verdict and Mary voting innocent . . . it's fishy, I tell you."

"Are you implying I asked him to do it?" Deidre said. "To seek her out because she was a juror?"

Gus raised his hands, trying to calm them. "That doesn't make sense, Joe. It's not like Deidre's life is on the line. No offense to Patti McCoy, but in the end, what does Deidre really care if she's found innocent or guilty?"

Ann chimed in. "Besides, she's not supposed to—none of

us are supposed to—talk about the trial. To our families. To anyone."

Joe glared at Deidre. "Did you tell your husband about this trial?"

Deidre blushed—which to Abigail seemed an odd reaction. "I did not. And I resent you putting *me* on trial. I haven't done anything wrong."

"But your husband did wrong," Joe said.

Mary pushed at Joe's arm. "You leave her alone. This has nothing to do with her or the trial. My Orlando is going to get the surgery he needs because of her husband. That's a marvelous thing, not some conspiracy against you, Joe Krasinski."

"She's right," Ann said. "You're overreacting."

Joe leaned back in his chair as if giving in. "Well, anyway . . . talk about an impossible coincidence."

Mary raised her chin. "There's no such thing as a coincidence. It's a miracle."

The way Mary looked at Deidre, with a new kind of respect in her eyes . . . it was almost as if Mary was transferring Dr. Kelly's smarts to his wife. Abigail did wonder if Mary could be swayed to vote like Deidre was voting, just because of this new respect.

Gus pointed at Deidre, but his eyes were on Mary. "Not that I buy into anything Joe is saying, but when you first found out Deidre's husband was this famous surgeon, why didn't you just ask him to operate?"

Mary raised her right hand, fending off the question. "I heard his name but I didn't know who he really was. What he really did. How he could help my Orlando—for free."

Abigail stood. "Come on, people, we're getting off track."

Joe shook his head. "We're totally on track if she changes her vote to guilty because of this."

"So now I can't change my vote?" Mary said. "Ever?"

Joe cocked his head. "Not and make me believe it wasn't influenced by the chance for your kid to get an operation."

"One has nothing to do with the other," Mary said.

"In your dreams."

It did sound very . . . convenient. And the idea of a rich doctor at a garage sale . . . even his wife sounded skeptical.

"Let's take a vote right now and see how Mary votes," Joe said.

"You're not the foreman, Joe; Abigail is. You can't call a vote."

Joe looked to Abigail, who at that moment would have gladly relinquished the position. What had she been thinking taking on the job? Why did she always put herself out front?

She opened her mouth to speak, but Ken interrupted. "I agree we need a vote first thing. We've had the whole weekend to think about things. Maybe some of us have changed our minds."

"Have you?" Letisha asked.

"No."

"Well, neither have I."

Abigail crammed half a donut in her mouth, hoping a surge of sugar would get her through this. "I do think a vote is a good way to start."

"Ballots," Mary said. "I want ballots."

Joe pointed at her. "Because you're changing your vote!"

"Because we voted by ballot last time and I think that's the way we should do it."

"That takes too long," Ken said.

Ann pointed toward Abigail. "You're the foreman. What do you think?"

I think I want to get fired from this part. But Abigail said, "Pass out the paper and pens. Let's do this thing."

Sig had talked to Mary about her son? about operating on her son? And he'd met her at her garage sale?

Deidre wrote *Guilty* on the slip of paper and folded it in two. She waited for the basket to come around.

Even though she didn't like Joe, he was right about one thing: it was too much of a coincidence to be believed.

Which meant Sig had sought Mary out. But why?

The only reason that made any sense was that Sig had meant to influence Mary into changing her mind. But how did he know how she was voting?

She stopped with her coffee cup halfway to her lips. *The list I made and put on his pillow. He got the information from me.*

Suddenly Deidre remembered something Sig had said last Saturday, at Audrey's. He'd mentioned doing something stupid—nearly doing something stupid. Had he truly set out to contact the jurors in order to sway their vote? Had he contacted any others? No one had said anything. Not that they would have dared after Joe's third degree.

Deidre looked around the table at the others who'd previously voted innocent: Bobby, Joe, Ann, and Letisha.

Mary was hesitating writing down her vote. Deidre pretended not to look but could tell by the length of the word Mary wrote that she'd changed her vote to guilty.

Chalk one up to Dr. Kelly, savior of children.

Ken wasn't there. Not really. He wrote his guilty verdict on the slip of paper and put it in the basket, but if someone would have pressed him to vote innocent, he knew it wouldn't have taken a lot to make him change. Guilty. Innocent. Who was he to judge Patti McCoy when he himself was so guilty? The more he thought about it, the line that separated the two verdicts was blurred. Who wasn't guilty? Who was innocent?

Certainly not him.

Abigail read the ballots. "We have eight guilty and four—"

Joe slapped one hand on the table while pointing at Mary with the other. "You changed your vote! You can't do that."

Gus intervened. "Actually, someone has to change or we'll be here forever. This is all about compromise."

Ann shook her head. "No, it isn't. It can't be. We can't compromise in regard to Patti's life. It's not like compromising on whether we'll have sandwiches or pizza for lunch."

Jack raised a hand. "I vote for pizza."

"Me too," Jason said.

"Me three," Letisha said.

Ken let his mind wander. What did he care about food? His son was going to die, maybe later rather than sooner, but still . . .

"Ken?"

He looked up when he heard Abigail say his name. By the way people were staring at him it wasn't the first time she'd said it. "Yeah?"

"Is something wrong?" she asked.

"You don't seem all here," Susan said.

"What'd you do this weekend?" Letisha asked. "Bogeyed instead of boogied?" She laughed at her own joke.

"Actually I found out my son is going to die."

Silence.

He hadn't meant to say it out loud. The words had entered his mind as a private aside. No one had been more shocked to hear them than Ken.

"What does that mean?" Deidre asked.

Although he usually loved attention, their curious and kind eyes made him get up from his seat to fill his nearly full coffee cup. "I don't want to talk about it," he said to the wall while pouring. He added a packet of sugar though he usually liked it black.

"How old is your son?" Mary asked.

"Grown."

"Well then . . . ," Jack said.

Just the way he said it made Ken swing around to face them. "So because he's grown it doesn't count?"

Jack's head shook back and forth in short bursts. "No, I didn't mean—"

"Yes, you did," Ann said. "Because face it, there is something more poignant about a child dying rather than an adult."

Bobby shook his head. "A son's a son."

"What's wrong with him?" Gus asked.

"How much time does he have?" Jason asked.

Susan jumped on him. "That isn't a polite question."

Jason shrugged. "I was just wondering. I mean, if Ken has to leave the jury to go be with him or—"

"He probably has years," Ken said. "He has HIV. He might have years."

Silence.

"He's not gay. He was into drugs." As if that made it better?

"My brother's gay," Susan said.

"You want a medal?" Joe said.

"No, but—" Susan sighed. "Never mind."

"At least he's not dying soon," Jack said.

Jack's words rekindled Ken's anger. He returned to his seat. "Just because it's not happening tomorrow doesn't mean I can't be upset."

"Of course not," Abigail said. "But the crisis is somewhat . . ."

"Diluted," Gus said. When he received a glare from Ken, he added, "What? We all could be dead in years, disease or no disease."

Philip had said virtually the same thing.

Bobby nodded. "You have now. Now is what's important."

Abigail clapped her hands. "Enough, everyone. Let's get back to the matter at hand."

"We have gotten off track," Gus said.

"For good reason," Ann said. She offered Ken a wistful smile. "I'm sorry for your bad news, Ken. What's your son's name?"

"Philip."

She swept the table's occupants with a look. "We'll certainly say some prayers for Philip."

Ken was surprised when most heads nodded. In fact, all but Joe, Deidre, and Abigail made the nonverbal commitment to pray for his son. Maybe it was a good thing he'd slipped and brought it up.

Maybe it was a God thing.

———

I should have nodded.

When Ann had asked people to pray for Ken's son, Deidre had been caught off guard. By the time she noticed that almost everybody was agreeing to pray, it was too late.

That truck driver, Joe, that redneck . . . he hadn't nodded either. Deidre didn't want to be lumped in with him. The only other juror who'd remained still was Abigail. Deidre liked Abigail. She was a woman of zest and spunk. That she hadn't nodded saved Deidre from total humiliation.

But a question niggled at her mind: why hadn't she nodded? She prayed. Sometimes. And when Don had been sick she'd certainly been the recipient of prayers—not that they'd done much good. When Sig had performed surgery on Nelly she'd prayed during the operation. And that had turned out okay.

I'm a foul-weather prayer.

She didn't like the idea of it, and yet . . . couldn't the same be said about most people? Didn't most people coast along on their own devices until some crisis made them doubt and seek help elsewhere? Wasn't that why Sig had wanted to go to church yesterday?

I don't feel good enough to pray. I've done so much wrong. So terribly—

Deidre must have shook her head because Jack said, "No, Deidre? You don't want to discuss the vote?"

She sat forward, pushing thoughts of Sig and prayer and her own lack of faith aside. She had to pay attention. It was time to come to a verdict. It was time to be alert and make things go the way they needed to go.

She hoped God wouldn't notice.

The image of a toddler covering her face with her hands came to mind. *Daddy, you can't see me.*

———

Ever since Ann had brought up prayer, had suggested they pray for Ken's son, Bobby had felt guilty—for not praying for his extended family. When was the last time he'd prayed for his brother or sisters? Until Cass had come to town, when was the last time he'd even thought about them?

Some brother he was.

They'd grown up without his care or his prayers. They'd

gone through good times and bad without his knowledge. And by keeping their existence from his wife, he'd even prevented her prayers on their behalf. "The earnest prayer of a righteous person has great power and produces wonderful results."

Ah. There was the problem. He was far from righteous. So what good would his prayers have done anyway?

He pressed a finger onto his napkin, capturing a flake of fallen glaze from his donut. He licked it, slightly amazed that even such a small bit could carry so much taste.

Like a small bit of prayer.

"Bobby." Abigail drew him out of his reverie. "Tell us why you think Patti is innocent."

He didn't like their attention. He didn't like the way Jack's arms were crossed, ready for confrontation, or the way Deidre kept turning her pencil over and over, point to the table, eraser to the table, as if ready to write down the flaws of his opinion. When he looked to Mary and Susan—who'd started out on his side but who had defected to the guilty bench—they looked away. Even the eyes of his fellow innocent-voter Joe were full of challenge, as if a threat were present: *Don't blow this. We have to convince the others.* Only Letisha and Ann offered looks of compassion.

"Come on, Bobby," Letisha said. "You go first; then I'll go."

He wished it were the other way around.

"You go, Letisha," Jason said. "Bobby's not ready."

Was his face that transparent?

Transparent or not, Bobby was glad to let someone else go first.

Letisha shuffled her shoulders and took a big breath, clearly ready to give her opinion. "I think Patti's innocent because that two-timing, no-good Brett was the one who had the power. He conned her. He wasn't going to marry her. No way, no how."

"How do you know?"

"Because he's just like my Raymond." She snapped her fingers. "Been there, done that. One kid. No father."

"You had a kid by a guy who wouldn't marry you?" Susan asked.

"He's ten now. Cute as a button but unfortunately has Raymond's charming smile. I'm going to have to watch that boy, that's for sure."

Gus shook his head. "I still don't see why Brett's character—or lack thereof—would have anything to do with why you think Patti is innocent."

Letisha tapped a fingernail on the table. "It's that prosecutor too. That Jonathan Cummings—not Jon, mind you, but Jon-a-than, all fancy-schmancy. A slick talker. Reminds me of Jordie."

"I thought his name was Raymond," Susan said.

"Separate guy. But two peas in a puny pod. Both of them scabs on the sore of my love life."

Ann laughed. "Any boyfriends named Brett?"

"Not yet."

Joe took the floor. "My wife worked in a restaurant kitchen once, just like Patti. She used to have people treat her like scum, just like Brett treated Patti. And you would never believe the filth she had to clean up—for horrible pay. Brett took advantage of Patti, just like my wife's bosses took advantage of her."

"But that has nothing to do with the trial," Deidre said.

Ann interrupted. "Maybe not, but Patti being pregnant and Brett being the father—that had everything to do with why I think she's innocent. I have four kids. I would never hurt their father. Never."

"Even if he refused to marry you?" Mary asked.

"We've been married fourteen years."

Letisha shook her head. "Brett wasn't going to marry her. No way, no how."

Bobby thought of something. "My mother's name was Patricia."

When no one said anything he realized what a dumb statement he'd just made.

Jack pounced. "So you think because your mother had the same name as the defendant she couldn't be guilty?"

Joe waved his hands by his head. "It's a sign from God!"

Bobby crossed his arms. "Never mind. It was just an observation."

"A stupid one," Joe said.

"Hey, be nice," Susan said. "We're just talking here."

"Talking baloney."

"And your reason was better?" Gus said. "Patti is innocent because your wife worked in a restaurant?"

Abigail clapped her hands, taking control. "We appreciate hearing why you're voting Patti innocent, but . . . your reasons are wishful thinking. You *want* her to be innocent, but your decision has nothing to do with the evidence. It's based on your own prejudices."

"I am not prejudiced," Joe said.

"I am," Letisha said.

That got everyone's attention.

"Well, I am. We all are in our own way." She sat forward, spreading her hands on the table. "Personally, I don't care if you're white, green, or plaid, but I do have a problem with men who treat their women badly. I'm the biggest bigot there is against bossy, bullying, brutal men."

"What about Brett being treated badly?" Jack asked. "He's the one who's dead."

"Well . . . that's not good either."

People laughed.

"You know what I mean," she said.

Jack shook his head. "This isn't supposed to be about feelings. Feelings are what got us off track. This is about facts. Evidence."

"And gut instincts," Susan added.

Jack shrugged.

Abigail took advantage of the pause. "So what are the facts?"

Deidre held up her notepad. "I have all the forensic evidence written down."

"Go for it," Ken said.

Deidre read through the evidence. When she was through, Mary said, "But as for motivation . . . we go back to Patti being a woman scorned."

"We don't know that for sure," Ann said. "That's what the prosecution wants us to believe. Before going to his house, Patti hadn't told Brett about the baby. Maybe she never did. You're guessing."

"They argued a lot. They had a history of fighting," Susan added.

Ken, who'd been oddly quiet, spoke next. "She was the last one there. And she ran."

"Only guilty people run," Gus said.

"I don't know about that," Joe said. "One time when I was coming out of a bar, when some cops started coming toward me, I ran."

"Why?" Mary asked.

He shrugged. "I dunno. I hadn't done nothing."

Bobby found that hard to believe. Joe seemed the type who always skirted the edge of the law.

Deidre said, "I don't believe Patti's a cold-blooded killer, nor that she meant to kill Brett. It just happened." She cut marks into the side of her empty Styrofoam cup with a fingernail. "It was a crime of passion. People can get caught up in a moment and act like they'd never act normally." She put the cup down. "I believe that."

There were nods around the room. Then Abigail added, "It makes sense. She goes over there, they argue, he shuns her, she sees her entire future go down the tube, he gets cocky or rude and says something horrible. She's embarrassed and hurt and grabs the handiest thing—the bottle. She wants to shut him up, make him stop ruining her grand plans. Just seconds after she hits him, she regrets it. She screams. She thinks, *Oh no! What have I done?* And when she hears the sirens she realizes how it will look and runs." Abigail took a fresh breath. "It makes sense."

"It does," Deidre said.

Ann put her hands over her face. "I know. It does. I wish it didn't, but it does."

Jack perked up. "So you're changing your vote?"

She peeked out from between her fingers. "Probably." She put her hands down. "If I let myself think logically and just think of the evidence . . . she's guilty. She has to be."

Jack clapped once. "Yee-ha! Another one bites the dust."

"Can it, Jack," Joe said.

Susan raised a hand. "I think it comes down to this: unless someone else just happened to have a reason to kill Brett Lerner on that particular night and had impeccable timing to do it just before his girlfriend was coming over, it looks like the only possible killer is Patti."

Deidre looked to Letisha. "Right?"

Letisha sat back and waved her hands in surrender. "He still deserved it."

Deidre turned to Joe. "Right?"

"Maybe she was just in the wrong place at the wrong time."

Jack rolled his eyes. "Oh, please."

"Fine," Joe said. "I'm not dumb. I do see your point."

Deidre took a cleansing breath and Bobby felt her eyes. He was the last holdout. "Well, Bobby? What do you say?"

Jason laughed. "Other than his mother and Patti sharing the same name?"

Bobby ignored him. Although he didn't want to believe Patti was guilty, given so much evidence, and applying common sense . . .

"I guess I see your point too."

"Yee-ha again!" Jack said. He looked at Abigail. "Another vote is in order."

———

Deidre never believed it would be so easy. A verdict already?

Now came the hard part: being in the courtroom and seeing Patti get the news.

"Will the defendant rise?"

Patti's lawyer had to help her stand. He kept hold of her arm.

The judge looked to the bailiff. "Bailiff, the verdict please?"

The bailiff took the piece of paper from Abigail and brought it to the judge. Even though Deidre knew what it was going to say, her stomach clenched horribly. So much depended on this decision. Months of worry could be set aside. She'd gone through hell waiting for this day. This moment.

"The jury finds the defendant, Patricia Jo McCoy, guilty on the charge of voluntary manslaughter."

Patti fainted.

So be it.

It was finished.

Becky met Bobby at the door with a kiss and a hug. "I'm so sorry you had to find that poor girl guilty. So sorry."

Her compassion did not take away his own guilt. Although he'd offered sincere votes—both innocent and, finally, guilty—it had put him in a position he hoped to never repeat. Let God do the judging. Bobby had had enough.

"How are you doing, Beck? You look a little flushed."

Becky grinned. "I'm doing fine, and the flush is from excitement." She linked her hand through his arm and drew him toward the kitchen. "We have a surprise for you."

We?

Once in the doorway, Bobby saw Cass seated at the computer. "Hello, Brother. Guess what we've been doing."

Uh-oh. This sounded ominous.

"Look," Becky said, pointing to the computer screen. "Cass has created a Web site for your furniture."

There, before him, were professional-looking photos of the hutch in their dining room and the rocking chair he'd made for the kids—one photo with Teresa seated in it, one without.

"I put her in the picture for scale," Cass said.

"You took these?" Bobby asked.

"It's not that hard. I used your camera."

Not his camera. Becky was the one who always took the pictures in their family. She let go of his arm and retrieved their digital camera from the kitchen table. "Cass showed me how to crop and make pictures lighter or darker. It's not hard at all."

"Which means she can keep adding pictures as you make new pieces. And look at this one." She clicked on something. There was a photo of a dresser he'd made for the principal of the high school two years before.

"How did you get this?" he asked.

"Becky called them up and asked if we could come over. People were happy to help."

"People?"

Cass clicked through more Web pages. "We got four more photos and four testimonials about how wonderful your work is."

Bobby was appalled. "You asked our friends to say nice things?"

"We didn't have to ask, hon. Once we went to their homes, they practically oozed about your work. In fact, the principal's wife, Dora, is interested in having you make them a matching headboard."

"Here," Cass said, scrolling down. "I put the testimonials below the photos."

"And I can answer e-mails and take the orders," Becky said.

Orders?

"Don't give me that look, Brother. There will be orders."

He felt weak and took a seat at the table. "When and how am I going to complete these orders?"

Becky's face fell. "You said you were quitting one of your jobs so you'd have more time."

Caught by his own words. "It all sounds great, and I know you put a lot of work into it, but I need to make a living. I have a family to support and—"

Becky moved directly in front of him and lifted his chin with a finger. "There is no mortgage. We have enough to get by without you killing yourself by working three jobs."

"Jobs you don't like," Cass added.

"Besides, it's time you stopped avoiding the inevitable."

He hated when she looked at him like this. She was way too lovely. "And what's inevitable?"

She bent low, her eyes just inches from his. "That you stop playing the part of a nobody and accept that you are somebody. You are an artist and have a God-given talent that will bring joy to many people. It is your life's work. And it's time you realized it." She kissed him.

Bobby's throat tightened. "This isn't fair," he said. "You are not fair."

Becky cocked her head and nodded. "But I'm right."

And she was. Except on one point. His furniture might be more important than his day jobs. But it was not his life's work.

———

Deidre pulled into the garage and turned off the car. She sat in silence, not at all eager to go inside and have Sig congratulate her on a job well done, a verdict well placed. Would he want to go out to celebrate?

She winced at the very idea.

Deidre opened the kitchen door, bracing herself for a hearty "I heard!" or "Congratulations!"

She did not expect a long face, nor for Sig to pull her into his arms and say, "I'm so sorry."

She pushed herself away. "I thought you'd be happy."

He closed the door, then stuffed his hands in his pockets and shrugged. "So did I. But when I saw the news and watched the look on Patti's face as they read the verdict . . ."

"But her conviction assures your freedom."

"I know." He took hold of a cabinet handle above the kitchen desk and ran a thumb up and down its shape. "I should be thrilled. I don't know why I'm not."

A question had been burning within her all day. "Mary, one of the other jurors? She said she met you. Said you'd stopped by her garage sale and were doing some surgery on her son. What's all that about?"

Sig let out a breath. "When you left me the list of jurors the other night I looked up the addresses of the ones who'd voted innocent: Bobby, Mary, Joe, Ann, and Letisha. I planned to stop by their houses one by one and talk to them."

"About the trial?"

He shrugged. "I wasn't thinking straight. I was desperate. I had no idea how I would go about it or what I would say if I had the chance. I found myself sending up odd prayers that God would help me—which, of course, made no sense at all. God was not going to help me send an innocent girl to prison. That I prayed anyway shows you the bizarre state of my thoughts. I was pulling the string of my sanity taut, and if I wasn't careful—" He took a fresh breath. "I knew something had to give—soon—or I'd end up in a locked ward, babbling about hot tubs, blue bottles, and what-ifs."

"Did you talk to anyone besides Mary?"

"I drove past the house of Joe Krasinski but found a huge dog yanking on his chain in the front yard enough of a barrier to make me drive on. It didn't look like anyone was at home at Letisha Meyer's house. I'd about given up hope when I drove in front of the home of Mary. She lives over on Coney Avenue? A cute Cape Cod bungalow on a street canopied with pin oaks."

"I don't care about the architecture, Sig. What did you say to her?"

"Nothing about the trial. I promise. Turns out she was having a garage sale. I pulled up in front and got out. I was really nervous and nearly chickened out, but the sight of a couple kids playing eased my nerves. Kids. I can relate to kids."

"You must have said who you were. Mary told me she'd met my husband."

"I did introduce myself, but not because of the trial. She had a son, Orlando, about four, who was playing with soon-to-be-sold castoffs. When he ran up to his mother he held his right hand oddly. It was turned in, deformed. My mind flashed with medical terms for his condition. But before I could say anything, he asked my name—you know how some kids do—and before I could think otherwise, I said, 'Sigmund.' Then the mother mentioned that she'd heard about another Sigmund recently, the husband of another woman on a jury. You know the rest. We talked about her son, and I told her I was a surgeon and . . . you've been with me when I see a child in need. I offered my services to fix his hand."

Deidre had witnessed Sig talking to total strangers and ending up with a new patient—usually gratis.

"I know it was wrong, Deidre. And I'm glad it didn't turn out like I'd intended. But the little boy . . . some good did come from it. His mother said our meeting was God's doing."

"You weren't going there to do good."

"No, I wasn't. But good came from it." He hesitated. "And then an hour later Audrey called to say that you and Nelly had been in the store and . . . and then I called you and invited you to her house and—" He sighed deeply. "It was a very long day."

Deidre hung her purse on the hook by the door. For the first time she noticed Sig was wearing suit pants, a white shirt, and a tie. His good suit. "Why are you so dressed up? You didn't expect me to go out and celebrate, did—?"

"No, no," he said. "But we do have the mayor's award dinner tonight."

She closed her eyes and sighed deeply. "Oh, Sig. No."

"We have to go. I'm up for the award."

Humanitarian of the Year.

"I know you may not feel up to it," he said. "I don't feel up to it. But I have to go. We have to go. We're expected."

It was true. The donation benefits this award could elicit were immense. And Sig had a good shot at winning.

"I know it's bad timing," he said.

Resigned, Deidre headed upstairs. "Give me fifteen minutes."

Abigail dropped her purse and keys on the floor, kicked off her shoes, fell onto the couch, and put her feet on the coffee table. A stack of magazines toppled to the floor.

She let them lie. If her entire coffee table collapsed, she would have let it lie.

It all came down to this one sad fact: condemning someone to prison was the pits. And being the jury foreman, being the one to hand the bailiff the verdict? Double pits. Big pits. Deep pits.

She noticed her *Annie* script on the other end of the coffee table, halfway covered over by an *American Theatre* magazine. She hadn't even opened it since the read-through yesterday. Yes, she'd been busy, but everyone was busy. People had jobs and family to take up the hours of their day. In the end, that didn't matter. Lines had to be learned. Songs practiced.

It was daunting. She closed her eyes. Maybe if she relaxed for just a minute . . .

Abigail hated being late. It was so unprofessional. Sure, divas were late, stars were late, but at the moment she was neither and had learned that such rudeness didn't earn brownie points from either the director or the rest of the cast.

She'd always prided herself on being punctual—until she'd fallen asleep on the couch and awakened only because

Hayley pounded on her door. That she'd also made Hayley late . . . it was not good form.

Actually, being awake in essence was not the same as being awake in actuality. Abigail felt drugged, sluggish, and not at the top of her game. Going into the auditorium and seeing everyone else laughing, chatting, dancing, and singing with vibrant enthusiasm only made her more tired.

I'm too old for this.

She joined a group of women on stage as they sang through one of the chorus songs. "Sorry," she mouthed to the choral director. She took a place next to Margaret Timmons. Margaret smiled at her and held the music so Abigail could share until she got her own score open. Abigail began to sing, muffed a few notes—since she was sight-reading—but recovered quickly. Yet as the measures progressed, she found herself doing something she had never done.

She lip-synched, held back, and listened.

Next to her, Margaret had a lovely voice, full of character yet able to blend. It was evident she was truly a team player, not concerned with showing off and drawing attention to herself, but intent on doing whatever it took to make the play the best it could be.

What about you?

Abigail stopped singing completely, causing Margaret and the choral director to look in her direction. To cover herself, she coughed a few times and excused herself, pretending to need a drink of water.

But as she headed offstage, she came upon Tony, the director.

"Abigail. How's it going?"

It was a loaded question. "Can I talk with you a moment?" With his nod, Abigail found herself taking Tony's arm and leading him into the wings behind one of the side curtains.

"What's up?" he asked.

She wasn't sure but didn't wait to figure it out. "I would like you to give the Miss Hannigan part to Margaret Timmons."

Tony's shocked expression matched her own surprise. Had she really said that? Why had she said that?

"Is there a problem with rehearsals or—?"

"No, no," Abigail said. "It's not you at all. Or the facility. Or any of the cast or crew." She took a breath and allowed the truth to come out. "It's me. I'm too old for the part, Tony. You know that and I know that, and—"

"No, no—"

She raised a hand, stopping his words. "And what's best for the show is that Margaret take the part."

He studied her eyes, and she cringed at the knowledge that he was seeing a veritable river delta of lines around them.

"If you're sure," he said.

He hadn't argued with her—which was telling and a bit humiliating. But it reinforced her decision. "I'm sure."

Sandy, Tony's assistant, peeked around the edge of the curtain, her face confused at seeing the odd tête-à-tête. But she quickly recovered and said, "Excuse me, Tony, but the orphans are waiting."

"Go," Abigail said, giving him leave.

He kissed her cheek. "We'll miss you. And if you ever want to be in any show, in any capacity, call."

And he was gone. And she was done.

Curtain down. Fade to black.

———

Abigail did not stick around to see Margaret's reaction to the news that she now had the part. Her largesse only went so far.

After pulling Hayley aside and telling her what was going on, after assuring Hayley that Abigail would still be her coach and that her mother would be back to pick her up when rehearsal ended, Abigail fled the building. Her last glimpse revealed Tony pulling Margaret aside.

As the doors of the community theater clanged shut behind her, the source of Abigail's shiver extended beyond the cool autumn air. What had she done? She had never quit a production. Ever. Why now?

Because she was old. Because she was tired.

Because it was someone else's turn.

That was the key. Abigail had spent her entire life vying for center stage—in every situation. Put her on a committee, she wanted to be chairman. Let her sing in a group, she expected a solo. Take a group picture? Front row was always good.

And put me on a jury . . . you'd better make me foreman.

She got in her car but did not start the engine. "Why do I do that?"

Because she was a performer. Because she liked attention. Because she did have leadership talent. Because . . . she had nothing else in her life.

No one else.

Pooh. It did no good to get into that again. She'd made her choices. And a husband and family weren't two of them. It did no good to have regrets. Everybody suffered those. It was a waste of time to dwell.

I am who I am.

The thought coincided with Patti's words on the stand. Simple, sincere, unpretentious Patti. And at this particular moment in Abigail's life, this straightforward statement was as eloquent as the greatest monologue, written by the wisest playwright, for the most esteemed character.

If Patti was who *she* was . . . who was Abigail? Could she make the same statement about her own life?

Suddenly the interior of the car gained clarity as if in a spotlight. All the accoutrements of the old car she'd sat in hundreds, if not thousands, of times seemed clearer, more vivid. Real.

Abigail grabbed the steering wheel and gained an odd strength from the sturdy feel of it. She purposely moved in her seat, feeling cushion against hip and back. She smelled the remnants of a fast food bag, crumpled on the floor on the passenger side. All this was real. It wasn't anything special. It wasn't brilliant. It wasn't noteworthy.

But it was real. It had purpose right now.

Which is more than I have.

She leaned her head against her hands, closing her eyes. This time, there was no risk of sleep. And yet . . . in spite of her turmoil, she had an inkling that what she'd just done was the right thing. And a good thing.

At least for Margaret Timmons.

———

"And the award for Humanitarian of the Year goes to . . . Dr. Sigmund T. Kelly."

Applause and a few cheers.

To Sig's credit he looked genuinely surprised, and his speech revealed an uncharacteristic humility. He almost looked embarrassed, as if the award were too much. As if it were undeserved.

When Sig finished his extremely short acceptance speech and made his way back to their table, the mayor's wife said to Deidre, "You should be very proud."

She was.

But then, when Sig reached the table, he didn't sit down. He leaned toward her ear and said, "I'd like to go now."

"We can't go," Deidre whispered. "You won."

Sig shrugged. He actually shrugged. "Please," he said.

He pulled out her chair and with as little fanfare as possible, they left.

Sig, not creating fanfare? Not sticking around to bow to the kudos and praise?

Something wasn't right.

"But what's wrong with you?" Deidre asked for the third time as she paced between their bed and the window.

"I just couldn't stay there and accept congratulations for being a humanitarian." He sat slumped in the overstuffed chair.

"Since when?" she asked.

"You know very well since when."

"But that's over. Patti's going to jail. You have to let it go, Sig. You have important work to do at the founda—"

"I don't know." He shook his head.

He didn't know? *What* didn't he know?

Deidre sat on the ottoman at his feet. "I just spent hours and hours, days and days at a trial, using my influence to make it come out to your advantage . . . for the advantage of the foundation." She knew she was exaggerating. The guilty verdict had not been a struggle, but Sig didn't need to know that.

Sig rubbed the space between his eyes. "And I appreciate—"

"No, you don't. Not if you leave events early, not if you don't nurture the foundation's benefactors, not if you don't—"

"I'm sorry." To put a period on the moment, Sig leaned

forward, kissed her cheek, said, "I'll try to do better," and left
to get ready for bed.

———

Becky nuzzled against Bobby's shoulder. He pulled the blanket higher over her arm. "I'm sorry if Cass and I blindsided
you with the Web site," she said.

That's exactly what they'd done. "It's okay," he told her,
even though he wasn't sure it was.

He felt her let out a breath she'd been holding. "I'm so
excited to see what happens next. Aren't you?"

Excited was not the word he'd use to describe his feelings.
Fear, panic, doubt? Those were the emotions that flew through
his mind.

"I believe in you, Bobby. I believe in your talent."

At least somebody did.

———

Ken unlocked the door of his apartment and led the woman
inside. "This is the place."

She took a slow stroll through the entry, her fingers brush-
ing the edge of a plant on the phone stand, before turning to
face the photo of St. Andrews in Scotland.

"You golf?" she asked.

He was stunned by her question. Hadn't he told her that at
the bar? Certainly he'd told her that. Being a golfer, a golf pro,
was part of his pickup story line. "I played the circuit."

She stopped her meandering, her eyebrows raised. "Really."

He felt a rush. Now he would tell her who he was and
the famous people he knew, and it would make what was

certainly going to be a good evening great. "Want to see
my trophies?"

She chuckled. "At least you didn't say etchings."

He led her to a display case, opening the glass doors wide.
He pulled one out.

Instead of taking the trophy, she merely nodded at it. Then
she pointed to the year. "You were a golfer—1983. What are
you now?"

"I give lessons at the golf club. I could give you a good deal."

"I don't get to golf much. I'm too busy." She walked away
from the trophies, unbuttoning the cuffs of her blouse.

Well then. A down-to-business kind of woman. Ken put
the trophy back. "And what do you do again?"

"I'm the CFO of Stanford Industries." She removed her
watch.

"But that's out of Albuquerque, isn't it?"

"Yes, it is. I'm impressed you know that."

He shut the door of the cabinet with a solid click. "I didn't
know they had an office here."

"They don't. I told you I was just in town for a meeting."

Had she? He wasn't thinking too straight this evening.

She flicked off her heels and approached him. "Enough
talk, Kyle. Let's get down to some real business."

Kyle?

"It's Ken."

She shrugged and started to unbutton his shirt. "Whatever."

Suddenly, Ken grabbed her wrists. "Don't."

Looking at her so close . . . she had a myriad of lines
around her eyes that the subdued lights of the bar had not
revealed. She'd tried to cover them with makeup, but it didn't
work, creating instead a crepey, creepy look. A look of someone trying too hard.

Join the club.

He let go of her wrists and stepped away. "I'm sorry. I've changed my mind."

She laughed but came toward him again. "That's a woman's line."

Ken sidestepped her advance and moved to the door, which he opened. "Perhaps another time."

She stood there, staring at him a moment. But just a moment. That was all the regret his withdrawal elicited. Then she slipped her heels back on, took her watch and purse, and strolled past him into the hall. He braced himself for a parting barb.

He wasn't disappointed. "Just as well. Has-beens can be such a bore."

So be it. He closed the door.

The voices of two women plagued Ken that night. One a successful CFO, and the other a meek dishwasher, convicted of murder.

"Has-beens can be such a bore" met with *"I am who I am. I don't pretend to be anything more."*

One set of words had been heard just moments before, while the other had obviously been sitting in his mind, dormant, since Patti had taken the stand last Thursday. He'd never thought of her words before. Why now? Why had the businesswoman from Albuquerque made him think of Patti? The two women could not have been more different.

Ken picked up the remote for the TV but ended up tossing it down. He couldn't stand the inane banter of television right now. He couldn't let those words interfere with the words of the two women.

He strolled to the trophy case, opened it, and removed the

trophy he'd shown the CFO—the one that had condemned him to has-been-hood by its ancient date.

"What are you now?"

"Great," Ken said. "More words to haunt me."

But instead of putting the trophy away, he took it with him to the leather chair. He settled in, balancing it on the chair arm. The trophy stared at him, reminded him of what he'd been. Once.

I played the circuit. I was somebody.

Kind of. Sort of. He'd given it a shot. Such as it was.

"And since then, I've pretended."

It was unfortunate there was no one there to argue with him.

He hugged the trophy to his chest.

Ten

The LORD will work out
his plans for my life—
for your faithful love, O LORD,
endures forever. Don't abandon me,
for you made me.

PSALM 138:8

*D*eidre awakened with a start. She held her breath a moment, uncertain what had pulled her from sleep.

It was 3:15 a.m. The house was quiet. There were no sirens outside, no bumps in the night. Then why . . . ?

She turned over and saw that the bed was empty. Where was Sig?

The bathroom was dark, the door open.

Deidre got out of bed and tiptoed into the hall. She found herself barely breathing, her ears perked to catch any foreign sound. She passed Nelly's room, then the guest room, and paused at the top of the stairs. The foyer loomed below, the moonlight casting shadows of the mullions from the door's sidelights on the marble floor. The faint whirr of the refrigerator and the resonant ticktock of the grandfather clock in the living room prevented the silence from gaining true victory.

The only logical place Sig would be was his study, so she went downstairs to check. He was not there.

Had he left the house?

His keys were on the kitchen desk.

She moved toward the door to the finished basement but couldn't imagine Sig being down there in Karla's domain.

The basement was dark. She shut its door with a soft click.

This was ridiculous. She didn't know whether to be scared or angry. He had to be somewhere.

Deidre made another pass through every room on the first floor, flipping on lights, letting no shadow remained undisturbed. Then she went upstairs and did the same to the guest room. Pristine and untouched.

Next, to Nelly's room.

She quietly opened the door but did not flip on the light. It took a moment for her eyes to adjust, but then she saw Nelly asleep in bed, undisturbed by her mother's roaming.

Deidre was just about to close the door when she heard a soft "Hi."

She looked to the far corner, where a white wicker rocker held court among Nelly's stuffed animal kingdom. Deidre blinked. Sig?

She moved closer and found him clutching a pink rabbit to his chest—Rory the rabbit, Nelly's favorite, the first present Sig had ever bought for her. She leaned close so as not to disturb their daughter. "What are you doing?"

Sig glanced at Nelly wistfully. "I had to be with her. See her."

"Why?"

Suddenly, shaking his head, he put his hand over his eyes. Was he crying?

There was movement in the bed as Nelly stirred. She sat up and blinked at her parents, rubbing her eyes. "What's going on?"

That's what I want to know.

Sig went to the side of the bed, shushing her. "It's nothing. Go back to sleep."

But Nelly wasn't so easily appeased. She turned on her
bedside lamp, changing the grays of the room to their full
pink. She pointed at her clock. "It's the middle of the night.
Why are both of you in my room? Did somebody die?"

Sig sat on the edge of the bed. "Actually . . ."

What was he doing? Certainly he wouldn't tell. There was
no reason to tell.

"I've done something—"

Deidre rushed to him and put a hand on his shoulder,
trying to turn him away from their daughter. "Sig. No. Think.
You don't have to tell her—"

"Tell me what?" Nelly asked.

Deidre regretted her choice of words. She took Sig's
hand and tried to pull him to standing, but he wouldn't budge.
"Let's you and I go downstairs so Nelly can get back to—"

"No way." Nelly pulled her pillow into her lap. "I'm not
going back to sleep. Not until you tell me what you're talking
about. Does this have to do with why you've both been acting
so weird?"

Deidre couldn't believe this was happening. She walked
to the door, swinging it wide. "I'm leaving. I'm not going to
be a part of this—hurting her and causing her worry when she
doesn't need to know any of it. . . . It's over, Sig. Let it be."

"I can't," he said softly.

She returned to the bedside, hating that she *couldn't* leave
and let this play out without her. Deidre knelt beside her
husband, trying to draw his attention away from Nelly. "Sig,"
she said quietly, "you know decisions made in the middle of
the night usually aren't wise ones. Logic is always cockeyed,
skewed, and warped in the dark. Emotions rule. Not now, Sig.
Not now. Besides, *we* need to talk first."

He took her hands and looked at her with the eyes of
someone with extreme knowledge or peace or—

Sig stood and faced them both: faced their daughter, sitting up in her bed, confused yet waiting for answers, and faced his wife, kneeling on the floor beside the bed, desperate yet hoping for silence.

"I killed a man, Nelly. I'm going to the authorities and tell them so."

Deidre jumped to her feet. "Sig, no!"

"I have to. I can't let Patti take the blame for something I did."

Nelly looked up at them. "Patti? That lady in the trial?"

Sig nodded. "She's not guilty; I am."

Nelly shook her head. "That doesn't make sense. No, Daddy. You can't be guilty of something like that. You can't."

"I hit the man who died—with a bottle. Remember how you felt before you hit Damon with the soccer ball? I felt that way too, felt backed into a corner with no way out. But instead of causing a broken nose . . ." Sig took a fresh breath. "Then, instead of helping the man, I ran away. That other lady, Patti, she found him. But I'm the one who hurt him."

Nelly stumbled off the bed. She started crying and pulled at the Kansas City Chiefs T-shirt Sig often wore to bed. "Daddy, no. You told me that sometimes people are forced to do something they normally wouldn't do."

"That's true, but it doesn't make it right. What Nana said was correct: violence is never right."

"But you said people get one mistake like that per person, per lifetime. This is your one mistake."

"Hopefully that's true. But that doesn't mean I shouldn't be punished for it."

Nelly slumped onto the bed. "I wish . . . I wish you could take it back."

"So do I," Sig said. "But because I did it . . . I have to tell."

Talk about a bad dream. Deidre raised a hand to make a point. "So all my hard work on the jury, getting the guilty verdict, was for nothing? And what about the foundation? You're willing to throw away years and years of hard work to ease your conscience?"

"What kind of conscience would I be exhibiting if I didn't come forward? What kind of man could let another person take the blame that was his?" He sat beside Nelly and pulled her head to his chest. "I am not that kind of man."

Deidre hated seeing Nelly's face contorted with pain and confusion. No child should have to feel—

Suddenly Nelly sat erect. "You said he was a bully. What was he doing to you? Why did you hit him?"

Sig looked at Deidre and she could tell he was searching for the right words. "Do you know what blackmail is?"

"Sure, it's . . . no, I guess not."

"It's when someone knows something that will hurt you, and they want money to stay quiet. It's like Damon tried to do with you—he was going to say you cheated unless you paid him."

"But I didn't cheat. It was a lie."

Sig nodded. "And what Brett was going to say about me was a lie too. But to make things worse, I couldn't tell the truth about it because that would uncover another lie that *I* told years ago. . . ." He swallowed. "Lies beget lies, Nelly. That's a truth no one can ignore."

"Brett Lerner was a horrible man," Deidre said. "All he cared about was power and money and hurting people, making them squirm. Your father was defending his honor and his work and—"

"I was just as horrible as he was in that I got mad and frustrated and hit him over the head."

"But what was he going to say about you?" Nelly asked.

Sig looked down at the stuffed bunny in his hand as if just then realizing it was there. He handed it to his daughter. "Brett said I was having affairs with other women, being unfaithful to your mother."

"You weren't, were you?"

"I wasn't. But the woman he'd seen me with was a friend of mine, a former patient who would be very hurt if people thought she was . . . that kind of woman. I didn't want her to be hurt."

"And the foundation. The foundation would have been hurt too," Deidre added.

Sig sighed. "The foundation too. But that doesn't justify me hitting him—and leaving. Leaving without helping him was just as bad. Maybe worse. To see someone in pain, who needs help, and *not* help them . . . I condemn myself for that as much as anything." He took Nelly's hand in his. "That's another reason why I can't let Patti take the blame. *She* needs my help. I can't make the same mistake twice."

"But what about me, Daddy?"

"I'm doing this for you. To show you what kind of man I *really* am."

Which made Deidre question what kind of woman *she* really was. . . .

"The award last night was the tipping point. Humanitarian of the Year. How can I accept such an award when I took a life?" Sig said.

"But you've saved dozens of lives. Hundreds. Doesn't that count for anything?" Deidre said.

"It means I need to hold myself to a higher standard. If I pretend to be a man of honor, I must *be* a man of honor."

"This is madness."

"This is right." He kissed the top of Nelly's head. "I'm going to get dressed now and go to the hospital to check on my patients. After that I'm going to the foundation office to clear up a few things. Then I'll go to the police."

"But it's not even light," Nelly said.

"I can't wait. I have to start the process now."

Deidre's thoughts stalled. All that had happened, all he had said. *All you should have said.* "If you think we're going with you, we're not. I can't support—"

He came close and cupped Deidre's cheek in his hand. "I'm going alone. I created this problem and I will finish it."

Once Sig left the room, Deidre nestled her cheek into Nelly's hair and rocked her. "Shh, shh. It'll be all right."

She was glad Nelly didn't ask how.

———

Abigail opened her eyes from sleep. It only took her a moment to remember what had happened the night before: she had given away a lead in *Annie*.

She waited for the regret and what-have-I-done? panic to take hold.

Nothing.

Perhaps she wasn't awake enough.

She sat up in bed and, for good measure, swung her feet over the side until they touched the cold floor.

Nothing.

This wasn't right. She should feel horrible. She should have awakened with an intense need to call Tony Novotny and take it all back.

With a surge of rebellion, Abigail whipped off the covers and went into the kitchen. She put some water on for tea— making as much noise as possible. She put an English muffin in the toaster and got out the Nutella, planning to spread it like a thick quilt.

But once she'd accomplished all these things, once she was forced to wait in the silence for the tea and the muffin, she was confronted yet again with feeling . . . good.

As an actress she was a pro at tapping into emotion at will, or if not tapping into it, at least feigning real emotion with something applied. Yet try as she might, she could not conjure up disappointment, sorrow, distress, doubt, or even anger. In spite of her effort and skill, the emotions that had first greeted her upon waking accosted her now: satisfaction, acceptance, peace, and even relief.

There was a knock on her door. At first she was peeved. Who would come calling so early? But then she saw it was after eight o'clock. Obviously she hadn't spent the night tossing and turning.

It was Hayley. The girl stormed in, dressed for school. "How come you quit? Tell me!"

Oddly, Abigail did *not* feel her defenses rise. The toaster popped up and she strolled to the counter. "Want a muffin?"

"No, I don't want a muffin. I want to know why you gave up the best part in the whole play."

Abigail plucked the muffin out of the toaster and quickly dropped it to a plate. "The part wasn't me." She dipped a knife deep in the luscious Nutella.

"It was you. It was perfect for you. You played it before."

Abigail gave Hayley a look. "It *was* me, thirty years ago."

Hayley made a face, then plopped in the beanbag. "You could have done it."

Abigail licked her finger, poured some tea, then took her breakfast to the couch. "How did Margaret do?"

"Fine, but—" Hayley sighed dramatically. "She's not you."

Abigail smiled. "There's only one of those."

"I don't get it. I thought you wanted to be in the play."

"I did."

"With me."

"You were the main draw, girlie."

"Then why?"

Abigail put her plate on the coffee table, trying to find words that originated within herself, not on the page of a play. "I think I've been holding on to a part that no longer exists."

"What's that mean?"

She looked at the walls that were covered with playbills and photos of Abigail Buchanan, playing parts. They were the highlights of her life, lovely times, and they elicited warm memories. But they weren't a part of the here and now. "It's time to move on and just be me." *Whoever that is.*

"No more plays or movies or TV or anything?"

It's not like they're beating down the doors. "I won't say never. But I don't want to pursue it anymore. I don't want to push." A new word appeared, one she'd never thought she would say. "It's time to retire."

"You said you'd never retire. You said they'd have to scrape your dead body off the stage. You said—"

Abigail raised a hand. "I think it's better to go out before things get . . . messy. Don't you?"

Hayley shrugged. "So what are you going to do?"

Good question. "I don't know." She put a hand to her chest. "But I think it's going to be kind of exciting figuring that out."

With a sigh, Hayley gave in. Then she looked toward the kitchen. "Do you have apricot jam?"

"Help yourself."

―――――――

Bobby drove to work, totally unsure about what he had to do or how to do it. Yet the image of being able to go home and tell Becky, "I quit my job at Burger Madness" spurred him forward.

He knew what *she'd* do. She'd squeal and wrap her arms around his neck and kiss him and say, "I'm so happy for you!"

And she'd mean it.

His own happiness would follow. He hoped.

But it was more than happiness he was after. Ever since Cass had come back into his life, he'd done a lot of thinking about his past and how things had played out. Up until now he'd tried to ignore all that because it was painful and because it didn't play into the life he wanted to live. Yet like Becky had said, until he accepted his past as an essential part of who he was *now* . . . he wasn't playing any part well. He was only skimming the surface.

Who he was then wasn't who he was now.

Patti McCoy had said, "I am who I am." That was true. But Bobby had the feeling he hadn't figured out who he actually was. Now. At this point in his life.

Was he a burger jerk? A popcorn pusher? Or a taxi driver? Those weren't bad things, but they did not define who he was, nor did they seem to be a part of what he was supposed to *be*.

He was supposed to be a good husband and father. And to do that, he needed to fulfill his potential in all aspects of his life—which was wrapped around the God-given gift of his art.

Use it or lose it. To do less was an insult to the One who'd given him the gift.

He walked into Burger Madness and spotted his boss at the fryer. Bobby's stomach flipped.

But that was part of it too. If fulfilling one's destiny didn't cause a few butterflies, what would?

Bobby stepped forward and changed his life.

———

With the dawn of morning, with a house devoid of Sig, with her daughter exhausted from worry, panic set in.

Deidre wandered the house, seeing things she'd seen a
thousand times as if they were new: the picture of Venetian
gondolas they'd bought on their honeymoon, which hung
above the fireplace in the family room; the Windsor clock
that had been in Don's family for three generations—but that
was perpetually ten minutes slow—on the desk in the kitchen.
The photograph of their wedding, three years previous, with
a nine-year-old Nelly, dressed in the palest pink "princess
dress," standing proudly between them. And Sig's brown
leather jacket hanging on a peg near the garage, ready for a
weekend errand.

She took it now and held it to her face. The musky smell
of the leather was intermixed with the distinct smell of her
husband.

Who would not be back to wear it.

He was probably still at the hospital, making his rounds.
What was he telling his young patients? *"I won't be your
doctor anymore. I'm going to jail."*

It was absurd.

It was going to happen.

Unable to be still, Deidre continued wandering through
the trappings of the life she'd created and crafted.

Nabbed and grabbed, according to her needs.

Suddenly she did a three-sixty. Would they lose the house?
Deidre didn't have a job. Sig's income would be cut off.

And what of the foundation? Although there were other
doctors on staff, would the scandal of Sig's guilt destroy what
he'd so carefully formed?

What would happen when Patti was released?

What would happen if there was a new trial?

What would the papers and TV say?

She knew that one: the Kelly family would be bitten off,
chewed up, and spit out. "We'll lose everything."

Karla came around the corner. "Morning. What did you lose?"

Everything. "Nothing. I—"

"Is Nelly up?"

"She's not going to school today."

Karla's face showed concern. "Is she sick?"

"She had a hard night."

"How come?"

Deidre shook her head. No questions. She couldn't handle questions.

She couldn't handle any of it. And so . . . "If you'll excuse me, I have something I have to do."

Karla looked skeptical but, totally oblivious to the crisis at hand, said, "I'll make coffee."

Deidre hurried upstairs, got out two suitcases, and began filling them with clothes. How odd to look through her closet of lovely outfits and have to choose only a few. Yet it was surprisingly easy. She wouldn't need cocktail dresses on the run. Or silk suits. Or perky tennis clothes. She'd need simple clothes, clothes that would help her blend into a crowd—

And just be Dee-Dee again.

Halfway through her packing she remembered the wall safe behind the picture in the bedroom. Money and jewelry she could sell. She wouldn't be able to go far without those. She grabbed an empty black purse and took a detour from the clothes. She opened the safe and removed a few stacks of money. It wasn't neatly bound in counted packets, but by flipping through the fifties and hundreds, she figured there was nearly twenty thousand. She stuffed the money and the most valuable pieces of jewelry in the purse. Rubies, diamonds, pearls . . . all presents from her generous husband.

Deidre sped through the bathroom, dumping toiletries in a bag. She grabbed more clothes and stuffed them into the suitcase. Forget folding anything. Time was her enemy. They had to be gone before Sig went to the police. Before their world blew apart.

Knowing she'd missed plenty, she zipped the suitcase shut.

She took a piece of empty luggage into Nelly's room and began packing her things.

Nelly awakened and sat up. "What are you doing?"

"We're going on a little trip."

"A trip where?"

"I don't know yet."

Her face brightened. "Is Daddy going with us?"

"He can't. He told you—"

"I was hoping he'd change his mind." She pointed at a green top. "Mom, don't bring that."

"Then you do it. And bring a few books and stuffed animals . . . some pens and hair things."

"Are the police after us?" Nelly asked.

Deidre forced herself to slow down, to calm her child. "No, they're not after us. We didn't do any—" She couldn't finish the sentence. She knelt beside her daughter's bed. "I'm just afraid of what people will do and say when they find out about your dad. The press will probably come over and want us to talk about it and—"

And I was on the jury even though I knew Brett!

Suddenly Deidre realized that with Sig telling the truth, her own past would be revealed. And Nelly would find out Brett was her father, and Deidre would get in trouble with the courts for lying about her previous connection with him and—

"Faster, sweetie. We need to get going."

"What about Nana?"

Deidre felt the air go out of her. Karla. She couldn't leave Karla to deal with the aftermath of this mess.

"Nana will have to go with us."

"What do you mean, Sig is turning himself in? In for . . . what did you say?"

Although Deidre understood Karla's reaction to her initial, abbreviated explanation, she didn't have time to go through it in more detail. Deidre had found Karla relaxing on the deck's swing, a coffee mug in hand. *"Karla, I have something to tell you. . . ."*

"I can't go into it now," Deidre said. "But by the end of the day . . ."

Our lives will be changed forever.

Karla balanced the mug on her thigh. "And why was Sig being blackmailed?"

Deidre didn't have time for this. They had to *go.* "I promise I'll tell you everything *after* we get out of here. Please, Karla. We really have to leave right—"

Karla patted the seat beside her on the swing. "I am not going anywhere until I hear a good explanation. You want to hem and haw about it, fine, but it will only take up more of this ticking clock you're so concerned with. Hence, I suggest telling me the truth."

Reluctantly, Deidre sat. "Sig was blackmailed by Brett because Brett had seen him with Audrey and thought they were having an affair. An affair would hurt Sig's reputation in the community and hurt the foundation. Brett had done his homework. He knew this."

"Brett was a maître d', right?"

"At The Pines restaurant. As the host I'm sure he witnessed quite a few odd pairings of young women with older men. Although no one's come forward, I wouldn't be surprised if he blackmailed others before Sig. He could easily make it his business to find out who the men were and what they could offer him in return for his silence. Brett had seen a picture of me and Sig in the paper. That piqued his interest. And when I showed up at the resort after my big argument with Sig . . ."

"It sounds like you did more than run into him. It sounds like you talked—a lot."

"Not any more than necessary, I assure you. I'd heard he moved away, but to find out he was back in town . . . he asked way too many questions. Just the sight of him made my skin crawl. I didn't stay around him a moment longer than I had to. But apparently, it was long enough."

"Did he act like he knew about—" Karla nodded toward the house where Nelly was finishing her packing.

Deidre's memories took over. . . .

Brett had sat down at her table as if he had a right to be there. He'd smiled his smarmy smile. "Why are you here, Dee-Dee? Alone at a resort? Trouble in paradise?"

"Of course not. Go away, Brett. Leave me—"

"Actually, I'm not surprised you have trouble. I saw your hubby in here once. And another time around town with a young woman—not as old as you, by any means. I wonder what the Kelly Foundation would think about that."

She'd started to get up, but he'd taken her arm. "Sit. I've been wanting to talk with you. About other . . . things."

Just the way he'd said it made her expect the worse. Which is exactly what she'd gotten: "I read in one of the 'Dr. Kelly the saint' articles that you have a daughter. How old is she now? Twelve? But you've only been married to the great doctor three years; isn't that right?"

Deidre stood, toppling her chair. She hurried out of the restaurant, but not before Brett called after her, "I'll be in touch, Dee-Dee. I can hardly wait to meet your lovely daughter."

Deidre felt a hand on hers, drawing her back to the present. "Honey? Are you all right?"

"No, I'm not all right! That's why I want to get away from here. I've had enough. Enough for a lifetime." She stood, causing the swing to gyrate wildly. "I don't understand why so many bad things have happened to *me*. I grow up with a lousy father who wants nothing to do with me, I fall for a man who rapes me, I get pregnant, and Nelly is born with a bad hip. No sooner do I find a good man and start to be happy than he gets sick and dies. I'm left with bills and no future. I have to struggle to survive. But I do it and once again find a way out—through Sig. But just when I get my life turned around, Brett interferes and gets himself killed. By sheer chance I get called to *that* trial. I thought that piece of luck was the answer to everything. But now Sig is throwing it all away by confessing, leaving me alone. Again. The world's against me." She let out a deep sigh, waiting for sympathy. *"There there, everything will be all right."*

But Karla didn't say anything. She just rocked, up and back.

Deidre was about to repeat her litany when Karla said, "There seem to be an awful lot of *I*s and *me*s in that list."

Deidre didn't understand.

Karla took a sip of her coffee then said, "I know it's been hard, but most of the things you listed did not happen to just you, Deidre. Your mother is the one who married badly. Nelly is the one who had the bum hip and had to undergo surgery. Don was the one who died, and then you married well and gained a grand life. And though this Brett was not exactly an upstanding citizen, he did not *get himself* killed. From what you've said, Sig *is* guilty of hitting him. Your husband turning himself in reveals his honorable core."

"So I have no right to be upset? frustrated? angry?"

Karla shrugged. "Feel what you want. But as far as the world being out to get you, it's simply not so. I'll admit that the scales of fair and unfair can seem pretty off-kilter at times, but when we start feeling all woe-is-me, we have to remember who wins."

Deidre wanted to go inside and leave this discussion behind. She was open to hearing Karla's practical advice about what to do next, but she didn't want to hear a come-to-Jesus lecture. She took a step toward the door. "We have to go. Now."

"Don't run away, Deidre."

"But we have to—"

Karla patted the swing. "Come on now. Come back here."

Deidre felt completely trapped. Unable to leave. Unwilling to stay.

"One more minute," Karla said. "That's all I ask."

Reluctantly, Deidre returned to her seat.

Karla patted her knee. "Don't run from circumstances and don't run from *him,* Deidre. He knows where you are. You can't hide from God. You shouldn't try."

There it was again. That hiding-from-God theme. There seemed to be no escaping it. "But I don't know what to do."

"And you think running ahead of God's direction is the wisest choice?"

Actually, Deidre hadn't thought much about God at all. She'd left God behind when Don died. Except for a few snippets of prayer, she'd buried the Almighty along with her husband.

The sliding glass door opened enough for Nelly to pop her head out. "I'm packed." She took one look at her mother and grandmother and said, "Are we going or not?"

"We'll be inside in a minute, sweetie."

Nelly looked confused but closed the door.

Karla started the swing again. "As a parent you know what's best for Nelly, right?"

Although it sounded like a trick question, Deidre answered, "Of course."

"And as you're walking her up life's road, you'd like to show her the way. Lead her on the best pathways."

Deidre nodded.

"But if she runs ahead of you, thinking she knows best . . . she's going to make some whopper mistakes."

Point taken.

Karla shrugged. "Don't race ahead without getting directions, Dee-Dee. It only leads to a ton of unnecessary detours, potholes, and crashes."

Yes indeed. She'd already experienced a few of those.

"Jesus said, 'Follow me,' not 'Run on ahead and *I'll* follow *you*.'"

"I know that."

"Knowing ain't doing."

Touché.

"One more thing and then you can go or not go, as you choose. The trouble with being strong and capable is we start believing we know best. We forge ahead, glancing back at God when we think about it, checking to see if he's going to stop us. Some of the time, we don't even look back because we know—we *know*—he wouldn't approve and we don't want to be stopped."

It was a disheartening image because it was completely true. Deidre had been doing just this—and worse—for years.

Karla stood. "So. That said, how about some lunch?"

"But we have to . . . go."

Karla looked down at her. "Do we?"

She went inside, leaving Deidre alone.

Deidre was not good company. Too bad she couldn't run and hide from herself.

She pulled her knees to her chest, and after a few quick moments the swing adjusted and was still.

But Deidre wasn't. Not her heart, her mind, or her tears.

The tears surprised her. Why was she crying?

Let me count the ways.

Because her world had flipped upside down.

Because things hadn't turned out as she'd hoped.

Because Sig was going to jail.

Because *he* didn't deserve to go.

Not really.

She did.

Yes, her husband had hit Brett over the head with the wine bottle. Yes, Sig had dazed him. And yes, Sig had even run away.

But it was Deidre's secrets that had set everything in motion. If she hadn't kept Brett a secret all these years; if she'd told the truth to Nelly and Don and Sig and Karla . . . And then, after seeing Brett again, realizing he was up to no good, if only she'd come home from The Pines and talked to Sig, warned him that this awful man from her past might be making another appearance. Her honesty could have saved Brett's life and Sig's freedom.

She thought back to that night, to the moment when Sig had come in the back door after his meeting at Brett's house. She hadn't known about the meeting. If only she'd known ahead of time.

Sig had collapsed to his knees and started to sob. He was ashen. His head shook *no, no, no.*

Deidre ran to him. "Sig? What happened?"

He raised his chin, capturing her eyes with his. "I killed a man."

With her help he got to his feet and Deidre led him to the couch in the family room. "Sit. I'll get you some water."

When she returned to the couch, she found him clutching a pillow to his chest. He ignored the water. She pushed the newest issue of *Vogue* out of the way and sat on the coffee table, facing him.

He did not look up but stared into the space around his knees.

She touched one of those knees. "Sig . . . you said you killed a man. Tell me what happened."

"I didn't mean to. I mean, I never intended—"

"I'm sure you didn't." She had no idea what he was talking about. Had he botched an operation? Had he been involved in a car accident and driven away before the police arrived? She quickly ran out of options. "Tell me what happened."

He nodded, as though only then realizing he needed to explain himself. "I got a call from a man who threatened me . . . who was going to spread rumors about me that would hurt the foundation unless I paid—"

"Someone was blackmailing you?"

"He called me late yesterday and said he had some information that could ruin the foundation. I didn't believe him at first; I thought he was a crank, but then he mentioned Audrey's name and—" He looked away from her, as if ashamed.

"Who was he?"

"I don't know his last name, but his first name was Brett. He said we'd never met but he'd seen me and—" Sig stopped talking and stared at Deidre. "What's wrong?"

Brett? He was being blackmailed by Brett? Deidre managed to answer her husband by saying, "Go on."

"I met him, to pay him. At his house—which seemed

incredibly strange. But stranger still I found him sitting in his hot tub. It was so odd it was almost surreal. He was unbelievably arrogant and cocky. And then we argued and he turned nasty, baiting me, making me feel trapped, and I . . . I hit him over the head with a wine bottle."

Her mind raced. She could easily imagine Brett Lerner's cocky smoothness turning bad, pushing her husband to a breaking point. Brett was the king of manipulation and meanness. "Maybe you didn't kill . . . maybe he's not dead."

Sig's eyes flashed with hope. "He *was* alive when I ran, though he was cut. Dazed because I hit him—" Sig's right arm came alive and reenacted the hitting motion of wine bottle against head. But then the imaginary bottle was gone and Sig's hands found his own head. "I'm a doctor. I should have tried to save him. I took an oath." Suddenly he sprang to his feet. "We have to call 911. We have to save him!"

But I don't want him saved!

The thought of having Brett Lerner back in their lives where he might find out he was Nelly's father—or press the point if he already knew—to create a scenario where Sig might find out about all the lies *she* had told all these years. . . .

Deidre put calming hands on her husband's shoulders, pushing him back to sitting. "If you call the authorities, they'll have this number. They'll come talk to you. Ask questions." She was shocked by her own words. So cold. So calculating.

So necessary.

She couldn't let Sig talk to the police. If they knew he was involved, everything would be lost. Everything.

"I left him there." Sig started to stand. "I can't just . . . we need to get him help. I need to call the police, turn myself in."

Deidre thought of a trump card—the one thing even more important to Sig than his work. "If you call the police, it will ruin everything you've worked for. Do you want our daughter to think her father is a killer?"

His eyes were pathetic. "I am a killer."

She took his hands in hers, peering into his eyes. "You are a healer. You are a great man who has helped hundreds of people. Don't you want to keep being that man? If you go to the police, all that will end and hundreds of people will suffer."

He blinked as if letting the idea settle.

"Come on." Deidre led him toward the stairs. "Let's get you to bed."

She was relieved when he didn't argue. There was no more talk of calling 911. There was no more talk of killing.

Though, if the truth were known, Deidre clung to a hope of her own: that there *had* been a killing. For it was an undeniable fact that her life would be better if Brett Lerner were dead.

Deidre didn't like what it said about her character, but she'd slept well that night, eerily free from nightmares or what-ifs or even questions of what to do now.

She should have been worried.

She should have been upset.

But she wasn't.

She'd slept so soundly that she had no clue how Sig had slept. Only when she awakened and found him standing by the window, his eyes puffy and red, his face sagging, did she realize he had not slept well, if at all.

What did that say about *her*?

"I'm waiting for the paper," he said on that morning after. "I'm waiting to turn on the news. But I'm afraid."

She ran a hand through her hair and tried to blink the sleep from her eyes. "I'm up now. I'll be with you."

Sig nodded weakly and sat on the foot of the bed. He took the remote, then handed it to Deidre. "You do it."

Deidre turned to the regional stations, flipping until she found one in the middle of news. A fire at the mall. An accident on the interstate. Then finally . . .

"A man was found dead last night in Branson, drowned in a hot tub."

"Drowned?" Sig asked.

"The man's identity has not been released pending notification of relatives. Foul play is suspected and a woman has been taken in for questioning. We will bring you more information as—"

It was Deidre's turn. "Woman?"

"What woman?" Sig said. He pointed at the newscaster, who had moved to another story. He yelled at the screen, "What woman?"

Deidre was just as shocked as he was. But thrilled.

They would be all right. There was someone else to take the blame. . . .

For months they'd lived on the nervous hope of Patti's guilt, always afraid that someone had seen Sig at the scene, that he'd left behind some minute piece of evidence. They'd both been thankful it had been cold that night. Sig had worn gloves. His fingerprints were not on the bottle. The news said nothing about a man at the scene. Patti was their suspect. Patti was going to trial.

When Deidre had been called to jury duty and she'd had a chance to sit on Patti's trial . . .

Perfection.

Complication.

Confusion.

Condemnation.

Her thoughts finally back in the present, Deidre whispered the words, "She's innocent" and let them settle around the swing. The words did not need volume. Although they'd barely had any time to live with Patti's conviction, the reality of it weighed heavily.

As did the reality of this day: Sig was turning himself in.

I started all this. I'm the one who knew Brett. I'm the reason he came into our lives. I'm to blame for what happened.

Deidre suddenly stood, sending the porch swing ricocheting against her legs. She had to see Sig. She had to talk to him.

She had to do something.

———

"Meet me, Sig. You have to meet me now."

"But I'm just finishing up at the foundation offices. Then I was . . . you know."

"I know. But I have to talk to you now. Before . . . You owe me that much." Deidre knew this wasn't true. He didn't owe *her* anything. He'd already given her everything.

"Fine. Meet me in the parking lot of the foundation."

———

It was an inauspicious place to play out a life-changing moment. But how much better seated in a BMW rather than a VW.

Sig's face was drawn and haggard, the stress of the day evident. "So," he said once they were settled in the front seat. "I don't want a tearful good-bye, Deidre. This is hard enough without—"

"It's my fault. If anyone should go it should be me."

"Go where?"

"To prison."

He stared at her a moment, then laughed. "And why should you do that?"

She realized she had to go back in time, to the source of the lie that had dogged her for over twelve years. "I used to date Brett Lerner. Way back. Before I was married to Don."

He was silent, but just for a moment. "That's an odd coincidence, but I don't see why that matters. We both had lives before we met."

"It matters because it ended badly. Very badly, and Brett . . . the day before he called you, I ran into him down at the resort where he worked. He showed interest in my life. He . . . he was bad news. I knew that. He asked about our lives—though he already knew too much. It was like he'd been studying us."

"Studying?"

"He knew who you were, knew I was married to you. Knew we had money. Knew about the foundation and the work you do and how important fund-raising was to your work. And he'd seen you with Audrey and thought . . . thought what I thought about the two of you."

"That's why he was blackmailing me. He was going to tell everyone, and truth or not, it would have hurt the foundation. That's why I hit—" He looked straight ahead and gripped the steering wheel. "One lie. One bit of dishonesty. If I had been open about my botched operation on Audrey from the beginning, none of this would have—"

"It's not your fault!" Deidre's words rang through the car.

Sig looked at her. Waiting.

It was time for everything to come out of hiding. The truth, her past, and Deidre herself.

She angled her body toward his. Her hands moved to her cheeks, and with a start, she realized how much she wanted to use them to cover her face completely.

To hide behind them.

Daddy, you can't see me.

She forced her hands into her lap, where they clung to each other as though they were afraid of the words she was about to say. She began, "I hated Brett Lerner. Despised him."

"I wasn't thrilled with the man myself."

"But you didn't hate. I hated." She shuddered. "It's a horrible feeling, hate. It's an evil feeling. It's like . . . it's a crime against the soul. And it's been eating at me a long, long time. And now . . . it's time to finally hold myself accountable for all that I've done."

"You are not the one who caused his death. I am."

"But I—"

"What kind of man would I be if I let you take the blame for any part of this?"

He wasn't letting her say what needed to be said. "You'd be a free man."

"A guilty man. That doesn't change no matter how much you hated Brett, no matter what secret you've kept hidden. I need to let myself be *set* free."

"By going to jail?"

"By taking the punishment for my actions. I *will* go to prison, but I also will be free, Deidre. I've confessed; I've asked God to forgive me. And he has."

Nothing he could have said would have shocked her more. Sig and God? Sig confessing to God?

"I know I'm forgiven because he told me so." Sig put a hand to his chest. "I've felt such peace since I did that. And somehow I know the peace is his way of telling me everything will be all right."

Who was this man seated before her? Where was her pragmatic husband who put his work— "But what about your work? The foundation?"

"Although I started the foundation, it's larger than I am, larger than one man. I'm hoping people will forgive me, realize what I did was a crime of passion. But the truth is, it's still a crime. And unfortunately, the truth about Audrey will come out too. I have a lot to atone for."

"No one needs to know about Audrey, about her operation."

"Everyone needs to know. It's the only way."

Deidre didn't know what else to say. "I still don't understand why you're doing this."

He pointed up. "I'm doing it for him, but he's not making me do it. That's the point, I guess. He's given us free will to do the right thing. Or not."

The right thing is for me to tell you all about Brett and me, about Nelly, about how I married you for the wrong reasons and have only pretended to love you when you deserved so much more.

But Deidre couldn't do it. The man sitting before her exuded peace. If she laid her sins upon him now, that peace would be destroyed. Sig was clinging to his newfound faith *and* the elements of their life he believed to be true. If she told him she was a victim of rape, that Nelly was the daughter of the man he had killed, that Deidre had married Don *and* Sig for the wrong reasons . . . Her confession may have assuaged her own guilt, but it would also inflict a deep crack in the foundation that was holding Sig together.

To confess now would be the epitome of selfishness. And though she'd previously lived a life focused on self, at this moment she had to do the selfless thing.

By remaining silent.

By keeping her secrets awhile longer.

"I need to go," Sig said.

Her time for confession had come. And gone. The final

decision was taken away from her. All she could say was, "I'm so sorry, Sig. So sorry for everything."

"As am I." Sig ran a hand up and down her back. "I guess God finally has me where he wants me. Broken. Contrite. But hopefully of use to him. Somehow." He took her hand, brought it to his lips, and kissed it. "I really love you, Deidre. You know that, don't you?"

Deidre didn't know. Hadn't allowed herself to know. But for his sake, she nodded. "I'll go with you to the police station if you'd like."

"I'd rather do this alone."

They held each other one more time.

As Deidre drove home after her meeting with Sig—her last meeting with Sig as a free man—she felt cheated. It was ridiculous, of course. Sig was the one who would have the most to endure. In public she could play the innocent wife who had been kept in the dark. No one had to know her connection to Brett. To the public it would be a simple case of blackmail gone bad. If the truth about Audrey came out, that too was something they could deal with. Since Sig's surgical mistake, he'd performed hundreds of successful surgeries—all over the world. It would not take much effort to elicit testimonials from happy parents of happy children singing his praises and overriding one mistake in the far-distant past.

Everything would be all right. Sig would take his punishment and might even emerge a hero of sorts. Society was weird that way. As long as anyone with any modicum of celebrity admitted their sins, they were forgiven and given another chance to be in the limelight, where they could be adored anew.

Whether the medical community would be so tolerant was another matter.

Deidre stopped at a traffic light and let her mind wander. Sig *would* come through this. And the peace he'd embraced would help him tackle the snags along the way.

But . . . "What about me?"

Her words, said alone in the car, sounded pitiful. And yet, what about her? She was rid of Brett Lerner. She never had to worry about him stepping back into her life, finding out Nelly was his, or any other mischief he might have caused.

But . . .

Where is my peace?

Not anywhere close. She had not received a chance to bare her soul, to come clean, to open the baggage of over a decade. She'd kept it all safely tucked away for Sig's sake—a mighty sacrifice that should earn her *something.* But in doing so, she remained burdened—more so now than before. For during her last meeting with Sig, when she'd wanted to tell him the truth, the whole truth, and nothing but the truth, she'd experienced a hint of the peace that release would have given her.

Only to have it yanked away so Sig could hold on to *his* peace.

The traffic light turned green and she continued toward home.

Alone.

———

Deidre dropped a frying pan to the floor and moments later mishandled its lid.

Karla looked up from the eggs she was whisking. "Bumbly fingers?"

Unexpectedly, her words were the last straw.

Deidre slumped to the kitchen floor, letting the pot and lid fall with her. Karla was immediately at her side.

"I can't do it," she said.

"I know it's going to be hard, honey. But Sig is determined and—"

"It's not fair."

"No, it's not but—"

Deidre didn't want her to offer that dreadful truism: *life isn't fair.* If Deidre heard those words, she would die right there on the kitchen floor. "Sig found peace and is off cleansing himself of his guilt, while I . . . I sit here with all my secrets still secrets from him."

With a glance toward the rest of the house, Karla sat on the floor beside her. "You mean the secret about Nelly?"

Deidre nodded. "That and more, more subtle things. Although I never thought I'd tell him any of it, since all of this—" she looked directly at her mother-in-law—"I want to feel what he feels. I want to feel that release, that peace, that feeling of it's-finally-over-and-I'm-free."

"If it's so important to you, why didn't you tell him?"

"Because he had enough to think about. You should have seen him, Karla. He was practically glowing, like a darkness had been lifted from him and he was a new person."

Karla nodded. "'If I had not confessed the sin in my heart, the Lord would not have listened.'"

Deidre pushed the pan away with a foot. It slid across the tile into some cabinets. "See? He confessed. God listened. And Sig's all better."

"He's forgiven."

Deidre blinked.

"He is, you know."

"That's what *he* said."

Karla nodded. She moved the lid out of the way. "You

know all of this, Deidre. Remember it. Jesus took the punishment for our sins so we could be forgiven."

The knowledge came from a lifetime ago, when she'd been married to Don—another man she'd deceived. "But I didn't get a chance to confess. Sig's in jail and I don't know when I'll have the opportunity to come clean and feel free of it."

This time, Karla shook her head. "It's not Sig you have to confess to—though that time *may* come. You can feel peace right now if you remember what Jesus said: 'Come to me, all of you who are weary and carry heavy burdens, and I will give you rest.'"

A snicker escaped.

"Deidre . . ."

She closed her eyes and leaned her head against the spice drawer. What Karla said was true. Deidre knew it was. But it wasn't something she dared tap into. *When one is living a lie, one can't confess the lie.*

Deidre felt Karla take her hand. "Come on, honey. You don't have to do it out loud, but do it. Now. I'll stay here with you and pray my own prayers while you take care of business with the Almighty. As far as telling Sig? I know it's hard, but leave the timing to God. He is never late and never early. Let him open the door for you to air the truth to Sig. Don't push."

"Don't run ahead."

Karla smiled. "You were listening."

"I do listen to you, Karla. Most of the time."

"Glad to hear it, but better than that . . . listen to God. Listen for him. He won't steer you wrong."

"You promise?"

She looked upward. "We both do."

Deidre realized how odd it was to empty her heart while

sitting on a not-terribly-clean kitchen floor, but she did it anyway.

Once she got going, the silent confession grew upon itself and Deidre found herself sobbing with shame, but also with release and relief.

Sometime during the process, Karla wrapped an arm around her and when Deidre said aloud a final, "Thank you, Lord" and pronounced an amen to the moment, the comforting arms of her mother-in-law felt very divine.

"The eternal God is your refuge, and his everlasting arms are under you."

———

He could have gone to work. He was supposed to go to work. But work was the last thing on Ken Doolittle's mind.

Or maybe the only thing.

Ever since kicking Ms. Aggressive from Albuquerque out of his apartment the night before, ever since waking up in his leather chair at 3 a.m. to find himself hugging his trophy to his chest, he'd been in bed, sheathed under the protective veil of the covers.

It's where he planned to stay until . . . forever, or until his hunger pangs got too nasty.

The phone rang and Ken held his breath to listen for the answering machine to pick up. *"Ken. Roger here. Where are you? I know that stupid trial is done. We expected you in today. If you don't call, I'll be forced to give Dan your lessons. Or . . . just get in here."*

Ken turned over, pulling a pillow to his torso. What was the use of going into work? It wasn't as if he was important to them. Dan had taken over during the trial and was obviously willing to keep taking Ken's clients.

The schmuck.

The phone rang again and Ken yelled at it, "Leave me alone! I'm not coming in. Don't you get it?"

But this time, even though he had no intention of answering it, he didn't wait to listen to the message from the bed. He was fully awake now. And hungry. A dozen fried eggs and a pound of bacon sounded suitably decadent. He was walking past the phone, mumbling about what Roger could do with his job, when another voice came on the line.

"Ken? It's Ronnie. I know you're not there—I know you're back at work—but I was wondering if you wanted to get together tonight. We haven't really talked since you found out the news about Philip and—"

Ken picked up the phone. "Ronnie. Hi."

"You're home?"

"I took the day off. Recovering from the trial."

"Did you hear my message? Can you get together this—?"

"Sure. Yes. That would be great." He was surprised at how great it sounded.

"Want to meet somewhere?"

The thought of leaving the apartment, even with Ronnie, was not appealing. "Come over here. Sevenish. I'll make dinner."

"Spaghetti I assume?"

"You know me too well."

A scary thought, all in all.

———

As he buttered the garlic bread, Ken felt joy. The realization made him stop his work, cock his head, and laugh. *When was the last time I felt joy?*

The answer to his question sapped a bit of the joy away—

for it had been far too long—but he was in such a good mood he didn't let that detail drag him down.

Ronnie was coming over. Ronnie was coming to dinner. It was a good day and would be an even better evening.

Her being his ex-wife was inconsequential. They'd had something good. Once. For a while. Until he'd blown it.

Today was a new start. He was on speaking terms with his son again. Yes, there was that HIV thing, but with a little effort Ken could set that aside for the sake of grabbing on to some happiness.

He got out the Lawry's Garlic Salt and began to sprinkle the bread, then thought better of it. No garlic. Not tonight.

———

Ronnie dabbed her mouth with her napkin. "That was wonderful, Ken. Although your repertoire is small, it's mighty delicious."

Ken offered her a nod. "Thank you, madam." He stood. "Ready for some dessert?"

"Surely you jest?"

"It's just spumoni ice cream."

"Maybe later."

He started to clear away the dishes. She put a hand on his, stopping him. "Leave those. Just sit. Talk to me."

"I have been talking to you."

She shook her head. "You've been talking *at* me. Talk *to* me, Ken. Tell me what's on your mind."

He sniggered. "Oh, you don't want to go *there*."

"But I do."

He sat down, both nervous at the prospect of talking at levels deeper than small talk and eager to do just that. He'd had so many thoughts pop in and out the past week. Most disconcerting. Where could he begin?

"You look . . . wistful," she said, studying him.

It was a word he'd never expected to be associated with. "I guess I am. A bit. I have regrets."

He expected her to raise her eyebrows, to mock him. Instead she said, "So do I."

He pounced on her confession. "What do you regret?"

She shook her head. "You go first. You're the one who's wistful."

He might as well get to the big one first. "I regret leaving you and Philip."

"I regret letting you leave."

"Really?"

"We had some good moments amid the traumatic times."

He nodded. "We just let the bad times take over."

She pushed her plate toward the center of the table, giving herself room to lean forward. "What else do you regret?"

Can I make you a list? "Actually, I regret not being a great golfer."

Ronnie seemed surprised. "You were very good." She pointed to the display case. "You won a lot of trophies."

Why did they mean so little right now? "I was a mediocre golfer. I could have done much better."

"Everyone can say that, no matter what their profession. Maybe the problem was you stopped short. Maybe you never reached your potential."

Then it hit him. Like a golf club to the gut. "Actually, I think I did reach my potential. I was the best golfer I could be. But the truth was, *that* wasn't very good."

"You tried hard."

It sounded as pathetic as it was. "Maybe that's what

makes it so hard. I tried and tried, but the real talent just wasn't there."

"Don't say that. You were very tal—"

He bolted from his chair. "Don't placate me, Ronnie! Don't try to make me feel good. I'm having a revelation here."

Ronnie's shocked look changed into a smile. "Sorry. You have the floor."

Ken felt like a fool. And yet . . . Ronnie had witnessed *fool* before. Many times. He took their plates to the kitchen, talking on the way. "The girl we just convicted of murder? That Patti McCoy?"

"I bet you're glad that's over."

He was, but didn't want to get sidetracked. "When she was on the stand she said something almost profound. She said, 'I am who I am. I don't pretend to be anything more.'"

"Sounds like a wise girl."

He set the plates in the sink and returned to his seat. "She does, doesn't she? Without a degree, breeding, or any grand life experiences. Yet in some ways she has her head together more than I do."

"You sound a bit of a snob, Ken."

"I was. I am. Oh, who knows? The point is, she knows who she is and isn't pretending to be anyone else." He put a hand to his chest. "I've been pretending my whole life, pretending to be somebody important and talented and special."

"Don't be so hard on—"

He took her hand. "Ronnie. Please. Just listen."

She squeezed his hand.

Suddenly Ken realized he had nothing more to say. "I'm done."

"No, you're not."

Yes, he was. He withdrew his hand. He didn't know what he was saying anyway. It was all a bunch of claptrap.

She took his hand back. "Hey. Look at me."

He did.

"Just be yourself, Ken."

"But I don't know who Ken is."

"Be a good man. Not a golfer, not a father, not a husband, not a one-night stand. What is *Ken* going to do with his life?"

"I have no idea." Then he *did* have an idea, one that had been brewing all day. "Let's get back together, Ronnie. Let's give it another try."

She looked as though he'd asked her to jump off a cliff.

"It's not *that* far-fetched," he said.

When she found her voice, she said, "We're not the same people we were."

He nodded vigorously. "I know. That's what makes it good. I want to change. I want to be better. I want to be that good man you think I can be."

She touched his cheek and he could smell her White Shoulders perfume. "Ken, I can't."

He pressed her hand against his cheek, not willing to let it go. "Don't say no. Not yet. Think about it." He thought of something else. "It will be good for Philip to see us together."

Ronnie pulled her hand away. "Philip is a grown man. He's not dependent on his parents being married in order to have us in his life." She took a fresh breath. "I can't be your lover, Ken. I can't be your wife. But I will be your friend. Till death do us part."

"That's not enough," he said. "What about all the changes I'm about to make? Doesn't that count for something?"

"You talk about being *somebody*. Fine. You are somebody. Right now. You are Philip's father."

"No, I'm not. I'm a terrible father. I wasn't there when he needed me."

"So fathering stops at age eighteen, or twenty-one? Be a

good father now. That's a somebody Philip and I both need. A somebody you need."

"I don't know what I need."

"Sure you do. You need change. So do it. For us. But also for you."

"I've been doing for *me* all my life. That's what's got me so messed up."

"There you're wrong. You haven't been doing for you; you've been doing for everyone else in that you've been consumed with what other people think. With appearances. With attaining that 'somebody' status." She found her purse and headed toward the door. "I'm glad you're on the road to finding the true Ken. But in the end, this journey is your own, dear man. Do you like Ken Doolittle? Are you proud of that man? Will you feel at ease standing before our Maker one-on-one?"

Now she was scaring him. "This isn't about dying; it's about living."

"Living is all about dying, Ken. Living so we know where we'll go after we die. Being accountable. Making concessions and confessions. Surrendering every aspect of ourselves to the One who's bigger than each of us. Bigger than even you."

He didn't know what to say.

Ronnie kissed his cheek. "Think about it."

———

"May I help you?"

Ken sat back against his pillows and cleared his throat. "I want to order the Montreux watch?"

"Number 38567?"

"Yeah, that's the one."

"Name please?"

Ken gave the info without thinking.

"Thank you, sir. You should receive your watch in two weeks. May I help you with anything else?"

"No, that's it."

He hung up. There. That felt good.

After all, a man couldn't have too many watches.

To keep track of time passing. Of a life passing him by.

He shut off the TV.

And the light.

And his conscience.

Eleven

Here on earth you will have
many trials and sorrows.
But take heart, because I have
overcome the world.

JOHN 16:33

An evening without Sig. A night. A morning.

A lifetime.

Deidre heard a key in the front door.

Nelly jumped up from the kitchen table and ran to answer it. "Maybe it's Daddy! Maybe they let him go."

Deidre and Karla followed—and were greeted by a surprised and embarrassed Agnes, their cleaning lady.

"Oh. Mrs. Kelly. I'm sorry. You're not usually home on Wednesday mornings so I'm used to using the key."

"Come in. It's fine. Come in."

Agnes came inside, lugging a handled tub of cleaning supplies. She closed the door with care, as if she didn't want to make a sound. Awkwardly, she looked at the three females before her. "I'm so sorry," she finally said. "When I heard on the news that Dr. Kelly had turned himself in for killing—"

"That's on the news?"

Agnes pointed toward the front door. "I heard it on the radio in my car. I almost turned around and went home, but then I thought that a clean house might be just what you need right now, so I came anyway." With a final nod she added, "Dr. Kelly didn't really do it, did he?"

The phone rang, saving Deidre from having to answer. She escaped into the kitchen. "Hello?"

"Is this Mrs. Kelly?"

"Yes."

"This is Wallace Jones from the *Daily News* and we were wondering if you would answer—"

She hung up. Her hand shook.

Karla was by her side, "Are you okay?"

"No."

"Me neither," Nelly said.

"Me neither," Karla said.

Deidre knew they needed to be alone. "Another day, Agnes?"

"Certainly, Mrs. Kelly. Just call."

Deidre let her out. Nelly attached herself to her mother's waist. "Everybody knows. Everybody."

"I'm afraid so, sweetie."

"I can't go to school ever again."

Deidre had let Nelly stay home yesterday, and again today, fearing the town would be awash in Sig's story. She wished she could tell Nelly everything would be all right, assure her that true friends would remain her friends, but there *was* no such assurance.

Karla stroked Nelly's hair. "Your daddy made a mistake, but he's owning up to it. That proves he's an honorable man. You should be very proud of him for that."

Nelly nodded, but it was halfhearted.

Deidre put her hand under her daughter's chin and offered her a wistful smile. "We'll make it through. Like we did before, after your father died."

Nelly hesitated a moment, her eyes searching her mother's. Finally she said, "This isn't the same as that."

No, it's not.

Karla took over. "Eventually things will go on as they were before."

"But Daddy won't be here."

Deidre answered, "You're right. Daddy won't be here. For a while. But he'll be back."

"When?"

"I don't know." She pulled Nelly under her arm and rested her chin against her head. "We have to be strong for him. And proud of him for stepping forward. Not many people would do that."

"I don't want to be strong." Nelly's words were without power.

"I'll help you. Nana will help you. We'll all help each other." Deidre felt a nudge to add one more helper to the list. She should tell Nelly that God would help them. And yet . . . old habits were hard to break. It would be awkward to mention God when Deidre hadn't mentioned him in years. It would be odd. Nelly might look at her weird and think, *Who do you think you are, talking about God stuff?* It would be—

In spite of her doubts and fears, the words spilled out. "God will help us get through this too, sweetie."

Nelly did not make a face. She did not bolt from the room. She surprised Deidre by nodding.

After which Karla smiled and put an arm around them both.

———

Deidre didn't want to be there.

Yet how could she not be at the courthouse? Besides, Nelly had insisted on accompanying her with a determination Deidre had rarely seen. "I have to see Daddy." Karla came too. They were a united front.

And so the three of them sat in the row nearest the defendant's chair—the chair where just two days previous Patti McCoy had sat to receive her false conviction.

But now, everything would be made right.

Actually, not at all, but it was the only way.

Nelly tugged at Deidre's sleeve and whispered, "There he is!" She moved to the edge of her chair as if holding herself back from leaping into her father's arms.

Sig immediately saw them and offered a weak wave and smile. He was led to his seat, where he reached back and took Nelly's outstretched hand for a brief moment before an officer stopped the contact. Sig gave Deidre her own smile. It was pensive and full of entreaty. *Forgive me. Forgive me.*

She could do nothing but smile back. The process was in motion. There was nothing anyone could do to stop it. You can't unring a bell, withdraw a confession, or . . . a lot of things.

The judge came in and everyone stood. Once settled he looked at Sig, then at the prosecutor's table, and said, "The court is satisfied with the signed confession of Sigmund T. Kelly and hereby sentences him to ten years for first-degree manslaughter."

Deidre heard a gasp and only after the fact realized it was her own.

Just that fast, the judge dismissed the court. They allowed Sig to hug his wife and daughter.

And it was done.

Deidre was glad to have Sig's lawyer, Tim Gothenburg, at her side as she was led out of the courthouse. And doubly glad that Karla had taken Nelly out a side entrance.

"Mrs. Kelly!" shouted a reporter.

Others rushed over.

Tim gave Deidre a slight nod. It was time to give the statement they'd carefully prepared. He set it up. "Mrs. Kelly will not answer any questions, but she does have a statement."

She was on. Deidre had gotten up early that morning to memorize it. "I am obviously very saddened by this turn of events but also very proud. My husband is an honorable man, who in a moment of instinctive emotion defended an attack on his life's work, the Kelly Pediatric Foundation. A man died, and we grieve that tragic fact. And as all actions have consequences, my husband has come forward to accept his. We regret any pain and suffering this has—"

"But, Mrs. Kelly, you were on the jury. You helped convict Patti McCoy of your husband's crime. Did you know he was guilty?"

"Did you somehow rig it in order to *be* on that jury?"

"Why didn't your husband come forward sooner?"

"Why didn't he stop Patti's trial?"

She had no answer for them that wouldn't elicit a dozen more questions. As for her own crime . . . she was not being held responsible for any wrongdoing for being on the jury when her husband was guilty of the crime because technically, she'd been coerced by Sig to pursue it. The court knew that much, but not that she knew Brett. She was not being held responsible because Sig had made it a part of his plea bargain to the court. He'd agreed to take the rap for everything as long as his wife was left alone.

The reporters' questions continued and one broke through the chaos: "Mrs. Kelly, did your husband and you conspire in all this?"

A surge of panic swept through her. She looked at Tim, seeking guidance. But before he could say anything, she said, "No comment" and hurried away.

No comment. No comment. The words of the guilty.
If they only knew.

———

Nelly sat on the family room couch, nestled under Karla's arm. The TV was off. The TV was the enemy.

Deidre stood at the edge of the room, uncertain what to do next.

"Well," Karla said. "That was unpleasant."

"It was horrible seeing Daddy led away. What do we do now, Mom?"

She had no idea. If allowed, she would have yelled to the room, *"It's not fair! I've had two husbands and lost two husbands! Two good men gone!"*

Then suddenly, she knew where she wanted to be. Needed to be.

If it might help *her,* what about Karla and Nelly?

It was worth a shot. Nothing positive could come out of sitting around, brooding.

"Get your coats on," she said.

"Why?"

"Just come."

———

Deidre wasn't a cemetery kind of person. She found them creepy and negative. But today, the cemetery was exactly what she needed. And as she walked along the grass-lined path under the canopy of trees, hand in hand with her daughter and mother-in-law, she was surprised to find calm accompanying her.

After confessing her guilt to God, and with the promise

that someday she might have the chance to confess to Sig, she had one more person to tell.

She reached her destination.

"Oh, dear," Karla said. "The flowers I brought last visit are gone."

Deidre didn't mention that she'd been negligent in ever bringing flowers. Nelly had asked to go to the grave that first Memorial Day after Don died, but Deidre had said no. A cemetery wasn't a proper place for a little child.

How about an older child?

She would see.

Deidre moved to the headstone and traced her husband's name: Donald Henry Polland. The feel of the cold carving against her fingers was nothing like her husband. Don had been soft and warm, without sharp edges.

My opposite.

They sat on a bench nearby and Deidre accepted the chill and hardness of the stone as appropriate to the cold, hard woman she'd become.

Yet she hadn't always been that way. When Don was alive she'd let his warmth rub off on her. But with his exit, she'd lost more than his presence. She'd lost his example, his encouragement, and the way he had of making her want to be more than she was. Better than she was.

But I've had other things to worry about beyond character. I've had to survive.

Baloney. She had to stop falling back on that excuse. Although it was true, and though times had been hard, that didn't give her the right to relinquish her character. Her attributes. Or the good person she'd almost become under Don's influence.

She drew in a deep breath and let out the words, "I forgot."

"Forgot what, Deidre?" It was Karla.

Deidre started. She wasn't sure why she'd said the words. What did they mean?

With her mental query, she received an answer. *You forgot who you were and became someone else.*

That was it. That was the key, the start of her downfall. For as she'd left Dee-Dee Polland behind and taken up the part of Deidre Kelly—with gusto—she hadn't added to the Dee-Dee that Don had helped her become; she'd abandoned her. She'd thrown out the baby with the bathwater, let go of the good she'd attained, virtually negating all the trials and struggles and victories that had begun the job of fine-tuning the woman who was Dee-Dee. She'd shut Dee-Dee in a closet, locked it, and started over as someone new.

But that someone new was without roots. By shunning everything from her old life, Deidre Kelly had been born an orphan from any life. She'd had no inheritance, birthright, or heritage. She'd become a woman without a past, with no source, baseline, or bedrock. It was as if Sig had plucked her and Nelly from the air, placed them in his lovely home, and said, "Begin."

But she hadn't known how to start, where to begin, or where she was going.

She still wasn't certain.

Karla had told her not to race ahead without getting direction and to stop thinking she knew best. The image Karla had created of walking ahead of God, not looking back because she knew he wouldn't approve . . .

I didn't want him to stop me. I didn't want anyone to stop me.

As if to punctuate her statement a sparrow lit on Don's headstone, bobbed its head a few times, then flew away.

The truth was, without Don to coax the good out of Dee-Dee, without him nudging her to rise to her potential, she'd rushed ahead with little thought to others or what was truly best. She'd rushed through the trappings of living a life, but she hadn't really lived. She hadn't grown. She hadn't prospered.

And in spite of the temptation to blame Sig and his busy career that often left her to fend alone, she couldn't. Was she totally dependent? Didn't she have a brain, a personality, a will of her own? Wasn't she responsible for her own destiny—sink or swim?

"What should we do now?" Nelly asked.

Karla took her hand. "Care for a prayer?"

"I think that might be perfect," Deidre said. And she meant it. For what could it hurt?

The three females held hands and bowed their heads. Karla did the talking for them. It was a prayer of contrition, a prayer asking for forgiveness and wisdom and discernment. It was a prayer for Sig, for Patti, for the three of them. Karla created a prayer cover over them all, tucking them in with a spiritual warmth that seemed to make everything more stable, more possible.

"And finally, God, help us see a plan in all this. Help us do what we're supposed to do. Help us never feel alone. Because we're not alone. We have each other and we have you. In Jesus' name, amen."

"Amen," Nelly said.

"Amen," Deidre said. She let go of their hands. "If you don't mind, I'd like to be here alone for a bit. I have some things to share with Don." She gave Karla a knowing look.

Karla put her arm around Nelly's shoulders. "Let's go find the oldest headstone."

Deidre waited until they were out of earshot. Then she began, "Don, there's something you need to know. Something I need to confess."

———

Deidre was done. Her confession to Don was complete and she felt better for it. She stood up from the bench and looked for Karla and Nelly. They were across the cemetery, headed toward the car. Nelly shuffled through fallen leaves under a canopy of red, gold, and orange. Except for the tombstones, it was a lovely sight.

Deidre did not return to the path but meandered toward the car by walking among the graves. Halfway there, she came around a grove of trees and spotted another mourner sitting beside a headstone. Although the cemetery had been empty before, someone else had joined them, visiting someone they loved.

Deidre did not wish to intrude, so she took a sharp right to give her privacy.

"Hey!"

Deidre stopped. Had the woman called to her? She backtracked tentatively.

Then she saw who it was.

Patti McCoy.

Patti had been sitting on the grass but now stood. She wore khaki pants and a pink blouse that was too big.

If only I could pretend I didn't see her.

It was too late for that.

Patti brushed off her knees. "Weren't you on the jury?"

Although Deidre could never imagine herself running through a cemetery . . . "Yes. I'm so sorry about all that hap—"

Patti shook her head once. "It's more than that. You're more than that. You're the wife of the man who killed my Brett. Are you Debbie?"

"Deidre." She let her correction stand as her affirmation. She had no idea what to say. The word *sorry* seemed absurd.

Patti held her arms across her chest as if she were cold. "I don't understand any of this. I mean, why did your husband kill Brett and how did you get on the jury and why didn't you say something and—" She repeated her first sentence. "I don't understand any of this."

"I know. I'm sorry. I'm sorry Sig . . . I'm sorry I didn't . . ." Deidre shrugged and immediately wished she could take the gesture back.

Patti stood silent a moment, as if studying her. Then she said, "Your husband is a good man."

Deidre felt her jaw drop. If she had written a hundred lines for Patti to say next, this would not have been one of them. "Yes, he is."

"I talked to him yesterday. When he was in jail."

"You did?"

She nodded. "I had to thank him. For coming forward. For getting me out."

But he killed the man you loved.

Patti looked down at the grave, and for the first time Deidre noticed whose it was: Brett Matthew Lerner.

She took a step back. Appalled. Horrified. The need to flee intensified. She couldn't breathe.

"I miss him," Patti said, gazing at the grave.

Suddenly a stream of words spilled out, as if a dam had broken. "How can you be so kind? Brett is dead because of—"

Patti got to her knees again, adjusting the blooms in the pot of gold mums on the grave. "I know. And I am mad. Sad. Frustrated. Confused." She looked up at Deidre. "But what good does it do? I was mad at being arrested for something I didn't do, mad at losing the baby, mad at being convicted." She shook her head slowly. "It ate me up. That first night after the conviction . . . I prayed a ton. I don't even remember what I prayed for, but it was the only thing that made me feel better.

Like somehow things would work out. And then they did. The next day your husband came forward."

Deidre didn't know what to say.

"I forgive him, you know. I forgive everyone. Even myself for being dumb enough to believe Brett's promises. I don't know how that would have worked out if he was still around, but . . ." She sighed.

"I'm sorry, Patti. For all of it."

"I know. It's all anybody can be. Sorry."

They stayed there a moment, the innocent woman kneeling on the grave and the guilty one standing nearby.

Then the latter walked away and did not look back.

He gave his life to free us from
every kind of sin, to cleanse us,
and to make us his very own people,
totally committed to doing good deeds.

TITUS 2:14

*B*obby leaned low, eyeballing the carving on the dresser leg. The point of the leaf was a little off. A little too wide. He positioned his chisel and sliced off an infinitesimal amount. But just enough.

Becky burst through the door of the shop, bringing with her a gust of winter wind. She quickly closed the door behind her. "Brrrrr! It's going to snow. I can feel it." On her hip sat their youngest, three-year-old Tally.

Bobby blew away the remnants of his chiseling and felt the edge. A little sandpaper would take care of its roughness. "What's up, you two?"

Becky pulled two pieces of paper from the pocket of her jacket. "Two more orders. A rocker and a hutch."

Bobby left his work behind. Sure enough, there were two more orders. One going to Vermont and the other to New Mexico. "If someone had told me I would be making furniture for people across the country . . ."

"I told you."

"Someone besides you."

She let Tally down in order to put her hands on her hips. "Isn't my word good enough for you?"

"I stand corrected." He kissed her, then Tally, who immediately sat down in the sawdust and started to play with the leftover pieces of wood. Sawdust was a part of their lives now—in the shop and even in the house.

Bobby looked back to the orders in hand. "I'm not sure I have time to do these, Beck. With the orders I got from people wanting things by Christmas—"

"These people aren't asking for Christmas. They'll wait. People wait for quality."

"You're going to give me a big head."

"Nonsense. Besides, you'll have lots of time to fill the new orders."

"Why is that?"

"Because you'll quit driving a cab."

It was his last outside job. He'd quit the theater concessions job a month after the trial when orders from his Web site had started to trickle in. But to give up his last stable employment . . .

She slipped her hand through his arm, pulling him close to her side. "Come on, Bobby. Why do you find your success so hard to believe?"

"Because it's success. And it's me."

Becky extended her hand to their daughter. "Come on, Tally-girl; want to help me butter the bread for lunch?"

At the mention of food, the scraps of wood were forgotten. Becky brushed off her daughter's backside and legs. "Lunch will be ready in a half hour."

This time when Becky left, the cold air that snuck in didn't affect Bobby. Her warmth lingered. As did her faith.

And his.

He picked up the chisel and got back to work.

———

"And who will give three hundred for this putter used by Tom Watson in the U.S. Open?" The auctioneer pointed to one bidder, then another, as the price rose.

Ken stood at the back of the ballroom and squeezed Ronnie's hand. "We're getting good prices," he whispered.

"It's good stuff. Thanks to you," she whispered back.

And it was true. Ken may not have ever been a big shot on the golf circuit, but he knew the big shots and was good at cajoling them into donating some of their golf items for charity auctions, like this one to benefit pediatric AIDS patients.

Philip popped his head in the door leading to the hall and motioned them over. It had been wonderful working with his son the past few years. And Ronnie. Although Ronnie stuck to her declaration that she couldn't be romantically involved with him anymore, she had held true to being his friend. His best friend.

As for the other women who'd always come and gone in Ken's life . . . somehow working for an AIDS charity and living a risky lifestyle didn't go together. At age fifty-eight he'd learned to behave himself. Besides, Philip had introduced him to a real nice woman at his church. Ken was taking it slow regarding that—and everything else. In most areas of life, Ken was not a fast mover.

They walked into the corridor. Philip was practically glowing. "Bill just came back to tell me we've already passed the fifty-thousand mark."

Ken was stunned. Although he knew the auction was going well, he'd had no idea— He looked down at the list of items up for bid. "We're only two-thirds through."

"I know. Isn't it cool?" Philip flashed his boyish smile.

Someone came out of the auditorium and called to them. "Ken! One of your trophies just went for two hundred."

A laugh escaped. "I am truly stunned."

"Don't be," Ronnie said. "You were somebody." She bumped her shoulder into his. "You are somebody."

Philip ran off to assume his auction duties, calling back to them. "We'll have to celebrate. I'll buy."

It was Ronnie's turn to laugh. "Will wonders never cease?"

Apparently not. Thank God.

———

Although she kept her face neutral, inside Abigail was screaming, *If I have to hear one more chubby old man sing "If I Were a Rich Man," badly . . .*

The latest auditioner finished. "Thank you, Mr. Montrose. We'll let you know." *Let you know you didn't make it.*

Jessica, Abigail's assistant, handed her the next tryout application, then called out a name. "Jack Crawford."

A burly man sauntered onto the stage. Abigail blinked. He looked familiar. Then she put the face and name with a place. "Jack from the trial, three years ago?" she asked.

"Yeah," he said, holding some music as a shield in front of him. "It's me."

"I didn't know you could sing."

"Actually, that has yet to be determined."

She nodded and waved a hand. "Go ahead. Show me what you've got."

He raised his music, adjusted his reading glasses, and began to sing.

Well.

No one was more surprised than Abigail—except maybe Jack himself. Uncharacteristically, she did not cut him off before he was through.

Jessica leaned toward her and whispered, "He's good."

Indeed he was.

And he wasn't the only acquaintance Abigail had heard sing today. Margaret Timmons—the woman to whom Abigail had given her part in *Annie*—tried out for the part of Golde. Margaret had a good chance of being cast.

As did Jack.

He finished his song and let out a huge sigh of relief. Blustery, cocky Jack the mechanic with the greasy fingernails was not Mr. Confidence now.

But he should be. Abigail sat forward in her chair. "Very good, Jack. You surprised me."

"I surprised me too. But when we were on the jury together, and I met you . . . you got me thinking about the theater again. I used to do this stuff. Eons ago. It took me a while to get up my nerve to try again, but . . . here I am."

"Good for you," she said. "We'll be contacting you about callbacks."

"Thanks."

As he left the stage, Abigail put a big nine—out of ten—on his sheet.

Jessica glanced at it. "Do we have a Tevye?" she asked.

"Could be."

It was nice playing a part on this side of the stage. Very satisfying.

"Next!"

———

"He's coming!"

Deidre and Karla got out of their car. Fifteen-year-old Nelly rushed to the prison gate. Sig walked toward them with a small bag of belongings tucked under his arm.

Nelly waved. "Dad!"

His face lit up and he waved back.

Karla moved around to Deidre's side. "You can wave too, you know."

"I'm too nervous to wave. Three years, Karla. It's been three years."

Karla slipped her hand around Deidre's elbow. "You'll be fine. You'll both be fine."

Deidre didn't have time to agree—or argue—for at that moment Sig came through the gate that led from imprisonment to freedom.

Nelly ran into his arms. He picked her up off the ground and swung her around. "My girl. My dear, dear girl."

Nelly was crying. "We've missed you, Dad. We've missed you so much."

He kissed both her cheeks, drinking her in with his eyes. "And I you."

Then it was Deidre's turn. She did not run into Sig's arms, nor he into hers. They stood a few feet apart and looked at each other.

"Hi," she said.

"Hi," he said.

Karla threw her hands into the air. "Hi? You can do better than that."

They hugged awkwardly. Sig was skinnier than before. Less substantial. Less strong.

Deidre hoped the last wasn't true. Because getting out of prison early for good behavior was the easy part. Facing the people in town, dealing with a reduced lifestyle of a smaller house, economical cars, and no money for international travel would certainly be difficult. And no foundation work. Perhaps that was the hardest of all.

The Kelly Pediatric Foundation had wisely changed its

name to the Helping Hands Pediatric Foundation. The other doctors on staff were continuing the good work Sig had started. Continuing without him.

"I'm okay with that," Sig had told her more than once. "I didn't give them much choice. The work must continue. The work is larger than one man."

Admirable words. Gracious words.

And sincere words.

Deidre believed him. It was only her own disappointment that tinged his benevolence. *She* missed the foundation. She missed being the wife of its founder. And though she'd often complained about the fund-raising and social events, she missed those too.

"Shall we go home?" Sig said.

"Shotgun!" Nelly said.

Sig took Deidre's hand and kissed it. He spoke to Nelly, but his eyes were on his wife. "Not this time, Daughter. I'd like my wife in the seat beside me, as it should be."

With her nerves still raging, Deidre took her proper place.

———

The Kellys—and Karla—enjoyed an amazing dinner that had taken the women three days to prepare. The kitchen in their much-smaller house was minimal, so they'd suffered a lot of bumping into each other, but they'd gotten it done. And now they'd all eaten past the point of comfort.

Dinner accomplished, Karla and Nelly made themselves scarce in their bedrooms upstairs, leaving Sig and Deidre alone in the family room.

"Want some more tea?" Deidre asked.

Sig patted the couch beside him. "I want you. Here. Beside me. As close as possible."

Deidre hesitated, and it wasn't because she didn't long for his presence or his touch.

Because she did.

She sat beside him. He put his arm around her and cuddled close. "Mmm," he said. "Human contact. You don't realize how much you can miss a simple thing like a hug."

Deidre closed her eyes and tried to enjoy the moment. Tried to relax in his arms. Tried to let happiness—

"What's wrong?" he asked.

"Nothing," she said.

He gently pushed her away in order to see her face. "Tell me."

There was something about his eyes that told her he truly wanted to know. But that didn't dispel her hesitancy.

He glanced about the room. "Do you mind the smaller house that much?"

"No, it's fine. It's plenty big."

"Do you mind the idea of me being just a regular doctor? Starting a practice from scratch?"

"No. If you're happy, I'm—" She stopped herself. She ached to let him know what was on her mind. For three years she'd waited for God to give her an opening to tell Sig the whole truth. But every time she'd thought *This is it*, something had happened or been said to change the direction of the moment. Would the same thing happen again today?

Sig angled his body toward hers, bringing one leg onto the cushion between them. He looked ready to listen.

She waited for the phone to ring, for Nelly to interrupt them, for Sig to talk about the weather . . . some detour to the subject that begged for release.

Sig sat in silence. He studied her face. He took her hand. "What's troubling you, Deidre?"

And with that one question, her prison gate was opened.

She rushed through before it clanged shut. "Me," she said.
"I'm troubling me. The me who I am is troubling me."

He smiled and swept a stray strand of her hair behind her
ear. "I love who you are."

She shook her head adamantly. "You shouldn't. Not at
all. I'm not the woman you think I am, Sig, or the woman you
thought I was."

"So your name is Mary or Linda or Brunhilde or
something?"

"Don't," she said. "This is serious."

"Then just say it. Whatever's on your mind. We've already
lived a nightmare. Nothing you say can be worse than what
I've put us through."

Wanna bet?

Her old impulse to run returned. How many times had she
fought this battle against flight? How many times would she
fight it in the future?

But she was still here. Still around. That said something.

Sig put a hand on her knee. "I love you. Does that help?"

Actually . . .

Deidre sprang from the couch and moved so the coffee
table sat between them. "No, it doesn't help. Because you
shouldn't love me. You should hate me. Despise me."

"Why would I—?"

She raised a hand, stopping him. "You wanted to hear
what's bothering me; you're going to hear it. All of it. It's
been eating at me for three years—if not longer than that." She
sighed. "I am a master at ignorance, at not allowing myself
to see what's wrong, at pretending I'm handling everything
wonderfully when I'm not handling anything at all. This
stupid need I have to control—"

"Deidre, just tell me."

Her hands were at her sides, making fists. She tucked

them across her chest. "First off, I did more than just date Brett Lerner. I . . . he raped me. Nelly is his child."

Through all her practice sessions regarding what she would say—and how she would say it when the chance arose—never had she thought about stating it in such a blunt manner.

Sig just sat there. Then his mouth dropped open and his head started to shake in short bursts of *no.*

"It's true, Sig. He raped me; I got pregnant and had the baby."

"But I thought Don—"

"Don *was* her father. In every sense but one. Even he didn't know about Brett. He knew Nelly was my child from a previous relationship, but he didn't know the circumstances behind her conception. I couldn't tell anyone that. I couldn't risk Nelly ever finding out she was the child of rape."

"It wasn't her fault."

"I know. It was mine. I was the one who trusted Brett, who was too stupid or naive to realize the type of man he was."

"You could have told *me* about it."

"The secret was old by the time I met you . . . and then you fell in love with Nelly and—"

"I fell in love with you. . . ."

Why was it so hard for her to accept that? "You shouldn't have loved me, Sig. That's the other secret I've kept from you. Because I didn't love you. I was a widow with no money and few hopes for the future. Nelly needed a father. Nelly needed an operation. I used you to get the two of us out of a bad situation."

"I know."

She took a step back. "What?"

"I know that you were interested in me for what I could do to better your life—and Nelly's."

"Then why did you marry me?"

"Because I fell in love with *you*. And Nelly. And because of that, I wanted to give you all the things you didn't have. I wanted to give you everything *I* had."

"Even if I didn't deserve—?" Deidre put a hand to her mouth, stifling a sob.

He went to her and pulled her into his arms. "Love has nothing to do with what we deserve. It just is. And when it shows up we need to embrace it as tightly as possible. And cherish it. And help it to grow. That's more important than any career, any project, even any calling. 'Three things will last forever—faith, hope, and love—and the greatest of these is love.' You and Nelly and Karla are my family. You are why I'm here."

"But—"

He tipped her chin upward. "But nothing. 'We love each other because he loved us first.' Without stipulation, reservation, or even logic. Can you accept that?"

"I am accepting it. I have been. A little at a time."

"What if I spend the rest of our lives helping you accept it?"

"It may take that long."

"Then I'll enjoy the process."

He leaned down and kissed her.

And she kissed him back.

Live a life filled with love,

following the example of Christ.

He loved us and offered himself as a sacrifice for us,

a pleasing aroma to God.

EPHESIANS 5:2

Scripture Verses in *Solemnly Swear*

Discussion Questions

1. In chapter 3, Abigail sits beside Bobby during a break. She is surprised to find him listening to classical music. We impose stereotypes upon others and have them inflicted upon ourselves. Yet stereotypes exist because there often *is* an element of truth in them. How do you see stereotypes played out in your daily life? Who has surprised you?

2. All the characters in *Solemnly Swear* play a part: Bobby (the Nobody) pretends to be less than he is. Ken (the Somebody) acts more important than he is. Abigail (the Has-Been) acts like the fame of her past is all there is. Deidre (the User) pretends her past choices are acceptable because she acted in order to obtain a secure life for herself and her child. Did these characters choose the parts they play or have they been unwillingly cast into the parts by circumstances? How does playing these parts keep them from achieving their true purpose? What part do you play? Are you playing it willingly? What is the danger in playing a part?

3. The emotional scars of Deidre's past led to her marry two men for the wrong reasons. Put yourself in her shoes. Go back years before, to the time when she first dealt with Brett. . . . What other choices could she have made? How might her life have been different? better? worse? What do you think of the choices she *did* make?

4. Fear is an underlying emotion for each character. What do each of them fear? (Deidre? Bobby? Abigail? Ken?) What do you fear? How can that fear be relieved?

5. Each of the characters seeks control. How important is control in your life? Have you learned to surrender control to Christ? If so, how? If not, why not?

6. Deidre tries to hide part of her life from God. Only when she stops the game does she find release. When have you hidden something from God? What was the result? What are you still hiding from him? What's holding you back from being honest with him?

7. Deidre is guilty of running ahead with her own plans, unwilling to hear what God has in mind. Name a time you've run ahead, wanting your own way. What happened? Did you finally let God catch up with you and lead? What happened then?

8. Sig is a good man who helps children. Yet with Brett he makes a huge mistake. What do you think about his initial decision to try to hide his guilt and let another—a person whose life didn't have as much obvious "worth" as his own—take the blame? What do you think about his decision to come forward? What do you think would have happened if he had *not* come forward? What would you have done in his situation?

9. The Kellys have to deal with the issue of violence with Brett and also with Nelly's bully. Is violence ever justified?

10. Many of the characters have painful pasts or have made choices they regret. Forgiving others and ourselves is one way to move on. How have you dealt with painful issues from your own past? What issue still dogs you? How can you move on, free of its power?

11. In chapter 11 Deidre realizes she should tell Nelly that God is there to help, yet she hesitates because she hadn't talked about God for years. She was afraid of Nelly's reaction. When have you been afraid to talk about God issues? Why? Did you do it anyway? How did it turn out?

12. Bobby has trouble believing his God-given talent has worth. He is unwilling to let God "do his stuff." What talent are you hiding or diminishing from its true potential? What's the worst that could happen if you committed to using your gifts fully? What's the best?

13. In the epilogue Sig alludes to God's unconditional love when he tells Deidre that "love has nothing to do with what we deserve. It just is." When have you loved someone when they didn't deserve it? When have you received love when you didn't deserve it? Who needs your love now? How have you felt God's unconditional love in your life?

A Note from the Author

Dear Reader,

Shakespeare said, "All the world's a stage, and all the men and women merely players: they have their exits and their entrances; and one man in his time plays many parts." Some good parts and some bad. Some in public and some in private. The trouble arises when the distinction between our public persona and our private one is vast. At such times are we pretending to be something we aren't?

H. Jackson Browne said, "Our character is what we do when we think no one is looking." When the curtains are drawn, who am I? What kind of person am I? Am I better or worse than the person I present to the world?

In *Solemnly Swear* I wanted to create characters who were playing parts—who were stuck in a part. I wondered whether they would recognize that they weren't being true to their real selves. Would they come to see that the part they were playing wasn't as satisfying as they thought it was? Would they discover that being honest with themselves *about* themselves offered release and freedom? Would they feel the need to seek out their true part and purpose?

The biggest consequence to playing a part is believing it's who we are. We hide within our roles, sometimes not letting even God behind the curtain. We cover our eyes and think he can't see us, can't see what we're doing or what's in our hearts and minds. It's exhausting work, keeping all that a secret. Only when we let God in do we give him the chance to direct the development of our character and mold it into something pleasing to ourselves, the world, and most importantly, to him. He's the only one who can tighten the boundary between public and private, making me a stronger, unified person. I once wrote an article based on this phrase: "Characters live to be noticed; people with character notice how they live." Our best character is derived from and through him.

I must admit the journey I took while writing this book was not always pleasant. Although Abigail, Ken, and Bobby behaved, Deidre and Sig did not. They kept hiding from me, teasing me with "This is who I am. Really. I'm not kidding this time" only to repeatedly lead me astray. Actually, unlike most characters (most people) they pretended to be *worse* than they really were. Stern and hard, needing no one. They had chips on their shoulders, daring me to knock them off.

When they were misbehaving like that, I didn't like them much, but finally, after fighting with them through many edits, I broke through their patina of toughness and found their softer, vulnerable cores. And when I did, I was allowed to show you, the reader, the private times when they weren't the mighty doctor and the assured socialite. I liked them with their masks off because I empathized with them and understood them better.

Can we be creating similar problems in our own lives? Do we keep our masks on, denying our friends and loved ones access to our true selves? And if our true selves are devoid of admirable traits, shouldn't we do something about it?

The saving grace is that God knows us and loves us no matter what part we play. However, we will be able to love him (and ourselves) better if we are honest and open and let him in. We have nothing to lose and everything to gain. So do it. Honestly and candidly introduce yourself to the Almighty and see what happens. I promise you won't be disappointed.

"Now may our Lord Jesus Christ himself and God our

Father, who loved us and by his grace gave us eternal comfort and a wonderful hope, comfort you and strengthen you in every good thing you do and say" (2 Thessalonians 2:16-17).

Blessings on your journey as you let God cast you in just the right part.

Nancy Moser

About the Author

NANCY MOSER is the best-selling author of seventeen novels including *The Good Nearby, Mozart's Sister,* and the Christy award–winning *Time Lottery.* She also coauthored the Sister Circle series with Campus Crusade cofounder Vonette Bright. Nancy is a motivational speaker, and information about her Said So Sister Seminar can be found at www.nancymoser.com and www.sistercircles.com. Nancy and her husband, Mark, have three children and live in the Midwest.

Turn the page for an exciting preview
from *The Good Nearby* by Nancy Moser.

Available now at bookstores and online.

TYNDALE
FICTION

www.tyndalefiction.com

CP0190

Margery Lamborn hated to lie. And yet . . .

What choice did she have?

She looked at her husband as he lathered his face to shave. Mick was waiting for her answer to the question "What are you doing up so early?" As a cocktail waitress at the Chug & Chew she rarely got up before nine.

Except today.

She couldn't risk meeting his eyes so she turned her back to the mirror and folded the bath towel that he'd wadded into the space between towel bar and wall. She adjusted the volume on the radio that sat on the clothes hamper. She didn't need any competition from Kelly Clarkson even if the girl was singing about playing it safe by staying on the sidewalk. Margery could certainly relate to that one.

"I have a few errands," she finally said.

"Don't write any checks. Rent's due."

"I won't."

"Speaking of money . . . can I have twenty from your tip stash? I owe Barry on a football bet."

She hated when Mick bet on sports, because he lost more than he won. If only he'd realize how hard she worked for that twenty dollars' worth of tips . . . what she put up with. The comments, the hands, the stares as she wore her skimpy bar-girl uniform. And a week ago, the drunk guy who'd pushed her up against her car when she was leaving and nearly—

"Marg? The money?"

She couldn't stall with the towel any longer. She faced him. "Sure. I'll leave it on the dresser."

"Good girl." His hand found her behind and he pulled her close enough to kiss. She pushed away, wiping the shaving cream from her face. So much for her carefully applied lipstick. Mick laughed.

Very funny.

She left the tiny bathroom of their double-wide and headed out before he could ask any more questions. If she'd been smart she would have made the appointment for later in the morning, long after he'd left for his mechanic's job. But when Dr. Quigley, the pharmacist at the drugstore, had said eight, who was Margery to argue?

Margery didn't *do* arguing. "Keep the peace" was her motto. Sometimes she felt as if the bulk of her life were spent in one continuous preventative act—looking ahead, checking the possible outcomes, guessing the consequences, constantly weighing and choosing the path of least resistance so the boat wouldn't be rocked and peaceful waters would cover the earth.

Mick never thought that way. He just lived. He just was. He didn't spend a moment thinking of what he would say, or how she would react to anything he might do. He just did it.

It was upsetting. How dare he coast through life clueless to the delicate balance between trouble and calm? Since he didn't care what effect his actions had on her, why should she care?

But she did. And amid her anger, she often envied him. To be so certain of his space, his identity, his moments . . . Margery took one moment at a time and weighed each one, hoping—just hoping—she'd get it right and wouldn't cause too much trouble *or* be called to suffer through something she'd messed up.

Her habit of walking the baseline made her current road risky. It wasn't that she hadn't looked ahead and imagined Mick's reaction to her trying to get a new job—that was as inevitable as a drunk spilling his drink—and if she told anyone else of her worry, they'd think she was overreacting big-time.

Which she probably was, but so be it.

Fifteen minutes after leaving the house, Margery parked in front of the drugstore, shut off the car, and leaned against the steering wheel, trying to find the courage to open the door and get out. Maybe she should forget the whole thing. Go home. Keep things as they were.

She fumbled putting the keys back in the ignition.

"Margery?"

She put a hand to her chest and sucked in a breath. An older woman with pumpkin-red hair and thick glasses peered in the open passenger window.

"You scared me," Margery said.

"It's a lifelong trait," the woman answered. "If you *are* Margery, I'm Gladys Quigley." She stood up straight, then stooped low again. "Actually, even if you aren't Margery, I'm still Gladys Quigley. Can't escape that if I tried. So now that we know who *I* am . . ."

"I'm Margery. Margery Lamborn."

"Punctual. Two brownie points." She jangled a crowded key chain.

Margery followed the woman inside Neighbor's Drugstore.

Dr. Quigley flipped on the lights. "Follow me to the office. We'll chat back there."

The office was tiny and contained a metal desk with a computer, two chairs, and a four-drawer file cabinet. What made it unusual were the travel posters that lined the room floor to ceiling, covering every inch of wall like wallpaper. Venice ran into Paris, which butted up to the Alps, with half of Mozambique cut off at the ceiling.

"You like?"

Margery turned full circle in order to see every wall. "Have you been to all these places?"

"Most." She pointed to the upper corner above the file cabinet. "Still working on Australia and New Zealand. If only they weren't so drattedly far away. Thirty-three hours on the plane. Though I love to fly, that one's pushing even my tolerance button. I mean, how many movies and pretzels can a person tolerate?"

"Movies?"

"On the plane. They'd probably show four. Maybe five."

"I didn't know they had movies on airplanes. 'Course, I've never been on a plane at all."

"You afraid of flying or something?"

"I don't think so. I just haven't had the chance to go anywhere."

"Anywhere *yet*," Dr. Quigley said. "You'll have a chance one of these days. If you make it a priority."

Priorities were rent, utilities, and food. Margery couldn't see how travel for fun would ever override any of that. Especially now since she was applying for a job as a checkout clerk that would mean a cut in pay. She and Mick would never have a better life if she took a step backward like this. Maybe the Chug & Chew wasn't so bad . . .

Suddenly full of doubt, Margery took a step toward the door. "I'm sorry, Dr. Quigley, but I've changed my mind. I can't apply for this job after all. I'm sorry for taking your time and—"

Dr. Quigley signaled time-out. "Whoa there, girl. What happened in the last five seconds that's making you run? I didn't scare you that bad, did I?"

Margery stopped in the doorway. "No, it's just that . . ." She ran a hand along the doorjamb.

"Out with it."

She didn't want to explain. She didn't even know this woman, though she sensed she might *like* to know her. "I really can't go into it."

"Oh pooh." Dr. Quigley pulled the guest chair close and patted it. "Sit. Though people have accused me of going over my allotted words per lifetime, I do know how to listen if I've a mind to. Which I do right now. So take advantage of it, girl. Sit and tell me what's going on."

To leave now would be rude. Besides, if Gladys Quigley had been around the world, maybe she knew a thing or two about life. What could it hurt? Margery was always open to suggestions.

She sat down and Dr. Quigley took a seat in the wheeled desk chair. "All right. Step one completed. Now fire away. How about starting out by telling me why you wanted to apply for this job in the first place."

Margery hesitated. Why *did* she want this job? "I . . . I like people."

"That's a job-interview answer. I want a real one."

Put off guard, Margery dug out the truth. "I want to quit my other job. I want a regular job."

"This other job is irregular?"

Margery looked past Dr. Quigley and focused on the Eiffel Tower. "I'm a cocktail waitress at the Chug & Chew."

"Can't say as I've partaken of their cuisine."

"Burgers, nachos, beer . . ."

"And . . . ?"

Margery sensed Dr. Quigley wasn't wanting an extended menu. "And skimpy outfits, guys hitting on me, me coming home smelling like booze and smoke, long hours, and never seeing Mick."

Dr. Quigley pulled Margery's left hand close and peered at the ring finger. "Mick's your boyfriend?"

"Husband."

She pointed at Margery's vacant ring finger. "No ring."

"We were only seventeen. There wasn't money for a ring."

Dr. Quigley's eyebrows rose. "You're a ways from seventeen now."

"I'm twenty-seven."

"There hasn't been a chance for him to get you a ring in ten years?"

It was a sore point that went far beyond lack of money. "He says he's bought me one."

"Where is it?"

Margery looked at the Roman Colosseum. If only she could escape there right now . . . "He has it. He told me he has it. He just hasn't found the right time to give it to me yet." *I haven't earned it yet.*

Dr. Quigley rubbed her forehead. "I'm guessing a discussion regarding your husband's lack of romantic skills would best be held another time. Let's get back to your job at the bar. You want to quit."

"I do. But I make decent money—with the tips." She looked at the purse in her lap. The stitching on the strap was coming out. "This job here . . . from what you said on the phone, this job pays less." She looked up and offered a smile. She didn't want to offend. "But it does have normal hours. I'm hoping Mick would like that." She shrugged, knowing he wouldn't care. "I'm hoping."

"How's your eyesight?"

It seemed an odd question, but maybe it had something to do with Dr. Quigley's thick glasses. "It's good. Real good."

The woman studied her, as if thinking things through. "To be honest it's not like I've had a lot of applicants. And if you've been handling the punks and jerks at the Chug & Chew I figure you can handle the normal folk who come in here for TUMS, film, and prescriptions. I like the idea of getting you away from that place. What if I pay you a bit above what I quoted before? How about eight bucks an hour to start? We'll talk about getting more after you've proven yourself."

Margery wanted to cry. She shook Dr. Quigley's hand vigorously. "I won't let you down. I won't."

"I know you won't, and call me Gladys. Later, you'll meet

Bernice, the other checkout clerk, and King. He's my partner and fellow pharmacist."

"King?"

Gladys rolled her eyes. "Dr. King Marlowe. He doesn't like the name much, but in his own way, it suits him. Not that he's high-and-mighty. Just the opposite. There's not a more down-to-earth, dependable partner than King. He's a widower with a son in college. Why another woman hasn't snagged him is a mystery he'd prefer I stop trying to solve—though I do my part by connecting him with eligibles."

"How old is he?" Margery asked.

Gladys smiled. "And here I thought you were married."

"I—" Margery felt herself blush—"I'm sorry. I shouldn't have asked."

"Oh, ask away; there are few secrets round here. King is fifty." She paused a moment. "Seems he pretty much spans the difference between your twenty-seven and my sixty-five. You'll like him. Most do." She stood. "Now, back to the basics . . . the hours vary, but most evenings we'll get you home to have dinner with your darling hubby. Can you start today?"

"Now?"

"Now is always good."

She had a job. A regular nine-to-five job.

Mick would be furious.

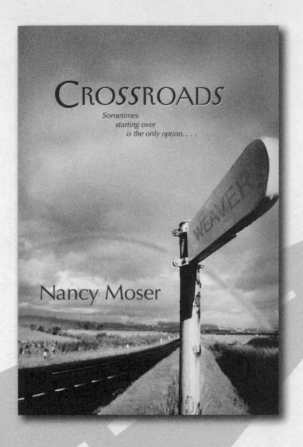

CROSSROADS

*Sometimes
starting over
is the only option. . . .*

Nancy Moser

Turn the page for an exciting preview
from *Crossroads* by Nancy Moser.

Available now at bookstores and online.

Be strong, and do the work.

1 CHRONICLES 28:10

September 2005

Eighty-one-year-old Madeline stormed into the middle of Weaver's main intersection, positioned herself directly beneath its only traffic light, spread her arms wide, and screamed, "I will not allow it!" Just to make sure every atom and chromosome of every person within range heard her proclamation, she turned one hundred and eighty degrees and did it again. "Do you hear me? I will not allow it!"

The light guiding the traffic traveling along Emma Street turned green, but there was no need for Madeline McHenry Weaver to move out of the way. The light could show its colors from now until Elvis returned and she would not have to move—for safety's sake anyway. Yet the truth was, she couldn't stand out here all day. If the heat of their Indian summer hot spell didn't get to her, her arthritis would. Annoying thing, getting old.

"You done yet?"

Web Stoddard sat at the corner on a bench that skirted the town's only park, with one arm draped over its back, his overall-clad legs crossed. The shoelace on his right work boot was untied and teased the sidewalk. He slowly shooed a fly away as if he didn't have anything better to do.

Which he didn't.

Which brought Madeline back to the problem at hand.

She waved her arms expansively, ignoring the light turning red. "No, I'm not done yet. And I won't be done until people start listening to me."

His right ankle danced a figure eight. "No people to hear, Maddy. It's too late."

She stomped a foot. "It's not too late! It can't be."

Web nodded toward the Weaver Mercantile opposite the bench. "Want to go sit at the soda fountain? I have a key."

"You have a key to every empty business in town. Don't abuse the privilege."

He nodded slowly, then grinned. "Want to go neck in the back of the hardware store?"

She crunched up her nose. "It smells like varnish and nails in there."

"Not a bad smell."

"You're obsessed with necking."

"When was the last time I mentioned it?"

She hated to be put on the spot. "But you *think* about it a lot."

"Last I heard, thinking 'tweren't a bad thing. And don't act like I'm pressuring you. The last time we kissed was 1942."

She looked past him toward the gazebo that sat in the middle of the town square. Even from here she could see that the floor was covered with the first sprinkling of gold, rust, and red leaves. Dead leaves. Blowing away, just like the town. Yet that's where she and Web had exchanged their last kiss. "October 22, 1942."

He smiled. "You remembered."

"You were abandoning me, going off to war."

"You were supposed to wait for me."

Ouch.

She took two steps toward the bank that she and her husband, Augustus, had owned. Yet proximity or distance from Web wouldn't make the past right itself. But how dare he bring it up at a time like this? She put her hands on her hips and glared at him.

"Gracious day. What a look. What did I do?" Web said.

"Here I am worrying about Weaver and you . . ." She let her head wag like a disappointed mother.

He sat up straight and his loose lace became sandwiched between shoe and sidewalk. "You need to let the town go, Maddy."

She shook her head.

He patted the bench. "Come over here."

She crossed her arms, hugging herself. She didn't want to be scolded, or worse yet, placated. "I will not let Weaver die on me."

His voice softened. "It already has."

Her arms let loose, taking in the expanse of the main street. "The town's going to turn one hundred next year. We can't let it expire at ninety-nine. It's . . . it's sacrilegious."

He squinted his left eye.

"Scandalous?"

"You're overreacting, plus taking it way too personal."

"It *is* personal. I'm a Weaver." As soon as she said the words she wished she could take them back. Her becoming a Weaver was directly related to her not waiting for Web's safe return from World War II.

He was charitable and let it slide. "Nothing lasts forever. Not even a family line," he said.

Ah. Sure. Rub it in. If only she and Augustus had had children . . .

"It's just you and me, kid," Web said, doing a pitiful Humphrey Bogart imitation.

But he spoke the truth. They were the only lifers left in town . . . which made her remember, there used to be another. "I can't believe the Sidcowskys left. We went to high school with Marabel."

"You can't blame them for moving to Wichita to be closer to their grandchildren."

Madeline strode to the curb in front of Sidcowsky's Hardware
and kicked it. The scuff in her shoe and pain in her toe were worth
it. "They're traitors, the lot of them. Abandoning their lifeblood,
their hometown that needs them. They are selfish beings, thinking
nothing of the greater good, only thinking—"

"The Sidcowskys are good people, but they, like others, came
to a crossroads and had to make a choice. The Sidcoswkys held on
way beyond when others left."

Madeline would concede the point—privately. She did a lot of
conceding in private. Although she hadn't let others see her panic,
that *was* the emotion holding her in a stranglehold this past year.
What had Queen Elizabeth called her horrible year when Windsor
Castle burned and she endured the scandal and divorce of her
wayward children? *Annus horribilus.* So it was.

Actually the demise of Weaver had not come about in a single
year's time. The disease that had eaten away at its foundation had
come slowly, like a cancer cell dividing and eating up the good,
only making itself known when it was too late. Townspeople
finding jobs elsewhere. People moving out; no one moving in.
People getting greedy or panicking when business slowed. Closing
up shop. Forgetting in their quest for more money, more success,
and more happiness, all that Weaver stood for: family, tradition,
safety, security, continuity.

Where was that continuity now? Where was the loyalty? It
wasn't strictly a Weaver problem. People did not stay employed
with one company their entire lives anymore. They didn't even
stay in one neighborhood, but hopped houses and even spouses as
if all were interchangeable and acceptable on the frantic road to
happiness. The truth was, Weaver's demise had killed her husband.

The doctor may have said it was his heart, but Madeline knew frustration and despair were the real—

"This town isn't the only town going through hard times, Maddy. People need to eat."

She pointed at the Sunshine Café on the opposite corner. "People could've eaten right there, until those quitters, the Andersons, moved out."

"Moved on, Maddy. People have to move on when they aren't making enough to live on. Big towns with big stores and big jobs. That's what people need."

She watched a squirrel scamper diagonally from the park to the bank just a few feet in front of her. It didn't even hesitate. Even the rodents knew there was no need for a traffic light in Weaver anymore.

Her shoulders slumped. What she *needed* was a long soak in a lavender-scented bath. What she *needed* was time—more years to accomplish what she wanted to accomplish. "They don't *need* those things they're after, Web. They *want* them. Big difference."

He came toward her, right there in the street. She let him come. She could use a hug. In the three years since Augustus had died, she'd relied on Web's arms to make her feel better when the world was uncooperative. Her cheek found his shoulder. The clasp to his overall strap bit into it, but she didn't care.

"It's not your responsibility, Maddy." He put a hand on the back of her head, and she closed her eyes to let the years slip away. Many, many years . . .

But then his words—instead of falling away as they gave comfort—hung back and started to jab like a bully offering a challenge.

Yes, she and Web had lived a lot of years here, shared a lot of history, but it wasn't time to rest on those laurels yet. There were too many years between them to brush off as being past and over. She may be old, but she wasn't dead yet.

She suddenly pushed away from him. "It *is* my responsibility, Web. You don't know . . ."

His faded blue eyes looked confused, as if he'd forgotten he'd just said those very words.

She repeated herself, growing impatient. "Weaver *is* my responsibility." She pointed at the street signs. "Emma Street is named after Augustus's great-grandmother, and Henry Avenue was named for *her* father. Every street in this town is named after a Weaver. They claimed it ninety-nine years ago and we've been here ever since. I'm the last Weaver standing and I will not go down without a fight!"

She noticed her arm was raised in a give-me-liberty-or-give-me-death position. She kept it there for effect.

"Ever hear of retirement, Maddy? Enjoying your golden years?"

She lowered her arm. "Oh, pooh. Use it or lose it." She started walking toward the Weaver Garden on the far edge of the park, right across from the Weaver mansion. She often did her best cogitating among the flowers.

When she didn't hear footsteps coming after her she turned back and found Web still standing in the middle of the abandoned street. "You coming?"

He put his hands in his pockets. "Depends. Exactly *what* are you planning to do?"

"I'm going to save Weaver, silly. And after I do, we're going to have the best and biggest one-hundredth birthday celebration this town has ever seen." Web's shaking head riled her. "I *will* save

Weaver, Web Stoddard. The question is: will you help me?"

Web's sigh was eaten up by the drone of the cicadas overhead. "What do you have in mind?"

Madeline had never let technicalities stop her before, and she certainly wasn't about to start now. She put her hands on her hips. "Are you in or out?"

"You need to explain—"

She took a step toward her best friend. "I don't need to do anything of the sort. I need a yes from you. Now."

"Before I even know the question?"

"Exactly."

"You're not being fair, Maddy."

She planted her feet dramatically and waited. *Come on, Web. Do this for me. For Weaver. For us.*

Web's head shook no even as he said, "Yes. Yes, I'm in."

Bravo.

It was a start.

Madeline grabbed hold with both hands and shook the chest-high, wrought-iron gate leading to the Weaver Garden. "Put this on your fix-it list, Web. Lately, I can't open this thing."

"I've fixed it multiple times." He moved to give it a try.

Presto. It opened.

She stood back, incredulous, and watched as he swung it back and forth. "How do you do that?"

He rubbed his fingers together. "Finesse. You should try it sometime."

From what she could figure, there was no reason she shouldn't be able to open the gate herself. Yet lately she never could. And he couldn't leave it open for her unless they wanted dogs to dig up the bulbs or a stray deer to munch at the leaves.

He let her go in first. She strolled along the circular path with purple asters on her left and pink roses on her right. He caught up with her and duplicated her stance, clasping his hands behind his back. The asters gave way to a strong stand of mums and orange tiger lilies bowing in the breeze.

"So. What are you going to do?" he finally asked.

Though she wasn't sure, she shared the idea that was centermost on her mind. "Buy it up. All of it."

"You're going to buy up the entire town?"

His doubt fueled her. "You betcha. Every single property that's for sale—and maybe a few that aren't."

"But that will cost—"

"Millions."

"You have millions?"

Her stomach did a backflip, but she simply shrugged and walked away. "A few."

He came after her. "A few million?"

"Give or take."

"What are you going to do with all that property? The few who've stayed behind already have homes, and as far as I know there's no line of people at the edge of town wanting to move in. And *I* certainly don't have the inclination to take care of all those properties. Keeping up with all the to-dos of the public areas is enough for these old bones."

She hated when he got all practical on her. If only he'd let her finish. "I'm going to buy it up, then give it away."

"What?"

She pointed to a honeysuckle bush, long past its flowering stage. "You need to trim that up. It's gangly."

"Yes, yes, I'll add it to the list. You can't mean you're planning to give away property, Maddy. Really give it away?"

She raised her chin. "I most certainly do."

He eyed her, then sighed. "Unfortunately, I know that look. Your mind is set in stone with deep foundations that can't be moved. Not that I haven't tried a few thousand times."

"Then stop trying."

He shoved his hands into his pockets and gave her his aw-shucks smile. "Actually, I'm proud of you."

She looked at him warily. "What's the catch?"

"Jesus told the rich man to give up everything and follow him. By giving away the town you're doing what he said, giving up the things that stand between you and him. That makes me proud. Jesus too."

She raised a hand as a stop sign. "If you know what's good for you, you and Jesus better back away and keep your veiled compliments to yourself. I'm not following him; I'm following me. What I give up, I give up for my sake, not his. Because *I* want to."

Web sighed. "You always have done what you wanted."

But not always gotten what I wanted.

Web bent over and plucked a weed from between the lilies and slipped it in his pocket. "But come on, Maddy. Think this through. If anything, buy it up and sell it again—even at a loss. That way you'd get some of your money back and still get people to move here."

"But that negates my purpose."

"Which is?"

She faced him head-on. "To revitalize Weaver. My way. Not just attract people looking for a bargain but—"

Web laughed. "You don't think *giving* property away will attract people looking for a bargain?"

She leaned toward a golden mum and pinched wilted blooms. She straightened and took a deep breath, raising her face to the breeze. And suddenly, she didn't feel like the elderly matriarch of Weaver anymore, but like a young Madeline, cheeks flushed, wind whipping through her auburn hair, her eyes flashing with life, an attentive man at her beck and call. . . .

With a shake of her head she left such romantic memories aside. "Pay attention to me, Web, because what I'm going to say . . . a lot of it is going to fall on your shoulders because I can't do it alone. Just like it's always been, it's you and me." She started to pace the path, her hands accentuating her words. "I'm not going to give Weaver to just anybody. This will not be an Oklahoma Land Rush without the rush. No, indeed, I'm going to take applications."

"Like a job application?"

"Exactly like a job application. In fact, I will make a list of specific positions that need to be filled. We don't want a town populated with twenty lawyers or a dozen ditchdiggers, do we? We don't want people to have to look elsewhere for employment. We want them to work here, right?"

"Yup. Suppose so."

"I've told you not to say *yup*. It makes you sound uneducated." She started to pace again. "I'm going to make a list of professions: a doctor, teacher, peace officer, grocer—"

"Pastor."

"If there's room. And we'll put ads in national newspapers and get on national television, on talk shows."

"Television? Who's going to go on TV?"

She pinched her lower lip and thought out loud. "I suppose we could get some pretty model to draw the younger crowd, but honestly, is that our target? Though we need a mix of ages to move here, the more mature candidates will be best. And *they* won't be put off by maturity—by me. I'll do it. So I'm old? I'm rich. I'm—"

"Bossy?"

"Since when is that a bad thing? At any rate, they'll listen to me. And they'll apply. You mark my words; they'll apply in droves."

"What will we ask them on the application?"

She turned back the way they'd come. "Come to the house. We have work to do."

"But the mailbox at the police station needs fixing. Somebody drove over it."

She paused amid the vivid splashes of color. "You want to save Weaver or not?"

He sighed. "I'm coming."

As if he had a choice.